MERE MORTALS

By Neil Ravin
M.D.
INFORMED CONSENT
SEVEN NORTH
EVIDENCE
MERE MORTALS

MERE MORTALS

Neil Ravin

Delacorte Press

Published by
Delacorte Press
Bantam Doubleday Dell Publishing Group, Inc.
666 Fifth Avenue
New York, New York 10103

Each character in this novel is entirely fictional. No
reference to any living person is intended or should be
inferred.

Grateful acknowledgment is made for permission to reprint
excerpts from the following:
"Doctor My Eyes" by Jackson Browne © 1970–1972 by
Atlantic Music Corp.-Open Window Music. All Rights
Reserved. International Copyright Secured.
"Desolation Row" by Bob Dylan © 1965 Warner Bros.
Inc. All Rights Reserved. Used by Permission.
"Like a Rolling Stone" by Bob Dylan © 1965 Warner Bros.
Inc. All Rights Reserved. Used by Permission.
"I Dreamed I Saw St. Augustine" by Bob Dylan © 1968 by
Dwarf Music. All Rights Reserved. International Copyright
Secured. Reprinted by Permission.
"Fire and Rain" by James Taylor © Country Road Music
and SBK Blackwood Music Inc. All Rights Controlled and
Administered by SBK Blackwood Music Inc. All Rights
Reserved. International Copyright Secured. Used by
Permission.

Designed by Rhea Braunstein

Library of Congress Cataloging in Publication Data
Ravin, Neil.
    Mere mortals / Neil Ravin.
       p.   cm.
    ISBN 0-385-29767-X
    I. Title.
PS3568.A84M4   1989
813'.54—dc19   89-30539
                                                  CIP

Manufactured in the United States of America
Published simultaneously in Canada

October 1989
10 9 8 7 6 5 4 3 2 1
BG

101332

*FOR ELIAS AND REID
TWO PRETTY SLICK KIDS*

ACKNOWLEDGMENTS

Jackie Farber, Editor

Surgeon Extraordinaire,
Louis Levitt

Love—is anterior to Life—
Posterior—to Death.

—EMILY DICKINSON

BOOK I

The Black Hole
of New York

Oh, I've seen fire
And I've seen rain

—JAMES TAYLOR

— 1 —

ENDINGS

I had not thought it would end this way. I had imagined the sirens sounding, the radio announcement heard driving in the car, the mad dash home to the kids, time enough for despair, panic, a last hug, then the boom and the mushroom cloud. Something cataclysmic, something impersonal.

Caroline's vision was less apocalyptic. Caroline always said she'd die in a car crash.

She dismissed the mushroom cloud as anything to worry about. "If that happens," she said, "I just hope it's over in a blinding flash. I'll take the kids outside and we'll be vaporized before we know what hit us. No, a car crash. That's what it'll be."

I did not notice the blood at first. It didn't occur to me until much later that I had been unconscious. My first thought on regaining this world was about the car. Now I'll have to buy a new car. And with what money?

Then I noticed Caroline. She was curled up on the floor, her head in the seat beside me as if she were asleep. And the blood hardly mattered.

What mattered was the sound.

I extricated myself from my seat belt and tried to get over to her, to sit her up, but she was curled into a ball, mouth open, a low guttural sound leaking out, a sound I'd never heard from that mouth. Not through labor, not through the many nights, not from her. From patients years before. At Whipple, where we'd both heard sounds you never forget, but never a sound like that from Caroline.

Her eyes were closed, but I could see the globes through the lids—her eyes had rolled upward. There was a dent in her forehead, and from that, a wash of blood down her face.

Blood. We were both well acquainted with blood. I hardly noticed it. She just wouldn't uncurl. And she would not talk to me. A moment before it was Caroline, and now she was so different. Now she wasn't really with me. She was damaged inside her skull.

We were in big trouble.

And it was really happening. To her. To me.

One moment we're talking about the party. Then headlights coming at us in our lane. Caroline saying, "Uh-oh." Now this.

My door wouldn't open, and I crawled over her and opened hers. I noticed the windshield. It had that cobwebbed fracture a head makes striking glass at thirty miles an hour.

No, no, no. Don't let it happen this way, not like this, not with Max at home and Caroline having told him "I always come back."

Not on an asphalt road under a streetlight.

Caroline had always said it would be a car crash, all breezy and unconcerned when we played the how-will-you-die game, never really believing it could happen to us, immortal and lucky as we were. How many times had we said to each other, "There but for the grace of God go you and I"? And now it was us going down the same path. Caroline, at least, headed down that path. To join the great majority.

She had said, "I'll die in a car crash is how I'll die."

But she never mentioned I'd be with her.

WHIPPLE

Before the kids, before the house and the mortgage, before car payments and life insurance and IRAs and financial planning, before Washington and invitations to country clubs, there was Whipple. In March of my last year as a medical resident, I was assigned to the Whipple Hospital for Cancer and Related Conditions, where, as the house staff wags said, the Mets Always Win—*mets* as in *metastases*. (I guess you had to be there. It was funny then.) Given the choice, I'd have preferred a trip down the Amazon without a mosquito net to one month at Whipple. For weeks before I was due to set foot on a Whipple ward I awoke in a black gloom and went through my days like a condemned man.

When the house staff was in an especially derisive mood, they called it "I. F. Whipple," or simply "The Big IF," an allusion to the "Internationally Famed Whipple Hospital," which was what the newspapers always called it, as if the "internationally famed" were part of the name. The best cancer hospital in the world.

Whipple was the night howl of the Medical Center.

It was one of three separate hospitals occupying adjacent blocks and it stood as a begrimed brick structure across from the sparkling white stone of the Manhattan Hospital proper. The Whipple brick may once have been red, but when I knew it, it was some dark-stained color that wasn't really a color at all. The stain may have come from within, like the final stain on the bedclothes of so many of its patients. The wards, too, were dingy and gray, no matter what color they had once been, and the patients gray when they weren't yellowed by jaundice, and everything, even the white uniforms, took on that dim, hopeless shadow that Whipple seemed to cast. The physical bleakness of the place was such a contrast to the crispness and polish "across street" at the Great White Tower, as Manhattan Hospital was called, and the grayness knew no limits, not just the floors, the windows, the very air, but it penetrated the spirits of those who worked there. It was a cancer hospital, after all, and that reality pervaded the place.

Someone should have hung up the "Abandon All Hope" sign, but, of course, the patients never would give up hope. *Dum spiro, spero.* What else did they have? And for the doctors, no sign was necessary.

The only consolation was not being an intern anymore, which, next to being a patient at Whipple, was the worst thing you could be. I was a senior resident, an officer in the war on cancer, still in the trenches, but I had status. I was beyond internship, beyond junior residency, dues paid and I had learned things: I was capable of getting a septic leuk through the night, able to bail out an intern with a patient foaming over in pulmonary edema. I knew enough to plug my finger in the dike and get through until morning.

The first time I ever talked to Caroline was over the phone. She said, "Your intern is over here trying to kill someone."

I said, "Anyone I know?"

"A patient," she said. "If he were trying to kill another intern I wouldn't have called."

When I arrived on the ward, Caroline was nowhere to be seen, but the intern was writing in the nurses' station and he looked up shamefacedly and mumbled something to the effect he was glad to see me. He was so glad to see me, he hadn't bothered calling to say he was in trouble, you understand. The intern was glad to see me the way a grade school bully is glad to see the principal on the playground. He was furious that Caroline had called.

"Did she call you?" he rasped. "Behind my back? That bimbo nurse." He spoke with the vaguest Middle-European accent, and I had to laugh hearing him come up with *bimbo.* He ran a hand through his lank blond hair. "I got everything under control. No problem. I guarantee you that calcium is normal in the a.m. I can't believe she called you."

Caroline had been correct, of course: the intern was trying to kill this particular patient. Unwittingly, of course. But that would have been less than complete consolation to the patient.

The patient had multiple myeloma and a calcium that had not quite yet set a new indoor record for Whipple Hospital. The intern had decided it was time to lower the calcium posthaste, and he had ordered intravenous phosphate.

"The thing is," I said, "you give this guy IV phosphate and he could be seriously dead by morning. Calcium phosphate precipitates in all the wrong places—heart, brain, unto death."

"But I looked it up—in Harrison's."

"Textbooks are five years out of date the day they're published," I said soothingly. "At the IF Whipple hypercalcemic crisis gets treated with mithramycin, saline, and Lasix."

"That's what the bimbo nurse told me."

"She's probably seen half a dozen residents cancel IV phosphate orders written by interns."

The intern went off to change his orders. I thought I might investigate the bimbo nurse, who had a very nice telephone voice and who had, after all, saved the patient, not to mention my neck. I would have had to explain the IV phosphate the next morning at attending rounds.

She was in the nurses' station, standing in front of the medication cart, checking a card file on top of the cart. She did not look up when I came in. I spun into a chair and clasped my hands behind my head and studied her. She was trying to pretend she didn't know I was sitting there staring at her legs. They were worth a stare. She was not doing a convincing job of ignoring me. Every so often she checked me out of the corner of her eye.

In those days, I could fall asleep instantly at any moment: standing in a cafeteria line, waiting for an elevator. Given a comfortable chair, there had to be a good reason to stay awake, especially after midnight. At a glance, she looked like a good reason.

I waited for her to look up and say something.

Finally, without looking up, she said, "Don't you have a home?"

"Pardon me?" I said.

"The action's over for tonight."

I stole a glance at her name tag: Caroline Bates, RN, Head Nurse.

She looked young to be a head nurse, and didn't have the disappointed-in-love look common among that species. And she was working the night shift, an assignment head nurses avoided like the plague.

"Excuse me for staring," I said. "I just never saw a head nurse on the ward after midnight before."

She liked that. She tried not to show it, but even on that short acquaintance, I could see she did. I had appealed to her professional pride. The night shift was a very scary shift at Whipple: you had very little in the way of help when things went wrong, and at Whipple things often went wrong in the worst ways.

"Staring," she said, "hardly describes the attention you were giving my legs."

"They deserve all the attention they get."

She shook her head slowly and I realized I had said the wrong thing. "Okay, bright eyes, I am positively swept off my feet," she said. "But I've got work to do, and it's past your bedtime."

She was done with me. She turned on her heels and walked out of the station. I watched her walk down the dark hallway, in and out of the light thrown from the overhead fixtures. She had a very pretty walk, toes slightly out. There was something very spare and tight about her construction. I watched her glide down the hall away from me, making rounds with her flashlight.

It was late and I was tired and headachey and I felt grimy and sleep was the sweetest sound on earth. But I was determined not to let Caroline Bates, RN, Head Nurse arouse my interest, then just turn and walk away.

I trotted down to the kitchen at the other end of the hall and was back in the nurses' station before she returned.

When she arrived, I was in my chair, and I held up a malted milkshake toward her. The malteds were for the cachectic patients who were eaten alive by their highly metabolic tumors, and they were considered great delicacies by the interns and nurses. The hospital kitchen staff realized how much everyone loved the malteds and instituted a system to insure only bona fide patients got them. Each had to be specially ordered and each had a patient's name stamped on it in purple ink. I had one for her and one for me.

She said: "What's this?"

"A malted," I said. "Five stars for the malteds. Only thing at Whipple that rates it."

"They're for the patients," she said flatly. "I'm not going to drink someone's milkshake. What's he going to eat?"

I liked her for that. The wages of guilt: drink a patient's milkshake and think of the poor patient, wasting away.

"Look at the name on it," I said.

"I'm not drinking it," she said.

"Look at the name," I said.

She read the name and she smiled. "He's dead."

"Died this morning," I said. "I check the death certificate list every morning and order up a malted for each dearly departed. The guy that malted belongs to will never miss it."

She flipped an appraising look in my direction and examined the malted. A smile played around the corners of her mouth, just enough to get my hopes up, but then it slipped away. Then she snapped off the plastic lid and studied me with an expression that was neither friendly nor hostile from behind the rim as she sipped it.

"I bet you work this milkshake routine on all the girls," she said.

"No, I pick and choose."

She thought about that for a moment and said: "Well, maybe you have one or two redeeming qualities."

"I need to redeem myself?"

"Wasn't that your intern who almost blasted my patient with IV phosphate?"

"We straightened that out," I said. "He canceled the order."

"Oh, no, Doctor. *We* did not straighten that out. *I* straightened that intern out." She smiled when she said that, but she wasn't giving an inch. "I was under the impression," she said, eyes medium to hard, "riding herd on the intern was the senior resident's job."

"I'm not psychic," I said, feeling the heat crawl up my neck to my face. "I can't know about dumb orders unless someone tells me."

"You can't know about dumb orders if you're not on the ward, if you're back in your apartment in bed."

I began thinking about grabbing back my malted. But I decided the soft answer turneth away wrath.

"How is that guy with the calcium?"

"He's cowering in his room," she said. "Afraid the doctors might launch another attack."

It did not take much in those sleep-deprived days to arouse my indignation and my sense that I had been massively mistreated.

"You can tell the patient the bad guys have finished tormenting him for the night," I said, hauling myself to my feet.

"Oh, he's not talking to me. I was the one who called the doctors in the first place."

That did it. It was too late an hour for me to put up with the doctor-as-aggressor, nurse-as-protector routine, even from a nurse with looks like hers. Good looks carried a certain currency, but she had spent it all.

I was beginning to think this Caroline Bates, RN, Head Nurse was not going to be the one who made it all worthwhile after all. She was turning into just another Whipple migraine, in a hurry.

"And now I suppose you're sorry," I said.

She studied me briefly, her brown eyes alert and luminous. Light brown, almost khaki-colored eyes. Very pretty. She radiated a sort of nervous energy, a twitchy kind of excitement, like a racehorse being coaxed into the starting gate.

"I'm glad he got his calcium treated," she said. "Personally, I could have done without the heated looks and the boyish charm from the resident on call."

"You sure got a line on me, and we've only just met."

"Oh, you know the Medical Center: a small town. Your reputation precedes you, Dr. O'Brien"—she knew my name. That was something. "Tongues wag," she continued before I could be too pleased. "You run around with the fast set. You've found a plentiful supply of willing nurses and you've tried them all without being too fussy."

Mother Superior, no less.

"Oh, of course," I said. "Lines form outside my door every night, all the willing nurses." I headed for the door.

"You don't have to be so clever," she said. "It's an overworked virtue around here."

"And you're the local authority on virtue."

"That's what I mean," she said. "About being too clever."

PROFESSOR TOOMEY

I don't know where Caroline got all that stuff about my frenetic bedroom life, really I don't. Well, maybe I do. I suppose I had been doing some catching up. I went to a small, cloistered all-male college in the wilds of New Hampshire. The only females I remember seeing those four years were fur-covered and had four legs. Medical school was less cloistered, but friendships of any kind were time-consuming and there was so much to learn and so little time to learn it. In medical school I learned how little I knew, and how helpless and worthless I was until I knew all the critical information there was to absorb.

But as an intern, you more or less fell in the way of women. My first day as an intern, I talked to more women than I had spoken with in four years in college. There were nurses, respiratory therapists, social workers, physical therapists, women doctors, ward clerks—women everywhere. Women who did not wait to be asked. Women who sought me out because I had learned things and because I had some authority. Women who, I suppose, might be described as willing.

We all lived together in hospital housing across the street from the hospitals. You ran into people: on elevators, on the sidewalk, at the two bars hospital people flooded into at the end of shifts, and given the proximity and the odd working hours, there was often the element of bedroom farce.

Of course, as with any place, there was always more speculation than realization.

The Medical Center was a small town, and as in any small town, you were observed. Notes were made. But things got exaggerated. My bedroom life for most of medical school, and certainly for internship, consisted of coming home and collapsing. If there had been anyone in my bed, I would have thrown her out. Sleep occupied a much higher place in my system of values than sex, during internship at least.

Personally, I never had anything against willing nurses. From where I stood, you took your pleasures where you found them, and felt grateful for the chance.

But to a certain extent, it was all just so much smoke. I went to the bars and sat around with the boys in white, made male noises and tried to remember what life was like outside the hospital, but I had the feeling we were just filling in the empty spaces. We had our rounds to do, our patients to see, our journals to read, our fellowships to apply for, and we wanted to be good doctors and to be thought of as good doctors. We progressed along the course, up the ladder from intern to junior to senior resident. But sometimes I wondered whether anything was really happening, in my life. There was always so much to do: for others, for patients, for the hospital, for medicine. There seemed to be no time left for yourself. You took your pleasures, all right, but so often it seemed a moment, in the void.

You never really mistook it for the making of a real connection.

And then there was this Caroline Bates in her sheer white uniform, looking so impossibly clean and pink and alive—so healthy. Watching her float down the hallway, I had been transfixed. She had to be the reason, that long-deferred, great reward.

Like so many of my fellow voyagers in that strange and trying odyssey called medical training, I had come to accept a certain article of faith: The reward awaits you. Through stinky organic chemistry labs in college, through deadly comparative anatomy lectures, the voice would be there: Your reward will come. Through aptly named gross anatomy labs and formaldehyde-marinaded cadavers in medical school, through the autopsy service where you gagged and retched and had bad dreams and told yourself to be tough, the voice would be there: Something's coming, something good. Somewhere in the long nights of internship, you began to suspect the voice was a fraud, and you'd been had, thoroughly and at length. And you realized you were not so young anymore, and a third of your life was gone, and you'd spent it staring into glassy-eyed death.

And then, sliding in and out of the shadows one night, in deepest, darkest Whipple Hospital for Incurable Disease, you saw something. White nurse's uniform, shiny honey-colored hair. The mysterious warbler that so often followed you into the wood.

The next morning, for the first time in a long time, I awoke before my alarm knocked me out of bed and I showered and shaved and hurried over to the hospital without really knowing why I was so eager to get there. Never before had I been in any sort of hurry to get to Whipple. I didn't even stop at the deli next door to my apartment house for my pint of Tropicana orange juice and my morning doughnut. I thought I might just go up to Caroline's ward and pour myself some coffee in the nurses' station.

She wasn't there.

She wasn't at rounds either, and she wasn't in the cafeteria at lunch when I carried my tray toward the table of a nurse with the same honey-colored hair and Dutch-boy cut: this nurse turned to look up at me and I saw she was not Caroline and I felt cheated and disappointed.

I was still missing her that next night when the intern paged me to her ward. The intern was Ludvik Novotny, the same intern who had tried to use the intravenous phosphate before Caroline intervened. The same patient whose calcium Ludvik had wanted to cure with IV phosphate was now acting up again.

They were all standing in the patient's room, Caroline, Ludvik, and the patient. Caroline looked at me with a flash in her eye and said, "We have a problem here."

The patient was a tall, dignified-looking gent with silver hair and high, fine cheekbones. His name was Patrick J. Toomey, and he had been a professor of classics at City College. When his mind was clear, which was less and less often lately, he was wry, erudite, and quite charming. But now he had multiple myeloma chewing up his bones, spilling calcium into his blood intermittently, scrambling up his brain, and now and again shorting out his cerebral circuits.

His eyes darted toward the door, which I now occupied, to the window, guarded by the intrepid Miss Bates, and to the intern. The professor looked trapped and desperate. His skin was as flushed as it could be, given his profound anemia. The pulse in his neck throbbed and perspiration beaded his upper lip.

I had seen him every morning on rounds but I had never seen him look more unhappy.

Now he looked at me and pointed accusingly at the intern:

"This young man refuses to allow me to leave my room. I am being held here against my will."

Just getting the words out left him breathless. I wished he would sit down. It looked like all he could do just to stay on his feet. I didn't want to have to break his fall with my body.

"You said you were going to jump out the window," sputtered Ludvik. "You were going to jump. I didn't hold you prisoner." Ludvik looked at me, hands spread, palms up. "He was going for the window. He was trying to jack it open."

Ludvik seemed to have some doubt about whom I was going to back.

I spoke to the professor. "The problem is," I told him, "you're on the ninth floor."

"Like Daedalus," said the professor, stretching his arms, "I shall spread my wings."

That stopped me.

"See what I've been up against here," Ludvik squawked, turning to me with palms held out. "He's trying to jump. You're fucking out of your mind, Mr. Toomey."

Caroline stepped forward. She looked like a lady who'd heard enough. She had a quickness about the eyes and plenty of steel in her, and she froze Ludvik with a hard look. She said, "We don't talk to patients like that around here." Then she turned and spoke sweetly to the professor: "You don't really want to run out on me?"

Toomey's face changed. He smiled, almost cooed. "Dear girl, would I ever do that? I'll be back. I just want to spread my wings and break free of this place for a while. It's stifling here. Roam these halls and all you see is misery and suffering, bony limbs, sunken eyes. Eyes without hope, eyes that say, 'Let me die.' Those two young men, both bald and both looking like living skeletons, who sit at the end of the hall and play cards all day, and they argue and throw their cards down and shriek at each other as if their silly card game mattered when they are dying. I must simply rise above this place. The worst place I've ever been. Except, perhaps, for Calcutta, in the war. I will fly. Like Daedalus. You may be my Icarus, and come with me."

The professor took a step toward the window, and Caroline stepped quickly to block him.

I smiled, watching Caroline. Okay, you're his pal—help him open the window so he can jump out and spread his wings.

"But you know what happened to Daedalus and Icarus," said Caroline. "In the end."

The professor considered the fate of Icarus and sat down on his bed.

"What do you want me to do?" he asked Caroline. He was finished with Ludvik and me.

"Just let the doctors explain what they want to do. If you don't want it, then you can decide."

That was my cue. I explained and he listened, looking at the floor, sighing. Finally he said, "Sounds like no fun at all."

Caroline explained why we wanted to do each test, what we were looking for, just as I had done, but it sounded much more convincing and less threatening coming from her, and the professor agreed.

We were finished doing the spinal tap and collecting the bloods within forty-five minutes, none too soon as far as the professor was concerned. Ludvik ran the bloods down to the lab and met me back at the small cluttered lab on the tenth floor, where we stained the spinal fluid with Gram's stain, turning our fingers blue and red, and then we dripped on the india ink for the cryptococcus stain. We looked at it under the microscope and cleaned up.

Ludvik was hungry and in a hurry. He wanted to get back to the ward and write the orders and cross the professor off his list of things to do. And he wanted, above all, to get to dinner before the cafeteria closed. I told him to go to the cafeteria. I'd go back and write the orders.

But Ludvik was having none of it. Whatever Caroline thought of him, Ludvik was not a bad intern. He was a physics major in college, and he still tended to think in numbers and he didn't smile much. When he got tired or frustrated, he occasionally lost his sense of perspective, as he had with Professor Toomey. But Ludvik was a soldier. He held his ground and he did not scamper out and hide in the toilet when patients started going down the tubes. He did his work, and he had a sense of pride: when you're an intern, you don't go to bed before your resident, and you don't leave the resident to write your orders for you on your own patient. You see it through until the job is finished.

I felt that way, too, when I was an intern. The professor was his case, after all.

"I'll write the orders," said Ludvik.

We walked back to the ward together. I could have trusted him to write the orders.

But he was headed to the ninth floor, to the professor's ward. To Caroline's ward. I thought I might just tag along.

DINNER AT HOTEL WHIPPLE

Caroline watched Ludvik scrawl his orders onto Mr. Toomey's order sheets and she stared after him as he charged out of the nurses' station headed for the cafeteria.

"Heaven forbid he should miss dinner," she said, looking after him.

"When you're an intern," I said, "the cafeteria is one of the three most important places in life. The other two are the toilet and your bed."

Caroline snorted.

"Ludvik's not so bad," I said. "He's a smart doc."

"He talks to his patients as if he were a drill sergeant," Caroline said. "He'd be better off in pathology, doing autopsies—his patients wouldn't mind him so much and his style would be better suited to his job."

"Ludvik's going to be a neurologist when he grows up," I told her. "His mother died of multiple sclerosis when he was in high school."

"Oh," said Caroline, looking suddenly pained. "I didn't know that."

"She was home until the very end, drooling all over herself. Incontinent of urine and stool."

"How very pleasant," said Caroline, eyes on the floor. She looked stricken. I didn't mean to make her feel that bad. I just wanted her to understand about Ludvik.

"So Ludvik went to medical school," I said. "Someday he'll be a neuron and he'll find a cure for MS. But now he's an intern, curing cancer, hating every minute. All things considered, Ludvik does okay."

"That depends on what you mean by okay," said Caroline, looking up. "He's humorless, and he never touches the patients except to examine them. He's one of those guys who was born middle-aged. And he has a nasty little mean streak in him when you question his authority."

"He's still a little unsure of himself."

"At least I can understand some of his grimness," Caroline said. "Watching them change your mother's diapers couldn't have been much fun."

"He saw more than that," I said. "She aspirated one day and died right in front of him."

Caroline's face fell abruptly, but she caught it just before it hit something hard and got messy. "I'll have to be more patient with Dr. Ludvik Novotny," she said. Her eyes had misted for a moment, but now she shook it off. "What'd you decide on Toomey?" she asked suddenly.

"I thought you'd never ask. We have, after much deliberation, arrived at a diagnosis."

"The diagnosis is no problem," said Caroline. "He's crazy. Acute craziness. Delirium, Ludvik called it."

"But why? What's making him crazy? That's the challenge."

"His calcium," said Caroline, very pleased with herself. She held up a yellow paper with Toomey's name and electrolytes written on it. The calcium was circled. "I called the lab while you were gone," she said.

"That," I said, "is not diagnosis. That is presumption."

Her grin tumbled toward ground and crashed somewhere. "Don't get snotty," she said, chin rising. "Just because I got the Dx before you did. While you were off playing in your laboratory, getting your fingers stained."

"So you're satisfied it's hypercalcemia making Mr. Toomey want to fly around the Upper East Side like Daedalus?"

"You'd be flying, too, if your calcium were thirteen."

"Okay, Miss Bates," I said, uncapping a pen, reaching for Toomey's orders. "Here's the pen. You write the orders, if you're so sure."

I unclipped the orders Ludvik had written and pushed the order book toward Caroline. "You write 'em. I'll cosign them. Anything you want. You think it's just his calcium, write whatever you like. Treat that calcium and tuck him in for the night. Won't worry any more about him tonight."

The first trace of doubt crossed her face. Her voice wavered and her chin dropped. "No."

"Now, suppose I told you Ludvik and I were just looking at the professor's spinal fluid and it was swimming with cryptococcus?"

I don't think I could have rocked her more with a right cross to the jaw. She reached out as if to steady herself on the med cart. "No," she said, with sudden desperation. "Don't tell me cryptococcus. I cannot take another crypto."

There had been a run on cryptococcal meningitis among the immunosuppressed patients on the ward lately. It was a nasty parasite and unpleasant to treat and the patients tended to die despite all efforts.

"As a matter of fact," I said, "Professor Toomey's particular spinal fluid was clean as a whistle."

"You creep," she said. She was trying to look annoyed, but a flicker of a smile betrayed her.

"The point is," I said, not wagging my finger and trying to keep the wag out of my voice, "you can't know he's goofy and wanting to fly around just because his calcium is high. It's a diagnosis of exclusion: Brother Ludvik and I have just spent an hour eliminating CNS infection, hyponatremia, hypoglycemia, and hypoxia. So that leaves calcium. It's not the answer. It's how you get there."

I thought I saw crinkles around her eyes, which would be all the smile I was going to get. "Academic rigor," she said. "I'm so impressed."

The thing is, she actually was impressed. You could see it. Her face changed, and her voice got friendlier.

"So he gets the Brendan O'Brien cocktail," she said. "Mithramycin, saline, and a twist of Lasix. Only I wouldn't write for mithramycin. I worry about platelets."

Caroline was repeating the local gospel, preached by the local octogenarian calcium maven, who was not a great fan of mithramycin.

"In this dose, mithramycin's not going to hurt anyone's platelets."

"Says who?"

"Stewart et al. *Annual Review of Medicine.*"

Another appraising look. She knew I wasn't bluffing. It was a genuine reference, all right. She was looking at me with real interest now.

"Then why is everyone afraid to use mithramycin?" she asked.

"Everyone isn't," I said. "Just the brainwashed minions at the world's greatest cancer center."

"And how did you manage to break out of that intellectual stagnation?"

"I read."

She smiled. It was a real smile this time, not one of her pin-you-to-the-wall smiles.

"So maybe you're not such an airhead," she said.

"Why were you so eager to believe that?"

"You sat there visually undressing me the other night—the old X-ray treatment, looking smug and oversexed."

"I am not smug and oversexed," I protested. "I am humble and overworked."

She crossed her arms, examined me slowly, in no particular hurry, with no particular expression, not one I could read anyway. She seemed to be waiting for me to say something, and when I didn't she said, "I see your problem."

"I've got a problem?"

"You're a counterpuncher," she said. She stopped and unfolded her arms and straightened her back and smiled as if she'd just found the soft spot and now she had me for the taking. "But you don't have any moves of your own."

"That's your diagnosis?"

"Call it a working hypothesis."

"Well," I said, and started to fidget and sweat, and I stared at my shoes. I can be so very quick and clever in the clinch.

"The cafeteria will close," she said. "By the time you figure out how to ask me."

"It already is closed."

She looked at her watch and shrugged.

"The vending machines never close," I said.

"Is that an invitation?"

So we ate dinner together.

She signed out to the other night nurse, going over the status of the various patients, their IVs, summarizing each perfectly in just a phrase—Mr. Jones was a little old woman about keeping his bed linens straight. Professor Toomey took flight with his calcium, but responded to calm explanations and a touch of mithramycin.

The other nurse looked at me the whole time Caroline spoke.

We were going to make local news, but Caroline didn't seem to mind.

We took the elevator down to the fourth floor. The shortest way to the vending room was to the left, but she turned sharply right, guiding me by the elbow. We took the long way.

In the vending machine room we changed our dollar bills for quarters in the bill changer and plopped the quarters into the machines for cheeseburgers, Dr Peppers and Nestlé bars.

Caroline stuffed the cheeseburgers into the microwave.

"Why did we come the long way here?" I asked her.

"It's nicer," she said. "More scenic."

The route we took had been empty corridors and closed doors.

"Nicer than going through the pediatric ward, you mean." I grinned at her.

"All those little kids," she said. "With leukemia and whatever the hell else they have, with the IVs sticking out of their scalp veins and jugulars."

"They seem to get used to it," I said.

"That's the worst part," she said. "They chase each other down the hall rolling their IV poles after them. They think it's normal to have leukemia and to grow up in a hospital."

I started to sit down at one of the nearby tables, but Caroline nodded toward the door.

"This occasion deserves a more elegant setting."

I followed her out, wondering where she intended to find elegance at Whipple Hospital.

Caroline led the way to a bank of elevators I'd never taken before, and when one arrived, she pushed me in and pushed a top button marked "P" and we rode a long way up and stepped out onto a short hallway with six closed doors. She pushed through one of these and switched on a light and I found myself in what looked like a well-appointed living room. Caroline walked through this and I followed her into a darkened bedroom. Opposite the door was an expansive window affording a dazzling panorama of the city lights. There were chairs and a dresser and a large bed with a headboard in the shadows of the room, much more furniture than any hospital room I'd ever seen, and I could make out the dim outlines of framed paintings on the wall. I had the idea those paintings wouldn't be prints. Those would be original objets d'art, unless I missed my guess.

I started to turn on the light, but Caroline said, "Don't. We are here for the view."

"And here I was getting my hopes up."

Caroline looked around her in the dark, as if she only just realized we were in a bedroom, and she laughed. "We are here to eat dinner."

We drew up two chairs to the window, and sat down with our little bags with microwaved cheeseburgers and sodas and candy bars in our laps and we looked out over the city.

"What is this place?" I asked.

"This is Hotel Whipple," she said with secret merriment. "The penthouse suites. Presently unoccupied."

"But I never heard of them."

"Of course you haven't." She laughed. "You weren't supposed to. But if your name is Morgan or Vanderbilt or Du Pont—someone who might donate a million for an ICU—and you need a bed at Whipple you're not going to be put on the same ward as the hoi polloi. You get put here."

"But who takes care of them?"

"No house staff," smiled Caroline. "Strictly private physicians and private duty nurses. Only the best nurses."

"Head nurses," I said, understanding how Caroline knew about all this.

"The crème de la crème."

"Nurse to the rich and famous."

"They get cancer too."

We sat there, shoulders almost but not quite touching, eating cheeseburgers and looking out the window. To the east we could see far across the river into Queens. The lights seemed to go on forever. The East River bridges were lighted and the lights reflected on the water. Looking south, we could see the lights of the twin towers of the World Trade Center and to the west the darkness of Central Park. The streets below us looked threadlike. The taillights of the cars made red currents in the streets.

"Isn't it gorgeous?" said Caroline in the dark.

"What is that way off there?"

"I'm not sure. Brooklyn, maybe."

"Brooklyn," I said. "Never seen Brooklyn before."

Even in the dark, I could see her astonishment. "How long you been in New York?"

"Seven years, including med school," I said. "But that's not really like living in New York."

She shook her head at the enormity of it all: seven years in New York and never seen Brooklyn.

"I've been to Central Park," I said.

"Intrepid traveler," she said.

I took a bite of my cheeseburger and looked around. "But doesn't this bother you?"

"Doesn't what bother me?"

"I mean, the special privilege. The class system of medical care. Like a cruise boat."

"I've got nothing against money," Caroline said. "I wouldn't feel guilty if I got rich someday."

"Get cozy with one of these old gomers and you just might. Marry him on his deathbed."

"Now there's a thought."

"I don't know," I said. "It just seems un-American, all this social stratification."

"What are you, some kind of communist?"

"Just shanty Irish."

"Oh, yes." She laughed. "With a private school education straight through medical school. Talk about a privileged life."

"I keep forgetting, you know all about me: my womanizing, my whole dissolute past."

We sat there looking at each other in the dark. I felt very far away from the hospital, from the stink of the wards and from the whir and push of Whipple. It was a little disorienting, really, as if we'd stepped on an airplane at the black hole of Calcutta and stepped off on the top of the world.

I started to ask her how long she'd been in New York—there was no trace of New York in her speech; she was obviously a refugee like me—when my beeper went off. I answered it from the bedside phone. It was Ludvik. His voice was several octaves higher, as it always got when he was frazzled. "Mrs. Johnson with the promyelocytic—she's hot as a pistol and now she's hypotensive. Septic probably. Gram negative maybe. And she's started to bleed from her puncture sites. I started the IVs for the antibiotics and I just can't get her to stop."

I told him I'd be right down.

"She's stable," said Ludvik. "I got a nurse applying pressure. I just wanted you to know."

"I'm on my way."

Caroline stood up as I was talking to him and gathered up wrappers and cans.

"Your favorite intern," I said. "With a septic leuk in DIC."

"It's awful about his mother," said Caroline. "But he doesn't seem to really like people. He's the kind of man who would have a dog he'd be very kind to, but he'd ignore his wife and kids."

We collected our things and walked back to the elevator.

We rode down to the ninth floor and Caroline got off. I stayed on and held the door as she turned to me.

"What time do you get off tonight?" I asked.

"Why?"

"Come to Gleasons for a beer."

"I drink wine," she said. "And I'm going to have my glass in a bath, with a good book about the filthy rich."

"Have your wine at Gleasons."

"It wouldn't be the same."

The elevator door started to shut against my restraining hand, and an obnoxious bleating sound emitted. I stepped out and let the elevator go.

We stood there looking at each other. Caroline waited for me to say whatever it was I got off the elevator to say. I couldn't think of a thing. I just didn't want to say good night.

"Go rescue your intern," she said finally. "Before he decides to get brilliant again."

"You're such a tough cookie," I said. "It's a wonder I have the nerve to talk to you."

"I haven't noticed you being much intimidated."

"Maybe," I said, "I just don't buy the act."

THE BOOK ON CAROLINE

With great effort I resisted the urge. I did not float by the ninth floor at midnight when I knew Caroline's shift would be ending. It was better strategy to stay away. Just when I was about to break down and drift over to Caroline's ward, a lady with breast cancer growing in her lung distracted me by turning slate-gray and gasping for air. Fluid compressed her lungs—pleural effusions—and she looked as if she might just die. Ludvik was her intern, and he scurried around grabbing all the things we needed to do a thoracentesis to drain off the fluid in a hurry while I stayed with her. By the time we got her in shape it was after midnight, and I still had to write a note in her chart, which is what I was doing when Forrest Fauquier paged.

Forrest had suffered through medical school and internship with me. We had shared on-call rooms, books, beers, nurses, and when we were interns, Forrest had admitted my mother to Whipple. He had a mind like a steel trap, the voice of a bassoon with laryngitis, and more libidinal drive than a college fraternity at spring vacation.

"Dr. O'Brien, I presume," Forrest cackled. "We are still in the hospital, are we not?"

"Sad to say," I admitted. "I'm on eight, just winding down."

"Wrong again, buddy. You are not winding down. You are about to get a second wind. There is more to life than death and disease."

"Not at Whipple."

"You are in big-time trouble, talking like that. I'm coming down to eight with two interns and we will carry you bodily to Gleasons."

"I'm going home. Can't run around with the fast set."

I could hear Forrest snort along the wire.

"Fast set, my ass. You should be so lucky to run with a fast crowd. At this Medical Center a three-legged trotter would be considered real speed."

"Only recently I was rebuked and rejected for running around with guys like you. The fast set. That's the book on Brendan O'Brien."

"You're making real progress," said Forrest sounding very pleased. "You'll tell me all about it at Gleasons."

"Not tonight."

"Olivia McGill," said Forrest, "is rumored to be on her way to Gleasons, even as we speak."

"Then I'm definitely going home."

"Now this is a sign of most serious pathology," squawked Forrest. "Lovely Olivia palpitates at the sound of your name and has been making no secret of it, and you're avoiding her. No red-blooded male in his right mind would do that."

"Good, you go to Gleasons. Stand in for me."

"Oh," said Forrest, playing games with his voice the way he could. "This is serious."

"I'm fine," I said, and hung up.

I still had hopes I could manage to bump into Caroline as she got off shift.

I took the elevator down to the hospital lobby. They locked all doors after midnight, so everyone had to enter and leave through the main lobby. I hung around there, not seeing Caroline. Forrest, however, spotted me as he stepped off the elevator. He broke into a broad grin and stalked over. He threw an arm around my neck.

"Come quietly now," he said. "Nobody's going to hurt you."

We walked the block to Gleasons and grabbed a corner booth with a good view of the door and the tables. Forrest ordered a pitcher of draft and surveyed the nurses and interns and residents crowding in as the shifts changed and rendered his unsolicited opinion on every woman in the place. We were both bone tired and talk quickly degenerated into what had happened with patients, what stupid things various hospital administrators and sundry professors had said, and general complaints about hospital bureaucracy.

"Dump MacDonald ought to be taken out and shot," said Forrest. "What brilliant dean of what medical school put his name on Dump's diploma?"

Dump MacDonald was widely reputed to be the dumbest human being ever to have been awarded an MD degree.

"They ought to take that dean out and shoot him too. And the guys here who let him on staff. Line them up too."

"You know that new wing they're building on Seventieth Street?"

"Yeah?"

"One of Dump's grateful patients," I said. "And the CCU got remodeled by another one of Dump's filthy rich and ever so grateful patients. He brings more money into the Center than any three attendings."

"And he's an embarrassment to every living doc in New York City. Ever seen his car?"

"I've heard."

"A fucking Rolls-Royce," growled Forrest, shaking his head. *"With* MD plates, just to rub it into the faces of the good people of New York City. I could puke every time I see it. Dump drives up First Avenue and every citizen he passes looks at that car with the MD plates and remembers that when he gets on a jury."

"In the real world, I am told, money makes the world go round."

"He can stick his money in his ear. Probably come out the other side, all the air in that head. The guy is a fucking moron. Did I tell you what he told me he was treating CHF with these days? Did I tell you this?"

"No, and I don't want to hear it."

"Propranolol," Forrest deadpanned. "I kid you not. He admits this nice little old lady in four-plus CHF and he tells me he wants to treat her with eighty of propranolol."

Propranolol is the one drug you do not want to give a patient with congestive heart failure.

"Did you let him?"

"Shit no. One of the nurses caught the order and called me."

"What would we do without nurses to save patients?"

Forrest gave me a strange and inquiring look for a moment and shook his head and hit himself on the forehead.

"Why am I talking about the hospital?" he croaked, his eyes bulging and swiveling in his head. "I didn't come here to talk shop. I came here in a testosterone storm. I came here to act badly, to give vent to my basest drives."

Forrest raked the room with a glowering stare, looking for a female on whom he could exercise his drives.

As if in answer to his search, Caroline stepped through the door with the night nurse from her floor. They stood in the doorway blinking in the dark bar, while their eyes adjusted, looking around them.

Forrest growled, "Well, what have we here?"

I was about to tell him when he said, "Miss Caroline Bates, ice princess. And who is this with her?"

"Ice princess?"

We watched Caroline and her friend stand in the doorway looking for a table, not seeing us. They slid into a table for two along the wall across from the bar.

"Why ice princess?"

Forrest shrugged. "Opinions differ."

"But why do you say that?"

"That's the book on her. Many have tried. None has succeeded, to Dr. Fauquier's knowledge," said Forrest. "But look at her friend. You think that's bottled blond or the real thing?"

"Who's tried?"

"What am I? The world almanac? You want to know, show some initiative: go over and meet her. Though from what I've heard, you'll be knocking your head against a wall. There is boyfriend speculation. Out-of-town boyfriend, rumor has it. Go ask her yourself."

"Maybe I will."

Forrest turned his attention back to me. "For once in this life, I'd like to see you put yourself out, like us normal mortals. You know what your basic problem is? You sit here expecting women to come to you. What really pisses me is how they usually do."

I sat there torn between the desire to investigate Caroline and the strong urge to escape unnoticed. On the one hand, there was the obvious question of the significance of her appearance at Gleasons, having just refused my invitation. She wanted to go home to bath and book, she said. Yet here she was. The significance of her presence might have everything or nothing to do with me.

One thing seemed likely: If Caroline had any doubts about the kind of crowd I ran around with, Forrest would put the nail in the coffin of my credibility as a solid citizen. Being discovered at large with Forrest Fauquier was not going to enhance my image with Caroline. I, of course, understood that beneath Forrest's Neanderthal exterior of loudmouthed profligate lay a quiet, self-effacing, unrepentant, thoroughgoing male chauvinist.

Forrest was busy examining Caroline's friend. He was rolling his mammoth body so that he was entirely under our table now, his head at a level that allowed him to look directly between the knees of Caroline's friend. Just about this time Caroline and her friend noticed him.

Forrest launched himself out of his chair in their direction.

I rose, weak-kneed, and tried to decide whether to follow or to attempt to slip out the door unnoticed, but he was careening directly toward their table. Forrest stomped over and planted both fists on their table, his shaggy shock of dark hair cascading in his face. Caroline's eyes dissected him with quick and unmerciful clarity. Her friend's expression was more receptive.

I arrived and hooked a hand on Forrest's shoulder, pulling him to a more erect and less confrontational posture.

"This," I said, "is Forrest Fauquier."

Caroline offered her hand and said, "Caroline Bates," with a straightforward force I liked.

Forrest invited them to join us in our booth, and before I could interject with some lame mention of the lateness of the hour and how I really had to be heading home, Forrest had them both ensconced at our table.

We listened as Forrest launched into his barroom routines. This neither required nor allowed very much in the way of audience participation; Forrest rambled on about the sad state of New York bars, the fortunes and prospects of the Knicks and the Rangers, the latest lunacies of hospital administrators. He had a broad repertoire, and he shifted among topics as he judged interest or lack of it in the eyes of the women.

Caroline listened with a smile that encouraged his monologue without endorsing it, trying, I thought, to find some indication that he wasn't really the drunken bar hound he sounded for all the world to be.

For the first time, I noticed her University of Virginia nursing school pin. It struck me, seeing that pin, how little I knew about her. That thought jarred me, because somehow I had assumed I knew all about her. I knew she hadn't grown up in New York, or at least I thought I knew that. She didn't take the city for granted, which made her a non-native. Watching her look out over the city from Hotel Whipple, I knew she had to come from somewhere else. Just living in New York was a kind of achievement for her, as it was for me. We had come here in quest of something. I might have thought I had come here to go to medical school and she might have come for a job, but we both had been dazzled and we had discovered that you don't just pass through this town unchanged. We were expatriates, and that status seemed to afford a sort of automatic intimacy.

There was a ring on her right fourth finger, a thin gold band with lapis inlay. It didn't look like a wedding band or an engagement ring. But working nurses didn't often wear rings—rings got caught on things and scratched—so the ring worried me.

Forrest was inveighing against the hospital administrators who had decreed that death certificates had to be filled out within fifteen minutes of every death, a policy that, considering the Whipple tradition of dying during rounds and at other inopportune moments, played havoc with the orderly running of a ward.

"C'est la guerre," Caroline said.

"De mal en pis," Forrest snorted.

Caroline said something that was much too quick for my French, and Forrest's eyes opened. He spoke good French, and about all I could pick up was that Caroline had learned hers in France.

She realized she was leaving her friend and me out of things and said, "My father was in the foreign service."

"You lived in France?" I asked.

"Paris, Marseilles. A foreign service brat. We moved a lot."

"Well, well," said Forrest. "You are an interesting wench."

"Yes." Caroline laughed. "Before you arrived, we were just telling each other we are the two most interesting women we know."

"Aren't we lucky?" Forrest said to me.

I liked the way Caroline had shifted the attention from herself to include her friend.

Forrest pumped the two of them for the details of their backgrounds with a skill I could never approach. I felt a little ashamed that I had not got nearly as much out of her when I had her alone at Hotel Whipple, but she seemed less guarded with Forrest. She seemed to play his game, not worried at all about what he might think of her answers.

Caroline was born in France, where her father had been posted, and she went to school in whatever country her father happened to be assigned to, until college. She spent two years at Barnard before leaving for the University of Virginia school of nursing before her junior year.

"You left Barnard?" asked Forrest, with real incredulity. "For nursing school?" Forrest had gone to Amherst from Andover and put great stock in the social cachet of name schools.

"It seemed," said Caroline, very dryly, "like a good idea at the time."

"And in retrospect?" Forrest asked. He had dropped his performance posture now. He was truly interested.

"No regrets," said Caroline. "I've never been unemployed. I've lived where I wanted."

I wondered about that. Dropping out of Barnard would not make sense financially, in the long run, unless she couldn't meet the tuition, in the short run. But her father was in the foreign service and ought to have been able to afford to put her through school, unless there were several kids in college at once.

"Do you have a big family?" I asked.

Everyone looked at me. The question seemed to come out of nowhere. I wished I had kept my mouth shut and allowed Forrest, who was good at these things, to get it all out of her. But I had spoken and there it was.

Caroline looked at me neutrally, and said, "Just me and my sister. She's in New York now too. Daddy's in London and Mother is somewhere in the South Pacific."

"Don't tell me," said Forrest, slow drawl, "she ran off to Tahiti with Marlon Brando."

"Close," laughed Caroline, her eyes meeting Forrest's. She was liking him better. I wanted to ask her something, but I would wind up sounding awkward again, and I didn't want to interrupt her story. "She ran off with a Dutch chargé d'affaires when we lived in Marseilles. I was eleven and my sister, the one I told you about who lives in the Village now, and waits on tables (Did I tell you that? She's an actress), my sister was eight. And Mommy ran off with the Dutchman. She took us with her, but we slowed them down. She sent us back to Daddy by night train."

"Sounds like quite a lady," I heard myself say.

Caroline looked over. She was smiling now, a very artificial smile, false as a paper flower, very pasted on. "Mother was the sweetheart of Sigma Chi at Cornell and never got over it. That's where they met, my parents. She was the campus queen, and Daddy was a basketball star, and they got married right after graduation and regretted it more or less immediately. She liked the traveling in the foreign service, but the life got dull. So she got herself swept away."

"And she left you in Europe?" I asked. I couldn't help it. "Put you on a train? Alone?"

"Oh, it wasn't all that bad," laughed Caroline. "She wrote our names and destination on cards and pinned one to each of our collars and Daddy met us at the other end."

"Where was that?" asked Forrest.

"Berlin. Daddy had been transferred."

"You traveled from Holland to Berlin by train at age eleven?" I said, trying to keep the astonishment out of my voice.

"From Madrid, actually. Mother and her friend had run off to take the sea air in Spain."

"And they dragged you along?" Forrest said.

"We were a drag, I imagine," said Caroline, draining her wineglass. "We stayed in hotels, and they went off in one room and we got stashed in another. It was a very depressing way to see Spain. Daddy never stayed in hotels. We always camped out in a tent with Daddy. All through Europe. We were glad to be sent back, my sister and I were."

"Across Europe, age eleven, by train," I echoed. It didn't seem possible. My mother would never let me turn the corner until she had arrived and could see around it.

"Oh, Europe isn't that big. We did get lost in Lyons, and I sat down on the train platform and cried until a conductor came by. He got all sympathetic and concerned. My French was better then, and I explained we couldn't find a train to Berlin. He read the cards on our collars and fixed up our tickets and off we went."

The kindness of strangers, I thought, and for the first time that night, managed to keep it to myself. Across Europe alone with your eight-year-old sister, and your mother in Spain with her new boyfriend.

"Did they get married?" asked Caroline's friend. "Your mother and the Dutchman?"

"No. She did marry a Dutchman, but another Dutchman, years later. I think she went through several Dutchmen and one or two Germans. Then she gained weight and her looks started to go, and she decided it was time to settle down and she married a Dutchman in the Dutch foreign service. Mother always liked a diplomat."

"And your father?"

"He never remarried."

We had run out of questions, or perhaps we were all just catching our breath. There ensued an uncomfortable silence during which we all stared at Caroline, her friend with a look of great fascination, Forrest with amusement and lively eyes, and I don't know how I looked at her, but I know I felt sorry for her, or sorry for that eleven-year-old kid on the train, with her eight-year-old sister in tow.

Caroline looked around and suddenly realized she had been doing all the talking and she looked a little flustered, and she made a curious gesture with her hand, closing the top button of her uniform blouse, as if she just realized her breast was exposed. She looked at her watch with too broad a move and said suddenly, "Lord, look at the time."

We left Gleasons together. Forrest and Caroline's friend split off at Sixty-eighth Street. Forrest threw me a look of febrile glee over his shoulder. Caroline's friend did look as if she was enjoying his company.

Caroline and I continued on. We walked uptown, toward my street. She walked with her hands in her pockets, her bag slung over her shoulder, looking in the dark windows of the stores.

"Your friend," she said. "Is he gay?"

That stopped me. I turned and looked at her. "Forrest?" I said, dumbfounded. "He may be a lot of things, but gay? No."

"Sounded like a lot of repressed homosexual panic."

"Why don't you ask him?"

"I might just do that."

We continued down the block toward my place. I kept thinking: Any minute she is going to stop and hail a cab and wave good night. But she turned the corner with me and we continued on toward York Avenue. I could see the doorman smoking a cigarette in front of the Whitney, my building. I caught glimpses of Caroline out of the corner of my eye. She was still smiling, still hands in pockets, still with me, step for step.

We reached the doorman. She smiled faintly, walking by the doorman, who looked past her and grinned broadly at me. We headed for the elevator.

We walked through the lobby while I tried desperately to think of something cool and casual to say, as if having Caroline Bates come home with me after midnight was nothing special. I could feel my face go hot and I knew I was glowing red.

She pushed the button for the elevator and we stood there not looking at each other, watching the lighted panel next to the elevator doors that showed which floor each car was on.

She was smiling now, looking very much amused by my disorder. I was having trouble swallowing, getting my Adam's apple to move with great effort.

The elevator arrived, doors opened, and we stepped in and I pressed twelve. The doors closed.

She pressed nine.

"We're neighbors," she said.

I was still trying to swallow. Nine came and the door opened and she stepped away from her side of the elevator and walked to the door.

"Sleep tight," she said, with a kind of twinkle.

I said good night and watched the doors close behind her.

6

THE ECU

Caroline joined us for rounds the next morning. Our team, two interns—Ludvik and another intern named Ira Bloomstein—and I, had thirteen patients on her ward. We had started the night before with fifteen, but two died during the night. They had died within fifteen minutes of each other, for which Ira was very grateful since it meant he was awakened only once the entire night, pronounced one patient dead, then the next, and went back to bed and slept until morning.

"Not a bad night really, all things considered," said Ira. "Just the two ECU transfers. Got it all done between two and three-thirty and then four hours sleep." Ira had a face like a thoughtful dolphin and he smiled contentedly, thinking of those four delicious hours of uninterrupted sleep, which for an intern represented a rare delicacy approximating the pleasure of a fine meal, well served.

"ECU?" Caroline asked. Her voice had an edge and she looked revved up, ready to engage the gears. I don't think I would have noticed it before, but now that I was more familiar with her moods and expressions, I could see the anger seething behind her eyes.

"Eternal Care Unit," I explained, wondering what had her nose out of joint. She seemed friendly enough until Ira had given his report.

"Cute," said Caroline with a look that conveyed her ire. "Real cute."

Ira looked at her uncomprehending. What Caroline hadn't liked was the "ECU" bit. That's the way we talked then. It seemed to help. "Distancing," the shrinks called it. But Caroline was having none of it that morning.

"Just say he died. Okay?" she said. "I can only take so much glibness in the morning."

Ira exchanged glances with Ludvik.

"Well, excuse me," he said, as if to say, get off my back.

"Let's make rounds," I said.

The first patient was a twenty-seven-year-old accountant named Vince Montebelli, who had widespread testicular carcinoma. Vince was growing testicular CA in his lung, in his spine, and in his skull. He was riddled with metastases. His chart was no thicker than the Manhattan telephone directory and thumbing through it the night I took over his case, the familiar story took shape: tumor that had responded to chemotherapy but then recurred. It would disappear in one spot and pop up somewhere else. Every time we sent him down for a new X ray we found the CA in a new place. Vince had very few negative studies.

"Just once," Vince told me, "I'd like you to look for it somewhere and tell me it's not there."

I had asked him the first time I examined him how he could absorb it all. One day he's living his life. The next day everything's changed.

"I still don't believe it," Vince told me. "I mean, I believe it up here"—pointing to his head— "but I don't really believe it. Three weeks ago I was sweating bullets over a bunch of accounts. The clients were calling, and I was chugging Maalox. I thought I had troubles then."

He fixed me with one of his strange and steady looks: "I walked out of that doctor's office—he had shown me my X rays—and I, like, staggered back to my office and collapsed in my chair and just sat there staring at the wall. I was freaked, you know? I kept thinking my doctor would come running in and say it was all a big mistake, somebody else's X ray. Phone calls were coming through; my secretary's coming in pissed as hell I haven't been picking up; my boss comes in and says we're late on some account and it was like I was looking at a movie of all this happening to me."

Now, six weeks later, he had that same look all the testicular CA patients acquired if they lived long enough: He was cachectic, temples and eyes sunken, the skin around the eyes dark and dead-looking. He was bald from one of his chemotherapy drugs and pale from another drug that ravaged his bone marrow and rendered him anemic and wiped out his white blood cells, making him prey to every bug that floated through the halls of Whipple.

Vince watched us approach, unsmiling, the way a zoo animal

behind bars watches his keepers, without rage, without fear, without hope.

He said, "I'm still here."

Ira was his intern. He said, "I don't think you're ready to check out of this hotel quite yet."

"The guests here," said Vince, "occasionally slip out the back door without notice." He smiled weakly.

Ira looked confused. They liked each other and often joked around on morning rounds—Ira was unflappable and joked around with everyone—but Ira didn't understand Vince's sudden morose turn.

Caroline said, "I'm real sorry about your buddy, Vince."

Vince's buddy was one of the patients who had died that previous night, one of the patients Ira said had gone to the ECU. His buddy had had testicular CA. It dawned on me that Vince would know the guy who died: they were on the same ward and they had the same disease.

"Yeah" was all Vince said, his eyes drifting off to a neutral corner of the room. "I'm sorry too."

"He was a nice guy," said Caroline.

Vince said nothing.

"They could never get him to respond, you know," Caroline said.

Vince spoke dully. "I know."

Patients didn't like hearing about other patients dying, especially if they died of the same disease.

But there are differences between your cases, Caroline was saying. Your tumor has responded to therapy, at least a little. His did not. Don't think because you have the same diagnosis you are condemned to the same ineluctable course. Don't give up hope.

Vince fought for control. "But, the thing is," he said. "I liked the guy."

He put his face in his hands and his shoulders shook with his sobs. Caroline patted him on the shoulder. There were five other patients in the room and they had been watching from their beds, but now they suddenly looked at the walls, the floor, their breakfast trays, anyplace but at Vince, five other patients lined up in their beds, trying to get past this scene.

Ira's jaw dropped and he put his hand on Vince's shoulder momentarily, and then he walked out of the room.

The rest of us followed Ira out into the hall.

"I didn't realize," said Ira.

"They used to play cards together," said Caroline. "Vince and your ECU transfer. They'd sit at the end of the hall and deal from the bottom of the deck and accuse each other of cheating. Now he is, as you put it, in the ECU."

We all shifted weight on our feet, leaning against the walls.

"I never knew the guy," Ira explained to Caroline. "First time I ever saw him was last night, and he was dead. From the looks of him, I thought he was probably better off."

Caroline said, "I suppose he may be. But Vince and he were buddies. They were admitted about the same time and they'd been through a lot together. Like in a war. You'd know about that."

Ira had commanded a navy longboat in the Mekong Delta before going to med school. He said: "Yeah. I feel like a shit."

"You didn't know," said Caroline.

Ira looked at the floor for a moment, then, collected and revived, he looked up, smiling. "Raskolnovich was around last night," said Ira, rolling his eyes. "He's got a new cure for testicular CA."

We all groaned.

Ira affected Raskolnovich's strange accent. " 'Sure t'ing dis time,' he says. Cisplatinum combination therapy. Do we have any patients for him?"

Raskolnovich was the mad oncology fellow. Every month he had a new cure for testicular carcinoma. Testicular carcinoma killed every last man who got it, but Raskolnovich was going to slay the dragon. It was just a matter of working out the right combination of drugs, said Raskolnovich. He was saying the same thing when I was an intern. He was spooking around the wards at dark hours even then, looking for patients to sign his informed-consent forms for his new, improved poison regimens. When there were no patients, he asked nurses to go to bed with him. Nobody took him seriously. He had long dark hair and spoke with an unplaceable accent and looked every bit the mad scientist. I asked him about the accent. Hungarian, he said. I had heard he was Argentine. He said that was true, but many Argentines are Hungarian. He also spoke Finnish and something he tried to pass off as English. I thought if anyone ever did find something for testicular CA, it would probably be someone like Raskolnovich. But he couldn't help anyone that night.

"Has he asked you yet?" I asked Caroline. "If you want to sign up for his protocol."

Caroline laughed. "I told him I thought I was low probability for getting testicular CA. I told him I'd take my chances," she said. " 'No problem,' he said. 'I got different protocol for nurses without testicles.' "

"He'd use you as a control subject."

Caroline laughed again. "He'd use me all right. I've heard about his special protocol for nurses."

It was good to have her laughing. It was bad enough doing rounds at Whipple without having a lot of friction among the staff. We were all supposed to be on the same side, after all.

We worked our way down the ward, in and out of the reeking rooms, listening to lungs, prodding at lymph nodes, avoiding the looks from patients who asked just the right questions for which there were no good answers.

Ludvik had a leukemic who had very few white cells and who spiked fevers every night. Like most patients who'd been around, the leukemic knew who had the power for which orders, and he asked me if we could stop doing blood cultures on him every time his fever spiked. He was running out of usable veins and the needle sticks from the blood cultures ruined what few he had left and we already had him on enough antibiotics to sterilize the East River. I agreed and Ludvik wrote the order to discontinue the blood cultures. Then Ludvik said it was Friday, and the leukemic's face screwed up in revolt.

"Oh, no," he moaned. "Not that finger again. I'm fine down there. I'd tell you if anything was wrong."

Fridays we did rectal exams on all the leukemics with low white cell counts to be sure they didn't have rectal abscesses, so they didn't get septic over the weekend. Ludvik started to put on his rubber glove.

"Do it after rounds," said Caroline. "Alone."

Ludvik looked to me. I looked at Caroline, whose face had tightened, and I nodded toward the hall.

We stepped out of the room.

"You can come back to do the rectals," said Caroline. "It's bad enough without an audience. Think how you'd feel."

"Twenty patients on this ward," Ludvik objected. "Eight leukemics. How're we gonna do all that and come back to do the rectals? Soon as we finish rounds my beeper's gonna start going off with three calls from the lab, two from the eighth floor, four from wherever. I'll never get back to do the rectals. Then we'd have eight septic leukemics this weekend. Better a little indignity than a lot of sepsis."

"We can't have eight leukemics getting septic this weekend," I told Caroline.

"Suit yourself," she said, exhaling, disgusted.

"Okay, so I'm Mister Insensitive," said Ludvik. "What am I supposed to do?"

"Do 'em after rounds," I told Ludvik. "Let's have some peace in the family, okay?"

Ludvik looked at Caroline with a green distillation of hate and shoved the glove back in his pocket. "I don't have the time for this," he said.

"If you don't have the time to do it right . . ." said Caroline, going red. "Oh, forget it."

I stepped between them. "Rounds," I said. "Remember? We are doing rounds."

We reached Professor Toomey's room. He was chipper and well oriented with a normal calcium now and he vigorously denied ever having wanted to jump out the window and circumnavigate the Upper East Side, and he looked at us as if we were crazy for asking whether or not he planned to jump out of his window now.

Mr. Toomey was in a private room. Usually these rooms were reserved for the sickest patients or for infectious patients. I asked Caroline how he rated one.

"We had him in a six-bedder," Caroline said, in her driest, most deadpan delivery. "But then one night his calcium went up and he got crazy and we found him urinating on his roommate's bed, with the roommate still in it. The professor was screaming, 'Fire! Fire!' He thought he was the fire brigade," she said. "We thought he'd do better in a single room."

7

THORACENTESIS

In and out of rooms: no one looked happy to see us. Ludvik pushed on the scalp of a leukemic and it gave way under his pressure and popped back up again. The neurosurgeons had cut away a three-inch-round hole in the skull and put in an Omaya reservoir, a rubber pond. Ludvik would come back later and push a needle attached to a syringe directly through the scalp and into the Omaya and inject amphotericin directly into the cerebrospinal fluid that bathed the brain, hoping to kill off the fungus living there. I'd seen Omaya reservoirs a hundred times, but it always gave me a chill to see that scalp indented and bounce back, a direct opening to the brain below. Omaya reservoirs were all the rage on that ward. Cryptococcus was making the rounds and the neurosurgeons were never far behind.

The next patient spoke only Spanish. We all shouted *"Respire profundo!"* at her and listened to her lungs, but we didn't know how to ask her if she was short of breath. Caroline asked her in very fluent Spanish, and then carried on at length. Watching her speak Spanish was strangely exciting, discovering this new part of her. She seemed so competent in a world where I could not even keep my head above water, speaking Spanish. And she made no great show of it. She acted as if any one of us could have done it. Caroline the foreign service brat. She'd probably speak Swahili next.

The patient had told Caroline she was, in fact, quite short of breath, which annoyed Ludvik greatly because she was his patient and he didn't have time to do the thoracentesis the patient clearly needed.

"Don't worry about it," I said. "I'll do it. You just call for the post-tap chest film and go down to look at it."

"No, she's my patient," said Ludvik heavily. "And you've got to get to morning report."

"Miss Bates will help me," I said. "We'll be done in no time."

Flicking me an appraising look, Caroline shrugged.

"Okay," she said. "If we can do it right now."

Rounds broke up. The interns went off to make their telephone calls and do their rectal exams and scutwork.

Caroline and I walked to the supply cart room and collected the thoracentesis tray and the blood gas kit.

"What makes you so sure she has an effusion?" Caroline asked.

"Talent," I said. "And first-class training."

"And the chest film you got on her last night."

"That too," I admitted. X rays made internists very much more talented.

We set up all the equipment at the bedside and Caroline explained everything to the patient. Caroline asked how I knew where to place the tube. I showed her how to tap out the effusion. She thumped on the patient's back until the note changed from the dull sound you get over a fluid-filled barrel to the deep, resonant sound you get over an air-filled drum. With a needle cap, I marked a spot well below the air-filled lung space, at the fluid level.

"The trick is to stick it into the part with the fluid sound," I said.

I pulled on sterile gloves and she poured out Betadine and I painted the patient's back with the amber disinfectant, using the spot we had identified as the bull's-eye. Then I unsheathed the big fourteen-gauge needle and told Caroline to pull on sterile gloves.

She looked at me, confused. She had assisted at thoracenteses, but she had never been told to put on sterile gloves. The nurse's role doesn't require it. She unwrapped a package and I watched her pull them on, carefully maintaining sterile technique.

"Does she speak any English?" I asked, nodding toward the patient.

"None."

I handed her the needle. We were standing behind the patient, who could not see what we were doing, and since she spoke no English, she could not understand what we were saying.

"What am I supposed to do with this?" Caroline asked.

I pointed at the mark on the back. "Just feel the rib, and go in over the top. The vessels run along the bottom of the rib, so you go in right over the top."

"You're nuts," she said. "I can't do that."

"Why not?"

"I've never done one."

"The cure for that is in your hand."

"I might stick it right in her lung. Give her a pneumothorax."

"You just tapped out the fluid line. You know you're going into fluid."

"I was just guessing."

"No, you know it. You just have to learn how to act on what you know."

You could see everything as it flashed across her face: astonishment, fear, delight, paranoia—I might just be a little insane—eagerness. Her eyes kept drifting toward the patient's back at the bull's-eye painted in Betadine. We did ten thoracenteses a week on her ward, but it was doctors' work, interns' work, more specifically. Nurses never did a thoracentesis. There was no reason of training or nature why a nurse could not do one. It was really very simple, if you knew how, but tasks were divided as if they were carved in stone at a place like Whipple.

"What is this?" she said. "You trying to put me in my place, or what?"

"I'm trying to teach you a new skill."

"It's a surgical technique."

"So, who am I? Denton Cooley? Interns learn this."

"Interns are doctors."

"Seymour Freudenberg's a doctor, a great and kind and learned doctor. Ludvik's a brand-new doctor. But who would you rather have doing your thoracentesis?"

"Ludvik," Caroline said, catching my drift. "Ludvik does three or four a week. Seymour hasn't done one in years."

"You don't need to be a mental giant or even a doctor to do a thoracentesis. You just need to know what you need to know and to have done a few to get the feel. It's like riding a bike. Once you do a few, you never forget how."

"But I'm never going to do this again, unless you're around. It's not a nursing procedure."

"You never know where you'll work, or what you'll have to do some night. So learn it. You may save a life, some night when nobody's answering pages."

She looked again at the bull's-eye.

"Interns do this five times a week. Each time they do it, they sweat bullets about hitting lung, knocking someone off with a pneumothorax. Do one yourself. Put yourself in an intern's shoes. It'll be educational."

She approached the back. She felt the rib and I checked her and she brought the needle to the skin and she swallowed hard, her Adam's apple bobbing up and down, and she plunged it in. Pleural fluid rushed out and I hooked up her catheter to the drainage bag and she looked at me with the look of a kid who'd just hooked her first fish.

Once we drained the fluid, I showed her how to do the blood gas. We bent the wrist back over the Curlex board, taped it to a short arm-board. Caroline felt for the radial artery. I showed her how to grease the glass syringe barrel with the heparin and how to keep heparin out of the needle and how to find the radial artery.

She got in the first stick. The glass plunger pumped up a centimeter with each heartbeat.

"How exciting," Caroline said. And for once, there was no irony in her voice. She watched that plunger rise with each heartbeat and she was thrilled. "I've seen this done a million times," she said.

But she had never done it herself, until that moment.

I popped the syringe into the cup filled with ice and ran it out to the ward secretary while Caroline remained with the patient to compress the artery for the required ten minutes. Then I walked back in and sat down on a chair next to Caroline, who was now captive to the artery compression schedule. She had learned thoracentesis and arterial blood gas and her face was flushed with the thrill of learning these things. She was very pleased with herself.

"You got Betadine all over your dress," I told her.

"Damn," she said. "And I'm out of spares. Usually keep one in my locker. Got vomited on Wednesday, and now I haven't got it."

"How do you stand it?"

"Stand what?"

"This place."

She looked at me as if I were making no sense at all.

"Whipple," I said, as if that was an explanation. "Everyone dies."

"It's such fun," she said, as if I was silly for asking. "Where else could I have learned two techniques—one of them potentially lifesaving—on the same morning?"

"It's the Black Hole of Calcutta. You heard the professor."

"Oh, yes, Professor Toomey. Well, I suppose you could see it that way. On bad days I do too. Then I think: What else would I like better? What should I do? Send off an application to Harvard Business School? Dress up in my power suit with my attaché case and go do battle in the world of big bucks and deals and organization men? For what? So I can buy a condo in East Hampton and pay a mortgage on some Upper East Side apartment? So I can look back ten years from now and say: What have I done? And have to answer: I made big bucks? And who did it matter to, except me and a few stockholders?"

I looked at her shiny hair, her clean, healthy skin.

"And who does your work matter to here?"

"This lady's breathing better now. It matters to her."

In Spanish, she asked the patient if she was breathing easier. The patient nodded and said yes.

"See?" said Caroline. "How many people can come home at the end of the day and say to themselves: I helped someone breathe today?"

"But you could do your good works anywhere. You don't have to work in this stinking, antiquated hole. Six-bedded rooms. Fatality abounding. No air-conditioning in the summer. You could work across the street, on one of those private wards in the Tower, even fancier than Hotel Whipple, with carpets on the floor and original art on the walls."

"The Tower? I thought the Tower was where all the Park Avenue docs dump their rich and famous patients to dry out."

"I thought you were the one who wanted to be filthy rich."

"I said I wouldn't mind it. But I wouldn't organize my life around it. I like doing what I do."

"Why did you leave Barnard?" I asked.

"I told you," she said. "To go to nursing school."

"But why? Even if you like nursing now, you couldn't have known before you did it. It's just not the kind of thing a Barnard girl would think of doing."

"This Barnard girl did."

"You said it was economically indicated, leaving college. Weren't your parents contributing?"

"My parents were not speaking. It's a long, boring story. I

needed to be able to support myself. Nursing sounded practical and noble and picturesque."

"What did your parents say?"

"My mother wrote saying she hoped it wouldn't affect my coming for Christmas in Amsterdam. My father . . . I'm not sure my father said anything, at the time."

I was already fifteen minutes late for morning report. I really did not want to leave. I wanted to sit down with Caroline over coffee and bagels and hear her whole life story.

"Have dinner with me tonight," I said. "Real dinner, at a real place. Not Gleasons."

"Real dinner? Now, there's an offer. But I can't tonight."

"Going out of town?"

She looked at me, disturbed, I thought. "Yes, actually." She paused a beat too long, studying me. "How did you know that?"

"Your dossier is on file," I said. "You are rumored to have business out of town. Regular business."

She drew in a breath and made her statement simply and without emotion. "I have a friend in Washington," she said. "If that's what you are referring to."

"So, your weekends are spoken for?"

She looked me in the eye. "Generally speaking," she said. "That is actually rather a touchy topic right now."

"I'll give you a ride to the airport."

"I take the train."

"To the train then."

"It's not worth the bother. I get a cab."

"It's no bother," I said. "It's Friday. I just happen to be driving downtown this evening."

"You'll never get out of here on time. My train's at five-thirty."

"I'll have you there."

"Look," she said. "You have arrived in my life pretty much at the wrong moment."

"I'd really better take you to the train."

"Bring my dossier," she said. "I need a good laugh."

8

DUMP MACDONALD AND SEYMOUR FREUDENBERG

Caroline's shift ended at three-thirty but she remained on her ward, giving reports to the nurses following her, charting on her patients, and getting in order all the details of running a busy ward for the weekend. It was four before she was ready to leave. I made it my business to hang around writing some of the longest notes ever inked into patients' charts at Whipple, waiting for her to pack it in. I wanted to talk to her before she left.

When she finally shrugged on her tweed jacket and swung her leather bag over her shoulder, I was lying in wait in the nurses' station.

She walked over and said, "You've been very diligent this afternoon."

"I'm always diligent," I said. "It just doesn't make the local press."

"You don't really want to drive me downtown, do you?" she asked suddenly.

I wanted nothing more than to be with her, than to drive her downtown if that was the way to be with her, but I had to do X-ray rounds, then chart rounds, and I never got out before six, usually not until seven, on Fridays. And she had a five-thirty train. I didn't see the logistics working.

"Look," I said. "What time does that five-thirty train put you in Washington?"

"Eight-thirty, nine."

"Then why not catch the shuttle at eight? You'd get there the same time. Then we could have dinner. Why eat those greasy Amtrak potato chips?"

She looked off for a moment as if she was doing some mental calculations, then her eyes came back into focus and she said, "If I can catch the eight o'clock shuttle, it'd work. But I absolutely must be on that plane."

"No problem," I said, trying not to look too pleased.

But I *was* pleased. I was delirious. I had wrested an hour from Washington, whoever that might be. Maybe I hadn't wrested anything. But I'd negotiated. I had an hour, maybe more, if I could get out of Whipple in good time. And I had the drive out to the airport with Caroline all to myself, which was another forty minutes. And I had her saying yes.

We set new standards for efficiency and speed doing rounds that afternoon. We did not wait for elevators: we ran up stairs. Ira nearly mutinied at the stairs—he wanted to get out early, but he drew the line at running up stairs. The X-ray file room, where we collected all the films on our patients, was always a bottleneck, and the clerk was even more torpid and indifferent than usual. She managed to find four of ten chest X rays we had to see. One of the missing films was on the Spanish lady whom Caroline and I had tapped that morning, and I had to be sure we hadn't punctured her lung and given her a pneumothorax, a collection of air between the lung and chest wall that can collapse a lung.

I made Ludvik swear a blood oath he would find the film and check it before he left the hospital, and he swore solemnly. Anything to get rounds over with early.

Chart runs were done with grim efficiency, none of the usual Friday afternoon chatter. We were all business, and we did business at a gallop.

Of course, whenever you got determined to accelerate, Whipple had a way of throwing curves and roadblocks at you. Halfway through chart rounds, Dump MacDonald swept in. It was Friday and Dump wanted to squeeze his notes into the charts, so it would look as if he'd actually come into the hospital each day to see his own patients, so he could bill the insurance companies for all the high-quality care he was not rendering. We all made sure to leave no empty lines between our notes and the notes immediately preceding, so Dump had to write in the margins. This particular evening, Dump decided we might appreciate the benefit of his vast and varied clinical experience and he held forth about the treatment of testicular carcinoma, about which he knew almost nothing and what he knew was wrong. I kept looking at my watch and thinking that every minute Dump rambled on was a minute I would not have with Caroline. I made polite noises about how we were all very interested but we had to continue reviewing our charts.

We made good progress until Seymour Freudenberg showed up. Seymour was an oncologist who was as good and admirable as Dump was bad and pathetic. He made rounds twice a day on his patients, and he was very nice to them. He wrote intelligent, well-organized notes that succinctly summarized the most complicated problems, and they were even legible.

When my mother needed an oncologist, I had asked Seymour to take care of her. She had loved Seymour right to the end. "Seymour Freudenberg," my mother had said, "is almost enough to make you believe in doctors."

When Seymour Freudenberg showed up, even if it was during chart rounds, you stopped what you were doing and asked him if you could be of any help.

"You guys are always a help," Seymour would always say. "You teach me things. You keep me nimble."

Of course, you couldn't teach Seymour anything. What Seymour didn't know about cancer hadn't been written. Seymour went off to do his rounds and we turned back to the charts.

Despite everything, we finished in record time. Ira and Ludvik were delighted to be finished so early.

"Young love," said Ira, "can move mountains. Look at us, we're all done. It's just all so romantic!" He sighed. Then he and Ludvik shared a knowing laugh.

As I said, at the Medical Center you were observed, no matter how hard you tried not to be.

I looked at my watch: it was already six. We had to leave for the airport by seven-fifteen. I ran for the stairwell and flew down nine flights, feeling guilty the whole way about all the things I'd probably missed trying to get out so early.

9

MANEUVERS

Caroline answered the door, wearing her raincoat. "I'd given up on you," she said. She looked happy to see me.

I looked at my watch casually, as if I hadn't been checking it every thirty seconds for the last hour. "Time flies," I said. "When you're having a good time."

"It does get away from you at Whipple," Caroline observed dryly. (I don't think she bought my act at all.) She knew I had to press hard to make it.

I stepped past her and grabbed her bag. Her apartment looked as if it had been ransacked: clothes everywhere, on the floor, on chairs, books strewn about. That was a part of her I was to get to know: her own indifference to disorder. It only concerned her as a matter of how other people might react. Left to herself, Caroline would never tidy up. She saw me looking around, and she switched off the light.

"I was in a hurry to get packed," she said.

We took the elevator to the garage and walked through the shadows to my car.

"Your very own garage space," she said. "You must be a very important person."

"I'm a saver of lives. A senior medical resident."

She looked at my banged-up heap, stripped of hubcaps, paint job like a case of measles, bumper reinforced with adhesive tape. "You really let the status go to your head, don't you?"

I threw her bag in the trunk. We walked up to the street.

A steady cold drizzle met us and there was the sound of the rain on the awning above us and the reflected light from the sidewalks, and the glistening street and the smell of the city in the rain.

"Wait here," I said. "I'll get an umbrella."

"No. Don't waste the time."

We started out into the rain. Caroline pulled her coat up over her head. I walked beside her and the water ran down my neck and soaked my legs, turning my white uniform pants translucent. We walked a block to McMaster's. We looked like a couple of shipwrecks by the time we arrived. They let us in anyway.

Caroline told the waiter we were in a hurry. He said the red snapper could be ready quickly and we took that. Caroline looked around. "Pretty place," she said. She had worn a pink sweater, and her skin was a glowing fresh pink color. The tablecloths and the color scheme of the restaurant were pink. Sitting there, she looked like a Mary Cassatt painting, with all her subtly blended shades of color. I began hoping we'd step outside to find the rain had changed into a blinding snowstorm, all airports closed.

The waiter brought a carafe of white wine and I poured us each a glass.

"You aren't from New York, are you?" she asked.

"No," I said, reaching for my wineglass. "Baltimore."

"And—let me guess—Daddy's a doctor, and all your brothers are doctors, except for the black sheep who went to law school."

"My father owns a garage."

Her wineglass stopped halfway to her lips.

"How many carburetors did it take to put you through college and medical school?"

"More than there are cars in Maryland. He took out a second mortgage on the house."

Her face changed.

"Your mother must have loved that, mortgaging her home on her son's education."

I thought about Caroline's mother, a mother who had run away.

I said, "She didn't mind." There was a silence. I said, "I never had your worries about the check arriving. I can't imagine that."

She exhaled sharply, "Well, my parents were hardly speaking. My tuition got lost in the shuffle."

"Who was supposed to send the check?"

"My father. He claims he thought he sent it to my mother. I think it was one of those lapses with a point."

"What point?"

"I got arrested in a war protest. This was seventy-one, you know. I was into long hair and love beads and about the only thing I am still proud of is that I marched against the war every chance I got. They had to get Dad out of a conference at the State Department to tell him I'd been arrested at a peace protest. Must have embarrassed the hell out of him. So my check got held up."

"And you wound up in nursing school?"

"I had vague notions of going over to Vietnam as a nurse, to spread mutiny and peace, but the war wound down before I graduated."

"Christ," I said. "How could your father ever look you in the eye again?"

Her surprise looked genuine. "How's that?"

"I mean, he didn't exactly support you."

"I can take care of myself. I don't need a sugar daddy."

"But you were just a college kid."

"In my family, we place a high value on self-reliance."

"I see," I said. But I really didn't see at the time.

"I had a lot of things most kids don't," she said. "Growing up."

"I get confused about your chronology. Go back to the beginning."

"To when? Barnard?"

"Start with birth. Work forward."

She laughed.

"You heard it all at Gleasons that night. I really had too much wine that night. You should have stopped me, you know. I was most embarrassed when I woke up the next morning."

She was born in France, during her father's first overseas assignment, and she grew up speaking French and English at home. Her father was determined she not become a typical American foreign service brat living in American compounds and never learning about the country she was living in. So she learned French in France, and later in Algeria, and she learned Italian in Italy, but she forgot it because she was only a year there. Then they moved to The Hague, where her mother began her fetish for Dutch diplomats, and the infamous trans-Europe child shuttle was launched. In Germany she learned German, and then back to Washington, D.C., where she went to high school, during which her parents' divorce became official. Her sister was dumped off with her father's sister in upstate New York and Caroline went off to Barnard. She declared herself an anthropology major.

"I took two courses with Margaret Mead," Caroline said. "As a freshman. Had to go talk to her and get special permission. She liked the idea I spoke all the languages. We had a lovely chat in her office. She served tea in stone cups from Samoa.''

Caroline thought she would grow up to be an anthropologist. Then the tuition checks stopped coming and she went to register for classes and she was told to see the registrar, who told her there was this problem with her tuition and room and board. The problem had, of course, been chronic, but some committee had met and Caroline was officially in limbo. Frantic letters and telegrams got sent to Daddy, who was then in Spain. He wrote back saying he thought Mother was handling the school bills. He certainly sent Mother enough money. Perhaps Mother had spent the money he sent for Caroline's schooling on her travels with her newest diplomat.

In the end, Caroline grew sick of it. Sick of the embarrassment of dealing with the college officials, sick of her roommates' sympathy, sick of worrying about whether she would come back to the dorm some afternoon and find all her belongings stacked in the lobby, evicted and kicked out.

She rushed off an application to the University of Virginia School of Nursing complete with the thirty-five-dollar application fee, which was a sizable capital expenditure, considering the dwindling state of her checking account. They wired back an acceptance pending an interview and she packed her trunk and hopped a bus to Charlottesville. Two years later, she graduated and Daddy came to the ceremony, acting befuddled, as if he thought she had been at Barnard the whole time, as if he was only now waking up to the fact that his daughter had been caught short and had to drop out.

Mother couldn't make graduation. She sent a long letter from Jakarta saying she never could stand the sight of blood herself, and grew faint at the sound of moans, but she congratulated her daughter and wished her all the best.

Caroline joined the Peace Corps, as a sort of belated gesture in Margaret Mead's direction, and "saw action," as she put it, in Honduras and Venezuela. It was in Honduras she met her boyfriend, to whom she referred as "my friend in Washington," who was finishing as she was beginning.

"He flew down from Georgetown, when he had vacations," she said.

I couldn't be sure what she meant by "Georgetown." Was he

going to school at Georgetown, or on the faculty? Or did she mean he lived in Georgetown, the neighborhood? She was maddeningly and tantalizingly vague about him. Intentionally, I supposed. I refused to play the game, to ask all about him. I simply sat and listened, and tried not to change my expression from one of benign, passionless interest.

She was all set to sign up for another tour with the Peace Corps when she got a telegram from Columbia Presbyterian Hospital in New York. Her sister, Isabel, had been admitted with a heroin overdose, and neither Daddy nor Mother could be found. Isabel had Caroline's address and didn't want her parents called anyway.

I was thinking about why Caroline was planning on signing up for another tour of duty when she had a boyfriend back in Washington who was flying down to see her and spending his vacations sloshing around the mud in Honduras. Was there more commitment on his part than on hers?

While I was considering this, I missed some of what she said about her sister, but when I tuned back in, Isabel was out of the hospital, living in SoHo, doing some modeling, and taking acting lessons and Caroline was working at Presbyterian and living on the Upper West Side. Neither sister had seen their mother for three years, which was fine with Isabel, but Caroline would have flown wherever she was invited. Daddy stopped by on layovers from Europe on his way to Washington. That is, he called on some of these layovers, and sometimes he took Caroline out to dinner. Sometimes he did not call, and Caroline got a letter mentioning that he had looked out of his airplane as he took off, and thought of her.

"And now you're going to want to know about my friend in Washington," she said.

Suddenly, I did not want to know. I did not want some sort of policy statement. It seemed better not to analyze, not to say too much. Just to enjoy each other and see where things led.

"No," I said. "Now I'm going to want to drive you to the airport."

She smiled knowingly. That annoyed me. I didn't like her sitting there looking as if she knew just what was going through my mind. I didn't know. Why should she? I didn't want her having that advantage.

She let me pay the bill, and we walked back to the garage and I

opened the door to the car for her and started up the car. We
wended our way up to the street, out into the wet night, down
York Avenue, black and glistening in the rain, past the Great
White Tower, past Whipple, down to the Fifty-ninth Street
Bridge, across to Queens. The traffic was moving well, and the
headlights and taillights of the cars sparkled in the rain.

Caroline said nothing. She just looked out her window and
smiled to herself. We arrived at the airport in plenty of time. I got
out with her, and I opened the trunk, and handed her her small
bag. She couldn't have packed a weekend's supply of anything in
there. She must have clothes in Washington.

She held the bag and said, "Don't come in," and kissed me on
the lips.

It wasn't exactly a peck. Longer than that. But it wasn't a long,
lingering preview of coming attractions either. It was just a kiss.
Good-bye. Nice to know you. Now I'm going off to the man you
wouldn't let me tell you about.

I watched her bounce off through the automatic glass doors, and
disappear into the crowd.

Then I flopped back into the car, slammed the door shut, leaned
over and locked her side, and drove back to the city feeling like a
grade A fool.

10

HAVING A WONDERFUL TIME

"Women," Forrest said, "are like razor blades. Use 'em and when they get dull, throw 'em out."

"Not even original, Forrest," I said. "Not even original."

We were sitting at the oak bar at Gleasons behind pitchers of draft, with plates of french fries. It was Saturday night and Caroline was in Washington with her boyfriend, whom she had met in the Peace Corps under the most romantic circumstances possible, and I was with Forrest and there were many unattached young ladies, most of whom were hospital people and therefore approachable. But I could not work up the motivation.

Forrest was staring covetously at my french fries. I shoved the plate in front of him.

"I've lost my appetite," I said.

"I give you the benefit of my own tortured insights, derived from long years of painful experience, and you reject it out of hand," said Forrest. "I don't know why I even associate with you." He was talking to the empty space in back of the bar, not to me. He was addressing the gods, the barman, whoever might want to listen to his semi-inebriated rantings. "Who am I kidding? I know exactly why I tolerate you. You're a fucking sexual magnet. I sit here and women just gravitate over here. They think you're safe, see. You look harmless. Fresh-faced, sweet. You attract 'em like honey attracts flies. Makes me fucking puke, 'cause you don't know what to do with the blessing the good Lord bestowed upon your face."

"What kind of guy would live in Washington anyway?" I said. "What is he? Some junior schlepper congressional aide? No, a lawyer. That's it. What else would you be if you lived in Washington?"

"I don't want to hear this," said Forrest; he looked over his shoulder, embarrassed.

"You don't think he's a doc, do you?" I looked at Forrest, who was now looking directly at the ceiling. "No, They don't have docs in Washington. Just lawyers and politicians and power lunches."

It made me feel better to have concluded that Caroline could not be spending the weekend with a physician. That could be serious competition, a doc. All lesser mortals could be edged out eventually, but a doc could be trouble: a surgeon especially, with someone like Caroline, who was so impressed by dedication, professional potency, competence, and all those good things surgeons have in such excess.

"She's down there with some senator," Forrest said. "And he's fucking her brains out."

"Forrest," I said. "Cut the suppressed homosexual panic routine."

"What!"

"Let's consider this problem rationally, methodically, systematically," I said. "We'll approach it with diagnostic objectivity."

"We've got one diagnosis," said Forrest, standing up. "You are having a fucking psychotic break."

"The possibilities are limited," I said. Being analytical seemed to help. Caroline Bates was a problem. This thing could be dissected, understood, and I would feel better. "This guy is either a surgeon, or he is not a surgeon."

Forrest took my arm carefully. "Now, just come quietly. Nobody's going to hurt you."

"If he is a surgeon, he could be serious competition." I continued, trying to ignore Forrest, who was growing more alarmed. "On the other hand, I have a two-hundred-fifty-mile advantage over him. He lives there, and Caroline lives here. She always has to come creeping back home, here, every Monday. And I live here. Waiting, like a spider in my web."

Forrest was waving madly now at a pair of nurses in mufti whom he spotted drinking Manhattans at a corner table. One of them stood up and came over.

"This man is very seriously ill," said Forrest, motioning with his hand in circles near his ear.

"Brendan," the nurse said. "You okay?"

I recognized her as the nurse we had met with Caroline in

Gleasons that night, the one who had gone off with Forrest. Her name was Sally Landau, and she was Caroline's friend.

"Why?" I asked her. "Would you fly forty minutes in the rain to spend a night in a grubby little cowtown, where the tallest building is an obelisk phallic symbol surrounded by nylon flags?"

Sally Landau looked from me to Forrest and back again.

"You all right?" she said.

"If you were a woman, and I was a man," I persisted. "And if I was hanging around, asking you out to dinner, driving you places, generally going out of my way to be pleasant and attentive, would you skip town for the weekend?"

"Oh," she said. "I see the problem."

"You do?" said Forrest, amazed.

"Caroline's in Washington this weekend," said Sally.

"With boyfriend," I said.

"She told you that?"

"She not going to fly off in a thunderstorm, take her chances on winding up as flaming wreckage all over Long Island, so she can drink tea with Aunt Minnie. She's with her boyfriend."

"What has she told you about him?" asked Sally.

I didn't like her caginess. She knew all about Caroline's boyfriend, that much was obvious, or she wouldn't have been so careful not to tell me anything I didn't already know.

"So who is this guy?" I asked. "Senator, surgeon, or slimeball?"

"Why don't you ask Caroline?"

"How well do you know Caroline?" I asked.

"We work together."

"And you go to Gleasons together, after work."

"Sometimes. That night we did. She felt like a drink."

"I had asked her that night to come to Gleasons. She said no."

Sally laughed. "Either she changed her mind or she wanted the drink but not with you."

"Assuming she knew I'd be there, and further assuming, perhaps an unwarranted assumption, but for the sake of discussion, assuming she wanted to see me that night I asked her to have a drink with me at Gleasons and she said no, I want to go home to a bath and a glass of wine, and then she shows up in Gleasons because she really is dying to see me again, just assuming for the sake of discussion, of course—why then would she then go fly off to Washington to this boyfriend in the middle of a fucking typhoon?"

"You're drunk," said Sally.

"I am just thinking out loud. You, however, do not want to engage in speculation, because you are being all cagey and calculating about your friend, which I respect. You go ahead and be a friend and don't tell me anything."

"Offhand I can think of about a dozen explanations," said Sally. "But look, you're a big boy now. Why play this she-loves-me-she-loves-me-not game? You want to know about her boyfriend? Ask the lady. You want to know if she wants to go out with you? Ask. Your problem is you're suffering from arrested development."

Forrest put his arm consolingly on my shoulder. "No woman is worth the trouble," he said.

Sally laughed at him. "Talk about arrested development," she said. "You are positively atavistic."

"Brainy cunt," laughed Forrest, running his hand over her rear end.

She grinned at him. They seemed to enjoy each other.

"I've got another friend for you tonight," said Sally, nodding at the woman she had left drinking beer at her corner table. This woman was lighting a cigarette and being careful not to look in our direction.

"I think I've had enough women for one life," I said, and headed for the door.

I heard Forrest's voice at my back. "In all your life," he roared, "you have not had enough women for one night!"

I don't remember the rest of that weekend. I think I spent Sunday wandering around Central Park, or maybe it was Greenwich Village. It didn't seem to make any difference.

11

MRS. ROUNDTREE

Monday morning, I did not happen to run into Caroline on the elevator at the Whitney, although I tried my best. The Whitney had four elevators and I did not manage to be on the right one at the right time to bump into her on her way to start the morning shift at Whipple. I lurked about the lobby until the doorman started staring at me, but I didn't see Caroline. That meant I had to wait until our team made its way to her ward on morning rounds. I was determined not to rush up there before rounds and sit around her nurses' station, panting like a dog in heat.

So you've been in Washington with your senator? Does that bother me? No, it does not bother me a whit. I am doing rounds. I am absorbed in my work. You have not entered my mind since I dropped you off at the airport.

Monday was bound to be a bad day. Our team was admitting Monday: we took all the new patients coming into the medical wards for twenty-four hours. I had more to worry about than Caroline Bates.

When we reached her ward, another staff nurse was waiting to do rounds with us. I didn't see Caroline but I restrained myself from asking about her. We did rounds and I went off to morning report not knowing whether Caroline was back from Washington, not knowing whether she had decided to stay down there and marry her senator, never again to return.

By the time I returned from report, Ira had already worked up our first admission.

"I think maybe you better go see her," Ira said, giving me a look. He wasn't smiling.

Her name was Barbara Roundtree. She was thirty-six years old, and had just got off the train from New Hope, Pennsylvania. She had three kids, a dog, a Volvo, a nice suburban life, and breast cancer. According to the letter her private doc sent with her, she had breast cancer just about everywhere you can have it.

"They did an EOD on her down there at some community hospital," said Ira. An EOD, an extent of disease evaluation, is usually pretty limited when done outside university hospital centers. We smirked a lot about the EODs coming from the community hospitals.

"This one's not half bad," Ira said. "Of course, they didn't think to look for metastases until after they had already lopped off her breast, but it's a community hospital, not the I. F. Whipple. And they did do a bone scan, which was positive as all hell—pelvis, tibia, lumbar spine, skull." Ira inhaled and said, significantly, "And they did a liver scan. She's growing breast there too."

Breast CA in the liver was thought to be the kiss of death at that time. What Ira was saying was, he didn't think there was much we could do for her.

"What's she here for?"

"She's got three kids. She's thirty-six years old. They hemmed and hawed a lot, down at the community hospital, but she got the message she's going to die. What would you do? She got on the train and she came to the best cancer hospital in the world: the Internationally Famous Whipple Hospital for Cancer and Related Conditions."

"She wants to be saved?"

"That's all." Ira shook his head. Then, "She's got three kids."

For Ira, having three kids was all the reason anyone needed to want to be saved, even if wanting to be saved made no sense at all. Having kids made all the difference, as far as Ira was concerned. It justified a certain amount of irrationality. It made otherwise incomprehensible actions totally understandable—like clinging to life when all hope was gone. At that time, before I had any kids of my own, I did not understand. Later, of course, I did, but not then. Then, it was just Ira being Ira.

So when Ira included in his brief summary of the salient points about Mrs. Roundtree the fact she had kids, that was the key point of information not to be missed or dismissed. I knew, the instant I heard Ira mention her kids, Ira was plugged in where Mrs. Roundtree was concerned, no matter how breezy or tough he sounded.

They had assigned Mrs. Roundtree to a private room. Usually the nurses saved the private rooms for patients who had frightening, contagious things. Sometimes they used a private room for a patient who was so agonal and wasted and near death that to shove her into one of those cramped six-bedded rooms with all the roommates staring at one another would precipitate a mass psychotic break. But they hadn't put Mrs. Roundtree in a private room for either of those reasons. The idea was to ease Mrs. Roundtree into Whipple.

It was a nursing decision, and Caroline Bates had taken one look at Mrs. Roundtree and led her to a private room.

Caroline was standing by her, the two of them chatting like old friends. Caroline looked up when I walked in and said, "Oh, here he is now."

Mrs. Roundtree looked up and smiled one of those reception line smiles, as if she were looking for someone she recognized, but she was going to try to fake it with those she didn't. She had clear pink skin and she looked very clean and fresh and un-Whipple, in her Talbots suit. She might have been checking into the Plaza for a weekend package deal of Broadway shows and dinner out with her husband. She was from the Real World, where most people did not have cancer, where shaved skulls with tubing running out was not a common sight, where people did not need Compazine to get through breakfast, and where life expectancy was measured in years as opposed to weeks.

At a glance, Caroline had done the right thing slipping her into the private room. Try dumping this lady into one of those stinky six-bedded rooms with three women made bald by chemotherapy, one yellow from her liver mets and another puking into her bedside commode, and she'd turn right around and hail the first cab back to the train station.

Caroline glided past me, passing closer than she needed to, so close, I caught a trail of her perfume. She said, "Be nice to this lovely lady. She's come a long way this morning." With that, she slid out the door, closing it behind her with a quick glance up at me, smiling to herself, as if she had played that as neatly as she pleased.

I never had a chance to act cool and nonchalant, and I never got to tell her how I hadn't missed her at all and hadn't thought about her for a minute after I dropped her off at the airport.

Mrs. Roundtree held out her hand and I shook it. It was a thin, cold hand, bruised from all the blood drawing they had done at her local hospital. She said: "Miss Bates told me all about you." I had the feeling she was talking to the wall behind me. I had the feeling she had been overwhelmed by the hospital, even in this sanctuary of a private room. I had the feeling she was just saying the same thing to everyone now.

Her husband, whom I had not noticed, stood up. He was a pale man, with unhealthy-looking indoor skin that made him look as if he'd been bled. He was getting his first shower of gray hairs at thirty-six—they would have sprouted since the surgeon told him his wife had breast cancer. He wore the standard dress fatigue uniform of the young suburban affluent set: L.L. Bean tattersall shirt under a herringbone tweed jacket, corduroy pants, and gum shoes with the rubber bottoms and leather uppers.

Looking at the two of them, you couldn't miss the unfocused look about their eyes, that stunned expression, as if they'd just been plucked out of the icy Atlantic, straight off the *Titanic,* but they knew they weren't safe even now.

Until this, the worst thing that had ever happened to either one of them was getting rejected by Harvard Business School, or having the BMW break down. This was something they hadn't been prepared for. They had been given the news you don't want to even think about, much less prepare yourself for.

Then they'd been told there is a place in New York that just might save them.

So here they were. You couldn't say they were happy, but they had some strong, vague hope. They were reacting, but they couldn't really concentrate or listen yet.

I stuck out my hand and shook Mr. Roundtree's hand and said my name. Sometimes if you can just do something plain, simple, and familiar, you can calm them down. It's better than slapping faces.

"I'm the resident who'll be helping with your wife."

"Miss Bates told us you'd take care of the day-to-day problems," said the husband. "I want to know where Dr. Freudenberg is. Our doctor in New Hope said Dr. Freudenberg would be my wife's doctor. All we've seen so far are interns and residents. When does the grand man sweep in and make an appearance?"

The good news was that Seymour Freudenberg was their attending. Seymour Freudenberg was not given to sweeping in anywhere. Seymour was humble and overworked and he was more

apt to amble in around nine p.m. and apologize about nine times
he couldn't get by earlier. Then he'd spend enough time to make
you understand why he never finished rounds until ten o'clock.

The bad news was Mr. Roundtree. If there is a denial phase that
makes you passive, and an anger phase that makes you hostile, it
was clear where he had arrived.

"Dr. Freudenberg is seeing patients in his office," I said. "He
makes rounds in the afternoon and again in the morning. We'll call
him and let him know your wife is here."

I tried to sound even and bland, saying that. Sometimes that
makes them even angrier, but sometimes it sets a tone of civility
that they accept.

Mr. Roundtree wasn't buying. "We came here because Dr.
Freudenberg is supposed to be a specialist. Why do we have to go
through all the warm-up acts?"

"The patients in this hospital have cancer," I said, just to wake
him up. "They tend to be very sick. Dr. Freudenberg can't be here
every minute. The interns and residents have to know your wife
too. If I'm called to see her at two a.m., I have to know her case."

"All you have to do is call Dr. Freudenberg. All you have to
know is how to dial his number."

"That's not the way it works," I said.

From Mrs. Roundtree's direction came a cool, sweet voice.
"Miss Bates said we were lucky to have you." Her voice came in
like a breeze. She seemed not to have heard a word her husband
had said. She just smiled sweetly.

Mr. Roundtree stepped over to her and put his hands on her
shoulders. "I'm sorry, Barb," he said.

I began to like him better. I even felt sorry for him. The guy
loved his wife, or he was one of the world's all-time great actors.
And he had been told, in so many words, that she was going to
die, unless the I.F. Whipple could pull a miracle out of somewhere. And all he'd seen were pretty ordinary-looking interns and
residents who asked all the same questions they'd asked in New
Hope.

"Don't mind me," said Mr. Roundtree. "I know you're trying
to help."

After the initial breast biopsy, they had tried to take some control of what was happening to them. They had discussed options
with their internist: lumpectomy versus simple mastectomy versus

modified radical. They had discussed adjuvant chemotherapy with the oncologist. They had interviewed several surgeons. I got the feeling they took a certain amount of satisfaction in rejecting the ones they rejected, as if the power to say no to those surgeons gave them the sense they were in the driver's seat: they were able to say no, we will not have this happen, we will have that. It gave them a feeling of controlling their own destiny.

Of course, they were in the driver's seat but they were not steering at all.

Mrs. Roundtree told about coming home after the mastectomy. "Richard was driving me home," she told me. "The kids were with us. I was in the backseat with Jason and Ashley, and we were getting closer and closer to our street and it all seemed so ordinary, driving home along familiar roads, and then I realized: It's not ordinary. I'm not the same. They've cut off my breast. And I started to cry. The kids got scared and pretty soon the whole car was sobbing." She said all this with a half smile, as if she found something vaguely ironic or amusing in the story, as if she were speaking of someone else, a distant aunt.

Then the pain came: low back pain and it wouldn't go away. Aspirin didn't touch it. They did a bone scan and found the reason: She had breast cancer chewing up a vertebra, impinging on a nerve root. And then, as Ira had said, they got around to doing a liver scan and she had it there too. And maybe in some places it hadn't been found yet.

"The surgeon told us he cured her," said Mr. Roundtree, more in frustration than complaint.

"This whole thing," I said, "must be quite a shock."

"If you had told me at Christmas we'd be here now . . ." said Mr. Roundtree, shaking his head, with a hard smile. His eyes glazed over, with visions of another, happier time, a few months and now light-years away. He said: "New Year's, we went out. Everything was fine. A nice time of life." His eyes traveled over my face. "Now this," he said. "Out of the blue."

He examined me carefully, curiously, as if I had answers for him.

"But I must have had it," said Mrs. Roundtree, "even then. I just didn't know it."

Their kids were four, six, and ten. Two boys and they got their girl on the third try. He was a lawyer. She had been a nurse, but she hadn't worked since her first baby.

"I worked in the happy part of the hospital," she said. "Labor and Delivery."

There was a flat area on her blouse where her left breast should have been—she had not had time to have a false breast made for her bra—but otherwise, to look at her, you could never have guessed she had cancer in so many places. She looked pretty and hopeful and so alive. It was hard to believe she had breast cancer in all those places Ira said they had found it.

I stood up to go.

Mr. Roundtree stood up and said, quite suddenly, "We've always been careful people." It was as if someone had pushed the sound button, and suddenly you could hear what was playing inside his head, as if the speakers had burst to life with the slip of a switch.

"Yes," I said. "I imagine you have."

Mrs. Roundtree said, "Careful is not the word for it. Whenever we fly without the kids, Roger and I take separate flights. Roger insists." Mrs. Roundtree laughed, and she looked at her husband with genuine amusement, as she must have looked at him so often before in the years of their marriage, before this crisis. Seeing her look at him with that mixture of mirth, affection, exasperation, and acceptance, I had an intimation of what they must have been like before disaster struck. Mr. Roundtree the worrier, the phobic, the controller, the kind of guy for whom life insurance, disability and overhead insurance, was not enough—he would have umbrella insurance, earthquake insurance, and disaster insurance. But I bet they never thought to insure Mrs. Roundtree. Who ever thinks to insure a mother? It's the men who die. Men get heart attacks and die young. Women are bedrock. They last forever.

Mrs. Roundtree was telling me about their travel procedures. "You know, separate flights: so if one plane crashes, the kids won't be orphaned. Can you imagine? We went to Aruba for our first romantic getaway together in years, without the kids. We took separate planes."

"Well," I said. "It makes sense."

Mr. Roundtree caught me with a look. "But what do you do

. . . how do you plan," he said, swallowing so his neck bulged, "for something like this?"

I said I didn't know and escaped out the door.

I stood in the hallway and breathed. There hadn't been enough air in Mrs. Roundtree's room. There would never be enough air in that particular room for me. That was the very same room where they had put my mother. I had spent too much time sitting by the bed in that room, looking out the window at the kids swarming over the little playground with the concrete dinosaur across the street.

"Playgrounds bored me when you were that age," my mother once told me as she watched the kids from her bed. "But now, I lie here and I can't wait for the kids to come out to play."

"I like that playground," I told her. "I like that dinosaur, whatever it is."

"Triceratops," my mother told me. "Three horns. You knew the names of all the dinosaurs when you were three."

"No kidding? I don't know any now."

"Oh, you knew them all," my mother said. "Now all you know are the names of diseases."

But things had changed since my mother was a patient on this floor. None of the nurses were the same. There was a new head nurse assigning patients to the single private rooms. And new patients with the same old problems.

In the nurses' station, I took Ira aside.

"We've got to talk about this Mrs. Roundtree," I said.

"Real nice lady," Ira said, pulling at his tunic collar. He looked sweaty and tired, and it was still morning and we had more than thirty hours yet, on call. He lit a cigarette for himself.

"Ira," I said. "How can you smoke?"

"The one thing I learned in Nam," he said, inhaling luxuriously, the dry skin around his eyes crinkling. "When the man upstairs says your time is up, it's gonna happen, no matter what. Until then, you might as well enjoy yourself." He grinned at me and blew out his smoke at the ceiling.

"This lady," I said, "has the potential to be big trouble."

"At least Freudenberg's her attending."

"Thank heaven," I said, "for small favors."

"Seymour's one of the few reasons to believe there may be something to all the greatest-cancer-hospital-in-the-world crap. You know?"

"Seymour's a good omen," I said.

"Oh, Christ," laughed Ira. "That again? O'Brien, I keep telling you: Everything is written. Nothing is luck."

Ira was trying to distract me with his metaphysics. He did that on admitting days when he didn't want to think about how many admissions he was going to get and how little sleep.

"This lady has everything going for her," I said. "Seymour Freudenberg and a private room."

"Her husband's a bit on the hostile side," Ira observed, grinning.

"You noticed that?"

"He wanted to know when Seymour was going to, and I quote, 'Get off his duff and come see my wife.' Seymour, who makes rounds twice a day and fucking never stops seeing patients and lives in this place. And this bozo's complaining because Seymour's not in the reception line at the door of the hospital the instant his wife arrives. He'll be complaining about the service next. Just you wait—he'll want to know where the ice water is. Caroline should've put her in a six-bedded room, just to sober them up."

"He's taken a pretty good hit. And he's new to this game. People say things. He thinks about it later, he'll feel silly," I said.

"Not this buzzard," said Ira. "He started building his case the minute he walked through the door. He'll be taking depositions any minute. We'll all be testifying about this case for years to come, even if we found the golden bullet and cured her. He'd have us for inflicting emotional trauma."

"What does Seymour want us to do for her?"

"I just got off the phone with him," Ira said. "She's going to be randomized to some protocol."

"So we just sit tight with her?"

"He wants us to complete the EOD."

As we were talking, Caroline slid into the room. She started leafing through the Medex files of patients' drugs on the medication cart, but she was listening to us.

"I told him she had an EOD already," Ira said, referring to the extent of disease evaluation Mrs. Roundtree had had at her local hospital.

"She's had part of an EOD," I said. "I didn't see the CT of her lung or her head, the LP, the bone marrow, the mammogram of the other breast."

"That's just what Freudenberg said."

I knew Freudenberg would want all that. He always had, when I was an intern taking care of his patients.

I said, "Great minds think alike."

"Okay," sighed Ira, reaching for the order book. "I'll write the orders. But damn if I can see how it's going to help her."

"She's got to have most of that for the protocol anyway," I said.

"As I said, it's not going to help her," Ira said. "It's just so she can be compared to everyone else in the protocol."

"Who knows?" I said. "She may get the lucky protocol that cures breast CA."

"And I might win the New York lottery and be made chief of medicine this afternoon," said Ira. He reached for the order book and started writing orders for Mrs. Roundtree's studies.

"She's got to have the entire program explained to her so there'll be no surprises," I told Ira. "You've got to tell her about each study, step by step so she doesn't sit in there worrying about what we're going to do to her next."

"She used to be a nurse," Ira objected. "She knows what all this stuff is."

"She worked in Labor and Delivery. She's never seen the inside of a CT scan and never had a bone marrow. Tell her all about the fun and games. And be as nice and lovable as you always are."

Ira stood up and saluted. "Aye, aye, skipper," he said, grinning. "I will educate this lady and probably scare the living shit out of her."

Ira went off to go over things with Mrs. Roundtree.

Caroline came over and sat down next to me.

"You talk to her husband at all?" she asked.

"He kept telling me that three months ago she was perfectly healthy," I said. "They had a nice life."

"He can't get over it," Caroline said. "His world was all planned and ordered and now it's just a shambles."

"Three kids, a dog, and a Volvo station wagon," I said. "Suburban life."

"Don't sound so superior," Caroline said. For a moment I was sure she was about to cry, thinking about Mrs. Roundtree.

"I thought you liked life in the big city," I said. "Young, single and female and free."

"Did I say that?" She looked at me curiously.

"Maybe I just read into things."

"Well, you're right," she said. "But sometimes, I can see the attraction of a slower pace, kids, PTA meetings, all those ordinary things. Especially when things have been really crazy around here. I can see the life of a Mrs. Roundtree in suburbia. This morning must have been awful for her. From sunlit lawns to the Black Hole. Isn't that what Professor Toomey called it? The Black Hole."

"Only now she's here, at the best cancer hospital in the world," I said. "Getting LPs, and bone marrows. By the time we're done with her, she'll think she'd have been better off if she'd stepped in front of a truck one day. At least it would have been all over in an instant. Would have been better that way."

"Better for her, maybe," said Caroline. "But not for her husband and kids. This way they'll have a chance to ease into the idea she's dying."

"No," I said. "Better for everyone she walks out the door one day and steps in front of a truck and it's all over."

"You just say that because you don't know. You don't see things from the other side of the bed."

I looked at her. "And you know how it feels?" I said. "From the other side of the bed?"

"I've been around here longer."

I let that slide. I was only too familiar with the view from the other side of the bed, and it was not a view you forget. But there didn't seem any point in talking about it.

"You think it's better, for her kids to watch her waste away? You know how she'll get. Solid tumor cachexia. Her kids won't even recognize her."

"They'll be ready for it when she dies," she said. "If you're going to lose your mother, better that it's slow, gradual, so you can accommodate to the idea."

"There's no good way to lose a mother," I said.

"Some are worse than others. Besides, by the time it happens, she'll be ready too. She's not ready now."

"That's for damn sure. She's got that hopeful, urgent look. *Le sale espoir.*"

"She's only had her diagnosis, what? Months. She doesn't have to understand everything at once."

My beeper went off. The number was for the fifth floor. It would be Ludvik calling with another admission. It was getting to be a bad day.

I dialed the number, looking at her. She stood there, arms folded, watching me speak into the phone.

"A Dump MacDonald gift," said Ludvik. He sounded tight. "Forty-year-old guy with AML who's failed every protocol, never could be induced. Now he's admitted septic and Dump says just put him to bed and hold his wife's hand."

"Sounds easy enough," I said.

"You should see this guy," said Ludvik. "You wouldn't say that."

I hung up and looked at Caroline.

"Just to make your day complete," she said. "Professor Toomey has a temp. And Vince Montebelli's gums are bleeding."

"Wonderful."

"Have lunch with me," she said, as if it were the only logical reaction to this disaster morning.

One thing about Caroline: She could keep you off balance. I never knew what to expect. Ask her to come for a beer and she turns you down cold, then shows up with a girlfriend. She spends the weekend with her true love in Washington and comes back and asks you to lunch. I suppose none of that happened by accident. Caroline had her strategies, and her timing was very good.

12

A CHOCOLATE DOUGHNUT

The admissions kept pouring in all morning: a forty-five-year-old man with malignant melanoma ulcerating messily all over his shoulder; a woman, lungs filling up with fluid from ovarian carcinoma metastases, gasping for breath, eyes bugging out, filled with panic; another woman: lung cancer and brain mets, vomiting. Around one o'clock things began to settle down, and I realized the cafeteria would close for lunch. I called Caroline and she said she'd meet me.

In the cafeteria, Caroline was nowhere to be seen and I went through the line and parked my tray at a table. I was suddenly hungry and wondered if I should wait for her or just go ahead and eat. Cafeteria etiquette for metropolitan hospitals. Hunger won out. I assaulted my Whippleburger.

"Sorry I'm late." I heard her voice as she slid into the seat next to me. There was an empty chair across the table, but she took the one next to me, and brushed me with her knees. Her tray looked bare with just a salad and a Coke. "Mr. Toomey decided to drink water from the toilet bowl and Vince Montebelli started vomiting blood," she said gaily, as if she were talking about something cute the dog did.

"Never fails," I said. "Everybody's quiet until the day we're admitting, then all hell breaks loose. Vince couldn't have done this number yesterday, when we had all the time in the world. Oh, no. He waits until today, when we are so bombed we don't know the patients without a program."

I started to get up, to go see Vince. Caroline tugged me back into my chair by my sleeve.

"Don't worry, your interns are on the job. Ludvik got a calcium on Toomey and a GI consult on Vince. You are the senior resident now: you don't have to put out all the fires by yourself. That's what the interns are for."

"Nice how they keep me informed."

"They were going to page you. I told them I'd tell you."

"You told them you were meeting me for lunch?"

"I said I was going to talk with you."

"They'll draw their own conclusions, if I know them."

I studied her. If she was bothered about the prospect of rampant speculation, she didn't show it. In fact, she seemed amused. Oh, well, she was the one with the boyfriend.

A patient, about four years old, wearing overalls and a T-shirt, appeared at the head of the food line. He rolled an IV pole behind him, with the IV in his forearm. Looked like they'd done a cut down to get the IV in. He was pretty nearly bald from his chemotherapy and they had painted some violet radiation therapy portal lines on the sides of his head for purposes of lining up the radiation machine they would aim at his brain. Leukemic cells could hide out behind the blood-brain barrier, out of reach by chemotherapy, so the kids got their brains irradiated. He might have had a brain tumor, but he was pale enough for leukemia, and the chemotherapy baldness and the IV pole made leukemia a better bet. Acute lymphocytic leukemia, ALL, the best and the worst of the leukemias: best because it's occasionally curable; worst because given that potential, you've always got to try.

Caroline watched him come through the line as she ate her salad.

"Oh, sweet little guy," she said. "And he's got ALL, don't you think? He's got his purple war paint on. They're radiating his little brain going after those sequestered cells."

He was a sick kid, thin and pale, and bruised from all the IVs and blood drawing. But he looked cheerful, and his parents were with him, looking like parents visiting their kid's new boarding school, trying to look pleased for him. They stopped at the dessert counter about ten feet from us and the kid looked over each of the pastries and pies very carefully and with great joy.

"I want the big chocolate one," said the kid, pointing to a big doughnut with conviction. "That's the one."

His mother looked with obvious misgivings, but the father, a big, burly man, said, "What the hell. Let the kid have a doughnut."

The mother took the doughnut to the cashier while the father and the kid headed for an empty table next to ours. I continued eating, but I watched them come.

I was thinking about the kid, about how none of the hospital people, nurses, doctors, techs, seemed to notice him. Patients were allowed in the cafeteria, although they usually ate in their rooms. I couldn't take my eyes off the kid.

As Caroline worked her way through her salad, she glanced over at the kid and his father taking their places at the table next to ours.

"You guys really are getting bombed today," said Caroline.

"I knew we would."

"Why?"

"Bad luck, admitting on a Monday."

"I would think Fridays would be worse: everybody getting nervous before the weekend, and all the attendings dumping off their problems."

"Mondays are bad luck at Whipple. Bad things happen."

Caroline put down her fork and stared at me with a smile of utter incredulity. "What do you do when there's a full moon? Hide under your bed?"

"I have my own superstitions," I said. "Based on my own observations."

"But that's irrational," said Caroline.

The mother arrived with the doughnut. The kid held it with both hands, as if it were the best doughnut he'd ever seen, and he bit into it. His mother watched with an expression that began as trepidation and slowly dissolved into pleasure, watching the gusto with which the kid was devouring his prize. Obviously, this was a rare concession to childhood fancy. His expression was pure joy. His father watched his kid enjoying himself.

Suddenly the kid vomited, without warning, without even being able to avert his head, so the doughnut popped up, macerated, on the tabletop in front of him. The kid looked embarrassed, and sad and disappointed. His mother froze with a look of sudden panic.

Caroline jumped up and darted to his table with a bunch of napkins before I could move.

"A little too much of a good thing," she said casually, as if kids vomited up doughnuts all the time in this cafeteria. "You okay?" I marveled at her easy way, which seemed to purge all the embarrassment and uneasiness from the situation.

The kid didn't look at her. He looked at his erstwhile doughnut, now an oozing, gelatinous heap on the tabletop. The kid looked very sad.

His mother, at least, could smile with Caroline, and rub her son's bald head, and try to pretend this was just another one of those many things kids at Whipple have to learn to shrug off. But you could see the mother was very close to caving in herself. She was just putting up a front for her kid.

"Don't worry about the table," Caroline said. "I'll take care of it." She went off to find a cafeteria worker.

The kid stood up and backed away from the mess on the tabletop. The mother rubbed his neck and guided him away—he was sobbing now—and they walked slowly out of the cafeteria, her arm around him, his head hung in defeat and frustration, pulling his IV pole along with him.

The father sat staring dully at the tabletop in front of him. I could only guess at what he must have been thinking. He looked up, and our eyes met.

He shook himself to attention, and he stood up and followed his wife and son out of the cafeteria.

I stepped over to the table and wiped it up using my own napkins and tray, and I carried the tray over to the window for dirty trays and stowed it.

"Hey, what's this shit!" the cafeteria worker in the window said.

"Vomit," I said.

"I don't touch that."

"Fine," I said. "Leave it there," and I walked back toward our table.

I could hear him shouting, "Don't leave that here. I don't touch no vomit."

Caroline arrived at the table with another cafeteria worker, who sponged off the tabletop with a disinfectant that smelled of pine oil at a distance of several yards.

Caroline sat down with me back at our table. She returned to her salad. I went to work on my french fries and offered her some, but she shook her head. We ate silently, with the smell of pine oil strong.

"How nice to be really hungry," said Caroline. "To be able to eat without vomiting."

She was attacking her salad.

"The simple things in life," I said. "A body free of chemotherapy, an appetite, and a morning without regurgitation."

She continued eating and I watched her. She could no more have sat at her own table and left that kid sitting there than she could have turned her back on a foundling left in a basket.

None of the doctors or nurses at any of the other tables around us had even glanced in that kid's direction, but everyone had seen what happened. Caroline had jumped over there, cheerful and helpful.

Working at Whipple had not eroded that capacity in her. People who work at places like Whipple become the most insulated of human beings. Someone falls in the hall, you observe for a moment; you decide whether or not you want to get involved, whether you want to expend the energy. There're just too many of them, too many cries for help. But whatever it was that happened to most people—and it was happening to me—had not happened to Caroline.

"I don't know how anyone can work in pediatric oncology," Caroline said.

"I don't know how anyone works in oncology, period," I said.

She looked up at me, and studied me for a moment. Oncology was her chosen field of nursing. She decided not to rise to the bait, and said, "What are you going into?"

"A nice happy field where everyone gets better. Where you actually cure people."

"That could only mean ID," she surmised correctly. Infectious disease, a field where the dragons had, for the most part, been slain. This was before AIDS. ID looked like a happy place to be, in those days.

"I can see the appeal," said Caroline. "Seems like everyone would want to do it."

"No, they have trouble filling fellowship slots some years."

"Why?"

"There's not much money in it."

"That doesn't bother you?"

"I won't starve."

We lifted our Cokes and drank and looked at each other. over the rims.

"When does your fellowship begin?" she asked.

I hesitated before I answered, then I thought, what the hell? It has to come out sooner or later.

"July first," I said. "I count the days."

"Where's your fellowship?" she asked, very casually, as if she was just being polite. But she was looking at me now. She had put her Coke down.

"Boston," I said quickly, as if I could throw it by her before she noticed.

I hated to admit it. The only advantage I had over her true love in Washington was proximity. Now that I was marked for departure, I lost that.

"Sounds wonderful," she said. Her tone was neutral, unreadable.

"Well, I've been in New York a long time. I figured I could use a two-year break."

"You think you'll come back?"

"I'm trying to set that up now," I lied.

We fell into silence again.

My beeper blurted. I answered from a wall phone. It was Ira. We were getting another admission.

"You're going to love this one," he said. "Another gift from Dump MacDonald."

"Wonderful."

"Sixty-four-year-old guy with metastatic pancreatic CA. Yellow as a canary. Liver full of it. Not making a whole lot of clotting factors, so, you guessed it: He's bleeding from every orifice and he yorks up a little every now and then just to make things exciting. He was sent home to die, but when the bleeding started his wife lost her nerve and shipped him back to us."

I did not want to think about this dump from Dump MacDonald right then. I was in serious discussion with Caroline Bates. "So what are we supposed to do?" I asked. "Just put him to bed?"

"Oh, you haven't heard the best part." Ira dropped his voice. "Dump wants us to keep this poor sucker alive until April first. April Fools' Day, appropriately enough."

"What?"

"He's got some kind of insurance policy that doesn't kick in until then, so he's got to be kept going, says Dump. I've got a good mind to call the chief res. I got a shitload to do already without this."

"I'll come over. Where are you?"

"Don't bother. I got to see him first. And the solid-tumor fellow's here talking to the heme fellow about it. Come in an hour. He's on eight."

I rejoined Caroline and told her about the admission.

"I told you Mondays were bad luck admitting days," I said.

"I can't believe the superstition. You go in for sticking pins into dolls and things like that?"

"I believe in luck. I put my left shoe on first, I have a bad day: fifteen sick as stink admissions, three deaths. I put my right shoe on first: three admissions for protocols, everyone's happy. You think after that I'm going to put on my left shoe first?"

"All that is is your attempt to control the uncontrollables," said Caroline, shaking the ice in her Coke, studying me. "Which shoe did you put on first today?"

"Right."

"And you're getting bombed anyway."

"If I'd put on the left first, we'd be getting bombed even worse."

She laughed and shook her head as if I were a hopeless case.

"Change my luck," I said, "Have dinner with me."

"I've already been to dinner with you."

"But I mean really go out. Not when you're on your way out of town and we've got to beat the clock."

"I'm not sure what you mean—'really go out.' "

"I mean, have dinner with me tomorrow. Chinatown. Little Italy. Somewhere more than two blocks from the hospital."

"You'll be in no shape tomorrow. You'll be lucky to get two hours sleep tonight, the rate you're going."

"I'll be fine."

"We'll see how you feel tomorrow."

Again, the beeper. Eternal intruder. It was Ira again.

"Hey, hey, you'll never guess what Vince Montebelli's up to."

"Surprise me."

"Did the lovely Miss Bates tell you?"

"She mentioned it."

"She said she was going to see you. I hope that means you're speaking to me from your apartment and nobody's got any clothes on."

"Actually, I am in the cafeteria and so is Miss Bates and we are fully uniformed, but my interns keep paging me with horror stories."

"Well, Vince opened up like a faucet," Ira said, unabashed. "He's got big-time DIC."

"Delightful."

"And the GI boys are down here. And, oh, I forgot. We took him down to the ICU. He starting vomiting blood in the elevator. I thought he was going to bleed out right then and there. And the elevator operator wants us to get off his elevator, 'cause he don't allow no blood in his elevator. I mean, I'm putting up with this tsouris while you're off in the cafeteria with the estimable Miss Bates."

"Builds character, big boy."

"That's what they used to say at the academy," laughed Ira. Ira had gone to the Naval Academy before they sent him to Vietnam and put him on a longboat. "We're pumping in fresh frozen and Pitocin into Vince down here."

"How's he look?"

"Like fucking at death's door."

"I'm on my way."

"Not to worry," said Ira. "Everything's under control. I just wanted to keep you informed—you bitch so much if I don't tell you things."

Caroline was right. It was going to be a long day and by the time it was all over the next evening I'd probably be in no shape to have dinner with anyone.

13

PROFESSOR DAEDALUS INSTRUCTS

Things got worse that day. Things always got worse before they got worse at Whipple, and then they kept on getting worse.

In the ICU, Vince was thoroughly plugged in. He looked like a broken marionette, a body dangled from strings. He had monitor wires and IV lines and catheters and his eyes were closed as if he didn't want to see any of it.

I leaned over the bed rail and whispered, "Vince?"

He opened his eyes and rolled them in my direction.

"Am I dying?" he asked. "Tell me. Don't bullshit me."

"He doesn't trust me," Ira said. "He says I'm too emotionally involved, poor deluded man."

Looking at Ira, it was clear Vince, sick as he was, could still see things clearly enough. Ira, for all his unflappability, was bright red in the face, and his eyes were all injected and right on the verge of brimming over.

"Hate to disappoint you, big boy," I told Vince. "But you are not quite ready to check out of this hotel, quite yet. You're going to have to put up with our bad company for a while longer."

The barest curl of a smile played at the corners of Vince's lips. "Don't kid around."

"We do not let people bleed out around this joint," I said. "Some have tried, but it's kind of a point of pride with us. With what you got, we never lose a patient. Nobody is allowed to die from bleeding."

"I'm scared shitless," said Vince. Tears welled up and rolled down into the deep hollows of his cheeks.

"I'm not kidding, Vince," I said. "Hell, hook me up to all these monitors and I'd think I was dying too. But you're not even close. You're fine."

"That's just what Bloomstein said."

"That's the party line. It's true, too."

"Can you ask Caroline to come down here?" Vince asked.

"Sure. You believe her, if she tells you you're okay?"

"Yeah."

"Believe her and not me?"

"Yeah."

"I am crushed, Vince."

"Why did this happen?"

"You got DIC, Vince. Everyone gets it eventually, if they hang out here long enough. Like gonorrhea in Subic Bay."

"Bloomstein said the same thing. Same line about Subic Bay."

"I got the line from him. Never been to Subic Bay myself."

"When you get out of here, Vince," said Ira, "I will personally make your reservation for Subic Bay. You'll see."

Vince started to cry.

Ira's mouth dropped open. "Vince, what's the matter?"

"I'm never getting out of here. I'm not going anywhere except the basement. The fucking Eternal Care Unit."

"Wrong," said Ira. "All wrong. You just had a little setback here. You're gonna be okay."

"What am I going to do in Subic Bay?" said Vince. "They cut off my balls."

"You got everything you need," said Ira. "You can still do the deed."

"Really?" asked Vince, his eyes open wide.

"Sure, didn't they tell you?"

"All I remember is they told me I had cancer."

"Well, it's true," said Ira. "You're going to Subic Bay, just as soon as you get out of here. You're gonna catch the worst case of clap a Whipple Hospital alumnus ever caught."

Vince closed his eyes, absorbing all this. For a moment, there was peace. The ICU was the quietest place at Whipple. There was just the sound of the respirators and the soft peeping of the cardiac monitors and it was all like soft background Muzak in a dentist's office.

Suddenly, my beeper went off with a Code Blue and the number of a room on the ninth floor.

"Kee-rist," Ira said. "That's Professor Toomey."

Vince opened his eyes, startled.

"It's not you, Vince," I said. "It's on another floor."

"Some other guy you knew wasn't in trouble," said Vince unhappily.

Ira had already bolted out of the ICU door. I backed out, waving to Vince, reassuring, trying to appear to be in no hurry. When I turned the corner, I broke into my Code Blue gallop.

Caroline and another nurse were wrapped around Professor Toomey's legs. He had decided this time he would not be denied, and he was perched on the windowsill, making vigorous efforts to launch himself into the wild blue yonder above First Avenue. He just might have succeeded, had it not been for the equally determined weight of Caroline on one leg and the other nurse on the other leg. Ludvik tried to pry the professor's fingers off the window. Ira had arrived before me and he stood with his chin in his hand, observing the scene.

"I will not be denied!" Toomey cried.

"I'm betting on you, Professor," said Ira.

"Shut up," said Ludvik, still working to disengage the professor's fingers.

We managed to carry the professor writhing to the bed, where we pinioned him with a Posey restraint and Caroline got the wrist and ankle restraints on him.

We all stood back to catch our breath and Caroline said, "I'm getting out of here, before something else happens." She slipped out the door.

"Must be his calcium again," said Ludvik, studying the professor.

Ludvik started to do all the things the professor needed and Ira and I were standing there wondering when the next admission was going to roll in when Caroline flew back into the room and said, "Mrs. Roundtree looks like she's going to die."

Caroline, if anything, had understated the case: Mrs. Roundtree was sitting forward, leaning against her bedside meal table, sucking air through her mouth, eyes bulging, face dusky and glistening.

Mr. Roundtree stood over her saying, "What is it? Say something!"

Ira and I pressed our stethoscopes on her back and heard no breath sounds at all. With each gasp, we advanced the stethoscopes toward her shoulder. It wasn't until more than two thirds of the way up that I could hear breath sounds.

"I already tapped it out," said Caroline. "It's a big one." She had already collected all the equipment we needed to do a thoracentesis.

"What is it?" asked Mr. Roundtree tremulously, from the far corner of the room.

"She has fluid compressing her lung," I said. "I'd like you to step into the hall."

"Does Dr. Freudenberg know about this?"

"I haven't called him," I said. "You really want me to wait until I call Dr. Freudenberg?"

Mr. Roundtree looked at his wife. You didn't need four years of medical school to know that delay was not in her best interests.

"Well, where the hell is he?" Mr. Roundtree barked. The words came out like pistol shots.

"Dr. Freudenberg?"

"Yes, Dr. Bigshot Freudenberg! The king of oncologists who we came all the way up here to have for our doctor."

Mrs. Roundtree was breathing hard, using all her neck and shoulder muscles to move air into the parts of her lung that hadn't been compressed and collapsed by her effusion.

"I imagine he's in his office at this hour, seeing patients," I said. "Where would you expect him to be?"

"I expect him to take care of my wife. I expect him to be here when she needs him!"

"We can't know when something like this is going to happen," I said. I wanted to add: What do you expect? Seymour Freudenberg to sit by your wife's bedside from admission to the day she's discharged? You're paying for a doctor, not a butler. But I didn't say any of that. It wouldn't have made the slightest impact on Mr. Roundtree. I said, "Do you want me to wait to speak with Dr. Freudenberg?"

Mr. Roundtree looked at his wife, who was gasping, heaving, clinging to the bedside table, and looking as if she might die at any moment.

"No," he said. "I suppose not."

Caroline took him off down the hall. Ira and I went to work. We had the fluid off very quickly.

Mrs. Roundtree coughed and then breathed in deeply. "Oh," she gasped, smiling weakly.

A respiratory therapy tech arrived, called I supposed by Caroline, since neither Ira nor I had had the time to think of it. The tech hooked up a Ventimask to the oxygen outlet and Mrs. Roundtree breathed into it.

"Oh, much better," she said, her skin pinking up nicely. "You guys are on my good list."

I left Ira with Mrs. Roundtree and walked back to the nurses' station.

Mr. Roundtree was standing there with Caroline and he leaped at me as I stepped through the door.

"How is she?" he said. He had a quaver in his voice and his eyes jumped all over my face, looking for clues to the news I brought. I knew then how surgeons feel after successful surgery, bringing the glad tidings to the family.

"She's fine," I said. "Go ask her yourself."

He flew past me and out the door.

I looked after him.

"The man loves his wife," Caroline said. "Can't hold that against him."

"We get a lot of husbands up here," I said. "Most of them behave better."

"Seymour Freudenberg wants you to call him."

"You did a nice job," I told Caroline. "With Mrs. Roundtree."

"All in a day's work," she said. "I am now a world-class chest thumper."

I phoned Freudenberg. "You're a giant, O'Brien," Freudenberg said. "Thanks."

"I think Mr. Roundtree was not too thrilled to have mere residents tapping his wife," I told him. "I think he would have preferred Michael De Bakey arriving by Learjet."

"You guys did as good a job as De Bakey could. You probably tap more chests every week than he does."

"She had an effusion a trained chimpanzee could have tapped," I said. That wasn't false modesty. Her effusion was medical student stuff. There was so much fluid, it would have been hard to hit anything else.

"Just be sure you check her post-tap film," said Freudenberg. "And Brendan, I know you're harried over there, but if you have the time, I'd appreciate it if you could talk to the husband. Half that hostility is he feels helpless and useless. He's used to feeling smart and now he feels dumb and insignificant. Make him feel important."

"For you, Dr. Freudenberg," I said, and we hung up.

When I hung up, Caroline had a telephone plastered to her ear and was copying down numbers. She handed me a paper with *Toomey* written on the top and a list of his lab numbers. His calcium had blasted off again.

"Let me guess," said Caroline. "Just let me guess what Mr. Toomey gets."

"He gets an Omaya reservoir, is what he gets," said Ludvik, stepping through the doorway.

Caroline's smile evaporated. Ludvik had just returned from looking at Toomey's spinal fluid under the microscope. He had seen scores of crypto swimming around. He had already called Infectious Disease, and Neurosurgery.

Professor Toomey was on his way to the Eternal Care Unit. We'd treat his meningitis and we'd do all the right things, and he would not last the week.

"No," Caroline said.

"He's got cryptococcus," said Ludvik, flatly.

"Well, don't sound so worked up about it," said Caroline, face blotching.

Ludvik was confused by her heat, and looked to me and back to Caroline.

"I am not worked up," Ludvik protested.

"Of course not," snapped Caroline. "It's just another crypto for you. You got the Dx and you won't even be late for dinner."

Ludvik stared at her, uncomprehendingly.

"What am I supposed to do?" he said. "Convince myself I didn't see the crypto? Maybe you'd like it better if I didn't even look for it."

I stood up and stepped between them.

"Now, now, ladies and gentlemen," I said. "We do have a patient to see."

We went to see him. He was lying in bed, strapped down but no longer fighting the restraints, looking calm and harmless. He seemed to be asleep. His respirations had quieted. In fact, it took me a few seconds to realize, he wasn't breathing at all.

We tried to resuscitate him. Called a code, brought the troops running. Pumped on his chest, intubated him, the whole nine yards.

Then the chief resident showed up and flipped through the chart as we were slapping in IVs and calling for bicarb and doing all the code-type things. He caught my eye.

"Uh" was all he said. What he meant was: Why are you doing this poor patient the grave disservice of trying to resuscitate him?

"Well, he only just got the crypt," I said. "He's been looking real good until today."

The chief res shook his head, and he was right. We all knew he was right.

"Okay," I said. "Thanks, everybody."

Caroline was passing the meds. She looked at me, stunned, uncomprehending. "But he was just talking to us," she said.

"He's got a calcium of sixteen," I said, defeated. The chief res was standing right there. "Myeloma unresponsive to therapy and cryptococcus in his CSF."

We called off the code.

Caroline and the nurses started to clean the room and they began to wrap up Mr. Toomey for the trip to the morgue. Ludvik went to call Dump MacDonald, who was Mr. Toomey's private doctor.

I felt useless.

I walked out to the nurses' station and poured myself coffee into a Styrofoam cup. The chief res was sitting there and I poured him one too.

"What's the story?" he said.

"We all liked the guy," I said. "He was just talking to us."

"According to the last note in the chart, he was just trying to take a flying leap out the window," said the chief res. "Who were you treating with that code, you or the patient?"

I shrugged. "Who knows? Maybe we could have got him past the crypt . . ."

"Brendan," said the chief res. He didn't say, Who are you trying to kid, but that's what he meant.

"It was worth a try," said Caroline, from the doorway.

"I'm sure he appreciated it," said the chief res, standing up, lumbering past her, out the door.

"Who the hell does he think he is?" said Caroline, looking after him, chin rising, color high.

"The voice of reason," I said.

"You didn't have to sound so apologetic," she said.

"I didn't think Professor Toomey would mind," I said.

14

DESOLATION ROW

Professor Toomey must have died toward the end of Caroline's shift. I don't remember seeing her again that day.

Caroline must have gone home soon after her shift ended at three-thirty in the afternoon and a new set of nurses for the evening shift came on. Seeing the nurses bring on the fresh troops was somehow demoralizing.

Ira, Ludvik, and I were sitting in the nurses' station on the eighth floor and nobody had paged. Nobody had died or bled out or arrested for at least thirty minutes, and I was getting nervous that things had been so calm.

"If things stay this quiet," Ira said, "we might even get to eat dinner tonight."

"That's right," I said. "Tempt fate."

Ira laughed.

"How'd you ever make it through Vietnam, Ira?" I asked. "Spitting into the wind, like that?"

"As I have often told you," he said. "If it is written, it is written. Ten admissions, two admissions. Six hours sleep or none."

"Nothing is written," I said. "It's all luck."

We sat there and I contemplated whether it could possibly have been written that Professor Toomey would die on this day in March, strapped down in bed in the most famous cancer hospital in the world, whether his multiple myeloma and his cryptococcus could all have been details of a more cosmic plan, and whether it was foreordained that I would have Mr. Roundtree as my special cross to bear for my last few weeks at the I. F. Whipple. We sat there, and I considered all this, and Ira smoked and Ludvik phoned for some lab results.

Then I thought about why Caroline had left that afternoon without saying good-bye. She was probably still angry about Professor Toomey. Angry that I called off the code so quickly, and angry that I had agreed with the chief res rather than fighting. And she was angry that Professor Toomey had died.

To hell with Caroline Bates.

I had other things to worry about than Caroline Bates.

We didn't seem to have enough fingers to keep all the leaks plugged that afternoon. Leukemics kept getting septic. Blood pressures were plummeting all over the place. Admissions kept arriving uninvited and in the back of my mind was always Vince Montebelli down in the ICU, capable of blowing out a bleeder anytime, and Mrs. Roundtree who could always reaccumulate fluid and stop breathing.

We tried getting organized to do X-ray rounds—we had a lot of X rays to see, including Mrs. Roundtree's chest film—but we kept getting interrupted. At five-thirty, we managed to make it to X Ray. I did not invite Mr. Roundtree to come look at his wife's X ray, although the thought crossed my mind. Seymour had asked me to include Mr. Roundtree, but there just wasn't time. We finished X-ray rounds by six.

"The cafeteria beckons," said Ira happily. "Lasagna night."

We raised a happy cheer and we all raced out to the elevator, visions of Whipple gourmet lasagna dancing before our eyes. Then the door opened and Seymour Freudenberg stepped out. I could hear Ira murmur, "Shit," under his breath. We all loved Seymour, but Ira knew he was going to have to kiss his lasagna good-bye.

"Just the young heroes I was hoping to find," said Seymour as the elevator door shut behind him. "Let's go see Mrs. Roundtree."

I told Ludvik to go on to the cafeteria. Mrs. Roundtree was not Ludvik's patient. He was not honor bound to go see her with her attending, as Ira and I were.

Ludvik didn't say a word. He just nodded and disappeared through the doorway to the stairwell. Ira and I waited for the elevator with Seymour and Ira looked at the ceiling and hummed under his breath.

Now, I want you to understand about Seymour. We really did love him. He was like some village priest, with whom you could never be yourself, whom you had to respect and admire. For Seymour Freudenberg, medicine was not a living, it was a calling. But right at that particular moment, when he stepped out of the elevator, the most important thing in the world to Ira and me was lasagna. Everything else could wait half an hour.

But you couldn't say that to Seymour.

Seymour saw patients all day, ate a tunafish sandwich in his car on the way to the hospital, and did rounds until all hours of the night. Then he got up the next morning and started all over again. How could you tell someone like Seymour to go ahead and do rounds without you, while you went off to lasagna night in the cafeteria, even if the Whipple Hospital cafeteria lasagna was the best lasagna in the entire borough of Manhattan?

"I asked him once," Ira told me once. "Don't you ever see your kids? And he says, 'At graduations. They know I'm a doctor.' And I say, 'But you're a father too.' And he says, the way he says it, 'Ira, there are only good doctors and bad docs. Either you're in it, or you are not.' "

Seymour had said something like that to me once. He had told me what a privilege it was to take care of my mother. I laughed, and said, "Some honor." And he looked at me—I'd never seen him more serious—and he said, "It is always an honor when a patient comes to you and puts her health in your hands. With your mother it was a special honor."

So there was no question of not trudging after Seymour and doing rounds until he decided everyone was tucked in for the night. But we were both thinking about that lasagna, knowing Ludvik wouldn't save us any.

The elevator arrived and we rode it up to nine, to see Mrs. Roundtree.

We paused outside Mrs. Roundtree's room.

"Her husband still here?" asked Seymour.

"He's camped out," said Ira.

Barbara Roundtree looked pink and happy and she was breathing nicely, and Mr. Roundtree had decided he liked Ira and me for saving his wife. They both beamed at us when we walked in with Seymour. Mrs. Roundtree was eating her lasagna dinner from her tray, and the aroma was almost enough to make me swoon. We had been on our feet all day, and there had been no time for lunch or even a trip down to the vending machines for a Coke. I could see Ira was drawn toward that tray. He stood right next to it, looking at it from the corners of his eyes.

"These young men," Barbara Roundtree told Seymour, "were very kind to me today."

"They are fine young physicians," said Seymour, who could say that sort of thing and get away with it. Ira's Adam's apple bobbed up and down. He was getting all choked up. Seymour had said he was a good doctor. Coming from anyone else, Ira would have laughed it off, but coming from Seymour, that meant something.

While Seymour was speaking, everyone had focused on him—everyone except Ira, who, I noticed, deftly filched a square of lasagna from Mrs. Roundtree's tray and popped it into his mouth. When he was hungry, Ira had no shame at all.

"But why did it happen?" Mr. Roundtree asked. "They said she had fluid in her lung. Does she have a tumor in her lung?"

"It's a good bet she does," said Freudenberg.

"Oh, God," said Barbara Roundtree, putting her face in her hands. "I hadn't let myself believe that. Good Lord, it's in my lungs now."

"That's something we can treat," said Freudenberg. "That's why you're here."

"But where else is it?" Mrs. Roundtree's face was imploring, the tears ran down. "In my lung? In my spine? Is it everywhere?"

Mrs. Roundtree's face was splotchy red, tears running down and dripping off her chin.

"We'll look for it and we'll find it and we'll treat it," said Freudenberg.

Mr. Roundtree put his arm around his wife. We left them there.

Freudenberg stood with us in the hallway. I checked my watch. The cafeteria would close in ten minutes.

"You guys know a patient named Montebelli?" Freudenberg asked.

"He's ours," said Ira gloomily, realizing that rounds with Seymour were likely to drag on and on, as usual. "Down in the ICU."

"I've been asked to see him," said Seymour. "Let's go down there."

We walked down the elevator and Ira hummed another Dylan tune, "And the Good Samaritan . . . He's getting ready for the show."

He didn't finish the song. He didn't have to. We had sung it together many a night: "He's going to the carnival tonight. On Desolation Row."

Raskolnovich, the mad oncology fellow, was in the ICU reading Vince's chart when we arrived.

"You will please call me?" Raskolnovich said, "When the autopsy is done on this Montebelli."

"We don't usually do those, until the patient dies," I said. "Even at I. F. Whipple."

"I understand this," smiled Raskolnovich. "But this one has now DIC and his chest X ray looks like a snowstorm and it won't be long. I need tumor for my rats. Sterile tumor."

Freudenberg said, "You know, theoretically, there should be good therapy for testicular CA. It's fast-growing, sensitive to several agents. It's like chorio. You cured chorio. Why can't you guys come up with a cure for testicular?"

Freudenberg was kidding, but he was serious too. We had all heard that Raskolnovich had some success with cisplatinum as part of a new combination drug therapy in a pilot study. And we had Vince, and about a dozen others just like him, who needed some good poisons posthaste. Vince was getting a combination of drugs that were simply labeled with a number: Nobody, not even Raskolnovich, knew which drugs were in Vince's packet, and nobody would find out, until the study was over and the codes were broken, or until Vince died, whichever came first.

"He's not on the good stuff," Ira told Raskolnovich. "He hasn't responded a flicker. His tumor hasn't batted an eye. He's getting the shit stuff. Probably the same stuff his buddy who already died got. You've been giving your good stuff to somebody else. Vince needs some good stuff."

But Raskolnovich was not about to break protocol. He wasn't sure about toxicities, and he wasn't absolutely sure his special supercombination, which had looked so good against testicular CA in the pilot study, was really as good as it looked. Several patients had died in the early-phase studies and it wasn't clear if the deaths were from drug therapy. Raskolnovich was keeping to his game plan and he wouldn't break the codes until he was sure. Not that Raskolnovich could have broken the protocol on his own, even if he wanted to. He was the driving force in the cisplatinum combination drug protocol, but it was a multicenter trial, funded by the National Institutes of Health. Rasko was part of a team—the quarterback—but still, he had to be a team player no matter how much he believed in his new combination, and he had to play by the rules.

Raskolnovich laughed and shoved Vince's chart at him. "First you get me tumor. Then I get you really good poisons." He disappeared out the door, lab coat flapping.

"That guy gives me the creeps," Ira said.

"You know what gives me the creeps?" said Freudenberg. He nodded toward Vince, sleeping in his bed, strung up in a tangle of IV lines and monitor wires. "That gives me the creeps."

There was a certain look patients got when too much had been done to them, when too many things had been sewn in with black surgical silk in too many places, a look that at a glance meant they just were not going to recover. Vince had that look now. The skin on his bald head was so pallid, it looked translucent, veins visible coursing beneath, except where subcutaneous bleeding had stained broad purple patches, and his temples were hollowed, his eyes sunken, and his lips crusted and bloody.

It was hard to believe that just a few weeks ago this body had belonged to a man who thought himself healthy.

Freudenberg was right. It was enough to give you the creeps. It was enough to make you put your right shoe on first every day and to carry a rabbit's foot or whatever you found worked. Caroline could be as rational as she cared to be. For my money, I'd bite my tongue, knock wood, and wonder every day why it was Vince in that bed and not me.

— 15 —

TOMORROW IS SUCH A LONG TIME

Nothing much happened that night. Vince Montebelli did not die or bleed or drop his blood pressure. Mrs. Roundtree did not reaccumulate her pleural effusion and her chest film showed we had managed to avoid puncturing her lung when we did the thoracentesis. Nothing much kept us up until four a.m., little details, checking potassium and platelet counts and hematocrits and hemoglobins and culturing up the hot leuks—all the details that had to be controlled, all the adjustments that kept things from getting away from you.

At five a.m., Ira looked at me and said, "What are you doing up at this hour? Go to your room." He had a point: no sense in both of us staying up all night. He was also a little bit sensitive. When you're an intern, you don't want to think your resident doesn't trust you enough to go to bed and leave the ward to your care. Ludvik was already in bed, and Ira would not do anything stupid, so I went off to find an on-call room.

There was one empty on the seventh floor, with the usual bare light bulb, the mattress that might pass for a concrete slab, the petrified pillow and the inevitable telephone, right next to the pillow. I was asleep the instant my head touched the pillow. I got a solid two hours sleep until Ira woke me for rounds at seven.

I showered and shaved in the on-call room and changed into the clean, pressed blue oxford shirt I had stowed in my black bag. I hadn't thought to pack a fresh tie, and the maroon-and-blue-striped one I had worn the day before was stained with blood and Betadine in spots, but it was a dark tie and it didn't look too bad.

Except for the puffiness around my eyes, I looked reasonably fresh and presentable. I brushed my teeth with mint toothpaste and rolled up my razor and toothbrush in my filthy yesterday's shirt and stuffed it back into my bag. I was ready to meet the day, ready for rounds, ready for Caroline Bates.

Ludvik and Ira were in the ICU. They were drinking coffee and Ira was examining the big three-foot-square clipboard with all Vince Montebelli's lab data and vital signs and urine output and IV input.

"He seized this morning around five," said Ira. "Gave him Valium and Dilantin and he stopped."

Vince was now postictal, the quiet state which often follows a grand mal seizure. He was not talking to anyone and it would be hours, maybe days, before we could tell whether or not he had anoxic brain damage. Ira said he'd already put in the neurology consult. Not that neurology could do much. Neurologists spend ninety percent of their time making diagnoses, pinpointing lesions nobody could do anything about. I don't know how anyone can be a neurologist.

"I called his sister," Ira said. "I don't think she understood much. I think she understood something bad had happened."

Ludvik looked at Vince, flaccid, bald, hooked up to all the wires and IVs and monitors. "He is definitely plugged in," Ludvik observed.

"Bread-and-butter neurology," said Ira. "You can have it, Ludvik. You can have it."

The three of us stood there, looking at Vince, and we all got more and more depressed.

"Internship only lasts a year," murmured Ira. Interns chanted that phrase as soldiers said the Twenty-third Psalm, for comfort. "And then we can grow up and be good doctors," said Ira. "Like Seymour Freudenberg, the eternal intern."

"I thought you liked Seymour."

"I love Seymour," said Ira. "But he depresses me."

The eighth floor went fast, with Ira and Ludvik nodding and blinking through most of it. My interns were not in good shape that morning. Between them, they had admitted thirteen new patients in the prior twenty-four hours. And we had twelve more hours left to tuck in everyone before we could go home.

Caroline was waiting for us on Nine with the clipboard with all the patients' temperatures, the "fever board," under her crossed arms.

"You had a lovely night," she said. "I heard all about it. Five admissions."

"Five admissions," snorted Ira. "Five on your floor. The team took thirteen hits overall." His hair was greasy and uncombed and he needed a shave, and you could smell him at four feet, and his uniform was smeared with blood and stool and Gram's stain and urine, and if I'd been a leukemic with a low white blood cell count, worried about catching infections, I would have started screaming if he got within fifteen feet of me. He looked like a Bowery bum. He looked like a Whipple intern after a bad night. Ludvik looked like a storm trooper just back from the Eastern front.

Caroline, on the other hand, looked wonderful, impossibly clean in her spotless white uniform, skin rosy and unblemished, eyes bright and glossy. She was wearing some sweet perfume and the effect was intoxicating. It was hard to believe anyone could look so undiseased and fresh and vibrant. Ira and Ludvik and I stared at her dumbly until she snapped us out of it.

"Come on, zombies," she said. "Duty calls."

We followed her into the first room and we made good progress down the hall, patient after patient.

We arrived at Mrs. Roundtree's room, and stopped outside. Ira told Ludvik about Mrs. Roundtree's brush with pleural effusion and sudden shortness of breath, which Ira referred to as "acute dyspnea."

"I've always loved that word *dyspnea*," said Caroline. "I might name a daughter Dyspnea some day. Dyspnea Bates."

I was the only one who smiled. Ira and Ludvik were in no mood, even for Caroline. They just stared at her.

"Okay," laughed Caroline. "I'll shut up."

"The effusions," said Ira. "Mean she's got it in her lungs now."

Caroline stopped kidding around, "This must seem so surreal to her," she said, speaking of Mrs. Roundtree. "Can you imagine? A few weeks ago she was carting her kids around to soccer games."

"That's all over," said Ira.

"O ye of little faith," said Caroline. "Dr. Freudenberg has a protocol."

"Ain't no protocol going to save this lady," said Ira. "Only she doesn't know it yet, and I'm not going to be the one to tell her."

There is no humoring an irritable, sleep-deprived intern. Such interns see truth with unmerciful clarity and they become snarly and belligerent when faced with denial, even when it comes from nurses.

Caroline knew all this and said nothing.

We filed in to see Mrs. Roundtree. Mrs. Roundtree was looking very pretty in her pink gown and she was breathing easily and we listened to her lungs and we heard no fluid.

"All clear," Ira told her.

"Then the fluid's all gone?" said Mrs. Roundtree, beaming.

"Gone," said Ira. "And there wasn't any on the X ray last night."

"Thank God," she said.

She took Ira's hand and smiled up at him. He tried to smile back and he glanced uncomfortably over at me. I smiled back. The lady feels good this morning. Why speak of things to come?

We stepped out into the hall and Caroline asked how Vince was doing in the ICU. Ira told her about his seizure.

Her face went blank. There was a short intake of air and she collected herself.

"Cancer," she said, "is the disease of nice people."

It was the old intern's saw: Heart disease gets the bastards. The nice people get cancer.

Rounds were over. Ludvik and Ira went off to make their phone calls to laboratories and Radiology and consult services and I was due at morning report. I stood there in the hallway, arranging my three-by-five cards, one for each new admission I had to present at report.

"The troops look demoralized," said Caroline.

"Internship gets depressing," I said. "It's supposed to make everything that comes after it seem good by comparison."

"It must work," Caroline said. "You look cheerful enough."

"Of course I am," I said. "You're having dinner with me tonight. I've got something to look forward to."

"You'll be lucky to be able to keep your eyes open by tonight."

"Dinner in Chinatown," I said, and walked off to take the stairs to morning report.

Report was wonderful. One of the best reports ever. Report is supposed to be a critical review of what you did for each of your new admissions, but with thirteen admissions, nobody was listening after the sixth case. I could have said I admitted six leukemics and sent them out to Lincoln Center with tickets to the opera and none of the six residents or the chief resident would have blinked: their eyes glazed over early, when they saw me lay out that stack of thirteen three-by-five cards. The professor who was supposed to provide the ultimate scrutiny of our handling of the new admissions, lapsed into semicoma early on and confined his remarks to murmuring, "Fascinating," after each case. By the time I'd finished, nobody had any more idea than I did who any of these new patients were or what we had done for them.

In the hallway, after report, Forrest stood next to me, smiling at the ceiling. The professor who had taken report was standing several feet away, and Forrest spoke under his breath so the professor couldn't hear.

"Aren't we lucky?" Forrest sighed. "To be training at the greatest cancer hospital in the world. I can hardly wait to get back to the mother ship."

By which he meant the Manhattan Hospital, where things worked right, where thirteen admissions would have been shared by four teams of interns and residents instead of one, and where you could get a full professor to come in at three a.m., if you needed one.

"Thirteen hits," he said. "The Grim Reaper was knocking on your door and all you had was Ira and Ludvik to fend him off."

"They're good interns," I said.

"They're good interns," said Forrest, "but they are only interns."

He was right, of course. You did feel alone at Whipple. We had been lucky to get through the night with so few casualties.

I walked back to the ward, elated, knowing I had two days before I had to do it all over again.

The morning passed and I might have had lunch. I don't remember. I do remember checking Mrs. Roundtree, after morning report. Her lungs were clear and she was breathing easily, but I had a dim, disquieting feeling that she didn't really remember who I was.

— 16 —

IF YOU KNEW BROOKLYN
LIKE I KNEW BROOKLYN

Later, I found myself in the nurses' station, staring at the phone. I knew I had a call to make, but I just could not think what it was. I could feel that cloud descending as it inevitably did after an admitting cycle. I drew my three-by-five cards out of my shirt pocket and unclipped the top card, which had the list. I always wrote down a list of things to do for the day after, so I wouldn't have to try to think and remember. Sometimes the system worked. Not this time. Nothing on the card made sense.

From behind my back, Caroline's voice said, "You don't really want to go out to dinner tonight. You must be wrecked."

She had a point there. My legs felt as if they were underwater and I ached all over. The smart thing to do was to admit she was right and ask for a rain check. I said, "I'm looking forward to it." That's how smart I was.

"You're mad."

"Chinatown."

"You will be out on your feet. You already are."

"I get a second wind around five," I said. "Or are you trying to back out gracefully?"

"I was just trying to let you off the hook."

"I'm not even wriggling."

The rest of the afternoon passed in a blur. Ludvik and Ira trudged down to Radiology for X-ray rounds with me and we took the elevator back to the wards to do chart rounds. They were glassy-eyed. I think we probably opened every chart and we must have looked at some of the lab values.

I paged Forrest before I left. He sounded grim. He was on call for the night.

"You sound awful," I told him.

"Six admissions," he rasped, in his funereal tone. "And it isn't even six yet."

"You're an iron man. You love it."

"I keep telling myself: I am not an intern. Things could be worse. I will eat at Gleasons tonight, like a gentleman. Meet me around seven."

"Can't."

"Oh, don't go home and crash," said Forrest. "That's so decadent. Eat dinner like a normal human being. Then you can go home and crash."

"I have a prior engagement."

"A hopeful sign. I hope Miss Bates is going to be spending some time *chez* O'Brien's."

"I'm having dinner with her tonight."

"What a giant! Thirteen admissions last night, and tonight, Miss Bates."

"It's all very tame: Chinatown. She has a boyfriend in Washington, remember."

"Chinatown? This sounds serious. Like an actual date."

"If I can stay awake for it."

"She could keep me awake," said Forrest. "I want a full report. I want excruciating detail."

Leaving Whipple at six that evening, I realized I had thirteen hours until I had to be back on the ward again. Pushing through the revolving door, I looked along the street running toward the West Side. The sky was turning magenta in the sunset. I thought: I have thirteen hours and I have Caroline Bates to play with. What a lucky human being I am.

Showering revived me a little. I ran the water from as hot as I could stand it to cold. That woke me up, but I knew it wouldn't last. As long as I did not sit down, I could stay awake.

I changed into my brown Harris Tweed jacket and pink oxford cloth shirt and blue jeans and threw on my raincoat and checked myself in the mirrored closet door. My fly was open. I corrected that. Did I have my wallet? Right inside pocket. What else do you need to go out to dinner? I stood there looking at myself. There seemed to be a dull buzz in my brain.

Did Professor Toomey die? When did that happen? Vince, something bad about him. Mrs. Roundtree was okay. Dinner. Caroline.

I took the elevator down to Caroline's apartment.

She answered the door and her surprise looked genuine.

"You weren't kidding," she said. "I thought you'd be in deep coma by now."

"I am feeling no pain. Let's go."

"You should be in bed."

"I can always sleep."

She asked me in, and her apartment looked as it had the first time I'd seen it: clothes and books everywhere, dishes piled in the sink.

"You ought to keep your door locked," I said. "Keeps the riff-raff from rifling through your things."

"I really didn't think you'd show up," she said. "The place is a mess."

The books struck me: Anne Tyler, Vladimir Nabokov, Larry McMurtry, scattered around but obviously read. Library books.

I don't remember walking to the subway, but I do remember the train roaring up, and us stepping on, avoiding the man with no legs who was scooting around on a wooden platform with wheels, and I remember him holding up a tin cup to each of us, and I remember Caroline tossing a quarter in his cup and I remember her saying, "Poor man," and me saying, "He probably makes more than I do, with that tin can," regretting it as soon as I said it, and the last thing I remember about that subway ride, I was telling Caroline we needed to get off at Canal Street.

The next thing I knew we were outside in the rain. It was a fine, misty rain and it was dark and we were nowhere near Canal Street.

"Where are we?"

"Brooklyn," said Caroline, with secret merriment. "You fell asleep. People moved away. They thought I was out with a drunk." She was laughing.

"Brooklyn?"

"You remember, we looked at Brooklyn that night, from Hotel Whipple. Actually, I think we were looking at Queens, but this is definitely Brooklyn."

"But this is supposed to be Chinatown. How did we get here?"

"The subway. You remember the subway."

We walked down some dark streets. That is, Caroline walked down the streets and I followed her. These were different from the streets on the East Side of Manhattan. The sidewalks were narrower and the people wore clothes, not costumes, and there were middle-aged couples strolling who probably had kids away in college, couples who had been married for years and who were left alone to keep each other company. We walked past restaurants, past people in trench coats holding umbrellas, through what looked like neighborhoods where people would know the grocer and they would know the cop on the beat. We strolled past town houses, down streets named Pierrepont and Remsen and suddenly the street ended and we were looking out at water, and there were oceangoing ships.

"Where are we?"

"Brooklyn Heights. This is called the Promenade."

There seemed to be a lot of water and a wide sidewalk running high above it and we leaned against the iron railing and we saw the mouth of the East River, Ellis Island, the illuminated Statue of Liberty, the lights on the big oceangoing ships, the skyline of lower Manhattan, the Brooklyn Bridge, with lights strung across like the lights on a house at Christmas. It was a dark night, wet and glistening, and the lights of the boats and the bridges and their reflections in the water were stunning.

"How do you feel?" asked Caroline.

"Very small."

She turned to look at me.

"Small?"

"Look at that. Ships from all over the world. Ellis Island, where my grandfather came in and got stuck in quarantine, and left with his suitcase and his ten dollars along with all the other potato famine refugees."

We were leaning on the iron railing and Caroline was listening and she turned and looked at me for a long moment. Her hair blew across her face, and I swept it back.

"And now look at his grandson," she said, "a soon-to-be filthy-rich doctor."

"I'll never be rich."

"Don't be so sure."

"No, I won't. I promised my grandfather."

"You won't be able to help yourself."

"As Seymour Freudenberg would say, that's not a central issue."

"What is the central issue?"

"Being a good doc," I said. "And as my grandfather would say, treating the workers."

"I knew you were a commie all along," Caroline said, laughing, but she stopped and looked seriously at me for a moment. Then she turned and we started to walk toward the flagpole, at the other end of the Promenade.

"You never talk about your parents."

"You heard about my dad and his garage."

"What about your mother?"

"My mother's dead."

"When?"

"Internship. She had myeloma. So she came up here, to the best cancer hospital in the world. She was on your ward. Before you, of course. Seymour was her attending. Forrest was her intern. He pronounced her."

"I see," she said. And she looked at me, as if she did see something.

This was not one of my favorite topics, and I was trying my best to get past it. Caroline got quiet, but she wasn't uncomfortable or awkward. She knew how to handle these things. She had plenty of practice at work.

"That must have been hard for you."

"It was just kind of an all-around difficult year."

She laughed and took my arm. "I can imagine."

"They put her in that room you gave Mrs. Roundtree," I said. "She died and they wrapped her up and sent her down to the morgue."

Caroline didn't say anything. We walked down the full length of the Promenade toward the bridge. We stopped to look out at the tip of Manhattan, with the twin towers we had seen that night from far-off Hotel Whipple. From this vantage they looked as if they could tip the whole island on its nose, right into the harbor.

I pointed vaguely in the direction of lower Manhattan. "That's where we were supposed to be," I said. "Chinatown."

"Oh," said Caroline. "You've been there before. This is an adventure."

I looked up the East River. "It is, at that."

"You like Brooklyn?"

"It's spectacular," I said. "You take me to the nicest places for dinner."

She looked at me again with that straight and steady gaze that might have unnerved me if I'd been less punchy. I just stared back at her dumbly. The wind off the water was blowing our hair around and she brushed mine off my face, and I thought I probably ought to kiss her, but I did not.

We walked to the end of the Promenade and Caroline turned us off to the path to the street.

She said, "Why didn't you kiss me?"

"Things are complicated enough already."

She continued walking by my side, looking at the path. Then she stopped, turned, and slowly brought her face close to mine and she kissed me.

I was surprised how gentle she was. And she was in no hurry to stop. I certainly was in no hurry. I would have stayed there all night.

She turned away and we continued walking.

She said: "He's a lawyer."

What do you say about your competition when he's a lawyer? I struggled for a few moments and said, "That's nice." I can be devilishly clever when pushed to the wall.

She laughed.

"It's not as bad as all that. He's a class-action lawyer. Public interest. His big case is against a public utility that won't hire single mothers."

"Sounds like a nice case."

"The single mothers appreciate him."

"I like him, too, if he's not suing doctors."

"His firm has a storefront office. They were all revolutionaries together at Stanford. They closed the school down once upon a time. Now they're tilting windmills in superior court."

I didn't say anything. I wondered what she was trying to say. She seemed proud of his rebellion and, at the same time, exasperated with him.

"Each man has his calling," I said.

She looked at me and laughed. "You can be very perceptive sometimes. You have an amazing intuitive sense."

That meant nothing to me. I said: "I thought your boyfriend was probably a surgeon."

She blinked and laughed. "Why?"

"I don't know. I guess I'm a pessimist."

"What are you talking about?"

"Nothing."

We reached the corner and I followed her down streets lighted by softer lights than they use in Manhattan. We moved in and out of shadows, down a street that, while it offered more haven for muggers, was also more inviting and more charming than those of the East Side with their maximum-security halogen lighting.

"Why a surgeon?" Caroline asked as we strolled through the shadows. "Why would you be a pessimist to think he was a surgeon?"

"I don't know," I said. "I say all kinds of things."

"You figured you might have a tough time prying me away from a surgeon? That's what you meant, wasn't it?"

She laughed out loud and shook her head and said: "You do get to the point."

She guided us to a restaurant that was dim and smoky and quietly busy. There was a jazzy pianist and a bass player.

They seated us together against a brick wall with a view of the whole place.

Sitting down in the warmth and the dark, after the chill night air, after thirteen admissions, and two hours sleep, my eyelids began their slow, ineluctable descent. I couldn't focus on the menu and I waited for Caroline to order and said, "Same for me."

It was nice sitting there, in the dark, touching shoulders with Caroline, drinking wine, saying nothing, listening to the music. There's a kind of personal closeness you get by simple proximity to a person that cannot be had by speech. I had first noticed it on rounds. Caroline naturally tended to stand a step closer to me, just a little farther away from everyone else. It seemed a sort of subconscious drift. I'm not sure any of the others could notice it, but it was a pattern that emerged so often, I was sure it was real. Now, sitting next to her, I felt very connected to her.

I don't think I ate much of whatever it was she had ordered. I paid with my credit card and made very sure I got it back and checked twice it was in my wallet. I was sure in my sleep-deprived drunk I would lose something.

"Let me look at that bill," Caroline said, after I'd signed it. "I don't trust you to do any calculations in your current pathetic state."

Somehow we got back to the Whitney. By subway, I imagine.

Caroline probably carried me on her back from the station. We were at the door of my apartment and I fumbled with the key and managed to unlock it.

I remember her walking me into the dark room and I remember her sliding my raincoat off me. And I remember her saying, "Poor baby."

And I remember her kissing my face. Not my lips, my face.

I awoke the next morning in my own bed, alone. No clothes. The alarm clock blaring. It was six-thirty and time to get showered and dressed. Time to get back to Whipple for rounds. My uniform jacket and pants and a shirt and tie were laid out on a chair near my bed.

There was a note from Caroline on the jacket: "Don't worry. You're still a virgin."

I must have been scintillating company for dinner.

IN THE PARIETAL LOBE

The next morning, I found Caroline drinking coffee in the nurses' station.

"How are you?" she asked, in that flat dry tone she could do so well.

"Oh," I said. "I'm alert and oriented."

"An improvement," she said, dropping her voice, "over last night."

We were alone together in the station. I looked around to be sure. It was a little thrilling to hear her allude to the night before. There was a taste of intimate collusion now, a secret we shared, made more exciting by the illicit and secret side of it.

"I thought I was doing pretty well," I said. "Until I woke up this morning."

She said nothing. She just sat back in her chair and draped one arm over the back and cast a sultry look in my direction, those khaki-colored irises glowing at me.

"Rarely have I had such service," I said. "Delivered home. Placed in bed. Undressed. Clothes arranged."

"Just good nursing care is all," she said, smiling.

"Yes, and I like the shirt-and-tie combination."

I was wearing what she had set out for me.

"You have lovely ties. But you always wear the same one."

"The dark ones hide the stains better."

"Oh, live dangerously. Wear a new tie."

Ira came in, headed directly for the coffee machine in the corner of the room, and poured himself some into a Styrofoam cup. His hair was wet from his shower and he was shaven and bleeding in spots and his eyes were bright. He gulped his coffee and grinned at us. "Anything that makes you feel this good," he said, "must cause cancer."

Ludvik arrived and we started rounds.

We worked our way down the hall, patient to patient, and things went relatively smoothly. Then we got to Mrs. Roundtree's room. Caroline stopped us outside the door.

"Mrs. Roundtree's kids are coming up from New Hope today," she said. "We're not sending her off the floor for any tests or anything today, right?"

Ira fished his three-by-five cards out of his pocket and drew out the one on Mrs. Roundtree. He said, "She's supposed to get her head CT. I'm not sure. Might be scheduled for today."

"No, it's tomorrow," said Caroline. "Now, her husband's going to have the kids here around ten."

"How many kids?" asked Ira.

"Three."

"She's a brave woman," said Ira. "I've got two. They outnumber you when there's two of them. Three is reckless."

"If there's one thing the Roundtrees are not," said Caroline, "it's reckless. They probably had each kid planned to the minute, with applications for nursery school already filled out."

"They are planners," said Ira.

"And today they have planned a visit for the kids with Mommy," said Caroline, nudging Ira. "So don't screw it up for them."

We filed into her room, Ludvik and Ira stood to her right and Caroline and I moved to her left. She smiled and I smiled back and I began to feel a little uncomfortable without at first knowing why.

Ira asked Mrs. Roundtree how she was and she ignored him and continued looking at me, and at Caroline, smiling pleasantly, and it dawned on me why she made me uneasy: She hadn't the foggiest idea who we were. She might have known we were doctors and nurses, but she clearly didn't recognize me. And she ought to have known me. Not just because I had helped tap her chest, and seen her daily, but the day before we had talked about the Triceratops concrete dinosaur in the playground across the street. She hadn't noticed it, but once I pointed it out she had said her kids would love to crawl over that Triceratops. Now she clearly didn't know me from Adam.

Ludvik stepped from his side of the bed toward the foot of the bed, directly in front of her. He was interested: you could see the fascination in his face. Caroline, on the other hand, looked confused and disturbed. She looked from Ludvik to me and back to

Ludvik again, as if things were happening too fast for her. She knew we had picked up on something, but she couldn't see it yet.

Ludvik moved across Mrs. Roundtree's midline and said good morning and she answered as if she had only just then noticed him.

"Please close your eyes," Ludvik said. "Tell me where I touch you." He touched her right leg and left hand.

"My hand," she said, raising her hand.

He went through it like that, and she reported every touch on the left side of her body but missed everything on the right.

Caroline caught my eye with the obvious question. Caroline did not know what Ludvik was doing, but she knew *he* knew what he was doing and she knew she didn't like whatever it was he was demonstrating.

Ludvik asked Mrs. Roundtree to open her eyes and he showed her a comb and asked her what it was.

"Well, it's a . . ." Her voice trailed off. She stared at it in consternation.

"What do you do with it?"

"Well, you comb your hair with it," she laughed, taking it and running it through her hair with her left hand.

"Then what is it called?"

She looked at the thing you comb your hair with and could not bring its name out of her brain to her lips.

Finally, Ludvik stepped directly in front of her and pulled his white uniform coat off his left shoulder, so it dangled opposite the right side of her visual field. He asked her if she noticed anything amiss. She did not. Ludvik moved to her left and she saw immediately. "Oh, yes. Of course. Your coat."

We all stood there in uneasy silence.

Caroline said, "I think we are making Mrs. Roundtree uncomfortable."

Ludvik waved her off. "It's you who's uncomfortable."

Mrs. Roundtree said, "There's something wrong, isn't there?"

"Yes," I said. "But we're getting to the bottom of it."

"I certainly hope so," she said, her face pinking, and tears brimming over and running down her cheeks.

Caroline pulled a tissue from her pocket and handed it to her and stood next to her, staring hate at Ludvik.

"I'm just not right," said Mrs. Roundtree. "I've been looking at this all morning." She held up a photo of her three kids. "I just can't make it out. And I know I should."

"You mean," Caroline said, "you can't see it clearly?"

"Oh, I can see it. It just doesn't ring a bell. I see the round things and an elliptical line below but I just can't make sense of it."

She had described the faces of her children, but she had no idea they were faces, much less the faces of her children.

Back in the hall, Caroline looked from Ira to Ludvik to me.

"You know what's wrong with her, don't you? All of you know."

"Parietal lobe met," said Ludvik, simply, without sympathy or triumph, just a statement of fact.

"What?" said Caroline.

"She got breast growing in her brain," Ludvik said. "Parietal lobe. She's got apraxia and selective aphasia. It's caught her visual sweep, too, so she only sees half a screen, the right side of her world is blanked out. It's got her sensory association area. She can get data in, but she can't connect it up and make sense of it. She doesn't recognize faces."

Ira and I had seen the professors of neurology go through the tricks Ludvik had just done with Mrs. Roundtree. But Ludvik had been the first to recognize what she had, and he had put it together. It might have been fun, if it hadn't meant that Mrs. Roundtree now had seedlings from her breast cancer growing in her brain. Radiation therapy might reduce the size of the met, but once you start growing tumor in your brain, you stop talking about protocols and hopes for cure. You talk about time left.

And that time would not be what you call quality time. She wouldn't be able to recognize people or things along the way. The world would become stranger and stranger to her. And the worst part of it was that she'd know it was happening. She'd remain aware of the gulf expanding around her.

"You mean," said Caroline, "she won't recognize her kids? Even if they stand in the same room with her, face-to-face? She won't even know her own kids?"

"Not likely," said Ludvik.

Then Caroline surprised us. She started to cry. Tears coursed down her cheeks and she pulled a tissue out of her pocket and she sniffed and gained control and she said, "I don't believe you."

She made me feel pretty small. Ira and Ludvik and I saw parietal lobe tumors and worse things a dozen times a day. All it meant was more work, more consults to call, more attendings to inform, more questions from relatives, more night wakenings. These things had become part of Whipple. They were just things that happened. We had stopped reacting. But here was Caroline wiping her eyes with her Kleenex, and thinking about Mr. Roundtree and Mrs. Roundtree and how they looked the day she got admitted, I felt like crying myself.

Ludvik eyed Caroline with a certain cool remove, and he said, "You had better intercept the husband and kids. What she needs is a CT and some radiation therapy."

"She is going to see her children," said Caroline, back straightening. "Today. No CT. No radiation therapy. Just kids. Today she is going to be a human being."

Ludvik looked to me for some rational intervention. I looked at Caroline, and it was obvious there was going to be only one winner in this contest. I shrugged at Ludvik. We pushed on with rounds.

Afterward, I pulled Caroline over. "You know, Ludvik, as obnoxious as he can be sometimes, can also be right."

"The kids are probably on the train right now," said Caroline. "What am I supposed to do? Daddy went home to get them and they're going to be getting more and more excited about seeing Mom with each passing mile. They're going to come prancing down the hall later this morning. What am I supposed to do? Tell them to come back tomorrow, after Mommy's had her CAT scan and her radiation therapy?"

"It's just that it may not go very well. She may not . . ."

"She has been dying to see her kids. I don't care if she does have a brain met. The met must have been there a while. It can wait one more day."

I turned to go. Then I had a thought. "Has she asked about her kids lately? I mean, today?"

Caroline hesitated, then: "She's been talking about seeing her kids since she arrived."

"But lately? You've heard her ask about them this morning?"

"I haven't had her as my patient since Monday. But she wants to see her kids. You heard her."

"I heard her," I said.

Caroline had dug in her heels. There was no arguing. I went to report.

18

CHILD'S PLAY

Caroline paged me out of Morning Report.

"Get down here," she said, and she hung up.

Ludvik was alone in the nurses' station when I galloped in.

"I told her to have those kids come another day," he said.

"What's the problem?"

"The kids have arrived," said Ludvik.

"Caroline just stat-paged me and told me to come right down."

"That's the problem," said Ludvik. "She's in there with the kids and the father, too, right now. Ira's in there too."

The scene in Mrs. Roundtree's room was crowded and noisy. Mrs. Roundtree was sitting in bed eyeing her four-year-old daughter, who was sobbing in the arms of her father in the far corner of the room. The other two kids stood near her elbow, on her good left side. The ten-year-old was trying to get her attention, saying, "Mom, don't you know me? It's Jason."

The six-year-old stuck his face in front of hers. "Mom! It's Zach, Mom!"

Ira was standing behind Zachary, with his hands on the kid's shoulders. Caroline had her hands on Mr. Roundtree's shoulders. Mr. Roundtree looked like he was near tears himself.

Ludvik and I had to find a place to stand.

"She doesn't seem to know them," Mr. Roundtree whispered to me, his face flushed and urgent.

"I'm Dr. O'Brien," I said, extending my hand to the ten-year-old. He had a firm little grip and he pumped my arm once or twice solemnly.

"I'm Jason Roundtree," he said in a clear but shaky voice.

"Why don't we go talk in the conference room?" I said. I looked over to Mr. Roundtree, who looked happy to have any excuse to leave the room.

"You might want to stay here for a moment," I told Caroline, "with Mrs. Roundtree."

We all filed out, leaving Caroline standing next to Mrs. Roundtree, who looked perplexed and disturbed. She had no idea who all these small people were who had come in and started crying.

"Ashley jumped on her bed and hugged her," Mr. Roundtree said under his breath as we walked down the hall. "She ignored her. It was like Ashley wasn't even there. Ashley kissed her cheek and Barbara didn't even look at her."

I didn't have to ask which cheek the child had kissed. I didn't have to ask from which side the child had approached her mother.

"And she clearly had no idea who Zach and Jason were," Mr. Roundtree continued. "I'm not even sure she knew me." He told me with a look of horror and disbelief.

We filed into the conference room, which had a metal table and chairs. Ira brought cups of water for the kids and coffee for Mr. Roundtree, and Ludvik stood at the head of the table and began speaking before I could collect my thoughts.

"Your mother," he said, his faint accent peeping through, "is not herself today. It's not easy to see your mother when she is not well."

"But she wasn't even happy to see us," said Zachary.

"She is happy, but she is confused," Ludvik said, smiling. "That is part of why she is here. When she is better, she will throw her arms around you and she won't believe you when you tell her about today, she won't remember it."

The two older kids seemed to be listening. The four-year-old sat in her father's lap and stared straight ahead.

"When your mother is asleep," Ludvik went on, "she can't hear you. Even though her eyes are open now, it's as if she is really asleep in some ways, because she cannot really see you."

Caroline slipped into the room behind Ludvik. She caught my eye as if to ask why I was letting Ludvik explain things.

The kids were listening to Ludvik intently.

"Later today, we are going to give your mother some treatment to make her better. It may take some time, but she will get better. And then she'll be so happy to see you, and she'll laugh at herself for not having been able to wake herself up to you today."

"She's asleep?" asked the middle kid. "Her eyes were open."

Ludvik smiled. "Part of her is asleep. Her eyes are open, but she can't see everything she wants to see."

"But she didn't even look at Ashley," said the eldest.

"She couldn't see Ashley. She doesn't look at anyone who sits on her right side. Ashley was sitting on her right. But you were on her left and she looked at you."

"But she didn't do anything. She just looked at me."

"Give her time," said Ludvik, smiling at him. "I know you came a long way today to see your mother. But you will have to be patient, which is so hard to be."

Ludvik's eyes seem to be focusing beyond the kids now, back years, I thought, to his own mother, to the day she had ceased to recognize him. He certainly seemed different with the kids. He had chosen his words so they could understand him. He knew just what to say. I would never have picked Ludvik for this delicate address to the family, but I could see now, none of us could have come close to him. He sounded kinder and different than I had ever heard him sound.

Caroline felt it too—you could see it in her face. We both stood staring at Ludvik, and at his small audience.

"Why don't you go back to her now," said Ludvik. "And kiss her good-bye for today. She may not be able to tell you, but she will be happy you have come."

The kids filed out of the room with their father behind them. Ira stood there with his mouth open, a smile half forming, staring at Ludvik. Caroline was staring at him too. But Ludvik didn't notice them. He was staring out the door, after those kids.

19

THE MAN ON THE ELEVATOR

Mr. Roundtree loaded his kids into a cab and headed for the train station. It had not been quite the visit with mother they had expected. We sent Mrs. Roundtree down to CT scan, which showed the metastasis in her brain, right where Ludvik said it would be, in the left parietal lobe. From CT scan, we trundled her off to radiation therapy, where they painted the purple lines on her scalp and face to mark the radiation ports, her "war paint," Caroline called it.

Neurology wrote a note in her chart, agreeing with everything Ludvik had said. Seymour Freudenberg arrived and went over the CAT scan with us and said, "Nice pickup, kids."

"It was really pretty obvious," said Ludvik, "if you were on the right side of the bed."

"Things usually are obvious," said Freudenberg, "if you think of them."

Ira said, "Poor lady. You heard about the scene with the kids?"

"Caroline Bates told me," Freudenberg said. He was smiling that sad smile of his. "I like Barbara Roundtree. Nice lady. Too bad."

"She's going down the tubes," said Ira. "And nothing's going to help now. Not the RT. Not the chemotherapy. It is all written now."

Freudenberg looked to me, lines creasing his leathery features. "These guys," he said, "have no faith in the power of science."

"They're interns," I said.

I did not see Caroline for what seemed like a long time after that scene with Ludvik and Mrs. Roundtree's kids. Trying to remember sequences of events at Whipple is like trying to remember the unfolding of a dream: things blur and the connections get lost. I just remember I didn't see her again until Friday evening.

We had finished chart rounds and listening to the interns sign out, I realized it was Friday, and, of course, I hadn't made any plans. At Whipple, I never thought beyond the next set of rounds.

Forrest paged: "Are we having dinner, or are we otherwise engaged tonight?"

"Otherwise engaged?"

"The lovely Miss Bates. Or is she in Washington?"

"Haven't seen her."

I told him I'd meet him at Gleasons.

I wandered out to the hall and washed my hands with the amber Betadine soap at the sink in front of the nurses' station. Pushing a medication cart toward me down the hall was Sally Landau, Caroline's wine-drinking friend. She was working the evening shift, passing out meds, stopping in front of each room, putting her poisons in little plastic cups, one cup for each patient. I ambled up to her. She was absorbed in popping pills and she didn't notice me until I was right on top of her. She looked up, startled, and smiled.

"Friday night," I said. "Ain't we got fun?"

She laughed. "Oh, definitely."

I don't know why I was standing there. I guess she was some kind of connection to Caroline. I must have been staring at her and she said, "Any progress in the campaign?"

"The campaign?"

"You know, on the home front. The Caroline Bates campaign."

"There's no campaign. She's got a boyfriend. We are merely colleagues. Colleagues, passing in the night."

"You are considerably more than that," she said, not smiling. "To Caroline."

I caught my breath and rolled my shoulders, as if that comment had not sent me into euphoric orbit.

"We hardly know each other," I said, watching Sally closely. "We have lunch in the cafeteria, that sort of thing."

Sally stopped with the pills and looked up, sly smile. "And dinner in Brooklyn Heights."

"She told you about that?"

"What do you think?"

"Well, then you know how the campaign goes. I slept through most of Brooklyn. She practically had to carry me home. She must have been real snowed."

"She was snowed enough."

Sally let that sail across my bow, and turned her attention back to her pills, as if she'd said nothing important.

"I was a total zombie."

"She was charmed."

"She was?"

Sally looked up. "She liked the part about your grandfather leaving Ellis Island with ten dollars in his pocket."

"No foolin'?" My head spun a little. An idle remark. If I'd been more awake, I'd never have said it. Might have thought it, but not said it.

"Listen, big boy," Sally said. "You know exactly what you're doing. And you're making progress. Now, if you've got what you want out of me, I've got about a thousand pills to push."

"She said she was charmed?"

"Beat it. I've already violated some pretty deep obligations of friendship."

You couldn't have caught me with a helium balloon on the way back to the Whitney after that little chat with Sally Landau. The two blocks between the hospital and the apartment building slid by beneath my feet and no shoe leather touched ground.

It was Friday night and Caroline was out of sight, probably winging her way toward Washington, but there was hope. She was charmed. She had told Sally Landau. On the other hand, she had not called before she left town. Not that she owed me a call. But it would have been a nice touch.

The doorman touched the brim of his hat as I walked past, as he usually did, but he did not smile. The doorman was my friend. He smiled whenever I walked by with Caroline. Oh, well, nobody likes working Friday night.

I saw Caroline first: she was standing in front of the elevators. Holding someone's hand.

He was taller than me, and his broad shoulders gave him the look of a lapsed collegiate athlete of some sort. A nice face with the bones showing through. He had a beard and his long, auburn hair just touched the collar of his gray herringbone jacket and his stonewashed jeans touched the tops of his tasseled loafers. He was expensively casual and he had just the sort of looks I would not have chosen for my competition. In college, guys who looked like him always dated the women I figured would be interested only in guys who looked like him.

The hand that wasn't enfolding Caroline's hand gripped a leather suitcase.

I stood behind them and Caroline didn't notice me. We all got on the elevator together, and she turned around to face the door and found herself face-to-face with me. Her eyes flared open, but there was no panic, and she did not release her grip from the hand that held hers. She smiled and said hello.

A brilliant hello, really. It meant nothing to her friend, but it said, "Hello, isn't this a fine mess?" to me.

He glanced over at me uninterestedly, and focused on the numbers lighting up above the elevator door.

They got off at nine, her floor. I watched them until the elevator doors shut them off.

Shower, shave, change clothes. Go meet Forrest. Don't think about that elevator. Push the button. Take the elevator down. Caroline and her friend weren't on this one. They were up in her apartment, getting reacquainted.

I had dinner with Forrest and we sat around Gleasons, drinking beer. I drank quite a lot of beer that night.

Oh, Caroline had been very snowed. Charmed.

"You're great company tonight," Forrest observed.

"I'm having a wonderful time."

"She off to Washington again?"

"Worse." I looked at him through my haze. "Washington is up here. In her apartment. In more than that, right about now."

"Repeat after me," Forrest said solemnly. "Women are no damn good."

There were lots of hospital people there that night. Four or five different women, nurses, other interns, joined us at our table at different times. There were always a lot of people at Gleasons.

Olivia McGill, a willing nurse if there ever was one, sat on my lap. She had oversize breasts she liked to rub in everyone's face and she reportedly was pretty free with them. Forrest had not had the pleasure, but he could not understand how I could pass up the opportunity.

Olivia was reasonably drunk and she kept wanting to sit in my lap and whisper in my ear. She said: "Where have you been all my life?"

I said: "Down among the dead men."

Olivia got distracted by a medical student in a sleeveless shirt and slipped off to present her breasts to more receptive hands. Other nurses, X-ray techs, lab techs, secretaries, and ward clerks floated by. There was a nurse anesthetist with whom I'd had an eye-to-eye relationship for a few weeks. She came in and sat with a nurse I knew. It was the perfect setup to meet her finally. I couldn't be bothered. Too much effort. Too little gain.

People stopped by our table to shoot the breeze with Forrest, who tried to include me. But after a while I just felt more and more alone, and I left.

I walked home, feeling stupid. Caroline had looked happy holding hands with her Washington lawyer. I was no more part of her life than Ira or Ludvik.

I was just a man on the elevator, riding up with Caroline and her boyfriend.

20

JUST LIKE A WOMAN

Some good things happened that weekend. Mrs. Roundtree got her radiation therapy and she began recognizing people again, which pleased Seymour Freudenberg and made her husband very happy. And Vince Montebelli did not die. In fact, he improved so much, they moved him out of the ICU and put him back in his room on Caroline's ward.

All this was duly reported on morning rounds, Monday.

But Caroline was not there to hear it. I had prepared myself for a major dramatic scene for our confrontation, but she had stage-managed things better. She simply was not there for my scene. The nurse who replaced her said she had the day off.

When she did appear, Tuesday, Caroline acted as if the elevator incident had never happened, as if she had not spent a long weekend in her apartment with her boyfriend. That made me angry at first: the least she could do was look embarrassed, or worried or something. But she acted as if nothing had happened. As if nothing had changed between us.

I decided the best thing to do was to freeze her out, and I started actively ignoring her. I did not look at her, except when she spoke directly to me, and I addressed my comments to Ira or to Ludvik or to both of them, without letting my eyes drift over to meet hers. As if in response, she moved into position standing right next to me, so I had to look at her occasionally or risk collision. My parry was to become very pleasant and polite, with many "excuses me's" and "please's," whenever it was necessary to move past her.

Rounds went smoothly enough, given the inconvenience of instituting this new formality that was supposed to unnerve Caroline and make her miss our easy intimacy. She remained bright and cheerful all through this, and I wasn't sure she had even noticed my attempts at the modified cold shoulder.

Then a very depressing thought dawned on me: Caroline wasn't contrite because Caroline did not think she owed me any apology for having a boyfriend, or for holding his hand in the elevator. She seemed blissfully unaware of my coolness because for her, nothing in our relationship had changed. Before our elevator ride, she was somebody else's girlfriend and I was just an amusing diversion, and the same was true afterward. Nothing had changed.

The more I thought about it, the worse I felt: I had no cause to feel wronged. I had no special claim on Caroline's attentions. She had not sworn fidelity or assigned me exclusive rights to her body and soul. In fact, she had not yet offered me either. She had simply been interested in me, and charmed. She did not owe me a thing. I owed her an apology.

It was Saint Patrick's Day, and the nurses had taped green and white crepe paper and shamrocks above the doors to all the patients' rooms and some of the nurses wore "Kiss Me, I'm Irish" buttons. I wished they hadn't done anything with the holiday. The crepe paper looked forlorn and dismal in those dingy halls, and the patients were in no shape to respond to all the efforts at good cheer. The whole show seemed to fall flat at Whipple: the effort had a false feeling that made it worse than no effort at all.

One of the nurses stuck a green plastic shillelagh behind my name tag, and kissed me on the cheek and bounced away, down the hall.

"Well, somebody loves you," said Ira.

With a name like mine, I often got that treatment on Saint Patrick's Day. I withdrew the shillelagh and stepped up next to Caroline and planted it behind her nameplate pinned over her left breast. A little shiver passed through me, being suddenly so close to her, and she looked up, and I thought she looked more than startled: she looked a little frightened, as if she half expected me to swing at her. I knew then she had picked up on my earlier efforts at deadly politeness.

I said: "Yours on loan," patting the shillelagh.

"Aren't you nice," she said. "You share everything."

She looked me straight in the eye when she said that. Ludvik and Ira were staring at her and at me. Caroline caught their looks and laughed. "Come on, zombies."

When we finished with the last patient, I turned to make my escape to morning report and found Caroline standing squarely between me and the door. Ira and Ludvik had already disappeared through it. It was just me, Caroline, and the six patients, who were more interested in their breakfast trays than watching a doctor talk to a nurse.

"I missed you," she said.

That was one of perhaps six hundred openings for which I was totally unprepared. I stood there like a dummy and tried to think of something bright and clever to say, but all that occurred to me was "You are?" I managed to keep my mouth shut and not say that. I just stared at her.

"I've got to talk to you," Caroline said.

"I'm late," I said. "For report."

"Lunch."

"I'm busy for lunch."

"Dinner, then."

"I'm busy for dinner," I said. "Saving lives, a full-time trade."

"I am going to talk to you," she said. "I know where you live."

"Page me for lunch, then."

She paged me a little past noon, but it wasn't for lunch and it wasn't for our talk. It was for Vince Montebelli.

"He's seizing again," she said.

He was doing that all right, and more. First he yorked up some blood, probably from his stomach—we couldn't tell; might have been from his lung—then he sucked the blood right down into his lung, a nasty business known as "aspiration." Then he started seizing, jerking around in his bed.

"He was talking to me," Caroline said. "He was saying how he never thought he'd get out of the ICU alive, but Dr. O'Brien had promised him he was definitely not going to die down there and Dr. O'Brien never lied."

We were standing in the hallway. Ira had trundled Vince off on a stretcher with the anesthesiologist and some nurse who had come up from the ICU. I was about to follow the troops down there but Caroline stopped me with a finger on my chest.

"He thinks the world of you," Caroline said.

"His judgment hasn't been too sharp lately," I said.

"He was doing fine, until just now."

"Vince is never doing fine. Vince is dying. Some days he does better than others, but he never does fine. He just keeps on dying at greater or lesser rates."

I left her in the hallway to chew on that little bit of wisdom and walked to the stairwell.

In the ICU, Ira was leaning over Vince, talking directly to his face, saying, "This is a big nothing, big boy. You're doing fine."

The amazing thing about Vince was how resilient he could be. He perked right up in the ICU and they pulled the tube out of his trachea, and by that afternoon, he could talk. Ira and Ludvik and I stopped at the ICU before X-ray rounds. Ira and Ludvik stayed at the nurses' station and I walked into his room and stood by his bed.

Vince looked up and said, "Where's Mom?"

His mother was dead, as far as I could remember. His sister was his only living relative. I said, "Where are you, Vince?"

"My room. Where's Anita?"

Anita was his sister.

"She's on her way. We called her."

"She at school?"

"At work, I think. She's coming."

"Work? She doesn't work. She's in school."

"Have it your way, Vince."

He looked around the room, through the glass window, out into the ICU center station where the nurses watched the monitors and where Ira was writing in his chart, and his face grew frightened.

"Where's Mom?" he asked again, his eyes crawling up and down my face. He shouted toward the open door, "Mom!"

At that moment, as if in answer to his call, Caroline walked through the door. But she wasn't Mom, and Vince knew it. In fact, just seeing her in her white uniform set him off.

"Mom!" he screamed. "Mom! Come up here, Mom!"

Caroline looked at me, alarmed.

"He wants his mom," I explained.

Vince looked back and forth between Caroline and me and suddenly burst into tears, buried his face in his hands, sobbing.

Caroline stepped over to him and put a hand on his shoulder.

"You'll be all right, Vince." But she knew he wasn't all right and she looked up to me, frightened.

"Oh, Jesus," sobbed Vince, looking up, then noticing the IV attached to his forearm. "Look what's happened to me."

"You're fine, now, Vince," I said, stepping over to protect that

IV. We had a hard time finding usable veins in Vince, and he had his fingers curled around the IV.

"But what is this?"

"It's just an IV, Vince," said Caroline.

"A what? Where the hell am I?"

"In the hospital," said Caroline.

"Oh, no!" Vince sobbed, tilting his face to the ceiling, tears coursing down his face. "Oh, please, no."

Caroline was becoming visibly disturbed. She was, in fact, just about ready to become unhinged. She could deal with Vince depressed, Vince angry, Vince in need of reassurance. But this was Vince delirious, and terrified and very sad, and she could not deal with him when he was beyond reason.

"Your mom's down in the kitchen, Vince," I told him. "Anita's going to be up in a little while. Just relax."

Vince jerked his head in my direction, tears of joy now. "Oh, thanks. When's Anita getting here?"

"In just a little while, Vince."

I pulled Caroline out of his room by her elbow.

"What's happened to him?"

"He thinks he's home, in his own room."

Caroline looked at Vince through the glass wall. "Maybe he's better off, thinking that. Poor Vince."

"He'd be better off if he really were in his own room, all the good we've done him."

Caroline swung her eyes back to me, coming out of her own thoughts. "Your problem is you lack perspective."

"Oh, do I? That's one thing I thought I had in abundance. The big picture."

"You think you'd just go gentle into that good night and have your death with dignity, serene and comfy. But you wouldn't."

"Speak for yourself," I said. "I wouldn't hang around in this ICU, getting jabbed for blood gases and getting 'scoped and catheterized."

"You'd do just what Vince is doing—you'd hang on by your fingernails. And so would I. I'd say: Put me on the respirator, make me a full code. I'm young and I don't want to die."

I looked at her. She was serious. I was astonished. If there was one conviction I thought we all shared, it was the undesirability of "the Whipple route." Didn't we all come away from the bedside shaking our heads, saying, "When my time comes, let me go," wondering why the attendings didn't have the fortitude simply to pull the plug?

We walked to the ICU door. Ira and Ludvik were standing up looking at me. They wanted to do rounds and finish up for the day.

Caroline said, "Stop by and see me. I'll be up late."

We were busy with Vince until eight that night. I walked home in the wet night air, thinking about nothing, letting my head clear. I did not stop off on Caroline's floor. I stayed in the elevator and continued straight on to my place.

To hell with Caroline Bates. To hell with her boyfriend. To hell with Whipple and to hell with testicular carcinoma.

I unlocked the door and it was like pulling a plug. Whatever hormones I had run on, epinephrine, norepinephrine, cortisol, all those good molecules made for stress had now run dry.

I went directly to the bathroom, and turned on the water for the bath. I peeled off my uniform and left it in a heap on the floor, walked out to the galleyway they called a kitchen, and flipped a can of beer out of the half refrigerator. Out to the stereo in the main room, two albums were already in place, ready to go. Dobie Gray started singing: "Drift Away." Mr. Gray had the right idea. I was all in favor of the whole concept. I grabbed a *New Yorker* from a pile on the floor and walked back to the bath, now steaming and full. I sank in.

Cold beer on a dry brain works quickly. Delirium set in. Disorientation, fog. Like Vince Montebelli. Poor Vince. Calling for his mother. I never did see his sister that day. I hoped Vince recognized her if and when she arrived. We had had our share of patients with perceptual problems lately: Professor Toomey, who thought he could fly. Mrs. Roundtree, who didn't know her kids. Now Vince Montebelli.

Sensory integration, Ludvik called it. They could take in the signals, but they couldn't make sense of them.

I had the same trouble with Caroline Bates, RN, Head Nurse.

Caroline Bates had a boyfriend. No thinking of Caroline. Read Pauline Kael. Read Elizabeth Drew. Smart ladies. Ladies with something to tell me about the world. Who needs the world? I'd had quite too much of the world. It was always running into perceptual problems, the world was.

There was a rapping at my chamber door.

I ignored it.

The possibilities were finite. One of them was Forrest. I was unavailable. Off duty and unavailable. Until seven in the a.m.

The rapping went on.

Perhaps Olivia McGill. Now there was a reason to stir. There was a lady with no perceptual problems at all. She knew exactly who she was, what she could do, and what she wanted.

More rapping.

Had to be Forrest. He was off tonight. He wanted to eat dinner at Gleasons. He would not go alone. Ignore him.

More and louder.

Forrest was not going to be deterred. It would take a confrontation. I stepped out and wrapped a towel around my waist, realizing as I did that Forrest never knocked like that. He pounded. And shouted. Generally Forrest sounded like a fire brigade breaking down the door.

I swung open the door, thinking too late I might have taken the time for a bathrobe. Standing there in her white nurse's uniform, with her heather tweed jacket, holding a large pizza box and a bottle of wine, was Caroline.

"Ask me in," she said, "or you will have an awful mess on your threshold."

I stepped back wordlessly, and she advanced.

My apartment, like most of the house staff apartments, was what is called in New York an "efficiency." The door opened onto a narrow passageway that contained the galley kitchen, oven, sink, refrigerator; and off this passageway the bathroom, and at the end of the passageway, the single room that contained a small dining room table, with two chairs, my desk, bed, and my two six-foot-tall bookcases.

Caroline's apartment was laid out just like it, and she knew her way around without a tour. She set the pizza and wine down on the galley counter and started opening drawers looking for dishes and utensils.

I retreated into the bathroom area, which also contained my closet, and closed the door and jumped into my jeans and pulled on a T-shirt and looked at my wet hair in the mirror and decided there was no point in getting all groomed and formal.

Caroline was at the table setting out plates and glasses and pizza. She handed me the bottle.

"Where's your bottle opener?"

"I'm not sure I have one."

She looked at me, astonished. "You don't have a corkscrew?"

I rubbed my ear, a nervous twitch I've never been able to control when I'm acutely embarrassed.

"I don't drink a lot of wine," I said. "I may have one somewhere."

I remembered my L.L. Bean knife with the corkscrew and was saved. The cork behaved and we had breathing red wine of some sort. I sat down at the table and she curled up in my brown burlap upholstered reading chair, which was crammed in next to the table at my elbow. Her knees were up and her hem slipped down toward her hips. She had very lovely legs and she knew how to display them. She watched me as she bit into her pizza.

We ate for a while, eyeing each other, until she finally said, "There's enough cholesterol in this thing to shorten your life by ten years."

I smiled and reached for another piece, "You're right," I said.

I looked at her and reached over with the wine bottle to refill her glass, keeping my eyes on hers. "We have the most elegant dinners," I said.

"What do you think of me?" she asked suddenly.

"I think," I said, "you're a good nurse, a kind person, and I think I should have listened when you said you had a train to catch."

She laughed, a pretty, tinkling laugh.

"The thing is," I said. "You've got this boyfriend."

"But the thing is," she said. "I've got this neighbor."

She stood up and came over and sat in my lap and kissed me.

"Well," I said. "You're full of surprises."

"You're not surprised. Nothing surprises the good Dr. O'Brien."

"You do. All the time," I said. "I can't figure you out. I never know what you're going to do next."

"Yes you can," she said, and she kissed me again. "You might even get to like it," she said.

"I don't want to develop a taste for you."

I stood up and she slid off me and took her seat in a chair by the table and I staggered around, looking for a neutral corner, and wound up sitting on my bed. She smiled again. She knew the effect she was having, and she was enjoying herself. She was stalking me now, looking for the right time, watching my guard sinking.

"How'd I do?" she said.

"You controlled it well," I said. "As usual."

She lifted her glass to her lips and looked over the rim at me as she drained it.

Then she stood up, and set the glass down on the table.

"Well, thanks for the memories," she said.

I looked at her. She had obviously planned two moves, one for my letting her go, one for if I jumped her and dragged her off to bed. She had to be willing to walk if I didn't move to keep her, and I didn't want that. But I didn't want to have to play into her plan.

I stepped past her to get to the door. She caught me as I tried and kissed me for real.

"Just to show you," she said, "I'm not always totally in control."

I edged her toward the bed, which was the one great advantage of living in an efficiency—you are never very far from the bed. I suppose that's why they call it an efficiency.

She was as quick getting my shirt off as I was with her dress. It unzipped down the front, and the view was even prettier than I had imagined. We fell back onto the bed. She kicked her panty hose down her legs and we were making good progress when she said, "You'll have to promise not to expect this on demand."

"Oh," I said. "You mean, I'm the local business."

"I mean," she said, "what I said."

I stood up and pulled my jeans on. "I know just what you mean."

She got herself back together, not looking happy. When she was dressed, she came over and kissed my cheek.

"I'm sorry," she said. "You're right. It's not fair. I don't seem to know how to behave with you."

"Oh, you know just how to behave," I said. "That's the problem."

I didn't want to look at her. If I kept looking at her, I'd start wanting her again, and the fog would descend, and I'd regret it in the morning. I turned away and looked out my window, down the street. It was dark and the headlights of cars moved toward the river. I looked across the street at the buildings opposite, also hospital housing. Lights blinked on and off in rooms of the apartments.

Caroline made her own decisions. I couldn't affect the outcome. I could not affect any of the outcomes. Maybe, as Ira said, it had nothing to do with luck. Maybe it was all written.

Thinking about this, I forgot all about Caroline, until I heard the door close behind her.

21

WHEN IT COMES TO BEING LUCKY

We did rounds together the next day and Caroline never blinked an eye. She said good morning as if we were two people who never saw each other outside of the ward, as if we were just a doctor and nurse who worked together. She was Nurse Bates and I was just Dr. O'Brien, her colleague. She was, as they say in the theater, into her part. She believed in her new role. She had immersed herself and become the new Nurse Bates with all the intimacy of an airline stewardess giving instructions on seat belts and oxygen masks.

Fine with me, Miss Bates. Be like that. We just work together.

Vince Montebelli had pulled another one of his patented from-the-valley-of-the-shadow-of-death routines and he was talking, greeting people by name and making all kinds of sense. He knew he was in the hospital and he knew he'd been down for the count, but he had no memory of his delirium the day before. He was back on Caroline's ward, out of the ICU and sitting pretty. His only complaint was about breakfast. It hurt to swallow. Ira looked down his throat and said, "Uh-oh."

Now, there were two things you learned never to say at Whipple: One of them was "uh-oh," and the other was "whoops."

Vince's eyes popped opened and he grabbed Ira's arm. "What's wrong? What'd you see?"

Ira realized his mistake and he patted Vince's bald pate. "Calm down, sailor," he said, grinning. "I didn't mean it like that. You got nothing that a little Nystatin mouthwash won't cure."

Vince knew all about Nystatin. "Not candida again," he said. Vince had had several bouts of that fungal infection before, when his white blood cells were knocked off by chemotherapy.

"You'll be fine," Ira said hoisting up a grin.

He had to work on the grin. He liked Vince and he liked Mrs. Roundtree, and lately he didn't seem quite as unflappable when either of them started going sour. I thought it was a good thing he'd be rotating back to the Real World, back to Manhattan Hospital at the end of the month. We'd all be going, Ludvik, Ira, and me, April first. But if I had to choose just one of us, I'd send Ira. Ludvik was better insulated. And it wasn't as bad for me, not being an intern.

We stepped in to see the next patient, another leukemic, who had bigger trouble. He had mucormycosis, another unpleasant fungus, chewing up his nose and lip. He looked like he'd been hit in the face with a rock. His upper lip was almost gone and his upper teeth and gums were exposed. He sounded like a foghorn, breathing through what was left of his nose. He belonged to Ludvik, who examined him while the rest of us stood near the door, wishing Ludvik would hurry. The smell of the mucor and the fetid flesh was stupefying.

Ludvik finished and we retreated to the hall.

"One thing I will not miss about Whipple," I said, "is mucormycosis."

"Hey, mucor is infectious disease," said Ira. "The fungi are going to be business for you. Fungi will pay your rent."

Ludvik looked at me, examining me with his expressionless eyes, processing the information he had just received. He said: "You're going into infectious disease?"

"He's got a fellowship," said Caroline so suddenly, we all turned and looked at her. "In Boston."

Ludvik and Ira stared at Caroline and then they stared at me. Ira knew I was thinking about doing ID, but he hadn't known I'd actually signed up.

"Well, congratulations," Ira said.

"I was in Boston once," said Ludvik. "It looked like a good place for infectious disease."

"The nice thing about infectious disease," said Ira, "is that everyone gets better. Except at Whipple, of course, where nobody's got any working white blood cells."

"Come off it," said Caroline. "Whipple's not that bad. You learn a lot here."

"Oh, yeah. No pain, no gain," Ira said.

"You guys," Caroline said. "The only reason you hate Whipple is that it humbles you."

"O'Brien is not bothered by humility," said Ira. "And he hates it as much as we do."

"Do you hate Whipple?" Caroline asked me.

"I like the malteds," I said.

"And the nursing staff," Ira added.

"Who could forget the nurses?" I said. "The nurses here are highly rated."

"Some more than others, apparently," Caroline said, not to me, to the air.

Ira and Ludvik exchanged quizzical looks. Uncomfortable silence ensued.

Ludvik broke it, trying his best to sound cheery and light. "Well, if one learns most from one's mistakes," Ludvik said, "I must have learned quite the most among us."

Caroline looked at him with something close to affection. "Why, Ludvik," she said. "You have almost redeemed yourself." Then to me, "Yes, I'd say I've had the same experience, lately, learning from my mistakes."

More pregnant pauses, and we moved on.

We filed into Mrs. Roundtree's room. Mr. Roundtree was standing by her bedside and he was smiling. Mrs. Roundtree was smiling, too, and she said, "Good morning, Caroline. Good morning, Dr. O'Brien."

"Wonders of radiotherapy," I heard Ira mutter.

The radiotherapy really had worked wonders. Mrs. Roundtree recognized people now, and Ludvik went over her neurological exam for us and most of her deficits were gone. Her husband watched Ludvik carefully, and he smiled as Mrs. Roundtree picked up the stimuli from both sides of her body. Ludvik showed her the photos of her kids and she named each one.

"I feel like driving right down to New Hope and getting the kids back up here," Mr. Roundtree said.

"You are positively a new woman," Caroline said.

"Can I get out of bed?"

"Absolutely," Ira said, writing the order to ambulate her. "Absolutely. We'll start today."

We left Mr. and Mrs. Roundtree behind and we gathered in the hallway out of earshot from her door.

"Did you see that?" Ira said, face bright and pink. "She's a full-blown, honest-to-Jesus miracle cure. Ludvik, did you see that?"

"She's much better," Ludvik said, unsmiling, not sharing Ira's enthusiasm.

I had to agree with Ludvik: Getting Mrs. Roundtree past a brain met was not exactly a therapeutic triumph. She was still loaded with breast CA, growing in lots of locations it did not belong.

"Do you realize?" said Ira. "We may actually be able to discharge a patient from Whipple. Maybe two, even, if Vince keeps getting better. I mean, instead of signing a death certificate on Mrs. Roundtree, I am going to write in her chart: Discharge. Home with husband."

We all looked at Ira for a moment, not knowing what to say. Ludvik looked at his watch and mumbled something about having calls to make, and he wandered off.

Ira looked after him, confused, and then to us. "She is getting better," he said. "You saw her. She can pick up all the stimuli. She knows her kids."

He looked eagerly from Caroline to me and back to Caroline.

"She really is a lot better," Caroline said. "Today."

"You mean, she's not out of the woods yet," said Ira. "Hell, I know that. But she's turned a corner. That brain met's zapped. Now all we got to do is finish her poison protocol and she's on her way home."

"That's right, Ira," I said. "We'll all sign out of this joint together. You, me, Ludvik, Vince, and Mrs. Roundtree."

"You come with us," Ira told Caroline. "Over to the Real World."

Caroline smiled. "I'll wait for you to come back here as a senior resident," she said. "Give me something to look forward to."

Caroline and I watched Ira walk off down the hall toward the nurses' station. He had orders to write and calls to make.

"I hadn't realized he liked her so much," Caroline said. "I hope she lasts until he rotates out of here."

"He's counting down the days."

Caroline looked up suddenly. "And you'll be going too."

"Sure."

"You're counting the days too."

"Yes and no."

"Why yes and no? I thought you couldn't wait to get out of here."

"Well, think of all the nice dinners I've had since coming to Whipple."

"I think about them all the time," said Caroline. "Not last night's, of course."

"Don't make too much of that," I said. "It was the end of a long, hard day."

"No, as Ludvik said, that's the way you learn things."

22

A PATHOLOGIC FRACTURE

Mrs. Roundtree was doing much too well. Even Caroline—who should have known better—started talking about how well she was doing, and nobody was knocking on wood.

And then, one day, it all came home to roost.

One fine Thursday morning, Mrs. Roundtree went for a walk in the hall with Caroline and she stepped forward on her right leg and everyone from one end of the hall to the other heard a crack like an oak tree snapping in high wind. Mrs. Roundtree went down like a rock.

It was a "pathologic fracture," of course, right through a metastasis. She had grown breast cancer in her right tibia bone, nice soft breast tumor where bone ought to be, right in a weight-bearing bone, like a rotten spot in a roof beam, and she stepped on her right foot and shifted the weight and she fractured right through.

"This is all my fault," Ira said, when I told him about it over the phone.

"How's that?"

"You saw her bone scan. You saw that met in her tibia. I should've radiated that tibia before I let her get out of bed and walk."

"Ira, you radiate for pain, not for peace of mind. She has mets all over her skeleton. What're ya gonna do? Whole body radiation? She's got three vertebrae with hot spots: you want to burn those too?"

"Well, but we could've radiated the tibia—any weight-bearing bone."

"You saw the plain films of her tibia. There was nothing there would've made you think she was going to fracture. Chrissake, Ira. You got guilt, go spend it somewhere else. You did everything you should've done and nothing you shouldn't have done. We're trying to practice good medicine, doc, not witchcraft. And radiating silent mets found only on scan is not smart medicine."

"Tell that to Mrs. Roundtree."

I waited for Ira to come up from ICU, where he had been busy with Vince Montebelli, who had been doing a command performance, and we went to see Mrs. Roundtree. I had ordered some morphine for her and she was riding the tide of eight milligrams, but she was still hurting.

"God, I cannot believe the pain," she said, tears washing down her cheeks.

Ira sat down next to her and held her hand. "I'm sorry about this."

"I could hear it crack," she said, staring at him, and you could see the horror in her eyes. "It was such an awful sound. I knew what happened, but I couldn't believe it."

"Did you hit your head when you fell?" Ira asked her.

"No, Caroline was right there. But why did this happen?"

"You had tumor in your tibia. The big bone in your lower leg. The tumor isn't as strong as normal bone. You put your weight on your leg and the break went right through the tumor. It's called a 'pathologic fracture.' "

"Did you know I had tumor there?"

"Yes."

"Do I have it other places?"

"You know you do."

"But other places that might break, like this?"

"We'll look at your other weight-bearing bones again," said Ira. "Just to be sure."

"Can you do me a super big favor?"

"Sure, anything."

"Will you call my husband? I just don't have the heart to call him with any more bad news."

"Well, actually, Mrs. Roundtree," Ira said, pulling his collar away from his neck, as if it had suddenly constricted. He looked over to me. "Actually, I was going to call Dr. Freudenberg. He might want to call your husband."

"I wish you'd do it," said Mrs. Roundtree. "He'd take it better coming from you."

"What's he got against Dr. Freudenberg?"

"Oh, you know. He's got to be angry at someone. And they

gave Dr. Freudenberg such a buildup, down in New Hope. You know, this man can save you. This man Freudenberg can walk on water. He puts his hands on you and your tumor evaporates. But my tumor isn't evaporating, is it?"

"No, not yet."

"Not yet," said Mrs. Roundtree. "Not ever."

Ira stared at her, bug-eyed. He looked down at his hands, in his lap. "No," he said. "I suppose not."

"So that's what my husband has against Dr. Freudenberg."

"I see," said Ira. "I'll call Dr. Freudenberg. I don't think he'll mind my calling your husband."

Seymour was quite happy to let Ira make the call: "Oh, by all means. Be my guest. Better take a Valium before you do."

"You're really going to call her husband?" I asked Ira.

"She asked me to."

"She could ask you to walk on your hands down York Avenue, that doesn't mean you have to do it."

"If Mrs. Roundtree asked me," said Ira, "I'd try."

"Well, I'm getting on the other phone. I don't want to miss this."

Ira had quite an audience for his call: he dialed from the nurses' station with Caroline listening on one line and me on another.

"What do you mean?" Mr. Roundtree said, voice low and monotone, the voice of a man holding on to his self-control by his fingernails. "What do you mean, she broke her leg?"

"She was walking down the hall and her bone snapped," Ira explained.

"Did she trip?"

"No, a nurse was with her. The bone snapped."

"For no reason? It simply snapped?"

"There is always a reason, Mr. Roundtree," Ira said calmly. He sounded reasonable, controlled, but his face was bright pink. "She probably fractured through a metastasis."

"Through a tumor in her bone, you mean."

"That's right."

"Didn't you know she had a tumor in her leg bone?"

"Yes."

"Then what did you have her up walking for?"

"She's had tumor in that bone since she had that bone scan in New Hope. Before that. She's been walking all that time."

"And nobody ever told us?"

"I don't know what you were told."

"Well, you never told us that."

"I've told you her bone scan showed tumor in multiple locations. I don't know that I've specifically mentioned the tibia. The important point is, knowing there're tumor cells in a bone doesn't mean you can't use that bone. In fact, putting it to rest may be the worst thing you can do."

"Worse than breaking it?"

"The X rays looked good. We thought fracture was unlikely."

"Looks like you were wrong again, Doctor."

Ira agreed he was wrong and hung up. Caroline and I sat there exhaling. Caroline started to laugh.

"You masochist," she said. "Ira, you are a wonderful and insane human being."

The orthopods set Mrs. Roundtree's leg and she started on crutches.

But the fracture turned out to be only the warm-up act for the real showstopper: within a week Mrs. Roundtree developed phlebitis, and what had been a painful leg with a broken bone ballooned into an exquisitely painful, red-hot leg with a broken bone, a leg throbbing with clotted-off inflamed pulsating deep veins. It's those deep veins, the ones that run right up against the bone, that get all aggravated and inflamed when the bone splinters through them. Those are most unforgiving veins, and when they get phlebitis, they make the fracture seem like nothing more than the sneeze before the pneumonia hits. Bones knit back together, but once the veins get hostile, they can really hold a grudge.

And nasty as the phlebitis can get, it doesn't hold a candle to the specter of pulmonary embolus. Leg vein clots have a distressing tendency to break loose and roar downstream and hit the lung like a runaway logjam. That's called a pulmonary embolus, and breathing through a lungful of clot can become impossible. Pulmonary emboli kill people, swiftly, efficiently, and without asking permission.

Keeping Mrs. Roundtree from forming clots gave Ira fits, what with chemotherapy wrecking her platelets: whenever Ira ordered just a little too much heparin, she started bleeding from her nose and from her bladder. When he gave her too little heparin, her leg blew up like a big red balloon. The whole process of keeping Mrs.

Roundtree humming down the narrow line between too little and too much coagulation drove Ira crazy, and it didn't do much for Mrs. Roundtree's disposition, but Ira finally got her regulated.

By Ira's last day at Whipple, Mrs. Roundtree's leg looked fine and her blood-clotting studies were all in line and Ira had her in great shape to hand over to her new intern.

23

BACK DOWN TO NEW HOPE

Ira's last day was a Monday, and Mrs. Roundtree was not quite ready for discharge. We all thought she'd be good enough with her crutches to go home by the end of the week.

"I wanted to be the one to write your discharge orders," Ira told her. "But now someone else will have that pleasure. No matter. Soon, Friday maybe, you'll be on a train to New Hope."

"Not soon enough for me," said Mrs. Roundtree, reaching for his hand. "But I'll miss you, Dr. Bloomstein. You got me past some tough times."

Ira grinned at her and tried to say something, but nothing came out. He swallowed hard and his eyes got misty and he put his hand on her head and patted her like a little kid.

"I really wanted to write her discharge orders," he said when we were in the hall.

"She adores you," said Caroline. "She really will miss you, you know."

"Yeah," said Ira. "She'll miss all her friends at Camp Whipple where she had such good times."

"You've been hanging around O'Brien too much," said Caroline. "Talking like that."

We worked our way halfway down the hall. Then Caroline realized she had left her fever board in Mrs. Roundtree's room. She went back for it and we waited for her in the hall. We leaned against the wall and I watched her rear end as she walked away from me. You could see the outline of her panties through the sheer white uniform dress and I indulged myself in one of the few pleasures of making rounds at Whipple. She disappeared into Mrs. Roundtree's room and suddenly she was out in the hall, waving, shouting for the crash cart.

Even when we reached her room, I still couldn't believe Mrs. Roundtree had coded. We had just been talking to her.

"She's so blue," Caroline said.

We started all the resuscitative maneuvers: Ira pumped the chest rhythmically, looking over to Caroline, who put her hand on the femoral pulse and nodded, and said, "Four plus," meaning Ira's compressions were delivering blood, ejecting it from the heart to the rest of the body. Ludvik, at her head, intubated her by slipping a plastic tube through her mouth, down her trachea—no mean feat while Ira was making her chest, head, and neck jump with each compression—but Ludvik got the tube in and he hooked it up to a rubber breathing bag and then he breathed her.

It was a very smooth arrest, technically speaking. The intubation had gone flawlessly, and I managed to get a couple of big four-teen-gauge lines into her, one subclavian and another femoral, with no misses. We had her hooked up and plugged in. Caroline slapped Bristojets of bicarbonate and epinephrine into my hand and I plunged these into Mrs. Roundtree's veins through my sol-idly anchored IVs. Then Caroline handed me a blood gas syringe and I drove it into Mrs. Roundtree's femoral pulse, which jumped each time Ira compressed her chest. The blood should have been bright cherry red, but it came out dark, depleted of oxygen.

I ran the EKG on six leads, and then we saw it.

"Big right shift," said Ludvik, who could see it even from his position by her head.

A big right shift meant Mrs. Roundtree's lung was full of clot and there wasn't a thing we could do for her.

Despite all Ira's heparin, Mrs. Roundtree's massive clots had silently, stealthily, and perversely formed, and some big clots had broken free and shot downstream and crashed into her lungs, where they logjammed, blocking all blood flow through the lung in one massive pulmonary embolus, and no matter how hard Ira pushed blood out of her heart, none of it got through to the lung. None of it got oxygenated.

And the brain needs oxygen to live.

Mrs. Roundtree just got more and more dead.

Everyone knew then we'd lost her. Everyone but Ira. And he would have known, too, if he could have let himself see it.

I stopped asking for medications, and Caroline looked at me hopelessly and we both looked at Ira, who was absorbed in pump-ing the chest. Ludvik, at her head, squeezed his bag less and less often, and he looked past frantically pumping Ira to me, for the word to stop. I nodded and Ludvik stopped breathing her. Ira continued pumping and only after some minutes, with all of us staring at him, did he look up and bark at Ludvik, "Breathe her! What's wrong with you?"

I stepped over to Ira and put a hand on his wet shoulder as he pumped. "It's over, Ira," I said.

Ira kept pumping. "No," he said. He kept pressing her lifeless chest and her arms flopped a little and he pumped again.

Mrs. Roundtree's eyes had that opaque sheen of the dead: all color had drained out of her face and she looked dead as wax fruit.

Ira kept pumping.

"Ira," I said. "Stop this."

Ira stopped pumping and looked at me over his shoulder and then he looked up at Caroline, who was looking at the floor.

Ludvik looked at Ira. Their eyes met, but Ludvik couldn't hold the contact, and he looked to me and then at Mrs. Roundtree, and then he walked out of the room.

Ira stood there looking at Mrs. Roundtree, eyes brimming, and his shoulders shook and he gulped.

Just then, Raskolnovich stepped into the room. He had heard the code announcement and he was here, as always, to search out tumor for his lab cultures. He stood there, long, lank hair falling over his face, fat, sweaty, and excited, and caught sight of Mrs. Roundtree and his eyes lit up.

"Oh, no, you don't," cried Ira, rushing around Mrs. Roundtree. "You fucking bastard!"

Raskolnovich was stunned to see Ira lunging for him and raised an arm to ward Ira off, uncomprehending.

"She's not even cold," Ira shouted. "You fucking bastard!"

I was on Ira's heels, and took him down with a shoulder-high tackle just as he swung for Raskolnovich. We both landed on the floor at Raskolnovich's feet. Caroline stepped between us and Raskolnovich, who retreated to the door in terror.

"What have I done?" he asked. He was genuinely astonished that anyone, least of all an intern he hardly knew, would want to bludgeon him to the floor. His amazement overcame his fear and he stood behind Caroline and asked again and again, "Why did you do that? What have I done?"

Ira's face was steaming and blotched red. "You fucking bastard!

You're not getting anything!" he cried from the floor, where I straddled him. "You hear me? Get the fuck out of here!"

"But we are friends," Raskolnovich said. "You and me. Good buddies."

"You want your pound of flesh, you dirty slimebag! You get the fuck out of here!" I had an arm through his elbows, behind his back.

Caroline caught Raskolnovich by the elbow and guided him out of the room while Raskolnovich desperately tried to make her understand he meant no harm, that he was Ira's good buddy, that there must be some mistake, as if he could just convince her, he could put the world in order again.

I put an arm around Ira's shoulder and dragged him off to the conference room. Caroline arrived with coffee in Styrofoam cups. Ira leaned forward and put his face in his hands. His thick, solid body was sweaty and he seemed to be fighting for control. He was shaking his head, looking at the floor, muttering, "Bastard. Fucking vulture."

Caroline held out a cup. He ignored her and pointed toward the conference room door and roared, *"Nobody!"* He caught his breath. "Nobody asks for an autopsy on that lady!" He looked from Caroline to me with a baleful glare, then back to the floor. "Nobody. Understand?"

"Sure, Ira."

We didn't say anything.

He looked at the floor and then back up to me and said, very softly, "Somebody's got to tell her husband."

"Yes."

Caroline handed him a cup and this time he took it.

He drank some coffee and looked at the floor. He couldn't look at us.

"I don't know what got into me," he said. "It's just I couldn't believe she did that. And then Rasko showed up. Fucking Rasko. Bastard."

"He didn't mean any harm," Caroline said.

"He's an asshole."

"You're on the same side, you know," Caroline said.

Ira looked up at her with a look of sheer incredulity. "Come on, Caroline. He's a fucking hyena."

"He's working on the same problem. Different perspective is all."

"He's a meat merchant. You know what he wants to do to that lady back there? He wants to slice her up down in the autopsy room. He doesn't want to know about her three kids or her husband or anything. All he wants is her fucking tumor. That's all. He's not interested in anything but his cell line cultures."

We didn't say anything. We just watched Ira. He gulped some more coffee.

"This stuff causes cancer," Ira said, smiling. "Mrs. Roundtree drank six cups a day. I told her. I told her it causes breast cancer. But she drank it anyway. She said, 'Don't take my last pleasure away from me.' "

"She was a nice lady," said Caroline.

"You shouldn't drink it either," Ira told Caroline. "You're mortal, too, you know."

"I'm cutting down."

"Back to New Hope," said Ira.

We didn't say anything.

"Damn funny name for a place," said Ira. "For her to come from."

An army of sluggish seconds crawled by and Ira shook his head and he seemed to have a silent conversation with himself. Then he said, "Okay, I'm okay now."

"You still want to kill Rasko?" asked Caroline.

"No," said Ira, half smiling. "He's just a vulture. He can't help himself."

"Okay," said Caroline, standing up.

"But if he ever sets foot across the street at the Manhattan Hospital"—Ira smiled malevolently—"I'll cut his fucking balls off."

"We need a psych consult," Caroline told me.

"I'm okay," said Ira. "Really."

"I'll call Freudenberg," I said. "He'll probably insist on calling Mr. Roundtree himself."

"Yeah," Ira said. "He'd do the tough part. That's Seymour all over."

"Then we'll do X-ray rounds, and then we'll do chart rounds and then we'll go to Gleasons and then we'll all go home."

"Yeah," said Ira. "That's what we'll do."

24

THE BIG PICTURE

Gleasons was filling up with the dinner crowd and I was contemplating the Book of Job and, in lighter moments, considering strategy for dealing with Caroline and her boyfriend when I saw her step through the door, look around in the darkness, and make directly for me. She slid into my booth and sat beside me.

Her smile was getting no cooperation from her eyes. She looked pale and worn and she said, "Buy me a drink."

I started to pour her a beer and she said, "I mean a real drink." She had a Manhattan. Then she had another.

"Did you buy Ira a beer?"

"Several."

"I'll miss him. I'll even miss Ludvik," she said. "They turned out to be pretty good interns. Ira, of course, is a sweetheart."

"He was still pretty down about Mrs. Roundtree."

Caroline grew quiet.

"Did Freudenberg tell her husband?" I asked.

"Yes. They came up and got her body and everything got taken care of."

"They going to do an autopsy?"

"I don't know," Caroline said. She did not look good. Her skin, usually a very healthy pink, looked pasty and she had a bled look.

"What's wrong?"

"Vince Montebelli's dead." she said. "Just before I left."

Then she pulled out a handkerchief and blew her nose and she looked at me.

"A real clean sweep," she said. "Grim Reaper made rounds on my ward today."

"I was just talking to him," I said. "Ira and I went by to say good-bye. He was fine."

"He was depressed," Caroline said.

"Well, hell. Aren't they all?"

"He slit his wrists," Caroline said, looking at me squarely. "Broke one of those heavy glass bacteriostatic water bottles and slit his wrists with one of the shards. Blood all over. I walked in and noticed his covers were bloodstained, and I thought some intern's drawn a culture and dropped a tube and not cleaned up. Then I pulled back the sheets."

I couldn't think of a thing to say. I was fresh out of glib remarks.

"I thought he was doing better," she said.

"We said good-bye to him tonight," I said. "He looked a little down. He said he didn't feel safe with a new intern and resident."

"Can you imagine how desperate you must feel, to do that?"

"I try not to think about it."

"I believe that," she said.

"Sometimes I wish Professor Toomey had managed to get out that window, you know?"

"You know, that whole act of yours grows old."

"I'm entirely serious. He ever tell you his Oedipus story?"

"No."

"He said Oedipus had been faked out by the gods. You know, they'd handed him his fate, and he'd tried like hell to resist it, but he wound up doing everything just as the gods had it planned."

"This sounds like the professor."

"I'm telling you, he told me this. So the gods are real smug. But then Oedipus takes a knife and cuts out his own eyes. The gods hadn't counted on that. See, Oedipus made his own fate. He controlled his own destiny. That's something you ought to appreciate."

"What's that crack supposed to mean?"

"Forget it."

We drank in silence for a while.

"What I mean is," I said. "At least Vince didn't die with a pack of house officers pumping on his chest, just the way we all figured he would."

Caroline stared at me with a look of genuine astonishment. "I take your point," she said. And she sounded like she did.

"I couldn't do what you do," I told her. "One month at Whipple and I'm wondering why I didn't go to law school. But you go in day after day, month after month. I don't know how you do it."

"It's not usually this bad."

"I wish Mrs. Roundtree's kids hadn't come up that time," I said. "I mean I wish I'd never met them."

"I know."

"Most of them, you never see them except in their flowered gowns. It's like they never had a life outside of the hospital. They're just patients. They were always sick and dying and they're supposed to go down the tubes. But Mrs. Roundtree was a real person. Like someone might have come from my neighborhood. I can just imagine that house tonight, down in New Hope. I can see those kids and Mr. Roundtree."

"Let's get out of here," Caroline said. "I need some air."

We walked up First Avenue, and over to Second, past the singles bars that still did a brisk business at that hour on a Friday night. I had a raincoat over my white uniform and Caroline wore her gray tweed jacket.

Coming in our direction was a couple in earnest and agitated conversation. The man looked very serious and was striding purposefully along, the woman on his arm looking just as intense.

"But it's not your weekend for the kids," the woman was saying.

"I know, but what can I do?" said the man.

"She always does this, just when we've made other plans. And I haven't been to East Hampton since last summer."

That's all I heard before they were by me.

"Second wife," said Caroline. "First wife's dumping the kids on him for the weekend and second wife there's accepted an invitation to East Hampton with friends who have no kids and they can't take his kids along for what is supposed to be an adults' weekend in the Hamptons."

"Big trouble," I said.

"They don't know what big trouble is," said Caroline.

We walked on, past the restaurants with the sidewalk extensions with windows they would remove in the summer to give the feeling of a sidewalk café. Young, pretty, affluent couples sat at the windows. Many were tanned in late March.

"Aruba," Caroline said, speaking of the tans on one especially dark couple. "Thirty-one or -two. Investment banker. She works as a management trainee for Chase Manhattan. He's at Citicorp now, but he was at Chase, which is where he met her. They're trying to decide whether to buy a place at Fire Island, but it's a commitment and they're not even married yet."

"More big trouble in the lives of the citizens of the Upper East Side," I said.

"Mr. Roundtree has big trouble tonight," Caroline said. "Not them. Not us."

We reached Eighty-sixth Street and turned back for home. Caroline had taken my arm somewhere blocks back, or we would have been separated by the flow of people.

"I don't know why I put up with you," she said. "Life is too short."

"Shorter for some than for others," I said.

"We are all of us merely mortal," Caroline said. "The important thing is to live every day as if you believed it."

Back at the Whitney, we got on the elevator together. Caroline's floor came and went. She remained on the elevator. When my floor came, she stepped off with me and walked down to my door with me.

"Don't," she said, when I started to object. "Let's not dicker tonight."

We took a shower. With lots of soap. The soap seemed important, don't ask me why. Shampoo and soap and hot water and we couldn't get clean enough. Then we dried off and went to bed.

What surprised me was how gentle she was. What really surprised me was how gentle I was. I was breaking all my rules, of course. But it didn't seem to matter. I didn't care about Washington or rules or next weekend or things to come. When you looked at the big picture, we had no problems.

25

SPRING

Caroline made one last trip down to Washington that spring, to "clean things up," with her boyfriend. Her ex-boyfriend.

"We are still friends," she said. "I don't cut off people I care about."

April came with its warm weather and its green buds and soft breezes and the only problem was deciding when and where to be happiest. During the week, we'd meet for lunch on the stone benches by the river and watch the big oceangoing ships pass by. Or we'd eat in the gardens at the Medical School across from Whipple. I was on a nine-to-five rotation, which seemed like part-time work after Whipple. When Caroline worked the day shift and was off at four, we could leave the Medical Center campus and strike out into the city. The days were getting longer and we headed for Central Park or walked down Madison Avenue and looked at the paintings in the windows of the small galleries.

"Someday," Caroline said, "when my ship comes in, I will have original art in my living room."

Among the many things I learned that spring was the unacceptability of hanging prints or copies of original art in your living room. Museum posters for exhibitions were acceptable, as long as they were clearly posters and not meant to look like originals.

"Better empty walls than fake art," Caroline said. "Which is just one step up from those paintings on black velvet of Elvis Presley."

As we spent more and more time together, I discovered how appallingly ignorant I was of the "basic essentials." Food, for example: frozen dinners were unacceptable. Dinner was a meal to be eaten sitting down, in a leisurely ceremonial fashion. Yogurt eaten from the container with a plastic spoon while waiting in line for a movie did not constitute dinner. Dinner meant a salad and something cooked—fish or chicken—with seasonings. Good dinners required wine, about which I was a near illiterate.

"The amazing thing about you," Caroline told me, "is that you are indifferent to real food. Tuna fish sandwich from the vending machine, dinner at Sign of the Dove, it's all the same to you." I did not find that amazing. She did. Which amazed me.

And restaurants—eating out was not simply a convenience but an experience. Food, service, price, atmosphere, but most especially the food, were all elements to be critically appraised. All that mattered to me was the company. Anywhere we ate together was splendid. But not for Caroline. "These are the things that make life sweet," she said, looking at me with a raised eyebrow. "Someday we'll go to Italy: teach you how to linger over a meal."

I did not know how to linger. Lingering was not one of those skills I had cultivated at the Medical Center. And I ate too fast. I knew nothing about wine. I had nothing to read in my apartment. Caroline brought her books and my apartment filled with books by authors I'd never read: John Barth, Larry McMurtry, Anne Tyler, John Irving, Jane Austen, Vladimir Nabokov. Caroline read in bed, every night, until her eyes rolled shut and the book fell out of her hand and landed on the floor.

Another discovery: I read too slowly. Of course, compared with Caroline, Evelyn Wood read slowly.

"You make your bed fast, clean your apartment fast. You eat much too fast. You walk as if you were in a race. But you read slower than a three-toed sloth."

Another item: I had no sense of adventure. "You read the same books over and over again. You've read *The Stranger* three times in the past two weeks."

"What's wrong with that? It's a good book."

"There are other good books."

"But I know I like this good book. Why chance a book I might not like?"

"That is the sign of a man who is afraid of new experience."

So I began reading books I'd never read.

"Try Hemingway. You'll like Hemingway."

"I never liked Hemingway, all those drunks and short sentences."

"When was the last time you read Hemingway?"

"High school."

"Try him again."

She was right about Hemingway. And about Raymond Chandler and Dashiell Hammett and about Larry McMurtry. (I never could see Nabokov.)

We did not live together, exactly. She cooked dinner and spent nights, but she had her own place. Which was fortunate. Caroline was never much on housekeeping. Her place always looked as if it had just been ransacked by foreign agents looking for something very small.

"You enjoy cleaning," she told me—another thing I never knew about myself—"it's part of your anal-compulsive fastidious nature. A good trait in a doctor. But a little hard to live with. I, however, do not enjoy cleaning relentlessly. Life goes by too quickly to spend it scrubbing tiles and organizing closets."

I had a lot to learn. For one thing, I had to learn how unobservant I was. I had to recognize this deficiency if there was to be any hope for me at all. I slipped out one morning before she was awake and had doughnuts and coffee waiting for her when she awoke. Coffee with cream. She nearly threw it at me.

"Christ, O'Brien." She looked at the coffee as if I had tried to poison her. "I drink it black. No cream. No sugar. How long have you known me?"

She poured it out. Later, she said, "Sorry. You were trying to be nice. But you are just *so* unobservant."

I was unobservant, it turned out, because I walked around lost in my own thoughts.

"You simply do not notice things," Caroline observed. "Because you are only rarely fully present. What were you thinking about, just now?"

We were sitting in front of the Plaza Hotel, drinking iced tea and eating Sabrett hot dogs we had bought from a street vendor.

"I was wondering whether these hot dogs were made from corn-fed or garbage-fed pigs."

"Did you notice who got out of that limousine, over there? Did you even see her walk up the steps into the hotel?"

"No, who?"

"I rest my case. Cybill Shepherd could walk right up and sit in your lap and you wouldn't notice. You'd be drifting off somewhere, thinking about the parasites in the horse manure."

"Was that who it was? Cybill Shepherd?"

"I am not telling."

"Actually, I *had* wondered about all that horse manure. I was thinking about the horse manure right before the hot dogs. I mean, I wonder if anyone's ever studied horse dung in New York City. Some of those horses don't look too healthy. I was just reading about this horse parasite that encysts in your brain."

Yet another item: I was insufficiently aware of current events. Caroline was more aware of the world around her than anyone I'd ever met. She read the newspaper every day, especially the local news, which is something I avoided. She was astonished I never read a paper.

"I read newspapers, once," I told her, "but then I started reading articles about breast cancer, herpes, things I know about, and they were awful. Full of distortion, inaccuracy. I figure it couldn't be only the medical stories they're screwing up. So why read newspapers?"

"Because, there is a whole world out there, outside the hospital," Caroline said. "And you are missing it."

It was true: the world was a bigger place than I had realized. Caroline could move about that greater world outside the hospital with such ease. She never seemed at a loss—she spoke Spanish on the subway to help a lost girl find her mother, French in Bloomingdale's, German on a street corner in Yorkville when a little old German lady couldn't figure out where to stand for her bus to The Bronx. Caroline could go anywhere, talk to anyone.

Caroline in a SoHo restaurant, laughing at me when they brought out the plate: "That's all there is," she said as I stared at it. It looked as if someone had eaten half the meal. "It's nouvelle cuisine. *Très chic.*"

The hospital had become the place I felt safe and comfortable. Before Caroline, on nights off, I'd drift up to the cardiac care unit and shoot the breeze with the nurses. Or I'd drop down to the emergency room, if I knew the resident on shift. I knew the stairwells and the underground passageways and the location of every canteen and coffee machine. I knew where they kept supplies and where the labs and bathrooms were. And I knew the people, the security guards, the aides, the staff, and they knew me. I never had to explain myself or say what I was doing there. The hospital was home.

Caroline led me out into the world.

When Caroline worked the night shift, we had dinner together and she went down to her own apartment and slept until ten and I didn't see her until dinner the next day. That time seemed empty and dull.

Not that I was bored at the hospital: the infectious disease rotation had become suddenly active. Three young men had been admitted within three weeks of each other with pneumocystis pneumonia, which is something I had previously seen only in the lymphoma patients at Whipple. But only one of these men had lymphoma, and that was an odd one, called Kaposi's. It was very strange, and fascinating, but they were just three isolated cases.

We were in my apartment reading, Caroline was in bed and I was at my desk going over articles on pneumocystis. I told her about the three young men.

"Sounds like the infectious disease service at Whipple," said Caroline. "Sounds like their pneumocystis is the least of their problems."

"What do you mean?"

"Pneumocystis is a pretty puny bug, as I understand it. What's wrong with these guys, they get infected with such a puny bug?"

"Maybe it's changed. Maybe it's mutated. Maybe pneumocystis has got more virulent. We got three healthy young men with it, sick as stink."

"Three?" Caroline said. "Lord, you've got yourself a regular epidemic."

Caroline's words were, of course, prophetic. Those were the first AIDS patients we saw at the Manhattan Hospital, only it wasn't called AIDS yet, and we had no idea how many more would follow. They were just three young men, two homosexuals and an IV drug abuser, afflicted by pneumocystis pneumonia, previously reserved for lymphoma patients or transplant patients with depressed immune systems. We had no idea we were witnessing the opening of a new epoch in medicine. But those three patients were just a curiosity then, and I gave them no more thought. I was too busy: I now had a life outside the hospital and her name was Caroline Bates.

With the warm days and with daylight saving time, we had more than two hours after work to explore the city. We took the bus down Second Avenue and watched the street life. We walked to Central Park, past the sailboat pond, past the Bethesda Fountain, over to the West Side, where you could eat well and not pay much at the Italian restaurants that dotted Columbus Avenue, before the street went upscale. I wanted to go back to Brooklyn Heights, but Caroline refused. "You must push yourself to do new things," she said.

"But I like the old things."

"O'Brien, live a little. Read a new book. Try a new restaurant. Walk through a new part of the city."

We ate in Yorkville, Turtle Bay, SoHo, the East Village, the West Village, Queens, The Bronx. We even took the ferry to Staten Island, one Saturday. I saw more of New York City between March and May of that year than I had seen the entire eight previous years.

It was the first time since senior year in medical school I'd actually had the time to live, more or less, on a Real World schedule, time to do more than go from ward to cafeteria to bed and back again. Nine to six seemed like bankers' hours to me. For Caroline, of course, the beat went on. She still worked that chaotic nurse schedule: three days, three evening shifts, three night shifts. She came home with stories about patients, about doctors, about the craziness that never changed at Whipple. But it became harder and harder to listen. I had made my break with Whipple. I didn't want to go over there, and would go only if it was the only way to have dinner with Caroline.

One night I nodded through a story about Raskolnovich, not hearing a word, thinking instead about how amazing it was Caroline could work every day among the bacteria and fungi so rampant at Whipple and yet her skin remained so unblemished, so pink and glowing. She realized I wasn't listening and said, "You don't want to hear about Whipple anymore, do you?"

"I want to hear about you."

"But Whipple bores you."

"Whipple was a battleground. I can't say Whipple ever bored me. I just have new things now."

"Well, it doesn't bore me."

"You're the advocate of the new. Adventure means change. Who said that?"

"Things always change at Whipple," Caroline said, not sounding entirely convinced herself. "New patients every day. New doctors. New nurses, just when you think you've got a decent staff to run the floor with. Christ, Meg Smith told me she was leaving in July. She's going off to Seattle with that solid-tumor Fellow. I didn't even know they were dating."

"And you don't ever feel the stirrings?" I asked. "Caroline Bates, foreign service brat, intrepid traveler, seeker of adventure."

"You're right, I should be an airline stewardess. Or what do they call them now? Flight attendants? It all adds up to the same thing: flying ass-wigglers. Keep the businessmen happy."

"So you have meaningful work and you sacrifice for it."

"Don't we all?"

"You can change the scene. They need nurses in Boston. They need nurses everywhere."

"Where could I be more needed than Whipple? Calcutta maybe. But they've already got Mother Teresa. No thank you, I'm doing fine here. I'm lucky to have a job like mine."

Another night, we were reading in bed. Caroline had discovered Barbara Pym and was not to be disturbed. She was deeply absorbed. I was rereading *A Moveable Feast* for the umpteenth time. I read aloud the part about having Paris as a young man, and if you have it then, it will always stay with you. I wasn't sure Caroline had heard a word until she snorted, "That's so much Hemingway."

"But it's true," I protested. "I feel that way about New York."

She rolled over and looked at me. "That's right," she said. "You won't have New York for much longer, will you?"

26

A PLACE IN BOSTON

Boston was something we never talked about. Boston was the place I was going without Caroline. But one Friday night I began to panic about having noplace to live in Boston.

"I've got to look for an apartment."

"Doesn't the hospital have housing?"

"It's not like here. You have to find your own. I've never had to find an apartment. I've always lived in a dorm or in hospital housing. How am I supposed to find an apartment?"

"It is daunting," Caroline said dryly. "Having to find yourself a place to live, at your tender age."

"I thought I might go up there and drive around."

"You mean, just drive around Beacon Hill and ask people you see on the streets if they have a spare room they'd like to rent?"

"I like that. Might work."

"You're hopeless."

"You've found apartments before. What do you do?"

"Try the newspaper," said Caroline. "Or try the local universities: they usually have card files on apartments for students."

"That's a wonderful idea."

"At this rate"—Caroline shook her head—"you're going to be living in a tent."

"Not if you help me. Come with me. It'll be fun."

"You don't need me to hold your hand." She said that softly, without a trace of reproach.

"Look, I'm going to Boston tomorrow. I'd consider it a kindness if you came with me."

It was a pretty trip, Merritt Parkway to New Haven and then Route 95 through Connecticut and Rhode Island. But as the hours passed, Boston began to seem a long way from New York.

"I didn't realize," I said, somewhere around Providence, "Boston was so far from New York."

"It's about as far as New York is from Washington," Caroline said, looking out her window. She was quiet most of the trip. The farther we got from New York, the quieter she got.

She was right about the card files at the universities. Even the hospital had one. We thumbed through it, looking for apartments in my price range.

"How much can you pay?" Caroline asked.

I told her.

"They are *paying* you for this fellowship?"

They were paying me about half of what I had made in New York as a resident.

"Boston's supposed to be a less expensive town than New York," I said. "It's a student town." The rents were less, but looking at the economics, it was clear I was about to enter the ranks of the working poor.

We looked at several places. None of the apartments looked right. We walked up a winding steep Beacon Hill street, toward the next address. It was a pretty early May day, and the breezes were wet and full of promise. Birds sang and trees with green buds were spaced along the streets and strollers roamed around with hands in pockets, breathing in the air.

"This town isn't so bad," Caroline said. "Lot of character."

A college-aged couple approached us and we fell silent, listening to their conversation: "Well, you can sense the dialectical tension," the boy was telling the girl, who was listening intently, "between him and Kierkegaard."

"It is a college town," I said, when they had passed.

"It really is different," Caroline said. "From New York."

"So tweedy," I said. "No glitz."

"You're going to fit right in," said Caroline. "All your Harris Tweed. This town fits your clothes: blue jeans and herringbone sport coats."

"Good taste abounds," I said, stopping to peer into an oak-paneled bar, with brass fixtures and leather-backed barstools.

"Now, now," said Caroline. "We have work to do. You need a place to live."

"One thing I will not miss is having to wait for elevators. Seems like I spent at least one year of the eight I lived in New York waiting for elevators." All of the apartments we had seen were walk-ups, usually the second floor of converted brownstones.

"It's all done on a very nice scale. Very civilized. Reminds me of London, or Oslo, maybe." Caroline said. "And the fall ought to be just gorgeous."

"Right," I said. "I'm going to be miserable."

27

THE SIMPLE CHOICES

We were standing on a corner. Caroline leaned her head against my chest and I smoothed her glossy hair and watched the honey-colored highlights catch the sunlight. I could feel my heart thudding against her forehead.

"You are going to be too busy to be miserable," said Caroline, still not looking up to meet my eyes. "People kill for high-powered fellowships. In Boston, no less. The medical Mecca. I'm thrilled for you."

"Come with me."

She turned away from me. "It's not that simple."

"What could be simpler?"

"What am I going to do? Come up here and starve on your stipend?"

"It doesn't have to be like that. Do whatever you want."

"Brendan." She almost never called me Brendan, except when she was very serious. "Talk sense."

"What could make more sense? We're happy. Let's stay together."

"Don't you understand? Internship, residency, are just like musical chairs. The music starts up again, and you've got to move on."

"I'm asking you to move on with me."

"You're just holding on, Brendan," she said, looking at me now. "You're just scared to go out into the real world. You've never had to do it. But you'll do just fine. You'll move into your apartment and you'll keep it immaculate as you always do, and you'll feel right at home and you'll go to the hospital and not come home for days at a time and you'll wonder why you ever wanted me around."

"Is that what you really think?"

"No," she said. "It's just, I can't simply pick up and follow you off into the sunset. It's not like we're college kids. I have a job."

"You really want to stay at Whipple, and wave good-bye and say 'Stay in touch,' have phone conversations and maybe visit on weekends and pretend we're still friends?"

"I'm not the one who's leaving."

"If I had any choice, I'd stay in New York and wash dishes to be near you."

"Don't say that. Don't ever say a thing like that. You are committed to your career. And you should be. You do what you have to do. And I do what I have to. But I can't follow you around."

"Then don't just follow me. Come to Boston and do it for yourself. Go to medical school."

Caroline looked off down the street. "Don't think I haven't thought of that."

"What's stopping you?"

"School takes money."

"Money's no problem."

She laughed. "Says he of the poverty-level stipend. You going to pay my tuition?"

"I've saved some. You could get loans."

"That is not the point," she said.

"I don't get it," I said. "I don't get the point."

"The point is," Caroline said, "I have always set my own course and been the captain of my own ship. You might not think much of Whipple, but I've got that ward running pretty nicely now, and it's taken a few years. Now I'm supposed to walk in and resign and tell them, 'Thanks a lot but where my heart leads I must follow.' "

"Sounds good to me."

"That's because you are the incurable romantic."

"Incurable disease," I said. "Your specialty."

"You," she said, putting her head against my chest again, "are my incurable disease."

28

THE AMBASSADOR

I signed a lease with a little old lady who seemed to think Caroline and I were married, but who never asked. The lady must have been in her eighties and had paper-thin, almost translucent skin. She fit Caroline's hypothesis that Boston was populated by the very old and the young, all the middle-aged having moved to New York.

The apartment was the entire third floor of an ancient but solid town house and it was more apartment than I really needed. Caroline said, "It's close to the hospital and you can afford it." And when the landlady was briefly out of hearing: "I saw only one roach, and he looked dead."

We drove back to New York talking happily, as if we'd settled something. But, of course, all we'd really settled was that I would not be on the street come July. The bigger issue remained an open question. But I remained optimistic.

Until the ambassador arrived.

He answered her phone one day, late May. I tried to keep the surprise out of my voice: here was this rich, masculine voice on the line, and when I asked for Caroline, he seemed amused and said, "I think she's somewhere here, lurking about."

Caroline came on the line: "My father's here." She sounded thrilled. "Come right down."

I had not had to deal with meeting fathers since high school. That was one experience I was glad to leave behind—all the fish-eye stares and phony warmth. Caroline was a big girl now, and she lived in her own apartment and the sexual-territorial aspect should no longer be a big issue.

And I was not some acneiform teenager in tight jeans. I was a bona fide physician, which ought to count for something.

I took the elevator downstairs with no special dread, but with a certain vague resignation and with some curiosity. I had heard enough by then to realize that the Washington lawyer had been no worry at all compared with Daddy: Daddy was the real measure of all men.

And Daddy was quite a man. I was not prepared for the sheer physical impact of his presence. It was easy to believe he had played basketball in college. And it was easy to believe he was a diplomat, and an important one. He looked like an ambassador, which was in fact his rank in the foreign service. Caroline occasionally referred to him as "the ambassador," and he really did look the part. He answered the door wearing a white shirt and dark Cornell tie, and a broad smile, holding a martini in his left hand and extending his right hand to me as if he had heard wonderful things about me and he was so glad to finally meet me in the flesh, which is exactly what he said. His little speech gave me the opportunity to examine him. He towered above both of us, full head of fair hair with white temples and forelock, deep facial creases, and a meaty handshake which gave the impression of restrained power.

"I understand you two had dinner plans," he said.

"Oh, nothing much," I said. "You'll have time to join us?"

"I wouldn't dream of intruding."

"Oh, Dad," Caroline said. She looked and sounded suddenly so young, imploring her father, with just a trace of a whine. I've always been fascinated how young my father looked in the presence of his father and how people in general seem to grow younger around their parents, but Caroline was an extreme case. The toughness and sting went right out of her. Caroline, who never seemed the least bit worried about whether she impressed anyone, was suddenly eager to please. She jumped up to refill his glass, laughed too eagerly at the mildest of his very dry observations; she did everything but bark and wag her tail.

He said, "You make a very good martini, Caroline. At least you learned something worthwhile along the way at all the fancy schools."

And she giggled like a schoolgirl.

I was surprised to hear him mention the fancy schools, and I looked at him, trying to see if there was a twinge of pain in his eyes as the mention of Caroline's schooling slipped out. Here was the man who had defaulted on Caroline's education, talking about her fancy schools. He caught me examining him and we looked at each other in mutual appraisal, and I could feel the power shift. The ambassador had problems of his own.

We did eat dinner together that night, of course. There was never any real question about that. Caroline ran through a list of restaurants for her father that comprised her top ten. These were restaurants we considered very special, and we saved them for important occasions. He picked a French one, La Petite Auberge.

"There's one by the same name in Newport, Rhode Island," he said. "Three stars. Really superb. If you're ever there."

"We just passed by Newport," said Caroline. "If we'd only known."

This surprised me, since I couldn't remember having been in Newport for years. Caroline could see the question forming in my face, and she added, "We were coming back from Boston."

"You're going to be doing your fellowship there," said the ambassador, looking at me.

I agreed I was.

"Nice town, Boston. In college, we used to eat at a place in Cambridge called the Brown Derby. Best prime rib I ever had. Probably gone by now. But I loved playing Harvard at Cambridge, thinking about that prime rib."

The restaurant was ten blocks uptown and we walked. The ambassador had a wonderful time along the way. He was a natural tourist, in the best sense of the word: he had an eye for the details of the city that escaped its inhabitants as they hurried from one point to another. Delighted by the stone masonry on a brownstone, he stood pointing out its features as an example of some sort of architectural era, and Caroline beamed like a schoolgirl. It wasn't that he was showing off; he really was fascinated. We halted while he stood transfixed as a car turned on a metal turntable in the private garage of another brownstone.

"It's like a big lazy Susan," he said, delighted. "Can you imagine spending all that money so you can drive your car out headfirst, rather than having to back it out onto the street? Only in America."

"If you saw the way people drive in this city," Caroline said. "You wouldn't wonder. Backing a car out onto the street in New York can be lethal."

"I don't know about New York," he said. "I'm never here that long. And usually I'm in the backseat of a cab, reading a paper.

But for my money'—and he nudged me—"Boston has the world's worst drivers. With the possible exception of Cairo during a sandstorm."

Something about the way he said that made me vaguely uneasy. We walked two more blocks, the ambassador bringing various items of interest to our attention along the way, before I could put my finger on what had disturbed me. He had spoken of Boston drivers as if only I would be interested. As if Caroline would not have to worry about Boston drivers.

They spoke a lot of French at the restaurant. The ambassador spoke French with the waiter, and soon the owner showed up and the ambassador spoke French with him. My own French, after five years through high school and college, was barely adequate to pick up the sense of the exchanges. The owner, I think, was from Bordeaux, and the ambassador had many friends in Bordeaux and had eaten many wonderful meals there. He introduced Caroline, who chatted away in her flawless accent. Then the ambassador introduced me to his newly made old friend, the owner.

"Nice to meet you," I said.

The owner looked more than disappointed—pained. I did not speak French. I suppose I could have said, *"Enchanté,"* or something French and appropriate, but that would have been a pose, and probably would have led to my being drawn into a conversation hopelessly beyond my reach.

The owner went away.

"My French is pretty bad," I explained.

"Americans don't cultivate languages," laughed the ambassador. "Even their own."

Wine, appetizers, breads, and salads started arriving.

Caroline and her father slipped into what was apparently a long-standing family ritual of evaluating the offerings. The escargots were "first rate," as was the bread. The salad was "clean and sharp, but unimaginative." And so on.

To me, it was just salad.

Around the time the main course arrived—I had ordered by pointing at the line on the menu and trying to pronounce *escalope de veau,*—the ambassador noticed that the conversation had been exclusively between himself and his daughter and he shifted his attention back to me.

"What is it you're going to be studying, in Boston?"

"Infectious disease," I said.

He found that enormously funny, and laughed until his face turned pink, while I sat there, slack-jawed, trying to understand the joke.

"I'm sorry," he said finally. "That just sounds like such a grandiose proposition. I mean, I could see studying pneumonia, or syphilis, or herpes—that's becoming something of a menace, isn't it?—but to carve out such a large piece of the pie. It's like the time I asked Caroline's mother what her major was—we were both sophomores in college—and she said 'Man.' I misunderstood her. I thought she had said 'Men.' But she was studying anthropology. You know, the proper study for man is Man? That's what she was alluding to. Of course, what she really meant was cultural anthropology. By the time she was a senior she was limiting her courses to a single tribe in New Guinea where the warriors ate the brains of their enemies and got some awful neurological disease."

"Kuru," I said, reflexively.

"Yes!" The ambassador's eyes lighted up, and he looked at Caroline, with great wonder. "That's it. I haven't heard that name for twenty years. And he knew it right off. Smart man." Then turning back to me, "Are you studying kuru?"

"I doubt I'll see much of it in Boston."

The ambassador laughed, a little too hard, I thought. "You don't know Boston. Hang around Harvard Yard, you want to see some brain cannibalism." He shook his head and carved his veal.

Caroline's face clouded during much of this. I thought about Caroline's majoring in anthropology, as had her mother before her. I had never seen a picture of Caroline's mother, and I wondered if they were much alike.

"But you must be limiting your study," the ambassador said. "I mean, doesn't infection constitute a rather large chunk of medicine? What else is there, after all? Heart disease. Surgery. Obstetrics. Pediatrics. And cancer. But infectious diseases cuts across all of those."

"It's a subspecialty, Dad."

We both looked at Caroline.

"Brendan's finished his specialty training, internal medicine. Now he does two years in subspecialty training. He learns about all infectious diseases known to man. He'll be called in consultation to see any patient in the hospital with an infectious disease."

"Sounds like you'll be a busy man."

"I won't see them all by myself," I said. "There are three other fellows."

"And you'll be figuring out what infections these patients have?"

"That's usually the easy part. The question is what to do about it."

"Penicillin," said the ambassador. "I could be an infectious disease consultant."

"Dad." Caroline laughed, scandalized. She seemed to enjoy her father, as if she were scolding a naughty but endearing child.

"Most bugs nowadays are resistant to penicillin. There must be a hundred antibiotics," she said.

"Well, I am behind the times. I can remember when penicillin was a miracle drug. During the war—the Second World War—they shipped all the penicillin to the boys at the front. Cured their gonorrhea. Meanwhile, if you were Stateside and had pneumonia, you could die of it, especially if you were a civilian or, heaven forbid, a diplomat."

"The problem then was supply," I said. "Now the industry's geared up. The big problem now is the bugs. They mutate and they get resistant to the drugs. So you have to keep up with the bugs and you have to find new drugs."

"That's your research, then?"

"I'm supposed to be working in a lab, mostly my second year, finding out the mechanism of action of one of the newer antibiotics."

"You mean, they use it but they don't know how it works?"

"All they know is that it kills the bugs. We want to know how it kills the bugs."

"How?"

"Some antibiotics break down a bug's cell wall. Some interfere with its ability to divide. Others do other things."

"But why would you care? I mean, either it works or it doesn't. What difference whether it's an arrow, a bullet, or an atom bomb?"

"Because if it's an atom bomb, it may do more harm than just hurt the bug."

"I see," said the ambassador. He stared at me with something that looked like curiosity. What kind of a man would be indifferent to the stonemasonry of the buildings in his neighborhood, uninterested in a lazy Susan large enough to turn a car, ignorant of French and wine and cheese and escargots, but willing to devote two years of his life to questions about whether a drug destroys the cell wall of a bacterium? It was all there in his face. He was looking at me much as Stanley might have looked at his first Zulu warrior, with a mixture of fascination, wariness, and incredulity.

We walked home together along First Avenue and I said good night in the elevator. The ambassador asked me to come for a night cap at his daughter's apartment. But I declined and winked good night at Caroline. She smiled back, half apologetically. She had subjected me to her father for an evening and she flashed that bashful look people our age use when they shrug their shoulders at their friends for the way their parents are.

But there was more to it than that. I had seen Caroline anew. And she had seen me through different lenses. I didn't speak French worth a damn. I hated travel and feared places where English is not spoken. And I was going to Boston. And somehow, I had the feeling I might just be going alone.

THE LESS SAID

"I think he liked you," Caroline said.

"You *think* he liked me?"

"Well, you met him. He hasn't spent his life in the diplomatic service for nothing. He keeps his own counsel."

"Even with you?"

"Especially with me," laughed Caroline. "He did say you were an intriguing young man."

"Intriguing," I snorted.

"Oh, he didn't say it like that."

I was sitting at my desk, reading an article about herpes simplex, which, as Caroline's father had pointed out, had recently become more of a problem.

Caroline was curled up in my reading chair, drinking wine with *The New York Times Magazine* in her lap. "What did you think of him?"

"Who?"

"My father."

I knew this was coming and I was prepared: "He's charming."

Caroline considered this for some minutes.

"You're right," she said.

I went back to herpes simplex.

"Do you mean he's charming and nothing more? Charming, as in congenial-but-lacking-substance? Or charming as in urbane and polished?"

I looked up at her.

"Well, charming can mean so many things," she said. "Charming as in winning, fascinating, appealing, glamorous even."

"Charming as in," I said, "intriguing."

As July approached, we were together whenever we were not at work. Rounds at the Manhattan Hospital had, for me, become dull and pointless. Not that the medicine was dull, it was simply that

my mind was elsewhere. My mind was in Boston. My mind followed Caroline to Whipple.

The medicine at Manhattan Hospital, in fact, was anything but
dull: we were seeing more and more young men with pneumocystis and two more with Kaposi's sarcoma. Murmurings had started
at the infectious disease conferences. The group at Manhattan
Hospital had kept pretty tight-lipped about our cases. Several
members of the section were working on a paper about this curious new syndrome and nobody wanted to say too much until the
paper was ready for publication. It was rumored a group in San
Francisco had seen a few cases like ours, and in academic medicine
loose lips sink manuscripts. Nobody wanted to let the world know
and have the whole thing become common knowledge before the
Manhattan Hospital group could get the credit for having been
the first to recognize what was happening. The infectious disease
group was all atwitter, and a certain amount of tension always
arises simply from being unable to talk about a thing.

There was quite a lot I couldn't talk about around that time. The
thing I most wanted to talk about was officially a nontopic: Caroline gave no indication she was coming with me. It became difficult talking about anything, trying to avoid that big topic, and the
more I avoided mentioning it, the bigger and more unavoidable it
got.

Forrest asked me three times a week what Caroline was going to
do. I always said she wasn't coming. Maybe later. But she didn't
want to give up her job.

"Job?" Forrest snorted. "You call working at Whipple a job?
That's S and M. That's no job. Mother Teresa herself wouldn't last
more than a six months at Whipple."

"Well, there's more to it."

Once I said it, I knew it was true. I just wasn't sure what more to
it there was.

"This is not the sort of thing you can analyze or make announce-
ments about," Caroline had said, soon after our return from the
apartment-hunting trip. "The best thing is not to push it, and the
less said the better."

We had done the best you could do, by her criteria, having said
nothing about it since.

*   *   *

In June, Forrest asked us out to East Hampton, where he had a share in a rented house. He and Sally Landau had gone out the night before, and they met Caroline and me at the train station, Saturday morning. We piled into Forrest's convertible, Forrest and Sally in front, Caroline and I in back, and Forrest gave us the tour through East Hampton, past the hillside graveyard above the pond, past the windmill, and down a long road lined with green boxwood hedges toward Three Mile Harbor.

"It's sublime," Caroline said.

"I love it," said Sally. "It's so New England. It's more New England than most of New England."

The mention of New England carried us toward dangerous territory. Talk about New England, next thing you know you might mention Boston. Caroline looked out at the road and I kept quiet, and we lapsed into our blank-out mode to avoid being brought face-to-face with The Subject. It happened so often, I hardly noticed. We had developed reflexes and slid to safer subjects.

"So," Forrest said as we cruised along in his convertible. "When's the big day?"

He had more or less to shout into the backseat, where Caroline seemed not to hear him, her hair streaming over her face in the breeze. Sally did not turn around, but she looked at us in the rearview mirror.

"June twenty-seventh," I said.

"That's next weekend!" shouted Forrest.

"Yeah," I said. "I'm really excited."

My apartment was in boxes and we had had to spend nights in Caroline's place, which, given the constant disarray in her apartment, was not much better than living in my place. Half the attraction of spending the weekend in the Hamptons was simply the escape from the clutter at the Whitney.

The rented house was lovely: weathered gray wood with decks everywhere, the main one looking across a marsh of reeds to the harbor. We spent the day riding bicycles around the town, down to the beach, eating picnic lunch, and riding some more. We didn't get back to the house until dark. Forrest got the charcoals going and we sat outside on the deck with the hamburgers grilling, drinking dark Dos Equis beer while Sally and Caroline created a salad in the kitchen.

I studied the stars. It was a cloudless night. The moon was nearly full, sharp and yellow.

Caroline stepped out on the deck, holding a glass of white wine, and she looked up at the blanket of stars spread out against the sky. "Oh, the life of the idle rich," she said. "I could get used to this."

She sat down in the canvas chair next to mine. Her shoulder touched mine.

"This tops even Hotel Whipple," she said. "Will you look at that sky."

Sally came out, carrying the salad and four wooden bowls. "Dinner is served," she said. She handed us each a bowl and we ate the wonderful concoction she and Caroline had mixed. There were clams in there, and radishes and cold asparagus and avocados and cheese and things I could not name and a vinaigrette dressing.

After the salad, Forrest distributed hamburgers on English muffins. More bottles of beer were handed around and we sat with our feet on the deck railing and finished the beer and watched the shooting stars and the far-off airplanes.

"The universe is vast," said Forrest, profoundly, waving his bottle at the universe spread out before us.

"Man is small," said Sally.

"Do you feel small, Brendan?" asked Caroline.

"Oh, sure. Tiny."

"Humility," said Caroline, "is so important." She leaned over and kissed my cheek. "You said you felt small that time on the Promenade, and my heart melted."

"An old line," Forrest observed. "But still effective."

"Oh, yes," laughed Caroline. She was laughing, but not in an ironic way. She sounded nostalgic. "I was putty in his hands. His grandfather came over during the potato famine and left Ellis Island with ten dollars in his pocket. O'Brien has a sense of his place in the universe, a sense of himself as part of a continuum."

"You know what O'Brien told me once?" said Forrest. "He said he was just a peculiar sequence of amino acids handed down in a watery medium through the millennia. How can you not love a guy who sees himself as an amino acid sequence?"

"You're right," said Caroline. "To know him is to love him."

"Why pick on me?" I said. "I'm just a sequence. I had no hand in it."

"I am not picking on you. I am appreciating you."

"It's about time," snorted Forrest. "You appreciated O'Brien."

"I appreciate Brendan," Caroline said, to the sky.

"But will you remember me when I'm gone?" I said. I don't know how that slipped out. I guess it was the beer, and the night. I don't know.

That shut everyone up. There ensued a silence so thick, a serrated knife couldn't have cut it.

Finally Caroline spoke. "I think this may require a walk on the beach."

"Take my car," said Forrest, holding up his keys. "Put the top down. Maybe the fresh night air will clear your heads. Christ knows, you could use it."

So we walked out to the car. I handed Caroline the keys.

"You drive," I told her. "This is your walk."

She drove too fast along the dark and winding road from Three Mile Harbor. The road was narrow and not well banked and I felt for my seat belt, but I did not clip it on. I was unwilling to risk, Caroline said. I refused to travel where English was not spoken. I would not try new foods. I was just as happy spending Sunday in my apartment reading *The New York Times* as I would be exploring Brooklyn or The Bronx. She had traveled the world with only a backpack. Her father had lived all over Europe and Africa and they both spoke lots of languages and they had never feared to tread on non-English-speaking soil. I made no move to buckle my seat belt. That night, I took my chances.

At Main Beach, the parking lot was surprisingly busy. We parked and left the top down. I hesitated a moment, thinking we ought to pull up the top and lock the car. But no, that was more of my "frantic caution," to use Caroline's phrase. We headed for the beach.

The moon threw a long yellow strip down the water toward the beach, and we walked near the water, where the sand was firm and easy to tread. Caroline walked with her hands behind her back. She was smiling, but I couldn't read her smile.

"This is a lovely mess," she said.

"I know. But as you once said, it's inevitable."

"It's not your fault, I know. I'm just pissed off I'm the one who's supposed to give up her job and follow you off into the sunset."

"A cynic knows the price of everything," I said. "And the value of nothing."

"Speak to me logically," Caroline said. "Tell me why I should leave the city I love, the job I love, the life I love, to go off with the man I love."

"You can't have everything."

"The world is full of men. There is only one New York, only one Whipple."

"Thank God for that."

"A week after you're gone, there'll be a new class of interns. Lots of fresh young meat to carve."

"You're right," I said. "Forget I ever asked you to come to Boston."

"You are not at all the man my father groomed me for."

"I know. I was your rebellion. Erase my memory from your mind."

"You won't travel. You won't try anything new. Next to you, Mr. Roundtree looks like Indiana Jones. Food is just something to keep your blood sugar in acceptable range. Wine makes you light-headed. Art is something you buy from Bloomingdale's. Ballet is for women with anorexia nervosa and amenorrhea. Africa is the land of parasites. The world is a dangerous place. You decompensate if the dishes aren't washed, all those unkilled bacteria growing on the forks. Microorganisms are everywhere on the rampage. You don't live a life, you live a phobia."

"I don't know why you hang out with me."

"Cancer is the fault of the people who take care of it. Whipple is a black pit that ought to be bombed."

"I'm hopeless. I can't keep my opinions to myself. I grieve over my own warped mind."

"You laugh, but it's a sickness. Look at that ocean. It's stunning. It's dark. It's beautiful. But do you see it? You look at that water and you see sharks and terrifying things waiting to eat you alive."

"The real world," I said, "is full of things eager to eat me. This is true."

"But there's more than danger, and you can't see past it."

"If you can't see the danger, you're not going to live to see much else."

Caroline shook her head and sighed. "Why do I put up with

this?" Then, not looking at me, "You know I gave them notice a month ago."

That stunned me. I stopped and looked at her.

"You're leaving Whipple?"

"I couldn't very well be a head nurse at Whipple and live in Boston. The shuttle isn't that reliable," she said. Her pupils were immense and shining in the night.

"You're coming with me?"

"I added up the pluses and the minuses."

"What was in the plus column?"

"Not 'what,' " she said, " 'Who.' "

"Oh."

"There were simply so many reasons to help you pack your truck and wave good-bye, I knew nothing could be that black and white."

"I see."

"Plus, I got into a master's program. Clinical oncology. At your very own institution. You'll be supporting me, more or less. Room and board, at least."

"No kidding?"

"You can still back out."

"Not a chance."

"It's not such a good deal for you. You get a messy roommate who's impoverished and who has to study a lot. I'll be no fun at all."

"You're really coming to Boston?"

"Yeah, I really am."

"But, why? Really."

"Instinct."

"Oh," I said. "Good reason."

We walked along the beach, looking at the dark sea, full of beautiful and carnivorous things, and we didn't say a word. There's not much discussion, when it comes down to instinct.

BOOK II

The Real World

I've seen sunny days
I thought would never end . . .

—JAMES TAYLOR

— 1 —

THE NEW YORK FADE

In the morning, I awoke before the alarm and slid out of bed, careful not to wake Caroline. My apartment was stacked high with boxes, with the only clear path a trail to the kitchen and bathroom. Caroline's apartment downstairs was packed as well.

Caroline was a very skillful packer. She has spent her childhood packing up and shipping out as her father got orders for new assignments. She had acquired a foreign service brat's astonishing skill for organizing a move. She wrapped glassware in newspapers and packed it all geometrically inside cardboard boxes collected from the incinerator room at the hospital. For a person who never showed any inclination to fold a shirt or hang up a dress, she was tougher than a drill sergeant on morning inspection when it came to packing boxes and organizing for shipping.

Caroline had organized us. I was simply following instructions. She had made me a clipboard with a checklist of orders, and she had her own clipboard with her own checklist. She had methodically planned for the consumption of perishables, arranged for mail forwarding, and she had every detail covered.

I did not shower, but pulled on my blue jeans and my Sears work boots and I let myself out of the apartment while she slept. I had my assignment, and I set out as ordered.

It was light out at that hour in July, but the East Side had not yet stirred. I walked to the subway, enjoying the quiet in the city, excited by the adventure, but a little sad too. There were certain times when it was hard not to love New York—fall, early spring, summer weekends, and any time very early in the morning in the residential neighborhoods, before they swarmed to life, when you felt you had the whole town to yourself.

And now I was leaving, and I felt sure I would never live here again.

The subway took me downtown and I walked through gray

streets in the coolness of the early morning and saw no one. The
address for the U-Haul place was a door, but there was no lot with
trucks.

The door was open, however, and there was a light in the office.
Behind the counter stood a big unshaven man with very thick
black hair, wearing a black T-shirt with a white Playboy bunny
logo over one breast, a gold chain around his thick neck with a
gold pendant that said "Guido." He was sucking on a dead stogie.

"You're up early," he wheezed. "If you're here with a gun,
you're outta luck. We haven't taken anything in yet." He grinned
at me with what I imagine he thought was a puckish smile. His
teeth were stained from the cigar.

"I'm here for a truck," I said. "Brendan O'Brien."

"Oh, yeah?" He found a clipboard under the counter and
plopped it on the desk and searched through the papers on top.
"O'Brien. O'Brien. Good Italian name like that I shouldn't forget.
Where you taking this truck?"

He continued to shuffle through papers, producing greasy fin-
gerprinted manila folders.

"Boston," I said.

"Boston?" he grunted. "Where else would an O'Brien be going? Micks run the entire fuckin' Commonwealth of Massachusetts."

He stopped shuffling papers and lifted up one and started reading, "Brendan O'Brien, *MD*?"

"Right."

He looked at me dubiously. "MD?" His boisterous air evaporated, and he became cagey and cool. "Like in 'medical doctor'? "

"That's right," I said. Why had Caroline added MD to my name
just to reserve a truck?

Guido looked at me appraisingly. Ira Bloomstein had once told
me, "O'Brien, once you write MD after your name, you become a
member of the tribe. You will learn what it feels like to be a Jew."

I had not understood, at the time, what Ira meant. In the hospital, it meant one thing to be called doctor, but in the larger world
it meant something else entirely. Once a person looked at me as
"MD," I ceased to become an individual with any distinguishable
traits. I became the representative of a race. Whatever resentments
he held toward that race were pulled out and heaped upon my
shoulders and the best I could hope for was to be considered an

exception. For a certain segment of the population, doctors are fat cats and scoundrels. Whatever he thought of me beforehand, for Guido it all changed once he saw that "MD."

Guido studied me, moving the stogie around in his mouth, a thought forming behind his eyes. "You an intern?"

"Was once."

"Bellevue?"

"The Manhattan Hospital."

"No kidding?" A smile broke out, a sly smile, with a twist of malice. "My mother-in-law died up there. Dr. O'Keiffer was her doc. Know him? Biggest heart man in New York. One of the top ten heart men in the country."

Always amazed me how many docs were one of the top ten. Where did they get that rating system to which patients referred with such belligerent insistence? Must make the dying easier, believing it happened at a top-ten hospital under the care of a top-ten cardiologist, or at the Internationally Famed Whipple, the best cancer hospital in the world. O'Keiffer was not a bad doc, about sixty. He probably was a good cardiologist once. Now he was burned out, headed toward retirement.

"You shoulda seen his bill," said Guido. "Fortunately for the family, the insurance covered the whole goddamned thing, or we woulda been in the poorhouse, you know what I mean? But you ain't got to that point yet, have you? You're still in the hospital all the time. You ain't bought your Rolls-Royce yet."

"If I had a Rolls-Royce," I said, "would I be moving by rented truck?"

"Hey, don't worry. You'll make yours. You'll have it and the year-round tan from all medical conferences on the cruise ships in the fuckin' Caribbean."

"I'm thrilled," I said. "Just thinking about it."

Guido grunted something like a laugh, but his eyes remained serious, and he continued to study me from under his eyebrows. "You're okay, Doc." Then he became all business and he produced a chewed-on Bic pen and he said, "Sign here. You want insurance?"

I signed for the insurance and I signed all the forms for the truck. He shouted into the back room, "Pedro!" and a dark kid who couldn't have been older than thirteen, with black hair hanging in his eyes, came out front and caught the keys Guido threw him and he went out the front door. Then he turned back to me. "What kind of doctor you gonna be?"

"I'm specializing," I said. "In infectious disease."

Big grin now. "Oh, now that I know about. I get the clap, I come to you. You give me a discount for old times' sake, on accounta I rented you a truck once."

"You got a deal."

"When you gonna be a real doctor?"

"Two more years," I said.

"Fucking A," he said, grin as broad as old Broadway. "How old are you now?"

"Twenty-nine."

"No wonder you guys're all in such a hurry to make a buck." He shook his head. "You got to make it before your first coronary."

Pedro arrived with the truck, bringing it to a screeching halt outside the door, pointed toward First Avenue. He could barely see over the dashboard, but he had driven the truck as if it were a Porsche. Seeing him handle the truck, I felt better: if he could wrestle this leviathan out of whatever hole they stored it, and get it here, I might have half a chance of piloting it uptown without killing someone.

Sitting behind the wheel, I wasn't so sure. Pedro and the big man stood on the stair stoop and watched me start it up and slowly let up the clutch and lurch into gear. I think they were laughing, but I had to keep my eyes on the road. This was the biggest thing I had ever driven. The steering wheel was flat, and you had to wrestle it to budge it. I was glad I had paid for the insurance.

I got uptown without being arrested, and taking the corner at Seventieth Street, I was astonished to see a sight I had not even dreamed of: a big gap right in front of the canopied entrance to the Whitney. This being the Saturday before July first, when new interns, residents, and Fellows had to move to their new hospitals en masse, I expected the Whitney to look like a castle under siege. But there it was, a parking space right in front, in the absolutely-no-parking, definitely-tow-you zone, which was ordinarily occupied by three or four parked vehicles before the doorman came on duty. I managed to wedge the truck more or less into it, with much creaking and groaning of the gears, so that only the front of the truck stuck out into the street. Even city buses could squeeze by if they went very slowly and if no one double-parked on the other side of the street.

The doorman smiled, when he saw me climb down.

"You got the prize this morning," he said.

Caroline was drinking coffee in the apartment with Forrest.

"That was fast," she said, seeing me. She wore a white T-shirt with "Red Sox" printed across the front and blue jean overalls and sneakers and she had pinned up her hair. I thought she look lovely.

"The lady is organized," said Forrest. "You see her clipboard here?"

"I got one just like it," I said, holding up mine.

Forrest shook his head. "I am truly impressed. She can come down here and move me in a couple of years."

"You'll never move, Forrest," laughed Caroline. "You'll stay forever at the Great White Tower."

"I'll live on Fifth Avenue," said Forrest. "Just you wait."

Forrest started to lift one of the book boxes and collapsed. He looked like a man trying to uproot a tree. "What've you got in here?"

"Books. Be careful with those."

"What the hell you move books for? They'll be out-of-date before you reach Boston."

Forrest was a great believer in the perishability of scientific knowledge.

We got three loads down the elevator before the place erupted, and twelve other former house officers of the Manhattan Medical Center got under way with their moves, their loads of boxes, and all their worldly possessions. Within an hour the street in front of the Whitney was choked with all the double-parked rented trucks.

Caroline looked around at all the mayhem and said, "It looks like refugees fleeing the approaching panzer divisions."

Our truck caused the least congestion, and I felt very lucky to have got the front-door space. A good omen, that empty parking space. I started to say that, but I knew Caroline would hoot about my superstitions, so I kept quiet.

After we loaded my bed and couch and bookcases, we went down to Caroline's apartment and loaded her things.

We loaded the truck in less than two hours. The sun was halfway up in the sky, and the truck was on the sunny side of the street.

Forrest and I were drenched with sweat and gasping in the already steamy morning, parched despite the several quarts of Gatorade and Coca-Cola Caroline had supplied. Caroline stood on the sidewalk, near the back of the truck, checking things off on her clipboard. Forrest hopped out of the truck and we closed the doors and clamped the lock.

"Sally wanted to say good-bye," Caroline said. "I better go call her. We're done early. She'll miss us."

"She's always late," growled Forrest. "She'd have missed the ark, and people would've gone the way of the unicorns."

"I heard that, you lunkhead!" It was Sally, hurrying toward us down the street, carrying a bottle of champagne. She was in uniform. She had slipped off the ward to say good-bye.

She hugged Caroline and she handed Forrest the bottle. Caroline climbed up into the cab of the truck and brought out Styrofoam cups she had set aside for this moment. She had it planned right down to the champagne. Forrest popped the cork.

A great horn-blaring erupted on the other side of the truck and a long cascade of oaths and invectives streamed forth. A cabbie was having trouble getting by our truck.

"Let him roast in hell," said Forrest. He poured champagne into each cup. We drained the cups.

Sally hugged Caroline again and they both started crying and wiping away tears.

"I shoulda brought my camera," said Forrest.

He looked a little teary-eyed himself.

"Thanks for the strong back this morning," I said. "I always knew you'd be good for some sort of work."

He stuck out his hand. "Two years from now, big boy. Two years, we help you move back into town. Fifth Avenue. Park Avenue office, Fifth Avenue residence."

"Sure," I said.

We shook on it, but we both knew better.

Caroline and I climbed into the cab of the truck and I started the engine and Caroline wiped her tears with a tissue and waved good-bye to Sally and Forrest and I eased the clutch and the truck shuddered under the weight of its load and lurched into the street.

In the big sideview mirror I could see the white brick Manhattan Hospital at the end of the street. I turned right, onto First Avenue and drove north, toward New England.

"I hope you know how to get us out of the city," Caroline said. "I got us this far. Now you're the pilot."

I turned right and headed down toward York Avenue and then right again and headed back downtown.

"Why are you turning around?" Caroline asked, snatching up her clipboard, checking it again. "What did we forget?"

"You'll see."

We rolled past the Manhattan Hospital, all white and glowing in the morning light. Nurses in white uniforms and interns and residents and technicians were flowing into the entrances. People were going to work. It felt very strange seeing them going to work as if nothing were different about this day.

Then Whipple loomed into view and I turned right again, and we took the block slowly. Caroline looked out her side as it went by. It was just a clump of buildings, a pile of bricks. I looked up to find the windows of Hotel Whipple and the windows of Caroline's ward, and Mrs. Roundtree's room, and Vince Montebelli's room and the window from which Professor Toomey had attempted to leap, but I was driving and I couldn't see much from the truck. I caught sight, briefly, of the Triceratops in the playground across from the hospital.

Caroline sat there, looking at Whipple go by us, transfixed. Then she faced forward and didn't look at it anymore.

I took the turn onto First Avenue and headed uptown, toward New England and out of the city.

LURCHING TOWARD ATHENS

We took the Willis Avenue Bridge out of the city, and I followed the signs to New England.

"Now I know how the pioneers must have felt," I said. "Pack up all you own, your woman by your side, your destiny ahead of you."

"Your U-Haul contract in your pocket," laughed Caroline.

"I saw Ira before I left. He asked me about you. He'd heard you'd quit Whipple. I told him you were moving to Boston, going back to school. I think he guessed we might be moving together. He told me to give you his regards if I happened to run across you."

"I really got to like Ira. He turned out to be a pussycat, under that glib exterior. I thought he was going to kill Raskolnovich that day Mrs. Roundtree died, though, remember?"

"I will never forget," I said. "There're a lot of things happened at Whipple I'll never forget."

Caroline looked at me, and she looked surprised.

"Like what?"

"Oh, everything, everybody: the professor, the times he tried to jump. And Vince Montebelli and Mrs. Roundtree. And Rasko. And meeting you, of course."

"That night Ludvik tried to blast the professor with the IV phosphate?"

"Who would've ever thunk it?" I said. "What great things can begin at such dark hours in such deep holes."

Caroline shook her head, smiling, but said nothing.

"You thought I was just another horny house officer, that night."

"Oh," Caroline said. "But you grew on me."

"Maybe Ira's right. He always said: It's all fate."

Caroline looked at me. "No," she said. "In the long run, men hit only what they aim at. Someone said that. I believe he was a wise man, whoever he was."

It was a hot, dyspneic day with the sky the color of skimmed milk and not enough sun to burn away the humidity. It felt like being submerged in a hot bath, and the only relief was from movement. Driving with the windows rolled down, a constant blast of hot air moved across our faces, enough to sustain consciousness. But whenever the traffic slowed to a crawl, the air circulation in the cab of the truck slowed and we were left gasping. When we got up to speed, it was easier to breathe, but the truck was not equipped with shock absorbers, to judge from the ride.

We crossed over into Connecticut and the sky became bluer and high white clouds appeared. It was just as hot in Connecticut, but the road seemed to open up more and you could see glimpses of the Long Island Sound from the roadway.

"Greenwich," Caroline said. "That's where Ira Bloomstein will wind up."

"Is he from there?"

"No, no," laughed Caroline. "Ira is from Brooklyn. But he will practice in Greenwich or Cos Cob or Darien or Westport, and he'll never feel like he belongs, but he'll be as happy as Ira can ever be."

We passed a hospital in Rhode Island, looming large and white over the roadway.

"What sort of place do you think that is?" asked Caroline.

"It is not," I said, "the mother ship."

"As opposed to the Massively Degenerate," said Caroline. "Forrest says that's what they call it, you know. The Massively Degenerate."

"Who calls it that?"

"The house staff there."

"What does Forrest know? He's never set foot out of the Great White Tower."

"Forrest hears things."

"Forrest hears things, all right."

"How do you know this place is so great? I mean, aside from the reputation?"

"They pay me so little. In academic medicine there is a strong inverse correlation between dollars and prestige. The more prestigious the hospital, the stronger the competition for places, the less they pay their Fellows."

"Then we should be very proud."

"It's all deferred gratification. Two years from now, you will have your master's in oncology nursing, and I will have my paper from the Massively Degenerate Hospital, and we will be, as they say, marketable. Unless they cure cancer and kill all the microorganisms in the next two years, we should be able to make a living."

"I was making a living before I met you," said Caroline. "I was happy."

"Aren't you happy now?"

"Happiness," laughed Caroline, "is a retrospective diagnosis."

"Well, I'm happy. I'm delirious."

"Yes, you've found your true calling behind the wheel of a truck."

"I'm happy you came with me."

"You'd be happy if Forrest had moved with you."

"Not the same thing," I said. "Not the same thing at all."

Caroline reached over and rubbed the back of my neck. "It is exciting," she said.

THE HOUSE ON JOY STREET

It was four-thirty when we hit the outskirts of Boston and the local drivers were casting off civilized inhibitions. I had driven my old heap up the week before to park it outside our new digs so we'd have our car in place, and now I was happy I had, because I had learned the way through the city on that trip and driving the truck was hard enough, without having to sort out which exits to take. Small cars careened in and out of the lanes around us.

"Welcome to Boston," said Caroline as a Honda zipped in front of us so close, I nearly put her into the windshield hitting the brakes. "Just take me directly to the hospital."

I succeeded in outraging the good citizens of the roadway by driving exactly the speed limit and no faster, and got many black looks and fists shaken at me and I could see the epithets on the lips of those I could not hear. Evidently, by driving the limit I had violated some local code of honor, throwing my fellow travelers into fits of righteous indignation. I felt like a public menace, a motorized pariah, but I was having a time steering that big boat through all the currents, and if I collided with anyone, I wanted at least not to be speeding at the time.

Around six o'clock, with the sky still light and the truck more or less in one piece, we pulled up in front of our new home on Joy Street. I moved my car from its space and backed in the truck, which fit halfway. Caroline got the keys from our landlady, who came out on the front porch with lemonade and offers to help.

"She must be eighty years old, and her husband pushing ninety," I told Caroline. "Let's not start off by having to resuscitate our landlords."

Caroline and I unloaded. The apartment was at the top of the house, the entire third floor, and it was hot. It was the books that brought me to my knees. Three flights with a seventy-pound book box and my legs felt like warm Jell-O.

We finally got the truck cleared out to the big pieces: the bed, the sofa, the dresser.

Caroline and I hoisted the bed and carried it upstairs. We rested on each landing and Caroline wiped the sweat from her eyes. Her arms were thin and not muscular, and I doubt she could have done more than three consecutive pushups at any time in her life. But she managed the bed. Her face was bright crimson by the third floor, but she never complained.

"Just let me catch my breath," she said.

We did the dresser, which, even with the drawers removed, was heavier than the bed, but less bulky, one step at a time. The sofa we left to last.

"Let's just leave it down here on the sidewalk," Caroline said. "We don't really need a sofa."

"It would be nice to have one on the sidewalk," I said. "For evening chats with the neighbors."

It was dusk now, and we were sitting on the sofa on the sidewalk, drinking lemonade in the gathering dark, when a medical resident in a short white jacket and white pants with a beeper on his belt came walking toward us along the sidewalk.

"Lemonade?" asked Caroline.

He did a double take and when he realized she had spoken to him, he grinned and said, "Did you say lemonade?"

"Fresh-squeezed," said Caroline. "First-class lemonade."

He watched us drink the lemonade our landlady had provided. "Sure," he said. "I love lemonade."

"It's upstairs," said Caroline. "Come on up."

He looked at her and his expression changed four or five times. Then he realized he was hooked.

"Just take one end of this thing," said Caroline, standing up.

The resident helped us wrestle the sofa up all three flights. He was very good-natured about it and once it was done, Caroline ran down and got him a big glass of lemonade.

His shirt was soaked through with sweat and his white pants were smudged gray from the underside of the couch, but he drank the lemonade and laughed about it. I asked him if he was from the Massively Degenerate and he said he was. He was a senior medical resident.

Caroline said, "Oh, Brendan's going to be doing ID there,"

with such a clear note of pride, she surprised me. "We are going to live on prestige."

The resident laughed. "That's what we all live on. Sure as hell, you cannot live on what they pay."

"You're an ID Fellow?" he asked me.

I told him I was, and it seemed strange to say that. Fellows were always such alien creatures to me, like Raskolnovich at Whipple. I had never been sure what they did with their time, what their responsibilities were, or what motivated them. Among the medical students, interns, and residents, the chain of command and the duties and responsibilities were so clear-cut, it was all very easy. Everyone from medical student onward knew his place with great precision. But nobody had ever explained Fellows to me.

"At the Degenerate," said the resident, "Fellows are gofers. They do all the legwork for all the research. They write all the consult notes, and they run down all the special studies and they hang out in the labs and they get their names on all the papers, like third or fourth author. But everyone in the world wants to do his fellowship at the Degenerate, so how bad could it be?"

I laughed at that. Everyone in *his* world wanted to do a fellowship at the Degenerate. Most people in the world had never heard of fellowships and some had not even heard of the Massively Degenerate Hospital in Boston, Massachusetts.

"Well," I said. "I guess I'll find out about fellowships."

He asked me where I came from, since obviously I had not done my internship and residency at the Degenerate. I told him and he smiled a tolerant smile.

"You must have been a star," he said.

"How do you mean?"

"Well, most of the Degenerate fellowships are filled from within. The place is very inbred. You know: we have the world's best medical school, from which we can choose the world's best interns and from those, the world's best residents. So when you look for Fellows, why go looking around at lesser institutions?"

"Lesser institutions!" Caroline snorted. She surged to her feet like a prizefighter at the bell, with blood in her eye. I stood up to block her path. "The Degenerate should be so lucky to be in the same league as the Internationally Famed Whipple Hospital."

"But you said you were from Manhattan Medical Center," the resident said with his palms held up.

"Whipple is part of the Center," I explained.

"Oh, well, of course, everyone knows Whipple," he said, apologetically.

That was the first time I saw that reaction to the Whipple name. Outside the Medical Center, where Whipple was a poor brother, a black sheep, its reputation far exceeded that of the mother institution, the Manhattan Hospital. It was always hard reconciling myself to the cachet that the name Whipple carried with people who didn't know any better. Caroline, of course, thought it only proper, but Whipple was the place people knew about when they knew about the Manhattan Medical Center.

"Caroline was a head nurse at Whipple," I said.

The resident looked impressed.

"You going to work at the Degenerate?"

"I'm in a master's program," she said. "Oncology."

"Oh, you're going to be one of those onc nurses," he said, smiling.

"Yes," said Caroline, with an irony I don't think he caught. "One of those."

"They sure make life easier," he said, as if he were speaking of some species of trained poodle. "Christ, I can never remember all the toxicities of the drugs and the onc nurses are always running around with their little toxicity cards, spotting the chemo toxicities on all the patients. How long is the program?"

"Two years," said Caroline.

"Two years! For one more you could go to law school."

"If I wanted to be a lawyer," said Caroline.

"We're all going to have to be lawyers," laughed the resident. "The way things are headed."

He said good night and left us there with our apartment full of boxes and displaced furniture.

"What a twit," said Caroline, after he'd gone.

"He helped us carry the sofa."

"He acted like nurses were some kind of lower form of life."

"I don't think he meant it like that."

"Yes, he did," she said, then she shook him off and she said, "Let's go take the truck back."

NEWNESS

We turned in the truck to the U-Haul place and then took my car to Cambridge, in search of the Brown Derby.

It was not far from Harvard Yard, and it was smoky and had exposed-brick walls. They brought us cold beer in a glass pitcher, beaded and frosty, and the beer tasted sharp and clean. We watched people come in and get seated. The men wore rumpled-looking seersucker jackets or short-sleeved shirts and the women with undyed gray-streaked hair pulled straight back and little or no makeup. The people had a more weathered, less manicured look than New Yorkers.

"We really are in a different city," said Caroline, looking at the people. "A different world."

Caroline nodded ever so slightly in the direction of our neighbors on the left. "Look at the book," she said.

The man had plopped a fat worn volume facedown on his table. The title was visible on the binding: *The Ethos of Athens. Patrick J. Toomey.*

"Do you think that's our own late great Professor Patrick J. Toomey?"

"Of course," said Caroline. "I have that book. Somewhere back in that pile of boxes in our apartment."

"I can't believe we live in this town."

"I know," Caroline said. "It doesn't seem real. I feel like we're just visiting. I'll feel that way until I find the grocery store, the pharmacy, the bank."

"Find one we can rob," I said. "That's the only way we'll make it."

We ate chili and Greek salads and we finished the pitcher of beer.

Then we drove back to the town house. It must have been a lovely building once. The walls met the ceilings about eight feet up at an oak molding. The floors were oak and the windows, now widely open, were six feet. The apartment had cooled off with the night breezes.

I assembled the bed and Caroline searched through the boxes and unpacked what we needed to take a shower and make up the bed. She brought out the blue flowered sheets.

"These are just the sheets for this occasion," Caroline said.

I looked at her for meaning.

"These were the sheets you had on your bed the first time I spent the night."

"No kidding?"

"Look me in the eye and tell me you don't remember."

I looked her in the eye. "I don't remember the sheets."

"What do you remember?"

"Everything else."

We could see the sky from our bed.

"What a strange and lovely sensation," Caroline said, lying with her hands under her head. "To be able to see the sky from your bed, and to hear street sounds."

In New York, neither of our apartments were high enough to be clear of obstruction from neighboring buildings. With the window open, in our new place we could hear the sounds of cars going by on the street below and we could hear voices of people going by: two teenagers calling across the street to each other as they walked away from us, their voices trailing off. In bed, the sheets felt cool and clean and we fell asleep quickly.

In the morning, the room was bright with sunlight and a robin called out from the tree outside our window. It was a beautiful way to wake up after so many years in the city, hearing a bird outside the window. It was cool enough by the window, although it felt as if it might get hot later with the sun.

Caroline lay on her back and she looked pale and quiet and asleep. I stayed in bed and looked around the room and I felt excited and happy and sad all at once. A little boy's adventure, driving away in a truck and waking up in another city. The sadness was missing New York.

But, of course, the best part of New York was lying beside me.

Looking at her sleeping there, I felt happy again. I touched her arm lightly. She was definitely there.

Without opening her eyes, Caroline said, "Is that bird in the room?"

"No, outside in the tree."

"Good," she said, eyes still closed. "I was afraid for a moment he might have a lease on this place too. I wouldn't put it past our landlady."

She opened her eyes.

"This place could use some curtains."

"A new list," I said.

"Oh, I have a very long list already. We have to explore our new neighborhood."

"Let's have a real lunch today," I said. "At some real place."

"Yes, let's do that. Then we'll explore the neighborhood a little and then we'll go over to the hospital, and spook around the Massively Degenerate, which is, after all, a first-rate place."

"You still on that poor guy from last night? He did help us with the sofa, after all. We'd have never got it up the stairs without him."

"He was a prince. And all for a glass of lemonade."

"I'm glad we have Sunday," Caroline said. "Let's not unpack. I can do that while you're at work."

"I'm not arguing."

"You must be sore today. You didn't have Forrest to help unload."

"What I didn't have," I said, "was an elevator."

"I noticed."

"You sure you don't want to unpack today?"

"Not a chance. What's the rush?"

"I'm just afraid," I said, "you won't be here when I get back."

"No," she said. "You're stuck with me now. I couldn't face another rental truck."

ECONOMIES

That summer I worked in the hospital and Caroline worked as a staff nurse on the oncology floor. Her academic program did not begin until September and she took two weeks to set up the apartment and she then went to work.

They were happy to have her at the hospital, with regular staff nurses wanting to go on vacation, especially when they found out she would work the three-thirty-to-midnight shift. Most nights, I was home by eight and she was gone. I phoned her at work.

"Dr. O'Brien?" she said. "I know your voice from somewhere. Are you that guy who lives in my apartment? The one who eats the cereal we're always running out of?"

"You know me. I'm the one who's asleep in your bed when you get home and who's gone when you wake up."

"Oh, that you? We really ought to go out to dinner sometime. Get to know each other."

"How's life at Cancer City?"

"It's not all that different from the I. F. Whipple. We got a lady admitted tonight from Newton reminded me of Mrs. Roundtree when she first came in. All bright and perky. You remember how she was, before she got her brain met."

"I hope she does better than Mrs. Roundtree."

"Who knows with breast. Breast does exactly what it wants to do."

"I miss you."

"Go for a walk by the river. That's what I'd be doing if I weren't working."

"Quit. We'll go for walks."

"Walks to debtors' prison."

Caroline had calculated it all down to the penny: my stipend would cover the rent, and one third of our food bill—providing we never ate in the hospital cafeteria but always brought peanut butter sandwiches for lunch. If we wanted a phone, groceries for the last eight months of the year, gas for the car, a newspaper, we both had to moonlight.

Friday and Saturday nights I worked in an emergency room in Charlestown. My first shift began at eight p.m. Friday night and lasted twelve hours. Saturday morning I'd get home just as Caroline was getting out of bed.

Caroline always wanted to hear about the ER. She had never worked in an ER and she had a very romantic notion of what emergency rooms are like. She'd sit in the bathroom with her coffee mug and talk to me through the curtain as I showered.

"Did you save lives?"

"Not a one."

"What did you see?"

"Five chest pains. Same number of lacerations. Barroom fights mostly, the lacerations. They always come in smelling like breweries and when you ask them how they cut themselves chin to chest, they say, 'I fell and hit the bar.' They all say the same thing."

"And you sewed them up?"

"Certainly. I'm getting to be good at sewing up drunks. They're better than the kids, though. The kids scream bloody murder and you have to tie them into this thing called a papoose to hold their arms down, unless their parents want to hold them, but then the father passes out and you've got two patients. Poor little kids."

"I don't want to hear about the kids."

"Kids are top-heavy. Always falling on their heads."

"Why are kids coming in during the night shift? They should be home in bed by the time you're on duty."

I turned the shower off and she handed me a towel.

"Most of them are just kids who've fallen at home. I guess some of them are probably abuse cases," I said. "There's this ninety-year-old nurse who's worked in the ER since the hospital was built in the First World War, and every time they haul in some kid with a scalp wound, she gives the parents the old fish-eye. Of course, most of the parents are more upset than the kids. They come in trembling, hugging the kid, and they don't want to let go and the kid's clinging to the mother and this old nurse is trying to pry the kid away so she can get him alone and ask him if his mother beats him."

"They ought to retire her but quick."

"If you couldn't stand to walk through the pediatric ward at Whipple, you'd have a tough time in the ER. More kids die from accidents than from cancer."

"I don't think I could work in an ER, if there were kids. Don't they have a separate ER for kids?"

"Not in community hospitals. We had one kid last night: his mother is unlocking the door on their third-floor walk-up. Kid is two years old, eighteen months, something like that. She's got a grocery bag in one hand and she turns to the door to put the key in the lock. The apartment has one of those staircases like ours— you look down between the banisters and you can see all the way to the ground floor. The kid manages to squeeze between the railings and takes a swan dive all the way down, three flights. Lands on his head."

Caroline's mouth dropped open and all the color drained from her face. She brought her hand up to cover her face and she began to cry. I don't know how I could have been so dumb: You did not tell Caroline horror stories about kids. I'd been depressed all night about that kid. Everyone felt terrible.

"Did he die?"

"Not last night. They took him off to the ICU and I called in some neurosurgeon. They did a CT of his head—even in this dip-shit little community hospital you can get a CT from the ER at night—and there was just nothing left in one piece inside that skull. The kid was there when I came in. The day-shift guy had seen him. This little old ninety-year-old nurse had started to grill the mother about how it happened."

"No!" Caroline looked suddenly fierce.

"Apparently the other nurses stepped right in and dragged her out of there pretty quick."

"That nurse should be shot."

"The mother had to be admitted. She was a basket case. Some-thing she'd probably done three times a week. Drag the kid and the grocery bag up those stairs, struggle with the lock. Of course, she should have put the bag down, held the kid, and unlocked the door."

"You didn't say that to her."

"I didn't say anything to her. I just took her blood pressure and gave her some Valium."

"Where was her husband?"

"Single mother. She had just picked the kid up from day care."

"Oh, God. Poor woman."

The whole idea of losing a kid like that seemed to overwhelm her. She looked off somewhere out of the corners of her eyes.

"Usually things aren't that bad," I said. "It's usually quiet for a couple of hours and then someone rolls in who fell on a bar."

Caroline snapped out of it and came back from wherever she was.

"So you can relax and put your feet up and shoot the breeze with the nurses and be king of the roost."

"Oh, yeah. They 'Doctor' me to death. They treat me like some visitor from another planet."

"So you're king of the Charlestown ER?"

"Until the car wrecks come in," I said. "Every time I hear they're bringing in a car wreck my stomach turns over."

"Why?"

"I've never put in a chest tube for pneumothorax. The chest surgeons did that at the Medical Center. Or bad fractures. What do I know about orthopedics? All I can do is call for help and hang on. It's like being an intern all over again. Except at the Medical Center help was always right there. At this place, you're calling some guy who lives forty-five minutes away and he doesn't want to get out of bed and he's just going to call in some orders for pain meds. Then he'll call the admitting office and tell them to admit the patient. Then he'll stroll by the next morning in see the patient. Even the orthopods do that. They won't come in to set a leg after midnight. Nice little hospital. It ain't the Manhattan Medical Center."

"Well, if you don't feel comfortable there," Caroline said, "don't do it." She said that with conviction but with dread. She was the one who had done the calculations. If I didn't work in the ER, we stopped eating around November.

"Ninety percent of the stuff that comes in, I'm okay. But it's not right. If we ever got a really bad car wreck, spleen rupture, or something, we'd be in big trouble. Emergency room medicine's a specialty by itself now."

"Christ, Brendan, if you don't feel qualified, don't do it."

"And how do we pay our landlady at the end of the month?"

"You'll find something else."

"Like what?"

"Like a nursing home. You could do that. No car wrecks. Just old gomers."

"That's exactly why nursing home jobs are such plums. All the nursing home jobs are grabbed up by guys who've been here for a while. New guys like me are lucky to get an ER. I've pretty much got to do an ER."

"Not if you think somebody might die some night because you were there instead of the kind of doc who should've been there."

"It would always be someone like me. These little community hospitals aren't going to shell out seventy-five thousand for an ER doc who can open a chest, when they get maybe one or two patients a year who need that. The hospital knows they got a nice little ER that sees mostly lacerations and flu and heart attacks and the big trauma stuff gets helicoptered off to the real trauma centers, unless someone staggers in with a blade in his belly or unless the cowboys drag somebody in."

"What cowboys?"

"You know, the paramedics. High school dropouts who take some six-week course on CPR and splinting and starting IVs, and then they get some certificate and a cloth badge, like in Boy Scouts, to sew on their sleeves. And the ambulance companies hire them and dress them up in these nice blue uniforms. And they sit around the ER, smoking and drinking coffee and telling stories about how they saved the mayor, or whoever, after he ran his Cadillac into the telephone pole."

"They sound charming."

"They'd be okay if they just went out and loaded the stretchers and brought in the victims, but oh, no. They get on the radio just like they've seen on TV or somewhere, with all this, 'Request permission to start IV.' And they get all disgruntled if you won't let them. Starting the IV is their big thing in life. Of course, it takes them about an hour and the IV's never working by the time they get the patient in."

"I hope you're nice to the cowboys."

"Oh, sure."

"What are the nurses like? They can't all be ninety."

"Mostly fifty with grandkids. Still wear their nursing hats."

"No! ER nurses? I'd think they'd be young and fetching."

"This is not your Massively Degenerate university-type hospital.

This is a little out-of-the-way community hospital trying to make a few shekels from the stray drunk trade."

"Maybe I ought to work there."

"You should. At least we'd see each other Fridays and Saturdays. We sure as hell don't see each other during the week."

"We have Sundays," Caroline said.

We kept Sunday night for ourselves. What memories I have of the city of Boston were Sunday nights, which Caroline always had planned. She never allowed us to settle into the same Sunday night routine, even though there was the risk that by trying a new restaurant or a new movie house we might be disappointed. The fact was, as long as we were together, it really didn't matter. We learned about the inexpensive movie houses near the colleges that ran classics and didn't cost much. She tallied up what each Sunday outing would cost and she was never much off.

She kept a hawk eye on the checking account and a firm hand on the wallet. I got my weekly dole and was not allowed to write checks for cash.

"What is this check for twenty dollars to the Department of Medicine?" she demanded.

I had hoped to slip that one by her. I had thought of a number of potentially acceptable lies, but in truth it was for a Massively Degenerate Hospital tie, with the hospital seal and the university seal embroidered into a maroon silk. I had to have one. It was an essential tie. I considered all the lies and then I told her the truth.

"Twenty dollars!" she gasped. "For a tie?"

"Not that many people even qualify to buy this tie."

"Twenty dollars."

"It's a keepsake. An heirloom. I'll probably pass it on to my firstborn son."

"Let me see this twenty-dollar tie."

I told her I didn't have it yet, which was not quite true. I had locked it in my drawer in my lab, knowing that she would want to inspect this extravagant tie to judge for herself whether it was worth twenty dollars, which could have paid for one of our Sunday nights.

"O'Brien, you'll break the bank yet."

What bank account we had was left over from the money I hadn't managed to spend in New York, and from the moonlighting.

I tried to stay out of her way that night of the tie confession.

"At least you don't drink," she said when we got into bed. "It could be worse."

"When I'm interviewing for jobs, after my fellowship," I told her, "I'll dazzle 'em with that tie."

"You'd dazzle them," she said, running her hand through my hair, "if you wore a sweatshirt."

— 6 —

THE NEW DRAGON

In the beginning, I was worried Caroline would flunk out. I could not see how a woman who could not remember to flush a toilet or screw the peanut butter jar top back on could remember the sequence of steps required to deliver intravenous adriamycin. Looking at the complete disarray of her desktop, I could not believe that she was capable of organizing a paper. When her classes began in September, I looked for some hopeful sign that she had resolved to get organized and become a methodical student, someone who could plan assignments, get chapters read on schedule, and complete papers on time. But, if anything, her desk looked more chaotic, if it is possible to go from complete disorder to even more disorder. But, to my stupefaction, by October I was finding an occasional term paper, stuffed into the magazine basket in the bathroom, or fallen behind the toaster, partially incinerated, embellished in the red ink of some instructor's hand, "Excellent discussion," or "Remarkable synthesis of a complicated subject." Caroline was apparently having no trouble with her coursework. She hadn't spent three years at Whipple for nothing. She knew some oncology.

She filled the apartment with library copies of *Cancer* and the *American Journal of Oncology,* and when she was reading one of these things you couldn't get her attention with a howitzer.

"How's it going?" I asked her one Sunday night, when we were out on our inviolate Night on the Town. Sunday nights, Caroline put down her journals and you could actually talk to her. "Learning anything?"

"All the time," she said. "It's wonderful having the time to read about all this stuff I'd seen before, but never really understood why they use which drugs and what they each do. School is really wasted on students. You should have to work first and then go to school to learn why you do things."

"Then you're enjoying it?"

"Immensely. I just feel so selfish."

"Selfish?"

"Oh, well, you know. Being a student is essentially a selfish occupation. The only one getting enriched by all this is me."

"And the nursing school."

"That too. But poor you. I never talk to you. And you make your own lunch and dinner. If peanut butter is ever found to be carcinogenic, you're a dead man from this year alone."

"I'm doing fine."

"Are you learning new things too?"

"Oh, lots."

"Having fun?"

"I wouldn't say that."

"Norman's lab no fun?"

Norman Giovanis was the chief of the Section of Infectious Disease. I worked in his lab attempting to find new ways to murder microorganisms.

"Oh, it's all right," I said. "But I never see patients. Just lab techs and petri dishes. The lab techs talk to the petri dishes as if they were people. 'Oh, and how is Mrs. Brown's pneumococcus this morning?' That kind of thing."

"You ought to come by Oncology. There're plenty of patients."

"But not my kind of patients. The Section of Infectious Disease pays my salary."

"That's why I think you ought to come around. Remember those patients you saw at the Medical Center? The ones with the pneumocystis? We've got some on the onc ward with Kaposi's sarcoma. Young guys with pneumocystis and Kaposi's."

"No kidding?"

"Three young men."

"Any of them homosexual?"

Caroline's mouth dropped open. "How'd you know that? They all three are."

"There was a paper in morbidity and mortality just before we left the Medical Center. Had 'em all talking in urgent whispers at the Great White Tower. They're going to submit their own paper to the *New England Journal* any day now, if they haven't already. Some group in San Francisco's seeing the same thing. The lid's going to blow off this real soon. It's some kind of new disease, probably a virus, kills your immune system dead. Pneumocystis—that's its calling card. Kaposi's is part of it, for reasons known only to God and the virus."

"These guys have candida esophagitis, the ones on my ward," said Caroline. "Lord, I hate that stuff. Remember how Vince Montebelli used to look in the mirror and make his own diagnosis every time he got candida esophagitis? That's what these guys do. Only they're not getting any chemotherapy. They've got no reason to have candida."

"There's a reason. We just don't know it yet."

"You ought to get out of that lab and come look at these guys."

"Norman would kill me dead if he found out I was sneaking out of the lab to see patients."

"Why?" Caroline could not understand anyone who did not put patients first, as the highest calling, the point of departure for all decent research.

"Because Norman is a laboratory animal. Norman says that all the great advances in human history have come from the laboratory. Penicillin, insulin, the polio vaccine, the oral contraceptive, all products of bench research. Clinical research is prostitution, according to Norman."

"I ought to have a talk with Norman."

"Just don't tell him about your patients."

"Why not?"

"If he doesn't know about them, he can't specifically forbid me from seeing them. If I sneak over there on my lunch hour and Norman's none the wiser, okay. But if he gets wind of it, I'll not be allowed to set foot on the onc ward."

"Buck up, Doctor. Are you a man or a mouse?"

"I am a lab animal. A white rat. I live in a lab and I eat little brown pellets, which they give me as a reward for good behavior. Positive reinforcement."

"So you'll come see my patients?"

"As long as you keep it quiet."

"Keep what quiet? I haven't heard a thing."

The next day I slipped out of the lab and donned a white coat and walked over to Caroline's ward. She was standing at a medication cart and she looked up and smiled when I approached her.

"There's only one left," she said. "The other two died last night."

"There'll be more," I said.

She took me down the hall to see the patient.

"He's like a leukemic," Caroline said. "Only worse. This thing's eating him up alive."

"It's a bad disease," I agreed.

We gowned and gloved and put on our masks and the paper hats that looked like shower caps and we went in to look over the patient. He was a forty-year-old choreographer for some Boston ballet company, and he was covered with blue nodules, which studded his skin. He lay in the subdued fluorescent light of his isolation room, like a creature from another planet, breathing fast and shallow with his pneumocystis pneumonia, unconscious, wasted—he couldn't have weighed more than ninety pounds, and he would have been more than one-sixty in full health. He looked like some newly hatched thing, helpless, fragile, alive, but just barely, and I shuddered just to look at him.

His head lolled off his pillow and he slumped to the right.

Caroline put her hand behind his head and positioned him back on his pillow. As she did, she noticed his IV and she said, "Well, that one's blown," and before I could say anything, she yanked out the IV. A rill of blood ran down his forearm, and Caroline, without thinking, stuck her thumb on the puncture site and stanched the flow while she looked around for a gauze pad.

"Christ," I said, knocking her hand away from the bleeding site. "Are you out of your mind?"

The mask covered her face up to her eyes, but you could see in them the surprise and anger. "What the hell?"

I found a gauze sponge, and taped it over the puncture site.

"This is infectious. You don't go sticking your finger on a puncture site."

"I'm wearing gloves."

"Fat lot of good that does. For all anyone knows, this thing, whatever it is, virus or whatever, slips right through latex."

"Oh, God," she said, rolling her eyes. "Another phobia."

"I'm serious. This isn't like AML or lung CA or breast. Those things were scary and did bad things to people, but it was always other people. This is something you can catch."

"Brendan, you're in the wrong line of work."

"Don't go sticking your finger over puncture sites. You work with this, you learn to be careful, more careful than you've ever been."

"Okay, hotshot," she said. "Now's your chance. Show me. Show me how careful you can be starting his IV, which he needs right now." She handed me an angiocath.

I looked at the IV in my hand and I looked at the patient, who looked agonal.

"What's he need an IV for?" I said. "Nothing's going to help him now."

She snatched the IV from my hand. "Okay, I'll start it."

"All right," I said. "For Chrissake."

"No, I'll do it, if you're so concerned."

I held the angiocath away from her and pulled on another pair of yellow latex gloves over the pair I was already wearing and I wished I had glasses. Every so often a vein sends out a spray and you get some in your eye or mouth. I was wearing a mask, but my eyes were unprotected. I tightened the tourniquet and felt for a vein, which was not easy, through two pairs of gloves. My hands were shaking.

"Hey," I heard Caroline say. "You're really upset. Forget it. You're right. What the hell good's an IV going to do him."

"He's still on protocol?"

"Sure."

"Then he needs an IV. How's he going to get his Bactrim without an IV."

"Let the tech start it."

I got in the first time and no blood washed over my gloves. Caroline hooked the line up and she fastened it down with tape. We walked out of the room.

"Nice going, O'Brien," Caroline said, when we were back out in the hall.

"Nothing to it," I said. "Just talent, long years of training, the heart of a lion and the eye of an eagle."

"And guts," she said, pulling off her mask, smiling.

"Aw, shucks."

"And you thought you were going into a happy subspecialty," she said, taking my arm. "Infectious disease, where all the dragons had been slain."

"New dragon," I said.

7

GREETINGS FROM THE REAL WORLD

That first February in Boston I was the coldest I have ever been. Our landlady did not believe in wasting money on oil or coal or whatever it was that was supposed to heat our apartment. We were not paying utilities, one of the many details about which I had not thought to ask. Caroline had thought about it and she had asked, and our rent included utilities.

"I thought that was a good deal," she said. "But it never occurred to me she might try to economize by simply not heating the place."

Since we had the top floor, and heat rises, we had plenty of heat in the warmer months, although we had no air conditioner. We had comforted ourselves with the thought that New England was a cold place and we would be grateful that heat rises during the long winter nights. But somehow, it didn't work that way. The third-floor windows were not equipped with storm windows, another one of those details that had somehow escaped me, and the temperature in our apartment rarely rose above fifty-five, to say nothing of the windchill factor when the gusts rattled through the cracks around the windows.

"I don't mind it when you're home," Caroline said. "Somehow it feels colder when I'm here alone."

"I don't think it ever got this cold in New York."

"We lived in hospital housing," Caroline said. "Those good solid high-rises, and they weren't heated by our landlady."

"And we had the money to go out to warm restaurants, in New York, when we were rich," I said.

But in Boston, we were both cold and poor and that makes you a little desperate.

"We can always go to bed," Caroline said.

We did that often and early, right after dinner, wearing sweaters and long underwear, and we huddled together and read. Some nights, the nights we could see our breath in the apartment air, we'd bundle up and walk over to the hospital library, where it was so warm, we fell asleep. Then we'd have to walk home in the dark when it was even colder.

In the mornings, Caroline would make coffee and she'd spread her books and journals and papers over the kitchen table and she'd get to work in a heavy sweater and a down vest. I'd walked to the hospital alone, thinking about the hot coffee the lab technician always had ready when I got there.

For the four-block trek to the hospital I felt like Zhivago crossing the frozen tundra. Sometimes the wind in Boston blows so hard, the snow simply cannot reach the ground, which is fortunate for Boston, because if all the snow reached the ground, they'd still be digging out in June.

It was on one of those bright mornings after a snow, when the sky cleared to that intense blue I've seen only in northern skies, and the sun was brilliant, and it reflected off the snow so brightly, tears came to my eyes, I set out for the hospital. The storm had passed, but the wind was stiff and dry and constant and I pushed out leaning forward into it, clutching the pea coat Caroline had bought me at Filene's basement when she discovered I did not own an overcoat. The wind pushed me back by the shoulders and tiny ice particles dermabraded my face and it was all I could do to keep moving one foot in front of the other. I thought they'd probably find me in the spring, when the snow melted. When I arrived at the hospital, I couldn't remember how I had got there.

I could smell the coffee in the hallway before I reached the lab. The lab technician was a wonderful human being who looked like she probably dressed up in black leather and did her hair up spiky and punk when she left work and then spent all night in smoky loud rock clubs before crawling back to work in the morning. She made the best coffee I've ever had.

"This stuff causes cancer," I said. "Anything this good must cause cancer."

"I wish it killed pneumocystis" she said. "They could feed it to the patients, and I wouldn't have to plate this crud out. Your new disease is complicating my life. We're going to need another tech, we keep getting so many of these in. I never seen so many pneumocystis cultures in a month."

I clasped my hot mug and felt the heat diffused into my fingers and I sat in my snow-blinded state watching the technician plate out some pneumocystis cultures, when my beeper went off.

Another pneumocystis patient, I thought. My beeper rarely went off when I was a Fellow. I was doing only one clinical project, the pneumocystis project, which was about the only thing anyone ever paged me about. Caroline was strictly forbidden to page me because I still got tachycardic and sweaty whenever my beeper went off, from conditioning at Whipple, and I relished the relative passivity of my beeper and didn't want it used casually. Most of the time I lurked about in the lab and tried to intimidate microorganisms with antibiotics, and the days were quiet, until another pneumocystis patient rolled in and stirred things up.

But this morning, it was Caroline. Her voice sounded odd and strained.

"I think you better come home," she said. "Right away."

"What's the matter?"

"There's a man here," she said. "Who wants to talk with you."

"About what?"

"Brendan," she said in her no-nonsense tone. "Come home."

And she hung up.

I didn't like the sound of her voice. The walk from the apartment to the hospital had been fifteen minutes against the wind. I made it home in five, falling only twice on the icy sidewalks.

The door to our apartment was unlocked and I put shoulder to it and blew through it, the door slamming back against the wall, narrowly missing a short fat man in a dark raincoat who reeled away from me toward the bright sunlight of the windows. I kept after him until he was pinned up against the wall and he caught his breath in his retreat and said, under his walrus mustache, "Dr. Brendan O'Brien?"

"Yes." I said. I had about four inches and fifteen pounds on him, and he looked ready to break and run.

He threw me an envelope, tipped his scrubby black waterproof hat, and slid by me out of the apartment.

"What is it?" asked Caroline, who had been standing by the archway to the kitchen, watching all this. She came over now, to look at the papers I drew from the envelope.

In the 𝕾𝖚𝖕𝖗𝖊𝖒𝖊 𝕮𝖔𝖚𝖗𝖙 𝖔𝖋 𝖙𝖍𝖊 𝕾𝖙𝖆𝖙𝖊 𝖔𝖋 𝕹𝖊𝖜 𝖀𝖔𝖗𝖐
𝕮𝖔𝖚𝖓𝖙𝖞 𝖔𝖋 New York

"What is this?" asked Caroline.

𝕳𝖔𝖚 𝖆𝖗𝖊 𝖍𝖊𝖗𝖊𝖇𝖞 𝖘𝖚𝖒𝖒𝖔𝖓𝖊𝖉...

"They want me to testify," I said. "I'm being subpoenaed."

RICHARD T. ROUNDTREE, Administrator of the goods and chattels and credits of Barbara S. Roundtree, deceased, and Richard T. Roundtree, individually, Plaintiffs

vs.

Seymour Freudenberg, MD
Phillip Brownwell, MD
Harold Golden, MD
Ira Bloomstein, MD
Brendan O'Brien, MD
and
The Corporation of the Whipple
Hospital for Cancer and Related Conditions
Defendants

"You're being sued!" Caroline said. "Let's sit down and read this thing."

Complaint

Plaintiff, complaining of the defendant herein, by his attorneys, Whitney, Sinai & Alridge, alleges upon information and belief, as follows

As for a first cause of action for conscious pain and suffering:

This went on for several pages in a language that bore some relationship to English but that was incomprehensible to me.

"Do you have any idea what they're talking about?" I asked Caroline, who was sitting next to me on the couch, reading over my shoulder.

"Mrs. Roundtree's husband is suing you," she said. "I cannot believe it."

Said defendant Brendan O'Brien further did hold himself out to be a specialist who would exercise that degree of skill and knowledge which is essentially possessed by similar specialists in the locality where he practices, and further to use his best and adequate judgment to exercise his skill and applying his said knowledge.

"When did I ever hold myself out to be a specialist?" I said.

"This is crazy," said Caroline. "There must be some mistake."

"I'll call Ira," I said. "He'll know what this is all about."

I went to the phone, but Caroline said, "Call from the hospital. Don't put this on our bill. We are poor enough, and from the looks of this, destined to be poorer."

I had not taken off my pea coat, and wandered toward the apartment door, still reading the court papers. Caroline came up from behind me and put her arm around me.

"Put it in your pocket and don't even think about it until you get back to the hospital," she said.

"I don't like this," I said. "They could take everything we've got."

Caroline laughed. "They can have it. If it means we won't need a U-Haul next time we move, plead guilty."

"How can you laugh?"

"It must be some sort of mistake, naming you. He probably wants Seymour. That's who he's after."

"But how could he sue Seymour? How could anyone sue Seymour? What did Seymour ever do to him?"

"His wife died."

"His wife had breast cancer."

"Call Ira," she said, mussing my hair. "And welcome to the Real World."

"But it's so unfair," I said.

"That's what Mr. Roundtree told me," she said. "About his wife getting breast cancer."

"Seymour Freudenberg didn't give his wife breast cancer."

"Go call Ira."

I walked back to the hospital in the blustery blinding day, feeling like a scolded child. I stood accused of something. Misrepresenting myself. Probably other things I'd find out about later, once I read through the whole complaint.

It didn't matter whether or not the complaints made any sense. I was not reacting with any rational part of myself. It was all conditioning. You didn't get to be a doctor by sniffing at authority. You went through a long, continuously applied process of learning how to accept the fact that you had done it all wrong so you could learn to do it better the next time. You learned how to absorb guilt and you let it use you to make you better. Only sometimes you hadn't done anything wrong and you still felt guilty, from habit.

I thought about Mrs. Roundtree and all the things we had been through with her, the brain met, her pathologic fracture, that nasty phlebitis, veins around the fracture swelling red and angry and full of clot, and all the worry with her heparin, and then her final hour, that big clot snapping free and hurtling into her lung, stuffing itself into her pulmonary arteries so she couldn't move any blood through her lungs.

And Ira pumping on her chest and not wanting to stop and Raskolnovich showing up and Ira going for him.

Now this.

And I got angry at myself for thinking about all this, for reviewing step by step everything we had done for her, because I knew I was falling into the trap the lawyers had set. I was doing just what Mr. Roundtree wanted me to do. I was remembering his wife, I was asking myself those excoriating questions I knew they would ask, even though I knew we had done everything anyone could have done for her.

But, of course, you never know that. There is always something more you could have done. And there is always that sticky doubt. There is always the possibility of error.

I could not put Mrs. Roundtree or those papers in my pocket out of mind. And that's what Mr. Roundtree wanted. That was his pound of flesh. He was making my blood pressure rise and my heart pound and my stomach do flips. He was saying: You wrapped up my wife's body and you sent her down to the morgue and you never gave her another thought. You never thought about what it was like for me and my kids waking up every morning without my wife. Well, now I'm going to make you think about that. It's going to matter to you, because I'm suing you for ten million dollars and you're going to pay that for the rest of your life.

I didn't know why he was doing it. Maybe we had hurt his

feelings. Maybe he had to be angry at someone. Maybe he just needed the money. Ten million dollars. That's what the last page said.

Where was I going to get ten million dollars? What do they do, follow you around for the rest of your life like Jean Valjean?

There is always something more you can do, but there's always a risk in doing it.

Try explaining that to a jury. A jury of my peers, loaded with guys like Guido the U-Haul man, who thought you got your Rolls-Royce with your diploma and hated you for it. Try making Guido understand about Mrs. Roundtree.

Maybe we could have got her out of the hospital and home, where her breast cancer could have killed her. But she had died. Everyone died at Whipple. There was no disgrace in that. We'd reviewed her case with all the mavens: with the ward attending, with Seymour Freudenberg, at mortality conference. Nobody had any bright ideas about what we could have done better. She'd just had bad luck. Bad luck and breast cancer.

Try and make Guido believe that. Just you try.

I didn't notice the cold the whole walk back to the hospital. It was only when I arrived that I noticed I hadn't even buttoned my pea jacket.

I walked up to the lab, holding the lawsuit tight inside my pocket. I didn't want it to fall out and be found in the stairwell. Then it'd be all over the Massively Degenerate: Brendan O'Brien sued!

When I reached the lab, the technician was still at work on the pneumocystis cultures, so I couldn't call Ira from the lab phone, or the tech would hear I was being sued.

Down the hall, there was an empty conference room. I hung out the "Conference in Session" sign and locked the door and dialed. The operator's voice came on and said that familiar name, "Manhattan Medical Center," and I felt a twinge of homesickness. I asked her to page Ira for me.

His voice came on the line as buoyant and clear as ever. "Hey, Professor!" he boomed. He obviously had not had his visit from the local paper server.

"Ira, how are you?"

"As ever, as ever. How is the frozen northland? And how is the lovely Miss Bates?"

"She sends you her regards," I said. "Ira, I've had some bad news."

Ira's voice became suddenly serious. "What is it?"

"I got served with a lawsuit today."

"Yeah?"

"Mrs. Roundtree."

"Oh, that," said Ira, great relief in his voice. "Christ, you had me worried for a moment there."

"You know about it?"

"Yeah, sure. Got the papers a week ago. Is that what you call bad news?"

"What would you call it? It's no honor."

"Brendan O'Brien." Ira laughed. "The big C is bad news. Hodgkin's is bad news. Little kids with AML are bad news. A lawsuit is just one of your professional pleasures. You have to pay your dues, you want to call yourself a doctor."

"But, Ira."

"Call the lawyers for the hospital. The Medical Center is self-insured. They got some lawyers. They'll take care of it. They don't want you anyway."

"Then why'd they put me on the suit?"

"Because they got nothing better to do. You recognize all the names on that suit?"

"No."

"That's because they named a physical therapist who wrote lots of notes in the chart. That's the Dr. Harold Golden or whoever. Poor schmuck does the PT on Mrs. Roundtree after she broke her leg and writes his notes in the chart every day and they name him too. Lawyers is all swabs, O'Brien. They don't know shit. They don't do shit for anybody. They don't contribute anything positive to the world. They just send you papers."

"Have you talked to Seymour about it?"

"You mean," Ira said slowly, "you haven't heard about Seymour?"

His voice had changed completely, and I felt my own mouth go suddenly dry. I sat down, clamping the receiver to my ear. "No," I said. "What about Seymour?"

"I thought you'd have heard." Ira's voice had dropped. "It was in the *Times* and all."

"What was?"

"Seymour died the day after Christmas."

The room swayed momentarily, and I pressed the receiver into my ear. "Died?"

"I'm sorry," Ira said. "I thought you knew. What a dumb schmuck I am. It's just that everybody down here knew. I kinda assumed the whole world knew."

"But what happened?"

"Hodgkin's," Ira said. "Can you believe that?"

"I can't believe he's dead."

"Yeah, I know. People still say, 'Seymour says . . . whatever,' as if he's still alive. Nobody can quite believe it."

"Remember?" I said. "He had a kid going to college: he was all worried about which one she'd choose."

"Yeah."

"Now he's never going to see her graduate."

"Yeah," said Ira. "It just didn't seem right, him dying. It made no sense whatsoever. Of course, he worked right up to the day he was admitted. He just wouldn't stop. Guys who took care of him said they had to just about tie him down: he would've done rounds in his pajamas."

"Remember how he always seemed to come in just when we were on our way to the cafeteria?"

"Yeah, I missed a lot of lasagna nights because of Seymour," said Ira. "But he taught me a load of medicine."

"It just seems so . . ." I couldn't think of the word.

"Random," Ira said. "Remember what we talked about that night after Mrs. Roundtree died? The world is like that."

"Yeah, I remember."

"A lot of guys went to the funeral. I was on, so I couldn't. I was just as happy, you want to know the truth. I hate those fucking funerals."

"At least he's out of it, the lawsuit," I said. "At least he was spared that."

"He may be, but his wife isn't."

"His wife? What's his wife got to do with it?"

"The lawyers, O'Brien. The lawyers don't let you off the hook just because you up and croak. They sue his estate, so his wife's stuck for it."

"No!"

"Oh, sure. Try putting your kid through Swarthmore and getting the tuition checks out when your husband's estate is tied up by a suit. Mr. Richard Roundtree wants his pound of flesh."

"Can't the hospital lawyers get this thing thrown out? I mean, don't we have any rights?"

"All we've got is a pure heart, big boy, and a mantle of good intentions. And we swathe ourselves in it, and we hope that twelve retired postal clerks on the jury can see it."

"But," I said.

"Don't think about it," Ira said. "I guess Caroline doesn't know about Seymour either."

"No."

"Break it to her gently," Ira said. "She really liked Seymour."

"I'll do that."

"So how is it, being an ID Fellow?"

"Okay. You like being a junior resident?"

"Every morning I wake up and I say, 'Thank you, God, for making me a junior assistant resident. Thank you for delivering me from internship.'"

"Everything ends eventually," I said. "Even internship."

"Yeah," said Ira. "Everything ends. Everybody ends. Even Seymour."

"Even Seymour."

"It is all written, big boy. That's why you got to live every day. You eat bagels, do rounds, learn medicine. On a good day, you get home before your kids are in bed. We are all merely mortals, big boy. If you don't learn that from being a doc, you haven't learned a thing."

We said good-bye and hung up.

I unlocked the door to the conference room and walked back to my lab and told the lab tech I had to go home for a few minutes.

Caroline was sitting at the kitchen table, reading journals.

"How was Ira?"

"Ira was Ira," I said. "Lawsuits don't bother him."

"You look worse than when you left," Caroline said, putting down her journal. "What's wrong?"

"Ira had some bad news of his own," I said. "About Seymour Freudenberg."

Her face went blank and I couldn't avoid her eyes. Ira had said to break it to her gently. How do you break something like that gently?

"Seymour died," I said. "Day after Christmas. Hodgkin's. He went real fast."

Caroline's head dropped. "Oh, God." She put her forehead on her hand and her shoulders shook and she sobbed. But after a long moment, she lifted her head and she reached out her hand for me. "How did Ira sound?"

"As Ira always sounds. He was sad about Seymour, though."

"You know," she said, "I think Seymour had Hodgkin's a long time. Back when we were still there."

"What?"

"He gave me a book of poetry once."

"Seymour? Poetry?"

"I still have it. Emily Dickinson."

"Seymour did that? This is a side of Seymour I never knew."

"Oh, that was Seymour all over. But now that I think about that book, I think it all makes sense, his not telling anybody about his Hodgkin's. One night, he was in to see a lady who was really agonal. The family's all hovering around and asking Seymour when she's going to get better and when she's coming home. Later, Seymour's in the nurses' station, and he looks at me and says, 'Can't they see she's dying? She's never going to get out of that bed?' And I said, 'Hope is the thing with feathers that perches in the soul.' And Seymour looks at me and smiles, and I think, well, now he thinks I'm crazy too. But the next night he brings in this volume of Emily Dickinson."

"That line was from Emily Dickinson?"

"Of course, and Seymour knew it. He said, 'She's a good poet for an oncology nurse to read.' That's all he said. But inside he wrote me an inscription, 'Because I could not stop for Death, he kindly stopped for me.' "

"So you think Seymour had it, even then. And he knew it? And he still went in every day and saw patients until all hours."

"What do you think?" Caroline asked. "What do you think, knowing Seymour?"

8

THE LUCKY ONES

The big papers describing the curious phenomenon ultimately recognized as AIDS appeared in December and January, and by March, Caroline was sure she had seen several more patients on her oncology ward with the syndrome, which had not yet been dubbed AIDS. Caroline called it "The Worse Than Bad Disease." But what it was, was AIDS. I sneaked down to her ward to see the patients and to enter them into my log. I had seen the disease in New York, and it was like reading the beginning of a detective story with a really good hook: I just couldn't put it down; I had to keep coming back and picking it up and following the story, guessing what was going to happen next.

My great fear was that Norman, my section chief, would catch wind of my little project. Norman was ever vigilant for signs in his Fellows suggesting a lack of dedication to the world of laboratory science, and in particular to Norman's world of microbacterial polysaccharide research. You could talk about the Celtics game or the Bruins, which Norman regarded as too absurd to be threatening, but mention some paper in another branch of infectious disease, and Norman would grow moody and silent and later he would mutter about your lack of "focus" on the important issues in infectious disease, namely the issues of polysaccharide biochemistry Norman was pursuing in his lab.

It snowed in April, which was depressing. Six AIDS patients had been admitted to the Massively Degenerate since the beginning of the year and I had surreptitiously followed them, and all six had died. That was even more depressing. They were so sick and so wasted and so dead by the time they died, I felt almost happy for them. And I felt relieved for their families, those who had families.

One of the patients, a thirty-year-old homosexual bartender, who had a very dry sense of humor until he got too sick to see much humor in anything, died alone, without ever having been visited by a single friend or family member. His parents lived in Wellesley, which wasn't far away.

"They simply abandoned their son," Caroline said. "How could you abandon your child?"

He had been on her ward because he developed Kaposi's sarcoma before he died and he had been entered into one of the oncology protocols. Caroline had taken care of him and she liked him as much as I did.

"His father is retired navy," I said. "I'm talking career officer. A captain or an admiral or something. He told me his father was a Great Santini type, real macho. Someone told his father that his son was dying of the homosexual disease. His father could never accept his son was a homosexual in the first place."

"If I had a kid and he were homosexual, I cannot imagine not wanting to see him again. Not having to be with him if he were sick."

At the end of April, the sun came out and there were a few warm days and the snow began to melt and you could walk around outside in your shirt sleeves and seventy degrees felt like the tropics and you knew it would get cold again for a few days, but basically, spring was coming.

Even on the lovely spring days, Caroline sequestered herself in the hospital library, working on term papers and reading for her examinations, which were coming in May. On a particularly splendid day, with the air soft and the buds pushing up through the topsoil and birds tweeting and the sky bright blue with wonderful tall clouds, I found her deep in the bowels of the library, bent over a journal. I had in mind talking her into a walk outside, and I sat down beside her but she ignored me. It's not that she ignored me: she was unaware I was there. She was concentrating completely on the article she was reading and I think a howitzer discharging at the next table would not have roused her. Caroline read slightly faster than the speed of light and remembered everything, and you could not dislodge her when she was in the act any more than you could pry apart a couple of dogs locked in.

She kept reading until she finished and when she looked up there were tears in her eyes. Now I had seen her moved to tears by a novel, by a story in a newspaper, even, but never had I seen anyone moved to tears by an article in the *American Journal of Oncology.*

She said, "Oh, you're here."

"You okay?"

She smiled and wiped her eyes. "It's just Raskolnovich," she said. "The bastard finally did it."

I was a little confused and disoriented and had to think for a moment who Raskolnovich was.

"What'd he do, finally?"

"He found the cure," Caroline said, eyes all glassy. "For testicular CA."

She held up her journal. It was an article with Raskolnovich as first author of a multicenter study: Combination cisplatinum therapy for testicular CA in twenty patients. Complete remissions. No signs of recurrence. No signs of tumor anywhere. Five patients followed for three years and still no sign of recurrent disease. Probable cure. *Cure:* that rarest of words in oncology.

"Too late for Vince Montebelli," said Caroline.

"Three years," I said. "Vince was alive. If only Rasko had randomized him to that protocol, he'd still be alive."

"I thought about that. Of course, there was no way Rasko could have known. If Vince had got his cancer just two years later, he'd still be doing taxes in The Bronx," Caroline said. "Can you imagine that disease gone? No more wards of baldheaded young men with testicular CA blanking out their chest X rays? No more Vince Montebellis?"

More tears. Tears of joy. How could you not love a woman who got teary-eyed over an article about cisplatinum therapy in some oncology journal?

But I knew what she meant. The thought of all those young men —we had always had three or four on service at Whipple—bald, chest X rays looking like a blizzard through the window, nothing normal identifiable, just white on white. And now all that was headed for the ash heap of bad memories.

"Makes me glad you're a doctor," Caroline said suddenly. "Makes me glad you're working on AIDS," she said. "You can have the lawyers and their Mercedeses. And you can have all the venture capitalists and Harvard MBAs. You keep working on your little disease. You'll do something you can look back on in twenty years and be proud."

"I should live so long," I said. "We both should."

"We are very lucky," she said. "We should always remember that. We are lucky beyond estimation, to be where we are."

"You're right," I said, and I did not knock on wood. And there was wood everywhere in that library.

9

THE CLINICAL COURSE

That May, Caroline finished her course work and took her exams and she was told she had done very well. Her classes did not begin again until late August.

"Relax," I told her. "Stay out of the library. See Boston."

She did this for about two weeks. She went to museums. She saw historic places. After two weeks, she began worrying about money again. She calculated our finances and projected for another twelve months and went back to work on the oncology ward as a float nurse, which usually meant nights or evenings, so we didn't see much of each other.

I was still moonlighting at the emergency room, Friday and Saturday nights. My first shift ended at eight Saturday morning and I drove home, showered, slept, ate dinner, drove back for the next twelve-hour shift. Sunday morning, I drove home again and crashed, but Caroline would wake me around noon and we had Sunday together.

Spring in Boston is a very sweet season, and those Sundays, the only problem was where to be happiest. In the warm June weather, we walked over to the river and spread out a blanket and I slept and she read Jane Austen or Barbara Pym or whomever she was currently inhaling, and we ate a picnic lunch. It was pleasant by the river, and we watched people, and we felt we were part of the city, for an afternoon.

We lived in such an enclave, really, in the hospital. Our only friends were hospital people, and most of them were married and had kids and lived in places like Brookline.

"I don't know what happens to people when they get married," said Caroline. We were lying on the brown wool army blanket on the grass in the sunshine, and there was a breeze off the river. "They just stop living and recede into themselves. They wall off the world as if they had spun a cocoon."

"What happens to them," I said. "Is they have kids. That changes them."

"Something changes them."

"We won't let that happen to us," I said.

"The first thing we won't let happen," laughed Caroline, "is the baby."

In July, we got two phone calls from New York. The first was from the lawyers for the hospital, who told me I had to come to New York to give a deposition in the case of Mrs. Roundtree and I was directed to show up a week later on a Wednesday morning. I squawked out a few objections and was informed that if I did not cooperate in my own defense, they would discharge me as their client and I'd have to hire my own. I checked with Norman and we shifted around some lab experiments we had scheduled, but the day before I was to go I thought to call to be sure the deposition was still on and the law associate gofer they had assigned to me said, "Oh, that was canceled. We'll have to reschedule."

I said, "Thanks for letting me know," with an irony which apparently escaped him, because he said, "You're welcome."

The other call was from Forrest and Sally.

"Yeah," said Sally. "You guessed it. The wedding's in August. You guys are invited. It's just family and select honored friends."

"Married?" Caroline said. She enunciated the word with great slowness, as if the concept overwhelmed her.

"There was this little problem with the diaphragm. So here we are with me about to become a mommy," said Sally. "You've got to come down or we won't go through with it."

"We need some friendly faces in the crowd," Forrest said. "This thing has all kinds of bad potential."

"Of course we'll come down!" said Caroline. "Sally, a mommy! I cannot believe it. I'm speechless."

"You're speechless," said Sally in her best dry voice. "Forrest was catatonic for five days. I thought he had stroked out. But he went to the hospital every morning, so I figured he was perfusing his brain."

"I was nothing like that," Forrest said. "I was and am very pleased. The little bugger will have full honors, when he arrives."

"We will be down to dance at your wedding," I said.

"We'll owe you one," said Forrest.

It was the first time we'd been out of Boston since we arrived in the U-Haul. The drive south on Route 95 in my old heap was a lot easier than the truck trip had been. We stopped for breakfast at Providence and took a detour down the east side of the Narragansett Bay to Newport, driving along the water most of the way, crossing the bridge to Jamestown Island in the middle of the bay and on to Kingston, and through that splendid farm country with all the stone fences, and the cows grazing in fields that ran right down to the water's edge, and then inland, past the ponds and the working potato farms with the big machines in the fields. We talked about taking a year off and living on a farm and we talked about buying a boat and learning to sail when we finished training and got rich.

We talked and talked. But we never talked about people who had decided to get married.

They had the wedding in some sort of a chapel. It was near the United Nations. There were maybe twenty people there. I was introduced to Forrest's parents beforehand. His mother was a tall gray-haired lady with a slightly yellow tinge to her skin, and his father had a very red nose. His mother said, "Well, Dr. O'Brien, we've heard so much about you," with a peculiar ironic emphasis on the *doctor.*

Forrest called the meeting to order and thanked everyone for coming and he said that he and Sally felt the time had come to acknowledge what had seemed obvious to them for some time, that they were in fact married "in all the important ways." They thought the practical thing to do now was to get this all legally recorded. Sally said she thought life with Forrest was complicated enough without bringing other people into it, but she had discovered that other people inevitably got brought into it, and she smiled at Caroline, about the baby, I presumed. And so, Sally said, she had agreed to "get properly registered by the state like a motor vehicle."

To do the honors, Forrest had inveigled some poor judge, who had the misfortune to find himself on the cardiac care unit a month earlier. He said Forrest and Sally were now officially married in the eyes of the State of New York.

The only conventional part of the whole business was an exchange of rings. (Forrest told me later he had bought the rings from "Some guy wearing a yarmulke down at the Diamond Exchange. You figure a guy wearing a yarmulke's not going to cheat you. Lightning bolt would come out of the sky and strike him dead. He was a real nice guy.") And they kissed and everybody shook hands.

It was really very nice, all done with a twinkle in the eye and a wink.

We piled into taxis afterward. Forrest's prep school roommate rode with us. We were among the few people our age at the wedding, and he attached himself to us. He gave the driver the address of Forrest's parents' apartment on Fifth Avenue, for the reception. "Nice little ceremony," he said. "No bullshit. Personally, I can't see marriage, philosophically. I'm with Sartre on that one. But, if you're going to do it, they did it about right."

Caroline examined him with one of her unreadable looks and smiled to herself. We arrived at the Fifth Avenue apartment, or I should say the Fifth Avenue territory belonging to Forrest's parents. They had an entire floor of a white stone building that looked as if it had been built by the Morgans or the Vanderbilts at a time when nobody worried about expense. There were detailed stone carvings and gargoyles and marble floors and the whole effect was somewhere between a Gothic cathedral and the Parthenon. And that was just the entrance. The apartment itself had more carved wood than I've seen any place this side of the Atlantic and the ceilings were high enough for a Ringling Brothers trapeze show.

Caroline and I admired the view of Central Park and drank champagne and we tried to ogle the place without being too obvious.

"Forrest comes from money," Caroline observed.

Forrest's preppy roommate was still attached to us and he said, "Oh, Forrest comes from real money. The sort that gets passed on in trusts. What I never could understand is why he went to medical school. He works in a hospital. And the stories he tells are so scatological."

The roommate was an investment banker.

"I can't imagine Forrest not being a doctor," I said.

"That's because you never knew him before medical school," said the roommate. "Our parents belonged to the same club, the Maidstone Club, in East Hampton. Forrest had a tan all summer, played tennis, golf. Now he never gets out of the hospital. His skin looks pasty. I've stopped calling him for lunch. He eats in some cafeteria.''

"Imagine," said Caroline, with a look to me. "Being able to afford a cafeteria.''

The roommate found this very funny. He laughed until his face turned pink. "I love it," he said, looking around. "Well, Forrest has always marched to his own drummer. He had to stand up to his old man and worse, to his mother, about this marriage. They thought she'd trapped him and all that.''

"Sally?" said Caroline, as if to say, how absurd.

"No, kidding," said the roommate earnestly, in his slightly breathless voice. "So Forrest wound up telling his parents, 'We are going ahead with the wedding. If you want to come, here's the date and here's the address.' They came around.''

"What'd they have against Sally?" I asked.

"Well, you know, she's just some nurse he met.''

Caroline's eyes grew cold and slitty, and I wasn't sure if she'd had enough champagne to be a real threat for throwing her glass at him, but I stepped between them.

"Oh, of course. I get it," I said. "Those nurses are just always wanting to pick off a doctor to marry. That's the only reason they go to nursing school.''

"Well, that's the way Forrest's parents looked at it," said the roommate, looking at me, unsure of how I meant that.

We managed to lose the roommate, by the expediency of excusing ourselves to find a bathroom. We found each other a few minutes later.

"What a flaming twit," Caroline said. "Look, there's Forrest's mother. Let's go look at her.''

She was standing with a martini in one hand and a cigarette, held palm outward, in the other. The hand holding the cigarette, extended back at the wrist, jerking erratically. The jerking was subtle, but perceptible.

"Oh, my," said Caroline, nodding at the wrist. "She's got a flap.''

What she had noticed, what we had both noticed, was the flapping at the wrist, a sign of severe liver dysfunction, of impending hepatic encephalopathy, a sign called asterixis.

Not long after, Forrest and Sally left and Caroline said it was time to go.

"You don't have to leave when the bride leaves," I said.

"I'm ready."

We walked out into the sunshine on Fifth Avenue. It was bright with the light reflecting off all the white stone buildings, and we crossed to the park side of the avenue, where it was shaded and green. We walked down the avenue, toward the Plaza Hotel.

Caroline said nothing.

"You okay?" I asked her.

"I don't know. I just got depressed. His parents and what they said about Sally. It made the whole thing seem so nasty. You can be okay together, until other people get in the way. We've had it easy. The world's left us alone."

"Oh, it's not so bad," I said. "Forrest told me, 'If you can get past the wedding, you know you have a strong relationship.' He laughed it off."

"We don't need a wedding to know that," Caroline said. "I feel very married and we've never had a wedding."

We continued down to the Plaza and we sat near the fountain, watching the coachmen come and go with their horse-drawn carriages. The horses looked worn-out, on their last legs.

"What is hard for me to believe," said Caroline, "is Sally being pregnant."

"She didn't look pregnant."

"I hope it doesn't change her. I can't imagine her not being able to think about anything but which stroller to buy and what diapers."

"Sally'll never be like that."

"Oh, I don't know. She's talking about quitting work when the kid's born."

"She'll go back eventually."

"That's what I told her, but she said, 'Oh, I don't know. They're only young once.' She's talking about becoming a housewife."

"Well, you know these nurses. The only reason they go to nursing school's so they can get married. Then they give up nursing without a second thought."

Caroline laughed and shook her head. "Christ," she said. "What a twit that guy was." Then she stopped laughing. "You wouldn't mind if I got pregnant and wanted to just sit home and eat bonbons and watch TV and rock a cradle?"

"You wouldn't do that."

"But suppose I did? That wouldn't bother you?"

"If you wanted to stay at home with a kid? No, it wouldn't."

She looked at me as if she were seeing me for the first time. "You really don't think what I do is important at all, do you?"

"What are you talking about?"

"You don't, do you?"

"I think your work is very important. So is being a mother."

"Anyone can be a mother. You think nursing is worth about as much as what those horses do."

"I never said that. You're just picking a fight. What are we arguing about?"

"My life," she said. She stared at the horse-drawn carriages, the horses looking tired and defeated.

"Harnessed," she said. "That's what mothers are."

"Caroline," I said. "That may be what Sally wants right now. You don't want that, not yet. Is it so inconceivable you might want all that some day, once you've done what you want to do with oncology?"

She studied me.

"And what do you want?"

"You."

She smiled. "You put things so nicely."

10

ROUTE 1 IN BRANFORD

On the way back to Boston, we got off I-95 in Branford and we took Route 1 for a few miles to look at the fields and the orchards and to see some of the real Connecticut. Coming around a bend, I saw a pickup truck straddling the road in a not so loving embrace with a green Jaguar. The pickup had plowed into the left door of the Jaguar, crossing the double yellow line to do it. There was glass and water sprayed out over the road and I hit the brakes. I didn't see anyone moving in either car or truck.

"It must have just happened," Caroline said. "There's no cops and nobody's standing outside the cars."

"Maybe they've all left."

"Pull over."

"Why?"

"You're a doctor. I'm a nurse. We might be able to help."

"Let the cowboys do it. What can we do on a road?"

"Pull over."

I pulled over, but I wasn't finished arguing. We had no equipment, nothing to work with, and I already had my name on one lawsuit. Caroline was out of her door before we'd come to a complete halt. She crossed the road to the wreck, leaving me, still complaining, to trail behind her.

I stopped objecting when we got to the Jaguar.

There were three teenage girls sitting in the front seat. The driver was conscious and had vomited in her own lap. The girl sitting next to her had hit the windshield and was on the floor of the car and the girl in the door seat on the other side was strapped into her seat belt screaming and terrified. I went around to the right side of the car and opened the door and told the screaming girl I was a doctor. She looked at me and did not stop screaming.

"Can you get out of this belt?" I asked her.

She stared at me, still screaming. I slapped her and she stopped.

I tried to unlock the belt but it wouldn't give. Caroline came up from behind me.

"Nobody in the pickup," she said. "He must have run for it. Smell the gas?"

"How can you miss it? Don't offer anybody a cigarette."

"We better get everyone out of the car."

"Not supposed to move anyone until you're sure she doesn't have a neck or cord injury," I said. "The cowboys taught me that. Full body immobilization."

"None of that is going to be very relevant," said Caroline, "if the car blows up."

She had a point. I had my L.L. Bean pocketknife attached to my keys and I cut the seat belt with it and freed the girl near the door. Caroline got her out and walked her across the road to the grass, where she laid her down. I slid in and scraped the girl who had been riding in the middle off the floor. She was conscious and her eyes were opened, but she had a laceration between her eyes and she was not answering questions.

"You okay?"

"Uhhhhh . . ."

"Can you see the fingers?" I held up two fingers.

"Uhhhhh . . ."

"Does your neck hurt?"

"Nuhhhh . . ."

"Lift your arms."

She lifted her arms, not far, not together, but she moved both of them. She could move her legs, too. She wasn't quadriplegic. She had that much going for her. She was even beginning to wake up a little.

"Does your belly hurt?" I said, pressing on the right and then on the left. She winced when I pressed the left side, and her belly tensed.

She said, "I'm going to be sick."

"Come out of the car."

She slid down the seat and Caroline was there to help her out. The smell of gasoline was getting thick enough to make anyone sick. I heard her vomit on the street. I was next to the driver now, who was sitting bolt upright looking straight forward, with vomit in her lap.

"You okay?"

"My dad's car."

"Anything hurt?"

"My shoulder, a little."

She wasn't wearing a seat belt, and she had hit the steering wheel and her forehead had a big bruised egg in the center. I got her out of the car and walked her across the road, where Caroline had the other two lying on their backs.

"Maybe one of us should go for help," I told Caroline.

"Enough cars have passed us. Someone will call the police."

"Don't count on it."

A police car arrived almost as soon as I said that. Shortly thereafter an ambulance arrived, lights flashing, siren blaring. Two skinny, pimply-faced adolescent paramedics jumped out, all excited, dragging lots of equipment, IV bags and poles and stretchers and immobilization braces. They seemed disappointed the girls were out of the car and already being attended.

I told them I thought the girl who had been riding in the middle had hit the gearshift with her abdomen and I thought she might have ruptured her spleen. That pleased the cowboys more and they put her on the stretcher and one of them ran back to the ambulance to radio ahead while the other pushed the stretcher to the ambulance with Caroline. I could hear the first paramedic shouting into his radio, "Ruptured spleen. Coming in. Full sound and lights."

They loaded the other two girls onto the ambulance with reasonable efficiency, although they did want to stop to put an IV in the driver, but I told them I'd start the IVs in the ambulance as we drove. The policeman wanted to interview me. I told him I had to stay with the girls.

We didn't start any IVs in the ambulance. The ride was too jerky and the girls had fine blood pressures and they were all awake. The middle girl started fading toward the end of the ride, though. She was the one with the tender spleen and by the time we arrived she seemed sleepy and less alert.

They took us to Yale–New Haven. They rolled the girls out of the ambulance and I went with the girl with the tender belly. I waited with her in the exam room while a nurse in a blue scrub suit took her blood pressure.

"You can wait outside now," the nurse said.

"I'm a doctor," I said. "I stopped on the road. I have to talk to the doctor."

"You can give me report."

"I have to hand her over to the care of another doctor."

The nurse looked at me hard for a moment.

"You've heard of abandonment," I said.

"Wait here."

A resident in whites stepped into the room a few minutes later. I told him what I thought about the spleen and I described how each girl looked at the scene and he listened with a patient smile but I got the impression he didn't really want to waste the time listening. The ER staff was evaluating the girls, and my roadside impressions didn't mean much. All he wanted to know was if any of them had been unconscious and if the windshield had been hit by any head, because he had to order a CT scan for anyone with evidence of a head injury.

The police were more interested. A young cop with jet black hair who looked like Al Pacino asked me for a complete chronology of what I had seen and what I had done from the instant I came upon the wreck until the moment I arrived at the ER. He asked me at least four times if I had seen the driver of the pickup truck. He kept calling me doctor, and he seemed a little incredulous I had stopped on the road, not having been involved in the accident.

"You didn't actually see the collision, then, Doctor?"

"No, I told you. I came around the curve and noticed the car and the truck stopped in the middle of the road, but I didn't even realize, at first, they had collided. When I got closer, I stopped."

"There were other cars ahead of you that kept on going around the wreck?"

"There might have been. I was focused on the wreck."

"But you would have wanted to avoid hitting cars that had slowed down in front of you."

"I was slowing down pretty much to a halt. I wasn't going to run into anyone."

"Were there cars in back of you, as you slowed?"

"Yes. I saw two in my rearview mirror. They had slowed. I pulled over to the side of the road and they went past."

He kept me going, from step to step, and when he was satisfied he said, "Did you know we have a Good Samaritan law in Connecticut?"

"What's that?"

"Nobody's ever been successfully sued for care rendered under emergency circumstances at the roadside in the state of Connecticut since the passage of the Good Samaritan Act of 1969," he said with great conviction. This had evidently been a subject of instruction for the local police.

I found Caroline talking to the parents of the girl who was driving, when I was finally finished talking to the policeman. She introduced me. The father was a prosperous-looking man with a flushed face. He was wearing a Ralph Lauren polo shirt and sailcloth slacks and boat shoes. The mother looked frazzled and kept twisting a pair of sunglasses and interrupting every few minutes to ask if her daughter was going to be all right. Her husband was very patient with her and he said, "The doctors are working on her now, Babs. They'll come out and talk with us when they know more," every time she asked.

I told the mother her daughter had seemed stunned but otherwise unharmed at the scene.

"We just saw the car," said the father. "It's hard to believe they weren't all three killed."

"No, they were okay. The one in the middle concerned me."

"Who was that, Stan?" the mother asked. "Was that Trudy?"

"I don't know."

"Short brown hair, bangs, bright blue eyes," I said.

"Trudy," said the mother. "That's Trudy."

"You'll let us know how the girls do," I said, starting Caroline toward the door. "You have our number?"

"What's he mean? 'How the girls do'? " asked the wife. "Aren't they going to be all right?"

"They'll be just fine. Yes, Doctor. And thank you so much for stopping and for all your help."

When we were back in the car, Caroline said, "I hope you don't mind my giving them your name."

"Their lawyer could get my name from the cops, if they want me," I said. "I don't think it matters: no one has ever successfully sued a doctor rendering care at the roadside in the state of Connecticut, since the Good Samaritan Act of 1969."

"How impressive. Who told you that?"

"I look these things up before I go out driving."

Caroline laughed. "For a moment there," she said. "You had me going."

We did, in fact, hear from the parents, about a week later. Their daughter did fine, as did the girl I had cut out of the seat belt. Neither was even admitted to the hospital.

Trudy was not as lucky. Her spleen was, in fact, ruptured and had to be removed, and her head CAT scan showed a bleed into the brain substance. As soon as the general surgeons got the spleen taken care of, the neurosurgeons went in and evacuated a big hematoma. She woke up and smiled at everyone, but she died two days later.

11

THE NEW DISEASE

There were more AIDS patients that August and even more in September. The intensive care unit swelled with them. Caroline's oncology ward had them. Nobody at the hospital was quite sure what to make of them. The virus had not yet been conclusively identified, but even then, it was clearly an infectious agent and the smart money was on virus.

"It's like the dawn of a new age," said Caroline. "I've never seen patients like this before. Even the leukemics, you figure you can get them into remission, give them some time. But these poor AIDS guys come in and proceed to go right down the tubes, and there's not a thing you can do for them."

"You know it, and I know it. I just wish Norman would wake up to it."

The chief of the Section of Infectious Disease, Norman Giovanis, or Norman, as everyone in the section called him, did not think AIDS was likely to be a very important disease.

"Has he seen the patients?" Caroline asked.

"Norman does not see patients. Norman goes to his laboratory and slays microorganisms. Or rather, he figures out what penicillin does to the polysaccharide coat of various bugs. If a bug does not have a polysaccharide coat, Norman is not interested. AIDS is a disease without a polysaccharide coat, and therefore, in Norman's mind, it is a mere fad. Nothing of lasting significance will ever come from studying it. And Norman is concerned not simply with New Knowledge, but with lasting significance."

"You still haven't told him what you're doing?"

"Norman knows each of his Fellows has other interests. He knows we all moonlight. He never asks what we do when we're not in the lab, as long as his work gets done. All Norman cares about is that I stay focused on the big things in life, like polysaccharide coats and Resistance Factor."

"Resistance Factor? Sounds like a Syrian terrorist group."

"*Au contraire.* Resistance factor is what strikes terror in the heart of every ID maven. It's the thing that bugs can pass on to their offspring that makes them resistant to antibiotics. Norman's greatest nightmare is that one day we're going to wake up and find all the bugs have it and none of our antibiotics work anymore."

"When he wakes up," Caroline said, "he's going to find out he's got a bigger nightmare already come to life."

"You may be right."

"Here's a bug, or a virus, that makes resistance factor unnecessary," Caroline said. "You strip someone of his immune system, no antibiotic's going to help him for long."

"That's what I've been telling Norman."

"What's Norman say?"

"He says, 'This too shall pass. Keep working on the pneumococcus.' "

"What's with this guy? He some kind of lightweight?"

"Norman's as brilliant a scientist as ever put eye to microscope. But he's like a lot of brilliant docs: he's not real smart."

"Bring him down to my ward," Caroline said. "I'll talk some sense into him."

I laughed. The idea of anyone, even Caroline, talking Norman into anything, was just too much. "Norman grew up a poor boy in Brooklyn. People told him he was too poor to go to college. He didn't listen. He went to Brooklyn College and published two papers in microbiology as an undergraduate. People have been telling him all his life he was wrong about this and that, and he never listened. Now he's a distinguished alumnus of Harvard Medical School, chief of the Section of Infectious Disease at the Massively Degenerate, and nobody can tell him anything."

"Sounds like you're just going to have to save Norman from himself," Caroline said.

If anyone could have done it, Caroline might have had a chance, but as it developed, events outstripped us. In November, the Chief went off to some federation for clinical research meeting in Washington and as soon as he got back, he called me into his office.

"O'Brien," he said, looking at me from under his overgrown eyebrows. "I know you've been spending time chasing down these AIDS patients."

He sat there in his chair for a moment and I watched him. He had very thick black hair, like a very thick lawn, rising from a solid line across a lowish, almost simian forehead. He had seen the last of his forties, but he wasn't graying at all, except, oddly, in his eyebrows, which were overgrown and which added to his furry look. He sat very still, but everything about him was alive, active, and intelligent.

I squirmed. I hemmed and hawed and I tried to minimize. He was about to lambaste me for wasting time on this AIDS thing. He had just got back from the meetings and he was visibly disturbed. He had discovered, I was sure, our lab had fallen behind the pack in resistance factor research, and it was all because his fellows were unfocused, distracted, and uncommitted.

And the fact was, I had been distracted. What I didn't want Norman to know was that I had been using departmental resources to abet my pet project: I had used departmental computer time to develop a program to follow the AIDS patients, who, all told, numbered fifty-two over the fourteen months I'd been tracking them. Norman could tolerate a little eccentricity in his Fellows, but he wasn't going to be amused by diversion of department resources.

It was time for some damage control. I said there were currently eleven AIDS patients in the house. His face clouded.

"I thought there might have been more," he said, almost to himself.

I said nothing.

He looked up. "Where's that notebook you were keeping?"

"Actually, sir, I thought it might take less time if I put it on the computer. It's just something I do after five. I run up there and log things in. It hardly takes any time at all."

"Let's go look at it."

We sat down in front of the screen and I called up all the current patients.

"No, I want to see all the patients since you started. Where are they?"

There was no way out now. The master display with all the patients showed it all: there were twenty columns of data on each of the patients and there were references to other files. I was trapped. Kiss good-bye to my AIDS watch. I was headed to the doghouse for shortchanging the vital polysaccharides. I called up the master display.

The Chief sat there staring at the screen, tracing the columns with his finger.

"You've got the medical record number on each one?"

"That's this column. I just drift by after I'm finished in the lab, and punch in some numbers. Maybe forty-five minutes a day. I could really do it during lunch. It really didn't take much time at all. Once I set up the program."

He swiveled in his chair and looked at me in astonishment. "You set up a program?"

"It really didn't take long. I just spun it out. Took a few hours one weekend, that's all."

"What's this?"

"Uh, that's the key to the narrative summary." The narrative summaries detailed the entire clinical course of each patient from admission until death. One look at a narrative summary and the Chief would see I had spent more than nights and weekends on AIDS.

"Flip up a narrative summary," he said with no expression at all.

I flipped it up and the screen filled with dates, numbers, drugs, the whole picture of what had happened to patient number twenty-four over his three-week hospitalization unto death. I sank into my chair and tried to disappear into a dot.

The Chief never took his eyes from the screen. He pulled a pipe from his jacket pocket and then he retrieved a tobacco pouch, loaded the pipe and lit it, and his eyes never left the screen.

But the curious thing was: His face was changing. He seemed to be growing excited. His eyes grew large and intense.

Then he turned to me again. "You've been doing this on every one of these patients? All fifty-two?"

"Yes, sir," I croaked.

"This isn't some diddly-shit hobby, O'Brien," he said. "You've put a lot of time into this thing."

There wasn't much I could say, with the screen full of data, blinking and winking in our faces.

"You never told me," he said.

"I wasn't sure there was all that much to it," I said.

"You were sure enough to carve off some computer time," he said, still staring at the screen. Then he swiveled in his chair and faced me. He was a short, stubby man, with a thick neck, and he looked about as movable as your average fireplug.

"O'Brien," he said. "You are, from this moment, officially relieved of all duties of your fellowship."

My head spun. This couldn't be. I had done my polysaccharide work. So I had a pet project. It was on my own time. Department computer time maybe, but my own time. I started to object, but he held out a hairy paw and stopped me.

"From now on," the Chief said, "your primary responsibility in this section is to follow every AIDS patient who sets foot in this hospital. Inpatient or outpatient. From emergency room to morgue, since the morgue is apparently their inevitable destination."

The Chief had got the word on AIDS in Washington.

"Until now," he said, "we have been wringing our hands about the possibility of bugs becoming resistant to antibiotics, about a return to the pre-antibiotic era."

"Yes, sir. That's a very important concern."

"Can you imagine, O'Brien, an era in which the patient is stripped of his immune system, so that even the most indolent bug becomes a potential killer?" He leaned over to look at me from under his bushy eyebrows. "This virus—it's got to be a virus—this virus can do that. This may be the dawning of a whole new era, the AIDS era."

"Great minds," I said. "Think alike."

"What's that?"

"Sure, Chief. This could be very big."

"Big," said the Chief. "Is not the word."

I raced home that night to tell Caroline about Norman and the AIDS assignment. She listened quietly, and when I was finished she shrugged and said, "You can't keep a good man down."

"But isn't it amazing?" I sputtered. "I'm thinking he's about to throw me out on my ear, and he turns around and hands me the whole project, more or less. No more polysaccharides. No more resistance factor. No more hiding the AIDS computer time from inquiring eyes. I can do an AIDS fellowship."

"But why would you want to?"

I looked at her, uncomprehending. "You know why."

"Humor me," she said. "Spell it out."

"It's the hottest thing in ID right now, and maybe for a long time."

"What does that mean?" Caroline said, studying me. "I mean, for you?"

"It means I don't have to spend all day in Norman's lab working on some dead-end polysaccharide. I can get back to the wards."

"I thought you were getting to appreciate the lab."

I couldn't understand her reserve. I had expected her to be dancing around the table with me.

"But AIDS is where the action is," I said. "And AIDS is on the wards, unless you have a virus lab. For now, AIDS is a clinical problem."

"You mean AIDS is what you're going to build your career on?"

That stopped me. I was beginning to see her point.

"No," I said. "You know the plan."

"I *thought* I knew your plan."

"It's still the same: I'm out of here when my two-year hitch is up. I haven't signed up for the duration of this war. The AIDS war is not going to be a short one."

She looked at me repressing a smile, raising an I-can-see-it-coming eyebrow.

"No, no, no," I said. "I will not be seduced. I am sallying forth into the real world, private practice, real patients, just as soon as I can."

"For a moment there," said Caroline, smile breaking through now, "I thought I detected a wave of enthusiasm sweeping you away."

"No way."

"Sweeping you toward a life of academic achievement and poverty at the Massively Degenerate, as so many before you have been swept away."

"Not this kid."

"I see."

"First of all, nobody's made the offer."

"Norman will."

"I wouldn't be interested."

"Oh, I see." Another knowing smile, even more annoying than the first.

"Of course I'm enthusiastic. I'm working on a project I like. One I began, more or less."

"Oh, I thought you were saving lives."

"Nobody's saving anybody at this stage. I'd be surprised if anybody's saving anybody with AIDS, five, even ten years from now. But if I've got to do research when I'm a Fellow, it may as well be in an area that's booming."

"Oh, AIDS is a growth industry, all right," laughed Caroline. "I can see that. And you're a star on the rise. You're going to be famous, at least around this joint."

"Fame will not turn my head," I said. "I stick to my plan. And my plan is private practice."

"Don't cut off your options," Caroline said. She was not smiling now. "If AIDS is what you want to do. But, as you once pointed out to me, AIDS is a catching thing. And people who catch it die with great regularity."

She was standing in front of me, but for once, she was not looking me in the eye.

"I'll be careful," I said. "You know how crazy I can be about being careful. I drive you crazy. I'm positively phobic, I'm so careful."

"Well, don't let me discourage you. If you want to devote your life to AIDS, you can do a lot of good."

"No, that's where you're wrong. The only place this battle's going to be won is in the laboratory. Some new Jonas Salk. Guys like me aren't going to slay this dragon. If I thought I might have a hand in that, I'd stay in. But I'm not. For what time I have left, I'd like to learn more about this thing. But then I wave good-bye."

"So you're going to be a local hero, and then walk?" said Caroline. "That's some plan."

"You think it's not going to be easy to walk away, once I get into it? Just watch me."

"Just remember," said Caroline. "You heard it here first."

"Would you be disappointed if I did? Stay at the Massive, I mean. Committed my life to academic inquiry and financial embarrassment?"

"If it's what you wanted, I'd be happy for you."

"I hate the whole thought of genteel poverty," I said. "Someday, I want to buy you a Mercedes and ensconce you in an obnoxiously large and tasteless house in the Great State of Suburbia."

Caroline's eyes widened and she looked genuinely startled. "Why?" she said, "would you want to do that?"

"Because . . ." I said. "I mean, after all the scraping and scrimping and being poor."

"Do you really imagine," Caroline said, "that matters to me?"

"Of course."

"But I've been very happy," she said. "I've never been so damn happy."

"You've never been so damn poor."

"Speak for yourself. Poverty's no honor, but I've been happy."

"Freezing in this apartment? You were Head Nurse, making a good salary. And you came to this."

She laughed and ran her fingers through my hair. "I have never regretted it. Not for a moment. Well, maybe for one moment. That U-Haul was daunting."

"And when your father invited us down to Washington?" I asked.

We couldn't afford the plane fare, that time, not even for Caroline alone. She told him she had to work at the hospital, which was true—she had to moonlight that weekend or we wouldn't have been able to meet the rent.

As she listened, her eyes grew more serious. "This sounds like what the shrinks call massive projection."

"Not by me," I said. "I've had everything I want. I got my Massively Degenerate necktie. I've got my computer program. And I've had you."

"In that order?"

"I'd put you way ahead of the computer program."

"But behind the tie?"

"For Chrissake, Caroline: that tie is going to be an heirloom."

Every Friday, the whole task force got together from eight to ten in the morning. There was plenty of work to go around. The AIDS field moved quickly and the journals had started filling with articles. The race was under way to identify the virus, but our group at the Massive was not equipped to enter that particular race. We were all pretty sure it was going to be a virus, and we were pretty sure that even once the virus had been characterized, it would be a long time before anything could be done to attack the virus or immunize against it.

Our problem was the more immediate one: the disease syndrome itself had to be characterized. It was important to define what the disease could do to patients. Did everyone die or did some people survive and become resistant? Were there silent carriers, as there were in salmonellosis, who weren't sick but who spread the disease? What was the incubation period? How did you detect it? There were new questions arising daily. Things were heating up.

"I saw Norman in the library today," Caroline told me. "He looked catatonic."

"We got scooped," I said.

"Oh?"

"I told Norman, we've been seeing all these Bactrim rashes in the AIDS patients. Sixty percent. We put 'em on Bactrim for their pneumocystis and they blossom in this mega rash within five weeks and we've got to stop the Bactrim."

"They're allergic?"

"Fine deductive mind you've got there."

"But they've got AIDS," Caroline said. "They're not supposed to have immune systems. What're they doing with allergy?"

"Now that's a very itchy question you got there," I said. "An apparent contradiction, *n'est-ce pas?* Allergy is a sort of hyperimmunity. An immune system revved up. Firing off at the wrong target, but firing. So what are these guys doing with allergies?"

"What did Norman say?"

"Norman said, and I quote, 'O'Brien, when it rains it pours. These poor schmucks are just out of luck.' "

"So some other group noticed the same thing?"

"Not just noticed, but reported the same thing in the *Annals.* Norman fell immediately into deep depression."

"Oh, poor Norman."

"Of course, this other group made sense of it: it turns out there's two arms of the immune system, and what they said was that when one arm is injured, as in AIDS, the other arm swings free. So you can get a hyperactive immune state in people with a half-crippled system. It makes sense. A clinical lesson."

"Well, then," said Caroline. "They deserve the glory."

"Norman doesn't see it that way."

"Of course not. Norman is competitive."

"He's got me writing up the psoriasis stuff. We've seen psoriasis flares in fifty-odd percent of the AIDS people. It's a me-too article, of course, just illustrates the same phenomenon. Psoriasis is autoimmune, just like allergic rashes. But Norman wants me to write it up. Raise the Massively Degenerate flag before the world."

"Thus is medical knowledge advanced," laughed Caroline. "On the bandwagon."

The task force meeting began with a review of the statistics I ran off on my computer the night before. As Caroline had predicted, I soon discovered the thrill of being a star at a research center. There was always excitement when the task force met: a roomful of graybeards, famous professors, and all their minions, and they listened, for the first twenty minutes, to the stuff I had collected and organized. My work was their beginning point. It was a heady sensation, giving that presentation every week.

And it didn't stop there. People asked me things. People I didn't know, but who knew me. They stopped me in the hall and asked me about things we had seen in AIDS. They asked me about things I had never seen in AIDS, and they listened seriously, intently, to every word I said. Two hundred people packed in the amphitheater to hear me give Grand Rounds, which I found particularly amusing since in forty minutes the best I could say was we knew very little at all about AIDS.

"Why did they applaud at the end?" asked Caroline, who had come to see the show. "You had just spent forty minutes telling them you didn't know anything about the disease except that it apparently kills every last person who gets it. And they applaud! Were they saying, 'Let's hear it for a really no-nonsense disease'? Or what? Why would you applaud after a lecture like that?"

"Did you applaud?"

"Of course," laughed Caroline. "But I love you."

"So do they."

She laughed even louder.

But it was true: the more I denied knowing anything of real value about it, the more people sought me out, as if they thought I was denying for the sole purpose of keeping the really important knowledge to myself. House officers stopped me in the cafeteria to say they had read my paper on psoriasis in AIDS. It was a very fine paper, they said. It was a good example of what you could learn about a disease from simple clinical observation and the application of simple logic: if one arm of the immune system were paralyzed, the other might swing free. Very clever.

"You'll never guess," Caroline told me, throwing down her books on the kitchen table. "The topic for oncology Grand Rounds today."

"AIDS."

"How'd you know?"

"The guy who gave it called me the other day for some slides. I take it he didn't give me credit."

"He did not," said Caroline, indignant. "What a swine."

"Oh, well. He's a professor. I'm just a Fellow."

"But you are the star Fellow!" she laughed. "Oh, well. No matter. He did give a very good talk, with your slides. Almost as good as your Grand Rounds, but, of course, without the élan. He had a different slant, however. Did you know that each and every one of us makes a few malignant cells, every day?"

"Yes, but if you don't have AIDS, your immune surveillance system picks off the little bastards and you don't get cancer."

"You know all this," said Caroline, astonished. "You are not supposed to know this. This is oncology. You are trespassing into my field."

"It's AIDS," I said. "And I am getting to be an AIDS maven."

12

FUTURESHOCK

The Christmas party for the section of Infectious Disease was held on a Friday afternoon in the conference room cum library and it spilled out into the corridor, where people stood around drinking spiked punch out of white Styrofoam cups. It being a Friday, both Caroline and I had to go moonlighting, but we put in the requisite appearance. Norman the Chief cornered Caroline by the spiked punch and I tried to work my way over to them, but, having become a star, I kept getting stopped by people who previously hadn't shown the slightest inclination to speak to me, but who now threw arms around my shoulders and wanted to talk about AIDS or simply to touch success.

Because of AIDS, I was being embraced by the group. In my initial role as a polysaccharide gnome, I had one or two friends among the Fellows, but I had been basically ignored, as most Fellows were, and very few of the faculty even knew my name. I was variously referred to as "Bryan," or "Ryan," or "O'Shaughnessy." But now, I could hardly make my way through the crowd with any more speed than Dustin Hoffman on opening night.

When I finally reached Caroline and the Chief, they were laughing like old friends.

"Norman didn't know you moonlighted," Caroline announced when I arrived.

It was "Norman," now. I was his Fellow and I called him "Sir," or at least "Chief," and I wasn't sure he approved of his Fellows moonlighting, although given what he paid us, I didn't see how he could seriously object.

"You are a busy man," said the Chief, smiling, friendly. "I hope, at least, you're digging up some patients for the project out there in the boonies."

I assured him I was and I said I was headed for the very emergency room in question at that moment and had to leave the party.

"Oh, by all means," said the Chief. "Go earn your shekel. I suppose we'll have to make it up to you later."

I thought about that last remark several times that night, and I thought about it as I was driving home from the ER the next morning, and I decided I still didn't know what he meant by it.

Caroline was up, drinking coffee, reading *Cancer* at the breakfast table when I got home Saturday morning. "What he meant," she said, "is that he expects you'll be a professor someday."

"What?"

"Oh, yes. We had quite a chummy little conversation. He thinks we're married or something. He told me all about his plans for your career. You're going to be a professor someday. Maybe you'll even be chief of Infectious Disease at the Massively Degenerate, when Norman gives up the throne."

"You two planned this all out?"

"That's not a certainty, you understand. But it's not beyond the realm of possibility."

"I'll try not to get my hopes up."

"Of course, you'd have to leave for a while. You'd have to do your time in the hinterlands for a while, which is de rigueur. You'll be chief of Medicine somewhere respectable for a few years, then when he's ready to retire, you might be offered his chair right back here at the Massive, and your life will be complete."

"Wonderful," I said. "I haven't thought past next week, and you guys have my whole life planned."

"Oh, that wasn't me talking. I didn't have a chance to say a word. This is all coming from Norman, unsolicited."

"And you simply nodded and drank eggnog."

"I was interested."

"Well, it's heartwarming to learn someone's looking out for my future."

"Somebody ought to," said Caroline. "Besides, Norman thinks you're wonderful."

"Oh, sure. This week."

"No reason to be so cynical. He feels he was the first to recognize your talent. After all, he picked you out of that bleak morass of mediocrity in one of those indistinguishable New York hospitals and made you a Fellow at the Massively Degenerate."

"Ah, a minute's success pays the failure of years. Who said that?"

"You have hardly been failing for years."

"I was not bound for glory until AIDS came around."

"So call it fate. Norman loves you. He wants you to be a great man someday, which, of course, means planting your roots in his own soil."

"He can have it. There's more to life than AIDS."

"One thing you can say for Norman: He's planning for your future, which puts him way ahead of you. Christ knows, somebody has to plan for it. You don't seem inclined."

She was right about that. Somewhere along the line from college to medical school to internship, I had lost the capacity to plot a future course, to project across time spans greater than twenty-four hours. I think it probably started during internship: they gave me an apartment; they told me when to work, when to go home, when to go on vacation, when to sleep and when to eat. And then at the Massively Degenerate, it was more of the same: between the AIDS expeditionary force and moonlighting, my time was organized. I did not sit back with my hands behind my head and think about what life might be like ten years down the road, or even ten days down the road. My time had been claimed and arranged. When you're on the treadmill, you do not sit down and reflect and project—you keep moving.

Caroline said, "In six months, you realize, you will be a free man."

I said, "What do you mean?"

"In six months," she said, "you will be a fully trained specialist in infectious disease. June thirtieth is the last day of your fellowship."

That came as something of a revelation. Of course, warm weather and June seemed far away, but thinking of it as only six months was simply stunning. After eight years of college and medical school, and five more years of internship, residency, and fellowship, I was about to be sprung.

"You can do anything you want," said Caroline.

She was right. And it was a dizzying notion. "You have a point," I said.

Caroline was studying me, and suddenly it occurred to me to ask her: "Have you thought about what you want to do?"

She got up, marched to the sink, and she did not look in my direction. Turning the water on full blast, she attacked the dishes as if she could scrub away my question.

I asked her again.

She said something so quietly, I could not hear her above the sound of the water and the clatter of the dishes.

I walked over and turned off the water. She still was not looking at me. She folded her arms and looked at the floor and said, very quietly: "I've got some options."

"What options?"

"Oh," she said, in exhalation. "A job."

"You've been applying for jobs?"

"Yes," she said, and then added in a rush, "at the National Institutes of Health."

"The NIH?" I echoed. "But that's Washington."

"Bethesda, Maryland, actually," she said, still not looking at me. "The National Cancer Institute."

"When did all this come up?"

"Brendan," Caroline said, meeting my eyes at last. "Wake up."

"But you never told me."

"Brendan, Brendan. The world turns. School days end. We go out into the Real World. We grow up. Personally, I'm really thrilled to get the offer."

"You don't sound thrilled."

"Oh, Brendan," she said, shaking her head, wiping her eyes, "the most they can offer at the Degenerate is a staff nurse position. I've asked. Christ, I have asked."

"Caroline, don't leave me."

"I could see this all coming, with Norman. I knew you'd want to stay. I've called all over Boston. I even tried the community hospitals. There's nothing like this thing at the NIH. I'd be running a program. Five protocols. I'd be like Raskolnovich, down there. We're going to be making breakthroughs."

"But we've been happy."

"Brendan, be reasonable."

"There's more to life than cancer, than the great towering work ethic. There's more to you than your job."

"Brendan, do you even know what you're doing? Have you made any plans at all?"

"I am going into private practice," I said, as if I had thought about this a great deal and had made up my mind ages ago.

"Oh, I see," she said, smiling. "And where are you going to practice?"

"I'm not sure yet. I haven't worked out the details."

"Brendan, life is made of details."

Now it was my turn not to be able to look at her. "I've been really stupid."

She stroked my head. "No, you've just been preoccupied, as usual."

"I don't know," I said. "Somehow, without really thinking about how it would happen, I figured we'd go back to New York eventually, and I'd go into practice with Forrest and you'd have babies."

"Someday," Caroline said, "I would love to have babies. But we are both in debt up to our eyeballs and now is not the time. If I have babies now, I will never go back to work."

"If you go to work, you may never have babies."

"There's plenty of time. The issue is not babies."

"What is the issue?"

"What I am saying," she said, stopping for an intake of breath, "is that we need to be practical."

"Don't go to the NIH, Caroline. The summers are dreadful down there."

"You are not thinking now," Caroline said. "You are just reacting. This is not the way to decide things."

"Tell me what the way is, to decide things."

"We will stop talking about all this for now," Caroline said, trying to sound very controlled and very determined, but the quaver in her voice gave her away. "And each of us will consider, in a moment of calm reflection, what to do."

She dabbed her eyes with a dish towel. They were brimming now, and mine were too.

I opened my mouth, but she raised her fingers to my lips. "No, wait. Let me finish. Right now, it appears, your work is here. You know it is. You can't leave the Massive. Norman will never let you leave. My work, it seems, is at the NIH."

"You're right," I said. "You cannot turn down NIH."

She looked surprised.

"I can't ask you to follow me around like some Dutch diplomat."

"No . . ."

"No, it's true. You are the same woman who gets moved to tears by an article on testicular carcinoma. And I've been selfish. No, the only thing that makes sense—"

"I know."

"Is for me to come with you."

She stared at me for a moment and said, "What did you say?"

"You moved to be with me once. Now it's my turn. I'm moving to Washington. I'll hang out my shingle in the nation's capital."

"But what about Norman? What about the AIDS project?"

"I'm not going to cure AIDS any more than you are going to cure cancer. There'll be plenty of people to do that work, and Boston isn't the only place to do it."

"You ought to think about it," Caroline said, trying to stifle a smile.

"I've thought about it."

"Can you face another U-Haul?"

"Sure, I'll call up Guido, in New York. He'll send up a truck."

"Are you sure about this? Better take some time."

"I'm sure I want to stay with you."

"But why?"

"I think," I said, "you kind of grew on me."

We went out for a walk in the cold January night, down by the hospital and around the neighborhood, past the taverns and past places we had saved for our Sunday nights together. It had snowed all day and it was still snowing, and the town was quiet under the white blanket, except for when a tavern door opened and we could hear laughing from the people inside.

We walked and walked and said nothing. We had come, as Caroline's father might have said, to an agreement in principle.

13

OF JONAS SALK AND
THE REAL WORLD

Every Friday morning, the AIDS task force meeting ended in a disorderly scattering of participants. I was usually able to escape to the computer room with one of the Fellows who had been assigned to the project, but after the first meeting in March, the Chief caught me by the elbow and directed me down the hall and into his office.

I had a pretty good idea what was coming, and I was as twitchy as a dowager with a full bladder and all the powder rooms occupied.

"What was that all about?" the Chief asked. His voice was controlled, but his eyes were dark and he was not happy.

"What was all what about?" I said, all innocence. That was the wrong ploy, and I could see it in his look, which turned suddenly molten. "Okay," I said. "I said it was a good idea to bring more people into the recruitment phase. It is a good idea."

"Administrative decisions are my job, O'Brien. When I want your opinion about how the study is organized, I'll ask. Don't go shooting off your mouth in task force meetings. Infectious Disease speaks with one voice. And that voice is mine."

"But the way you've got it now," I said, all conciliation and reason, "I'm the only one recruiting subjects."

"And that's the way I want it."

"But they're all worried about that."

"They just want a piece of the pie. ID got way out ahead of them on AIDS. They're all Johnny-come-latelies. We set the whole thing up and now they want to be sure they've got their hooks in the meat."

"At least let some other ID Fellows do some recruiting."

"Why? You feeling overburdened?"

"The whole project shouldn't depend on me."

"What's the matter? The responsibility overwhelms you, or what?"

There was no way to get out of it now. I had been dropping large-sized hints, but I had not been able to march myself into the Chief's office and sit down and confront him. But there were now only four months left.

"What happens," I said, "when I leave?"

The creases in the Chief's face deepened and his eyes burned under his bushy brow. "What do you mean?" he growled. "Leave?"

"I'm talking about July," I said.

"What about July?"

Caroline had warned me about this. "Norman," she'd said, "is going to apply pressure."

"What pressure?" I had said, ingenuously. "He doesn't have a thing over me. He's already signed my form for the boards. He can't hold up my fellowship diploma, not at this late date."

"He will find a way," Caroline said. "And I'm not sure he'd be so wrong."

Norman the Chief now examined me with a look which mixed disapprobation and respect, the sort of look a tycoon father might cast upon his only son who had just announced he was not going to take over the family steel mills but would handcraft surfboards in Malibu instead.

"What do you mean?" His voice was low and rumbling. "When you leave, in July?"

"When I leave, somebody has to be able to step in and take over."

"What leave? What are you talking about?"

"You know what I'm talking about."

"Humor me. Tell me about it."

"July first, my fellowship ends. The project—"

"Your fellowship ends," growled the Chief, "when I say so."

That wasn't much of a card, but he played it, just for the effect.

"My fellowship ends in July," I said.

"Am I hearing this right?" he said. "I thought I was working with someone who was committed here. I thought this thing mattered to you."

"It has and it does," I said. I thought I sounded cool as an alcohol bath, but my left foot was beginning to twitch and jump. "But all things end."

"If all you wanted to do was a little stint, put in your time, you could have done your fellowship at Islip General or Podunk. I gave you a spot in the best ID program in the country. You know how many applications we had for your spot? You know how many from just within this institution alone?"

I contemplated all those applications, and I reflected upon the intimate connection between academic reputation and financial distress.

The Chief was just getting warmed up. "But," he croaked, "I thought I saw something special in you. And you had me going for a while, you really did."

This was going to be worse than I had expected. There was nothing I could do but take it. It was going to be the full court press, in the style of the Best Medical Institution in the World.

"Yeah," said the Chief, leaning back and shoving his hand into his pocket, searching for a pipe, not finding it, patting other pockets, and growing more frantic, hands shaking, and all the while his eyes fastened on mine, his voice growing tremulous. "You had me suckered. I really thought you were the genuine article. I told people that, too. Told Caroline. Told the Dean. Told everyone. You saw this AIDS thing coming even before I did. You had it all organized. Remember how you made up that computer program? I looked at that list of patients you had organized and followed all by yourself, all on your own, when nobody would even listen to you. I thought, here is a guy with guts, a guy with vision, who is really going places. Here is a guy who is really going to do some significant work. Someday we'll all be saying, 'I worked with Brendan O'Brien. Yeah, I knew him when.'" He shook his head slowly. "I thought bringing this plague to heel meant something to you."

He paused to give me a chance to open my mouth and make things worse. I didn't take the bait.

"But no," he said, voice choked. "All you were interested in was putting in your time, taking your exam and getting your paper to hang up on your mahogany-paneled wall, in your sumptuous Park Avenue office, making sure your slice of the pie is a real big fat one."

He found his pipe on the ashtray near his elbow, paused to dip it into a rubber tobacco pouch and looked at me as he lit it. The whole sequence was silent and calculated and the seconds went by on tiptoe and I was shifting and squirming in my chair by the time he started speaking again.

"What is it you want from life, O'Brien? You want to spend twenty years driving fancy cars, spending weekends in your big place in the country and throwing tax deductible parties catered by little men in black tuxedos for all the guys who trade patients with you? You want your ten weeks vacation and your trips to Europe on the Cunard Line? Why didn't you go to business school, O'Brien?"

I sighed.

"I want to know," said the Chief. "Really, I want to know. What the hell did you think you were doing here these two years? I mean, you think you can just dabble in this pestilence and enter a few numbers into a computer and then, when the clock sounds, you just drop it all and let 'em all die and go to hell? And you go out and buy yourself a closetful of Brooks Brothers suits and never look back."

"It won't wash, Chief," I said. "I don't have to apologize to you or anyone for not wanting to live on grant money the rest of my life. There are many paths to heaven, Chief. I told you about Seymour Freudenberg. I should live to be half the doc he was."

"How many docs ever have the chance to make a really big contribution? Those guys you're talking about are living ordinary lives. They get their kicks from the little things in life: buying a new car, a bigger house, another suit. Those guys in private practice are there for a reason. Their chance went by them, and they know it. Either they never had the talent to really make it, or they never knew how, or they were just in the wrong place. It's not everyone who can be a Fleming and discover penicillin. But you've got the talent. You've got everything it takes."

"I'm not going to turn the tide against AIDS, Chief."

"How do you know? Suppose Pasteur had said that? Suppose he decided he'd rather spend his summers on the Riviera? It's not just gray matter that raises a guy to greatness, it's the values you live your life by. What are you gonna have, thirty years from now, you go into private practice?"

"A life," I said. "My own life."

"You don't think you could have a life here?"

"Not the kind I want."

"What the hell's that supposed to mean?"

"Chief, you own all the people in your section. Not because you're paying their salaries. They got to go to the NIH for that. But you control them. I'm just not much of a team player, not in the long run. I'm happy to have had a role here, but come July, I'm gone."

The Chief heaved a massive sigh and suddenly he looked very sad. He looked at the floor and then he looked up at me again, this time smiling sweetly.

"I heard Dave Garroway introduce Jonas Salk once," he said, as if we'd been talking about nothing more important than the cafeteria menu. "I ever tell you about that?"

"No," I said. I couldn't help myself, I was liking him again. There was a lot of theater in his rage, but there was something else, too. He would have no trouble finding another Fellow to replace me. I wasn't indispensable. But something about my choice was personally important to him: it was as if he were justifying his own life choices to me. If he could just convince me to spurn the world of private, commercial medicine, to embrace university life, he would be vindicated. My choice seemed the most important thing in the world to him.

"Yeah, Dave Garroway," said the Chief. "You're too young to remember him, but he was like Johnny Carson or maybe Walter Cronkite or someone. Dave Garroway gets up on the dais and he says he was getting dressed to come to this dinner to introduce Jonas Salk and he still hadn't figured out what he was going to say. And he's putting on his tuxedo and tying his bow tie and his little kid, seven years old, comes in and asks him what he's doing. His little kid knows the tux is special, see. So Garroway says, 'I'm going to introduce Jonas Salk.' And his kid says, 'Who's Jonas Salk?' And Garroway says, 'He's the man who came up with the vaccine, the cure for polio.' And the kid says, 'What's polio, Dad?' And by this time, of course, the whole audience is so quiet you can hear a pin drop and Garroway says, 'Can you imagine any seven-year-old of our generation who didn't know what polio was?' "

The Chief had tears in his eyes. I did, too, damned if I didn't. He let me think about Dave Garroway and Jonas Salk and the little kid who'd never even heard of polio.

"The history of man on this earth," the Chief said, "is, for the most part, pretty uninspiring. All those kings and dictators and strongmen: just a bunch of cavemen hitting each other over the head with clubs. I never could get very interested, you know? They were all doing pretty much the same thing, through the ages, for pretty much the same reasons, when you get right down to it. But there have been some men who've really made this world different. I'm not talking about changing some line on a map. I'm talking about guys who really changed life the way every little guy leads it. Jonas Salk was one of those men. You won't ever have to live with that fear that your kid's gonna wind up in some iron lung. And that guy Raskolnovich, Caroline was telling me about, the guy comes up with a new combination of the same old drugs we had on the shelf, but this combo works—and all those wards at Whipple Hospital filled with guys dying from testicular CA, all empty now."

I kept telling myself to just get through this, the way you sit through the preacher's eulogy at a funeral. Just sit there and take it and don't say a word.

"So don't make up your mind so fast," the Chief said. "You're a little angry with me, 'cause I butted into your life. I control people, you said. No, I don't control anyone. Everyone in this section is here because he agrees with me about one thing, and that's what's important in life is not how much your portfolio's worth. What you're worth in this life has nothing to do with your portfolio."

He let me go then.

That evening, I drove the long drive to the emergency room thinking how I wouldn't have to make that drive after July, and thinking how I wouldn't regret that one bit. I thought about my fellowship and I thought about Jonas Salk and I thought about Caroline and about Raskolnovich and about people I hadn't thought about for a long time. I damn near drove off the road, seeing faces I hadn't seen for ages. Vince Montebelli, Professor Toomey, and Mrs. Roundtree.

I sewed up three drunks in the ER that night, gave one old man penicillin for his pneumonia. If it hadn't been for some medical giant, there wouldn't have been penicillin and that old man probably would have died from his pneumonia. Around one a.m. a young homosexual rolled in, short of breath, chest X ray looking like a snowstorm. Probably pneumocystis pneumonia and AIDS. I called the Massively Degenerate and arranged for his transfer.

He asked me, "They can take care of me, huh, Doc?"

"Sure," I said. "They'll give you medicine for your pneumonia."

"But they'll get me better, right?"

And I thought, no. No, nobody at the Massively Degenerate will be able to do a thing to really make you better. We will treat the pneumonia, which will regress, this time, but eventually, the virus that stripped away your immune system will leave you naked in the world and you will die. And nobody at the World's Best Hospital will be able to do a thing about it.

The men who will find the cure will not find it in time for you. They will be men working in virus laboratories, maybe they'll be working with genetic splicing. But they won't be running around enlisting patients and following their blood counts on computer screens.

The next morning I drove home knowing that in July, I would be leaving Boston, pursuing an ordinary life in the Real World.

14

WRITE YOUR OWN TICKET

I was not the only Fellow trained by the Chief who had fallen from grace and left the ivory tower for that great seething caldron of commercial medicine. Spencer Clark Wriston III, MD, had preceded me, years before my defection from the ranks of the elect. Wriston had kissed good-bye the prospects of ascending to chairmanship, gaining editorial board membership, finding his place in medical history, winning the Nobel prize, being introduced by Dave Garroway—all of it—in favor of seeking the rewards of private practice.

The Chief, of course, never mentioned Spencer Clark Wriston III, but I found out. Dr. Wriston spoke to me from his car phone in Washington, D.C.

He said, "You can't learn anything by telephone. Come on down this weekend. We'll talk. It's a nice time now in Washington. Azaleas are in bloom."

"He said he'd meet me at his office at six," I told Caroline. "He said, 'Y'all come down. The azaleas are in bloom.'"

"It's the South," said Caroline. "You have to learn how to tolerate people who talk like that. He's going to offer you a job."

"Nonsense," I said. "He doesn't know the first thing about me," I said. "All he knows is I trained at the Massively Degenerate and he knows the Massively Degenerate is the best hospital in the world. He knows that because he trained there himself, and they spent two years drumming it into him."

But, underneath, I thought Caroline might just be right. Why, after all, would he invite me down? If he was simply trying to be polite, he could have said, "Drop in to see me once you move down." I was trying to suppress my own soaring hopes, but Caroline's unsolicited conclusion made it seem like kismet. "He's just being nice," I told her.

"He needs help. He's looking for some bright, well-trained

young infectious disease guy to help shoulder the burden. And you've got the right merit badges. You are a catch, a find, a rising star. He wants to bask in your luster."

"He's already got three young guys working with him. They just added the fourth last year."

"He's desperate," said Caroline. "He needs you. That's why he wants you to come down in person, so he can look you over. He's going to offer you a job," Caroline insisted smugly. "He's going to offer you a starting salary in six figures for the first year. Then full partnership. I can see it now: We'll be able to afford a subscription to *The Washington Post* and have it delivered to our door! It'll be so nice to have money again. One thing I've learned the past two years is that poverty is not romantic. It's just shabby and cold and ulcerogenic and no fun at all."

We both arranged to take off Saturday and we flattened our bank account for the plane fare down to Washington.

"This little trip is going to strain our cash flow," I said. "What with the loss of the weekend moonlighting income, the plane fare, whatever we spend down there."

"Consider it a business investment," said Caroline. "It takes money to make money."

She sounded very confident, but I knew she was worried about the cash too. We had to save for the move, and we were cutting things close as it was. We had decided it might be necessary for Caroline to move down to Bethesda and work for a month, to get her first paycheck so we could rent the U-Haul, but neither of us liked that idea, and we hadn't worked out the details.

"Maybe, if he offers you a job," said Caroline, "he'll offer to pay for the move."

"Oh, come on."

"No, I've heard they do that sometimes. They'll actually pay for a real mover to move you."

"From Boston to Washington? That'd be a thousand dollars, maybe."

"I'm telling you: Susie Goldstein's husband, what's his name? You know, in cardiology—they moved them to Texas, all expenses paid."

"He went to work for some big clinic. A hundred doctors. This is different."

"Maybe you should go to work for a big clinic."

"Do they have those in Washington?"

"That's one thing we'll find out."

From the air, the city looked like a postcard, all the monuments and famous buildings. It was much greener that time of year than Boston, and it looked very manicured.

We took the subway from the airport and got out at Foggy Bottom, face-to-face with the George Washington University Hospital.

"What an omen," said Caroline. "The first thing we see when actually setting foot in the city: a hospital."

"An omen, but good or bad?"

"Will you stop that? That hospital is a welcome mat."

The plan was to look at apartments, not necessarily to sign a lease, but to scout the terrain, until my appointment with Wriston. I was all for taking the subway out to Bethesda.

"Bethesda is the suburbs," Caroline said. "I will not live in the burbs."

"But your job is in Bethesda," I said. "And I am currently unemployed."

"This will change. Your practice will be downtown, and we will live in the city."

We headed for Georgetown. Caroline knew Washington, more or less, from her intervals in the city when her father was awaiting reassignment. We walked along Pennsylvania Avenue until it turned into M Street. It was a sunny spring day and I took off my raincoat and carried it. We had dressed too warmly. It was still cold in Boston, but it was spring in Washington. The sky was a single shade of blue. People were out on the sidewalks, enjoying the weather. Well-dressed couples our age strolled along in cotton shirts and sweaters, looking happy and affluent.

Georgetown rents were simply not to be believed. An apartment in Georgetown was out, although we did have a very nice lunch there at Au Pied de Cochon. Caroline looked over the real estate ads at the restaurant table and outlined our itinerary. We walked out of Georgetown and back to the subway. We looked at a few places on Connecticut Avenue.

"What a lovely street," said Caroline as we walked past the outdoor restaurants. Spencer Clark Wriston III knew what he was talking about: azaleas were in fact in bloom and a lot of other things were blooming and the city looked lush and green and quite wonderful.

"To think we can just move here," said Caroline. "No applications. No committee of admissions."

"At least one of us has a job," I said.

We walked along the broad sidewalks and looked at the grand old apartment buildings. We even went in a few, where they had vacancies. The prices were better than Georgetown and you got more for it, but they were still quadruple what we were paying in Boston.

"Makes our landlady look a lot better," said Caroline. "Even if she doesn't believe in heat in the winter."

The rents were better along Wisconsin Avenue. We walked toward the cathedral until we came to a cluster of brick buildings that looked like upscale army barracks.

"If this ad is right," said Caroline, "this is more our speed."

"I don't want to live here," I said, looking at the buildings.

"Let's look. We're not signing anything."

"What's the point?"

The first apartment they showed us was magnificent. They had redone the inside of the buildings, and the one they showed us was a three-floor walk-up, top floor, with skylights and a loft and polished hardwood floors and everything looked brand-new and there were big windows and the place was flooded with sunlight.

"It's only twice what we pay in Boston," said Caroline.

"It's just too much," I said. "I can't be an unemployed bum and have you supporting me in this kind of splendor. Let's look in Bethesda. Maybe they have some hovel there. Some humble garden apartment."

"I'd rather live in a tent. And I, at least, will be gainfully employed."

We wandered through the neighborhood around the apartment. Standing on Wisconsin Avenue, we heard the cathedral bells chiming.

"I love it," said Caroline, throwing her arms around me. "And Georgetown is only a mile that way. It's a wonderful neighborhood. Let's go sign that lease."

"Caroline, we've only just arrived."

We crossed Wisconsin Avenue and Caroline peered at an ugly brick building and laughed. "It's a nursing home." She dragged me toward it. "If you don't join Spencer Clark Wriston, the third, you can start your practice at the nursing home."

"A fate worse than death," I said.

"Let's go back and sign the lease." Caroline was glowing. She was grinning from ear to ear, holding my arm.

"Are you out of your mind?"

"We can afford it."

"But we ought to think about it."

"How many trips down here can we afford? We found a place we like and we can afford it. This may be the last time we can get down here."

"*You* can afford it. I'm a bum. If you lose your job, we're insolvent."

"Okay, I'll sign for it. You can be my tenant."

We went back and signed. They asked what I did for a living and Caroline did not laugh, although it took everything she had not to. I said I was a physician entering the private practice of medicine and they didn't ask any more questions, foolish people.

We walked back to the subway and Caroline said, "Don't worry about the money," she said. "We'll be okay. You'll see. Go to your appointment with Spencer Clark Wriston, the third."

15

THE TELEPHONIC PHYSICIAN

The waiting room for Dr. Spencer Clark Wriston III's office was just short of sumptuous: no extravagance, nothing that would make you ask what kinds of fees these guys must wring out of their ailing patients. Just simple, quiet quality and a great deal of tone. The carpet was some peach color, clean, deep, and soft, the sort of carpet you want to lie down on and roll around. There was original art on the walls, oils mostly, which picked up the peach motif and enriched it with shades of brown, green, all muted and very lovely. The lights were on, but there were no secretaries.

Spencer Clark Wriston III, MD, came out from behind a door to the waiting room and said, "I thought I heard someone prowling around out here. You must be Brendan."

He offered me a warm hand and I tried to study him without being too obvious. Blond, light blue eyes, ruddy cheeks and white teeth, impossible to guess his age, although I knew from my inquiries among the Degenerate faculty that he was just fifty. Gray suit, white shirt, Movado watch, everything understated, expensive. He offered me coffee, which I refused, and he led me back to his consulting office. I took a chair on the patient's side of his desk and he swung into his high-backed chair and we looked at each other across the desk.

"How was your flight?"

"Wonderful," I said. "Anytime the plane does not crash, I consider it a wonderful flight."

He laughed. "You're an easy man to please."

The phone rang on one of the four lines, a back line, I imagine.

He answered. It was evidently a call he was expecting, something about what antibiotic to use for a patient. He was talking to another doctor. His distraction with the phone call gave me a chance to examine his office walls, which were covered with the requisite diplomas: University of Maryland undergraduate, Medical College of Virginia, and the big Massively Degenerate diploma from his postgraduate training. He finished his call and hung up.

"It never ends," he said. "And I'm not even on call. I had plans to go see the Postimpressionist exhibit down at the National Gallery and come back to chat with you. But I made one mistake: I stopped off at the hospital and wrote a note. Never got out of the hospital. Should have known better. If they see you, they won't take no for an answer. Three consults, just making rounds."

"Sounds like you're busy."

"Oh." He laughed. "We are that. And more."

His group covered five hospitals: the Medical Center, across town, one university hospital, and three community hospitals, one in Virginia, one in Bethesda, and one in Gaithersburg. They were busy, all right, just driving between hospitals could take all day.

"The car phone is essential equipment." He laughed. "We each have one and one backup. If we ever lost the car phones, I don't know how we'd manage."

"But what happens if you get home from Gaithersburg and you're starting rounds in Arlington and a new consult rolls in back in Gaithersburg?"

"That's what the phone is for," laughed Spencer Clark Wriston III. "You can cover a lot of territory over the phone. Mostly it's just nurses out there in the community hospitals. I just admitted a lady with acute pyelo out at Gaithersburg, through the ER. The nurse called, says she's got a lady with left flank pain and a temp and a white count. I order the IVP and an hour later, nurse calls back and says it's a pyelo, and I call in the orders. You can do it. You just have to become very efficient."

Yes, I agreed, efficiency was essential. Being very efficient meant that the lady in Gaithersburg was admitted to the hospital, had an X ray of her kidney with contrast, which rarely, but not all that rarely, causes fatal allergic reactions, got an IV put in her arm and antibiotics pushed into that IV and was never examined by her doctor and would not even see him until the next morning. Telephone medicine. Big-time private practice in the nation's capital.

I could see even if Spencer Clark Wriston III offered me immediate full partnership in his group, starting the next day at a six-figure salary, I was not going to be able to accept. Busy is one thing. This was quite another.

I asked him about moonlighting jobs and he gave me a few

names I might check for contract work with the government. "But why do contract work?" he asked.

"Well, I'm new in town. I haven't trained here. I don't know any docs. It's going to take some time for me to get started, once I hang out a shingle."

"Aw, shucks, you're not going to have any trouble. You're an authority on AIDS, and AIDS is going to be big. Our group has five guys doing nothing but ID right now. We figure with AIDS, we're going to need to double that within five years. I hope to hell I'm wrong, of course, but this AIDS thing ain't going to just disappear like some bad dream. Every ID doc in town is going to be busy."

"How did you know I worked on AIDS?"

"Norman told me." He said. "You didn't think I'd invite you down here without talking to Norman first. Norman says you're first-rate."

I stopped myself from gulping and choking, and stammering, "He did?" I stared bugeyed at Wriston.

Wriston didn't seem to notice my surprise. He said: "Why don't you think about joining us?"

"I'd have to think about it," I said, having no intention of thinking about it. I was not going to be put in the position of having to cover five hospitals by telephone. Then I thought about Caroline, and about our flat bank account, and I thought about what she would say about not cutting off options and remaining pleasant. I said, "It's real nice of you."

"Of course, you'll want to meet the other guys in the group. We'd have to be sure we have a certain comfort level. But you're very well trained and meeting you now, I don't think there'd be any problem."

He'd hardly asked a question of me. Apparently questions had little to do with whether or not I'd be acceptable. He'd got my schools and training and report card from the Chief, and all that mattered was how I looked. Maybe whether I looked white, not black, and maybe it was my Brooks Brothers jacket. I didn't know.

I kept thinking about the Chief's giving me a good report. The Chief, who made me feel I had betrayed the deepest values of medical ethics by simply considering private practice, had given me his seal of approval.

"Well," I said, trying to force myself to think rather than simply react. Don't be impulsive. Don't be rash. Don't say what you feel. Say what you'll be happy for later. "This is something we both ought to think about."

We chatted about the Massively Degenerate and about the little sandwich shop around the corner from the hospital that Wriston was happy to learn was still in business. I walked past it every day, carrying my peanut butter and jelly sandwich. I couldn't afford to buy lunch there, even at the sandwich shop prices, but I didn't tell Spencer Clark Wriston III that.

He walked me to the elevator and we shook hands and said good-bye.

I met Caroline at a bar called the 21st Amendment on Pennsylvania Avenue. She was sitting alone at a booth near the bar and she waved me over and I slid in next to her and I saw her face was full of hope.

"Well?"

"He has a very pretty office. Peach carpet."

"Did he talk starting salary, stock options, or did he just ask about your research?"

"Actually, he knew all about my research before I stepped in the room."

Caroline beamed. "He reads the medical literature. A good sign."

"Not exactly: he got it all from Norman."

"Norman!" Caroline winced.

"Norman told him I was a good man."

Caroline's face softened. "Good old Norman." Then she studied me a bit and asked, "So what's the scoop? You didn't really like him, did you?"

"He's pleasant enough. He's just not exactly Seymour Freudenberg."

"Nobody's Seymour Freudenberg."

"I don't think I'll be joining Spencer Clark Wriston, the third, MD, in practice anytime soon."

Caroline stared at me over her Manhattan. She took a long sip and set her glass down. "Hello? Is this fear-of-insolvency O'Brien, turning down a golden opportunity?"

"He did give me some leads on some moonlighting jobs," I said. "All is not lost."

"But what about the job? Details."

I gave her details. I told her about the five hospitals, the telephone admission.

"He admitted this lady to the hospital," Caroline said, incredulous, "without even going in to see her? What kind of hospital would even let him do that?"

"Community hospitals. Spencer Clark covers two of them."

"Well, scratch Spencer Clark Wriston, the third, MD."

"What about our lease?"

"Let me worry about the lease. You'll work nursing homes and contract jobs until the word gets out you're in town and the world beats a path to your door."

"That could be a long wait, Caroline."

"I know," she said, looking off in the direction of the bar. "Nobody knows you here. If you're going into private practice, it's like opening a business." She sighed. "People have to know your name, if they're going to line up to buy your services. In New York, you'd have all your friends referring you patients. All those guys you trained with. You and Forrest would have a practice in no time. In Boston, you'd have a practice the instant you hung out a shingle. An AIDS practice, but a practice."

"I guess it looks like the nursing home after all."

"I can't stand the thought of your being unhappy down here," Caroline said. "Doing nursing homes, after all you've been through. All the high-powered training. Did you stay up all night at Whipple, pulling Vince Montebelli through gram-negative sepsis and DIC and bringing Professor Toomey down from outer space, so you could treat constipation in some nursing home? I hate thinking you've got to do that because of me."

"You did the same thing when we went to Boston."

"I did not. I loved my program. Of course, I'll spend the rest of my life paying off the loans, but I got a master's out of it. And now, I'm going to be doing just what I want, dream job."

"I'll find something."

"Yeah, nursing homes. While Spencer Wriston the third packs in the carriage trade in his plush downtown offices."

"What I don't understand is why he spreads himself so thin. I mean, from the looks of that place he can pay his bills. Why not keep the practice close to home?"

"He's after something you don't even think about yet. Something you don't know about: money."

"Yeah, but telephonic medicine?"

"I don't know," Caroline said. "Maybe this whole thing isn't such a good idea."

"Is that what you want?"

"No."

"You haven't heard me complaining about nursing homes, have you? I'd consider a nursing home real progress, after the emergency room."

She laughed. It was a nice, sweet, full-bodied laugh and she kept her eyes on me the whole time. "You're okay, O'Brien."

"You don't mind about the job, then? I suppose I ought to talk to them about it. Maybe the rest of them aren't like Wriston."

"Forget it," said Caroline. "Four guys covering five hospitals from Arlington to Gaithersburg: how good could they be? How much could they care?"

"I saw a copy of his daily schedule. He had it on his desk. I peeked at it while he was on the phone. It was his Friday schedule. He saw twenty-eight patients. One every fifteen minutes, and an hour off for lunch."

"He must think very deeply about those patients."

"If he does, he thinks very quickly."

"Twenty-eight patients a day." Caroline shook her head. "You think he knows who they are? You think he'd know one, if he bumped into her at a cocktail party?"

"I don't know," I said. "Maybe that's private practice."

"I cannot imagine Seymour Freudenberg ever scheduling a patient every fifteen minutes and flying by them all."

"It's the Real World."

"Not for you," said Caroline. "You stay pure. You do good medicine. We won't starve."

"It would be nice," I said. "To have money."

"Don't start off your medical career," said Caroline, "by selling out."

— 16 —

THE LIMA BEAN

Leaving Boston was not what I had expected. I had expected to have to sneak out under cover of night. But a week before July first, Norman's secretary told me the Chief wanted to see me. He was sitting behind his desk, with his back toward me, and he swung around in his swivel chair, and stood up when I came in. He took his pipe from his mouth and I couldn't tell from his expression whether he intended to throw it at me or if he just was preparing to say something. He said, "That's for you," and gestured with his pipe at a gift-wrapped box on his desk.

This was the first time I had been alone with Norman since my return from Washington. At conferences since then, he had been businesslike and wasted no emotion on me, and I was grateful he had decided to allow me simply to fade quietly from the scene. But here was a box for me, and it was gift-wrapped. I picked it up tentatively.

"Go ahead. Open it," he said. "It's not ticking."

I unwrapped a leather-bound volume and opened it. He had collected every journal article bearing my name and had them bound. Norman had collected them all and sent them off to the bindery. And he had a title page printed up: *Collected Works of Brendan O'Brien, MD.* Below this he had written, "If a little knowledge is dangerous, where is the man who has so much as to be out of danger?—T. H. Huxley."

As I held that collection of papers in my hand, it struck me how much we had done in two years, Norman, me, the whole department.

"I liked it better when you were yelling at me," I said. My voice cracked. "This is really more than I deserve."

"Don't I know it," Norman grunted, trying to sound irascible, but failing miserably. "You did a nice job here, Brendan," he said.

"Thanks."

"I'll miss having you around."

I mumbled something, I don't remember what, and I slinked out of there.

Caroline listened to the whole story that night, thumbing through the leather-bound volume, shaking her head.

She said, "I feel like I'm breaking up a marriage and a home."

"We really did do some good work," I said.

"Look," Caroline said. "Maybe you ought to stay. There's a Boston–Washington shuttle. Lots of couples do it."

"Oh, no. The world of Boston academia can turn without me." I wrapped my arms around her. "Infectious Diseases Enterprises is opening for business in the nation's capital, arriving by U-Haul trailer this July. You and I have a date with the Real World."

Moving was not so bad. We hired two Boston College kids to haul the furniture and do the muscle work, and that made all the difference. They hauled our stuff down three flights in Boston, and up three flights in Washington. Caroline started work, and I scouted around for office space, shook a lot of hands and pressed my card into the palm of anyone who was willing to take it.

By mid-July we had the apartment set up. Sundays, the tones of the cathedral bells floated through the windows and we read *The New York Times* together in our sunny living room. Then we walked down the steep hill into Georgetown, toward the river. The sidewalks were alive with women in brightly colored African dresses, men in turbans, and you could hear languages you couldn't even guess at all along the way.

On Caroline's salary, we could afford to eat in restaurants again.

"Lord, what a marvelous city," Caroline said. "There's no end to exotic cuisine."

I will be forever grateful for August and the Washington heat. Doctors leave Washington in droves in August, and no sooner had I introduced myself to three older physicians in my building than they asked if I'd like to cover their practices while they were out of town. Patients streamed into my waiting room and there were people writing my name on their checks. This was a very strange sensation at first, being handed a check for telling a woman she had a sinusitis and writing her two prescriptions. People paid me for telling them things I used to chat about in the hospital cafeteria.

"You'll learn to live with it," said Caroline.

I had a lot to learn about private practice. The first shock was that all those little things I had always taken for granted at the university hospitals, like office space, secretaries, phones, beepers, furniture, lab supplies, stationery, even the pictures you hang on your wall, all of them cost money. And the money in private practice comes from your patients, or, if you're lucky, from their insurance companies. Patients have a disarming way of waving their Blue Cross cards around as if they were credit cards. The trouble is, the great blue insurance companies in the sky do not guarantee payment.

Those first months, money cluttered up my mind. It was a relief to be able to sit across the desk from a patient and to listen to his symptoms and think about medicine. Cash flow, debt servicing, commercial space, income projections, hospital privileges, geographic positioning, independent practice associations, preferred provider organizations, were all new words and concepts, and I didn't have a clue.

"Ask your father," Caroline said. "He's run his own business. He ought to know about these things. Besides, we're all moved in and he lives forty minutes away and I've never met the man."

So we had my father down for dinner.

Caroline cooked and we had a very nice time and he extolled Caroline's food and he asked about Caroline's job and about my practice. But he didn't offer any direction, which, for my father, was something of a rarity. My father would give you advice on deep-sea fishing and he'd never set foot on a boat.

Caroline and I walked him out to his car to say good-bye. Then she made some excuse and she went back, leaving us alone.

"Only advice I got for you," my father told me, "is get a new car."

"Why? This one's still moving."

"Look at it." We were standing next to it in the parking lot. It was a pretty beat-up old heap. "Would you go to a doctor drives a car like this? You drive this thing into the doctors' parking lot at the hospital and other doctors see you, who's gonna refer you patients?"

"It's not the car, Dad. It's the brain that drives the car."

"Well, you'd know more about that. But I know people, and nothing succeeds like success."

"What's the verdict?" Caroline asked, as soon as I walked through the door.

"He thinks I need a new car."

Caroline washed dishes and I dried.

"No, I mean about tonight."

"He thinks you're a great cook."

"He likes me?"

"My father likes any woman who's a great cook."

"Oh, well," she said, "at least he didn't call me intriguing."

Caroline loved her job. She took the subway to work, and I picked her up, and she was always surrounded by doctors and patients and I could see from those glimpses she had become an important part of the team. I, on the other hand, had become a hermit. Solo practice is an isolated, lonely pursuit, especially when you don't have enough business to justify hiring employees. I did hire a secretary, and patients occasionally wandered in, just often enough to keep me from folding my tent. But I did not feel needed, and after so many years at busy hospitals, that was a disturbing sensation. But I had prospects, and Caroline kept telling me not to worry, and I really enjoyed those few lost souls who strayed into my office. I had time to organize my slide collection for the lectures I only rarely got invited to give, and I had time to read the journals, to follow what Norman and the group back at the Massive were doing.

And I had time for Caroline. In the evenings and on weekends, we went exploring. Down Massachusetts Avenue, there was the Vice-President's house, with all its comings and goings, and farther along were the embassies: the sprawling British consulate with the statue of Churchill, the South African Chancery with the lines of protesters. Caroline loved walking through a neighborhood called Cleveland Park with all the Victorian homes with their turrets and verandas. The trees there were big oaks and elms and an occasional sycamore, and in the summer the light came through their leaves green and filtered, but in the winter they threw long shadows. It reminded us of New England.

"Do you think we'll ever live in one of those?" Caroline said, one Sunday in early March. We were standing in front of a big one, with a wraparound screened-in porch. It had snowed, and there was that quiet snow can bring.

"Not at the rate I'm going," I said. "You don't start off with one of those anyway. You buy a starter home in AU Park, when you have your first kid."

"Maybe we ought to walk over to AU Park."

I went on, perfectly oblivious of what she was trying to say.

"I don't know how people ever buy houses. You've got to project so far ahead."

"We ought to be looking now," she said.

"I thought you liked our place."

"I love our place, but it's a three-floor walk-up and I can't see doing that with a bag of groceries in one arm, dragging junior with the other."

This took a while to sink in. We walked another block as the idea gained shape in my mind and finally grabbed hold.

"You trying to tell me something?"

Her eyes were shining.

"Yes, you idiot."

"You're kidding, of course."

"Do I look like I'm kidding?"

She did not look as if she was kidding.

"You're late this month?"

"I am late and I'm going to get later," she said. "Two beta HCGs do not lie."

She had done the blood tests at work.

"Oh," I said.

"Is that 'Oh,' as in 'Oh, golly, how great!' or 'Oh,' as in 'Christ, she's pregnant. Now what?' "

"Just, oh."

"This really doesn't have to change things," Caroline said. "About us, I mean."

I stopped and looked at her.

"I cannot believe what an idiot I am," she said. "That diaphragm is five years old and they tell you to check it every two."

I wasn't sure what to say.

"You're not worried, are you? Because I'm not at all worried. This doesn't have to change anything. We'll be just the same."

"Of course we will. We'll be fine. All three of us."

"You seem pretty calm," she said, eyeing me. "I thought you'd faint dead away. I could not believe it. I am like clockwork, and then suddenly, no period."

"It is pretty hard to believe."

"Not for me. It was the nausea, every morning. But it didn't occur to me, for a week."

"You've been nauseated?"

"Vomiting every morning the last three days. I was so afraid you'd hear me."

"Afraid? Why?"

"Then you'd know. You'd figure it out."

"What did you think I'd do?"

"I didn't know. I thought you'd feel trapped."

"Trapped?"

"Do you?"

"Why?"

"Because, you don't have to. I can have it. You don't need to. You don't have to have anything to do with it."

"Are you out of your mind?"

"It's all my fault. I don't know how I could be so stupid."

"You are not stupid. You're just pregnant. Think of it as a gift."

She took my arm and said, "That's a very nice thing to say."

We turned around and headed back for our apartment.

"How long have you known?" I asked.

"About a week."

"Why didn't you tell me?"

"I don't know. I didn't know what to do. I knew I had to keep it. I just couldn't do away with it."

"But why didn't you tell me?"

"I felt I'd let you down."

"You don't need an obstetrician. You need a psychiatrist."

"You have so much to worry about, right now. I thought you'd go right off the deep end. You've been so worried about the money. But you don't have to. I have it all figured out. I can take maternity leave for six weeks, and we can make it."

"We'll make it. Kids aren't that expensive."

"I looked in a book," she said. "It's about the size of a large pea. Maybe a lima bean."

"A lima bean?"

"Oh, Brendan," she said suddenly. "What're we going to do?" For once it was Caroline who seemed at a loss.

"I think the lima bean might appreciate it if we got married."

"But it's all so tacky, getting stamped and registered."

"We'd better do it anyway," I said. "For the lima bean."

We walked, and our apartment came into view.

"I could go off and just have it."

"My son? I should say not. He will be brought into the world in happiness and I intend to be there to be the first to shake his hand."

"What makes you so sure it's a he?"

"That's all we ever have in my family."

"And you're not at all disturbed?"

"Disturbed? We are talking about new life, the passing on of genetic material, immortality. Why should I be upset? Except, of course, I haven't the faintest idea how we're going to afford this lima bean."

Caroline laughed. "We'll make it. People who drive cabs have kids."

"They probably make a profit. My practice . . ."

"The lima bean will not starve."

We arrived at the stoop in front of our apartment and Caroline sat down and rested her elbows on her knees and her chin in her hands.

"You really think we ought to get married?" she said. "It's so conventional."

"Being parents is conventional."

"I never thought of us as conventional."

"I know."

"I thought of us as so special, we didn't need anything else."

"I know."

"Let's not change."

"We won't."

"Then it won't matter we're married. We'll be just the same as we've always been. Just us."

"You're right," I said. "None of it matters. All that matters is us."

"The three of us," she said.

17

THE FLYING NEWT

"Many marriages," Forrest told me over the phone, long-distance, "have survived the wedding."

As far as I was concerned, whatever Caroline's family wanted was fine with me. This was Caroline's party and I was just happy to be invited.

Caroline made up a list and hand-lettered invitations with her italic pen and mailed them off. It was a short list: her sister, Forrest and Sally, two nurses she worked with, the only living grandparents either of us had—her father's parents—my father, and her parents.

The wedding was set for May and one Friday evening in early April, I came home to find Caroline beaming like a sophomore who'd just been asked to the senior prom.

"Dad's coming," she said. "He called. He's in Ankara, but he's coming. He said he thought we could use a reception room at the State Department for the ceremony."

"I thought we were just having champagne and hors d'oeuvres."

"My eighty-three-year-old grandmother is coming down from Owego for this. You can't just have a cocktail party."

"Anything from your mother?"

"No," she said. There was a mixture of pain and anger there, heavily weighted toward the pain.

Three days later, Caroline was in tears when I got home. She was standing at the stove, working over a big pot of her special clam chowder. At first I thought she'd been slicing onions—her eyes were red and she was sniffing back a runny nose and wiping her hand across her face.

"Mom wrote," she said, motioning to a letter on the dining room table.

"I'm so thrilled for you," it began. It was written in lavender ink on light green stationery in a very-well-formed hand.

"May is such a lovely month in Washington, and I so much wish I could be there to give you a big hug and kiss on your wedding day. Jan Hendrick and I have just arrived in Jakarta and the entire Dutch mission here is in such disarray. They don't even have ready our permanent digs—a lovely Victorian like our house in Amsterdam, with turrets and a great sweeping screened-in porch. You can imagine what a snit I'm in, with all I have to do to get into the house, and things in storage at the dock, and they not even ready for us. They've got us living in a three-room apartment with no air-conditioning, just those Casablanca-type ceiling fans. The ambassador pulled me aside at the reception and said he'd have us in our house if he had to call in the navy and don't run off. The wife of the chargé d'affaires simply fled back to Holland a week after she arrived because of the heat and morale has been awful. So I cannot let the team down and skip town, especially on such short notice. I just cannot be there, not in body, at least. But you know I'll be there in spirit, cheering you on, and I'll look at my clock (if I can figure out the international dateline) and drink a glass of champagne at four o'clock, May 21, and wish you all the very best. I love you very much and I'm so proud of you and so happy for you. I'm so looking forward to meeting Brendan. You are both hereby instructed to honeymoon in Jakarta."

I put the letter down and went back into the kitchen and poured each of us a glass of burgundy.

"Sounds like she'd love to come," I said.

Caroline didn't say anything.

"I guess it is short notice," I said. "As she says."

"You don't know my mother," she said.

I agreed. After all, I had never met her mother. So I agreed. But I felt as if I knew her mother, really. I just didn't see any point in arguing about it.

"She could have been living in Chevy Chase and we could have set the wedding for December and it would have still been short notice, if she had a better offer for that date," said Caroline. "She'd miss my wedding for tickets to the Redskins."

I drank my burgundy and watched her. Her neck was bright

scarlet, the way it always got when she was trying not to get really angry.

"This is getting blown out of all scale," I told her. "First, we were just going to go down and register at some county office. Then we were going to have a few friends over for cocktails. Then the families got invited. So here we've got a full-scale event and now you're all upset."

"We can still call the whole thing off," said Caroline. She was hot now.

"Nothing is getting called off," I said. I shoved the burgundy toward her.

"I don't drink," she said. "Not until the newt is born."

Caroline estimated the kid had grown. He was now about the size of a newt, and we had taken to referring to it as "the newt," or simply "Newt," or sometimes "NOB," for Newt O'Brien.

"It's awfully nice of your father," I said. "To come all the way from Turkey or wherever the hell he really is."

"Daddy wouldn't miss this for the world," Caroline said. "He's finally getting one of his daughters married off."

The ceremony was actually rather elegant. It didn't occur to me until the judge turned to me to ask if I took Caroline for my lawful wedded and all that, that this gathering was a wedding. Caroline had hired some college students to play a cello, flute, and violin and we were all gathered there together in some room with a crystal chandelier at the State Department—they just about stripped you naked getting you through security—and the judge kept it mercifully brief.

The judge was a woman Caroline had met through some tenuous NIH connection. I don't think the judge had cancer. She had been brought to the oncology ward for some sort of legal pronouncement on one of the patients. Caroline had charmed her and snared her into doing the wedding. She said, "You may not love each other, every day, but I hope you always like each other." She may have said some other things, but that was all I remember.

I had wanted to say my own vow, to do it all ourselves and have the judge just bless the whole thing with holy water or whatever she thought appropriate, but Caroline said, "My eighty-three-year-old grandmother is going to have trouble enough coping with a non-church wedding. Let's just let the judge say her bit and get out."

It was painless enough. We said all the words and I kissed the bride and Caroline's grandmother kissed my cheek and her father shook my hand and my father kissed Caroline's cheek and we all drank too much champagne, except Caroline, who just held her glass and sipped demurely, not wanting to overdose the newt.

Forrest stood by me and said, "Count your blessings, big boy: her mother might have come."

Had her mother come, I'm not sure we would have been able to find her in the crowd. The guest list had ballooned in the last week before the ceremony as Caroline started saying, "The room is so big, it'll seem empty."

So the invitations went out and people flew in and it was great fun and a little surreal, seeing everyone from different phases of our lives in the same room at the same time.

Ira Bloomstein strode up and shook my hand. "Does my heart good," he said, smiling that dolphin smile, "to see something good come out of that time in the Whipple gulag. Seymour Freudenberg should be here."

"I wish he could be," I said.

And Norman the Chief flew down from the Massively Degenerate. "Well, you made one smart decision," he said, nodding toward Caroline. "How's life in the Real World?"

And Caroline's sister was there, a sultry young thing in violet and green. She came up, dragging an NIH oncologist, and gave me a boozy kiss and kissed Caroline, and she said, "This dashing young physician has offered to drive me to the airport. I think I might just take him home with me."

Caroline walked off with her sister and they talked and her sister must have said something to Caroline about their mother not being there. Don't let it bother you, that kind of thing. They both started to laugh and then cry. Then they came back, wiping away tears, and they kissed good-bye and Caroline's sister kissed their father good-bye and she left with her dashing young physician.

The champagne went fast and the hors d'oeuvres followed quickly and people stayed to talk until the security people started clearing their throats in unison, and the party broke up.

Caroline, Forrest, Sally, and Caroline's father, my father, and I went to a Middle Eastern restaurant where we sat on pillows on the floor and they had no menu but just brought food and we had a lovely meal. Afterward, we shook hands with my father on the sidewalk and said good-bye to Forrest and Sally, who hugged and kissed Caroline, which got them both crying.

My father got his car and drove it around to where we were standing in front of the restaurant and Forrest and Sally got in and we watched them drive away with my father, who was giving them a ride to the airport.

Caroline's father rode with us. We dropped him off at his hotel. Caroline got out with him and kissed him good-bye. More tears and handshakes and she got back in the car and we drove off.

We drove down Pennsylvania Avenue, past the White House, and headed for home.

"Nice wedding," I said.

"I hope it wasn't too much excitement for the newt," said Caroline, looking down at her belly, patting our little friend in utero. "I fed him his first champagne tonight."

"He's probably very happy right now," I said. "High as a kite and doesn't know what hit him."

"Like his parents," said Caroline. "Just like his parents."

18

TO THE MAX

In order to be awarded a medical degree in the state of New York, where I went to medical school, you had to deliver eight babies. During my obstetrics rotation, my first delivery was a cesarean section for fetal distress, which, if you have ever seen one, you know is not for the fainthearted. The obstetricians cut open that belly and get down to the baby in one big hurry and they don't fuss a lot about delicacies like hemostasis and tying off bleeders. The medical student gets shoved out of the way and you stand there holding retractors, trying not to faint. By the time I had my eight deliveries under my belt I had seen three c-sections for distress and three other less urgent c-sections and only two normal vaginal deliveries.

So I brought a certain amount of trepidation to the prospect of Caroline's delivery.

"You are so phobic," she laughed. "Having a baby is the most natural thing in the world. Women used to go off and squat in the bush."

"Well, you're delivering in a hospital, and from what I remember, that can get to be pretty exciting."

"We will prepare ourselves," said Caroline.

Preparing ourselves meant going to puff-and-pant classes every Wednesday night for six weeks. I tried, I really did. I tried transforming myself into a focal point without laughing while Caroline practiced panting in my face, never without laughing. We trudged off every Wednesday night for six weeks to listen to what-happened-to-me, you'll-never-believe stories as told by the puff-and-pant instructor and by one of the women in the group who had had three deliveries already, but she now had a new husband and she was putting him through the course, which she used as a stage for a sort of dramatic recital about each of her prior deliveries.

"The first thing they always try to do to you," the mother-of-

three told us, "is to slam in this intravenous needle about the size
of the Holland Tunnel in your arm. They broke one off in my arm
with Jimmy, my second, and I thought I'd never stop bleeding.
And then they try to draw about two gallons of blood, right?
You're in agony, I mean big-time pain, and they're slashing away
at your arm and blood's all over the place. Jerry, that's my first
husband, just about puked right there."

Those puff-and-pant classes were a refresher course about what
people who are not part of the medical world really think about
doctors. Caroline and I had agreed to keep our medical degrees to
ourselves. We were there to learn and we didn't want assumptions
made about what we knew. And we did learn. We learned hospitals are places where they try to inflict the maximal pain in the
shortest amount of time; modern medicine is the attempt to con-
vert every simple biologic process into a complex technological
feat; hospitals treat patients like machines on an assembly line;
hospitals try to drug patients into submission; doctors do not care
about patients; what doctors really care about is making money;
nurses know nothing except how to change bedpans; obstetricians
want to do cesarean sections on every patient because they can
charge more money for c-sections; technology is bad; it's a wonder
any baby ever makes it out of the uterus alive and it's a wonder
any mother survives delivery and the only reason either ever does
is that birthing is such a marvelously simple process, even modern
medicine can't foul it up.

"Don't let them put the fetal monitor on you," mother-of-three
told us. "That's how they get you to agree to a cesarean section.
They put the monitor on you and then they come in and look at
these graphs and all the squiggly lines and they shake their heads
and they say, 'Oh, this is really bad.' And by this time, you're
about to have a heart attack. What's wrong with my baby? And
they say, 'This monitor shows we better do a cesarean section.'
Get out your checkbook, they're going to operate."

"Did you have a cesarean section?" Caroline asked mother-of-
three.

"Yes. With my first, but they let me have the next two naturally.
But with my first, this was just when they began letting the fathers
in the delivery room for sections and Jerry—that's my first husband—Jerry went and got dressed up in the green scrub suit they
gave him, so he looked just like all the doctors. He was supposed

to come sit by my head and hold my hand while they did the surgery, but Jerry didn't know. He just wanders in the room and he doesn't know where to go or what to do and I can't see him 'cause they've put this screen up.

"So one of the nurses thinks Jerry's a medical student and she pulls him over to the table and helps him into his sterile gloves and he doesn't know how to get them on, and she's saying, 'Don't they teach you guys anything in class?' And he thinks she means puff-and-pant class. Then they give him a place next to the obstetrician, who doesn't recognize him 'cause he's got this hat and surgical mask on, and the obstetrician hands him a retractor to hold and slashes open my belly and he keeps telling Jerry, 'Pull harder, son. Didn't they teach you how to do this?' And Jerry's thinking, 'No, they certainly did not. All they taught us was how to breathe.'

"And meanwhile the surgeon's got down to the womb and there's blood all over the place and Jerry's starting to sway, but he's holding up and about the time they're about to cut open the womb and get the kid out I'm saying, 'Anybody seen my husband?' And I hear Jerry's voice. 'Right here, honey.' And all the doctors and nurses look up and realize who this klutz is they thought was a medical student. I think it was then and there our marriage started on its decline."

"I should imagine," said Caroline.

"After that, I hear they got special scrub suits for the fathers, bright red or something, so everyone could tell who the father was."

We were safely in the car, after the class, and Caroline said, "Poor Jerry."

"I hope you don't need a c-section," I said. "I'm not sure I'd be up to scrubbing in."

"Oh, I won't need a c-section. I'll pop the kid right out."

"Hope for the best, prepare for the worst."

"Dr. Gloom and Doom," laughed Caroline. "We've got the crib and the dresser at Crib n' Cradle and you won't even let me bring it home and set up the room."

"There'll be plenty of time for that. I'll have it all ready."

"Apparently you are not the only neurotic father-to-be in Washington," Caroline said. "The salesman knew immediately when I told him we'd buy it now but not pick it up for a month or two. He said, 'Not until the baby's born,' with this knowing smile."

And then there was the amniocentesis, a procedure I had never seen done before they did it on Caroline. First, they did the sonogram to find the newt, which was a strange feeling, watching him move around and squirm. Caroline was surprised by how much the needle hurt, and afterward she had a lot of cramping as we drove home in the car.

"Maybe this wasn't such a hot idea," she said. "Now that I've seen the little twerp moving. I'm not so sure I could go through an abortion, even if the chromosomes look bad."

"We'll cross that bridge then," I said.

Fortunately, that was one bridge we didn't have to cross. The chromosomes looked fine.

Only after we got the amnio report did I allow Caroline to get out the name books. I was determined to not tempt fate. We would have no baby furniture in the house until after the delivery and we planned no names until the amnio report. Caroline, of course, had been looking at names for months, but I refused to discuss it.

By early November, Caroline was getting very tired of being pregnant. "This grows old," she said. "I grow old."

At night, I'd press the base of her spine with the heel of my hand to help her low back pain. She could only lie on her side, and shifting position in bed was a major maneuver.

"Feel this," she said one night.

I put my hand on her belly and felt the unmistakable outline of a heel, which pulled away from my grasp.

"Come out here and try that," I called in to him. "Your mother's tired of this dicking around."

Then one Sunday morning, she woke up in labor. She insisted it was false labor at first, but when the contractions were five minutes apart we called the number for the hospital and they told us to come right in.

At the hospital, a nurse-midwife met us and she took Caroline into a room and examined her. She told me, "She's six centimeters. It shouldn't be long now."

I walked in and sat by Caroline. A contraction hit her and she started puffing and panting through it.

"Christ," she said when it was over. "Damned if that breathing doesn't help."

"Want a focal point?" I asked. That had become a joke between us. We couldn't stare into each other's eyes the way they told you without laughing. She started to laugh and another contraction hit. You could see her belly rise and move like shifting lava under a volcano.

"Oh, oh, oh." Then, "That was a good one. Poor baby. He must be getting squeezed in there."

"What can I do?"

"A hundred milligrams of morphine sulfate, IV stat," she said as another contraction hit. That would be a lethal dose. She was only kidding. She meant: Put me out of my misery. Take me out and shoot me.

She breathed and puffed and took a deep breath when it ended.

"Your cleansing breath," I laughed. That's what they called it in puff-and-pant classes.

"You laugh," she gasped. "It helps."

A woman wearing green scrubs came in then. She had very clean-looking skin and she looked remarkably wide-awake and fresh, considering the early hour. She was the obstetrician and she asked how Caroline was and she laughed a lot.

"You're a doctor?" she asked me.

"Yes."

"Internist?"

"Yes."

"Infectious disease," I heard Caroline put in, between contractions.

"She's a nurse," I said. "An onc nurse."

"Well," the obstetrician laughed. "You guys will soon have new titles: Mommy and Daddy."

"I'll believe it when I see it," I said.

One epidural and two hours later she was ready to go. They moved her down to the delivery room on a stretcher.

Then they let her push. Her contractions were coming hard and fast, but you could see the uterus moving down toward the perineum with each contraction. She held her breath and the veins in her forehead stood out and she pushed and her face turned blue-red and I thought, Lord, don't let her have a berry aneurysm inside that brain of hers, because if she does, she's going to burst it. She kept on pushing and I could see all the eyes in the room shifting down below, to the southern exposure, where something was beginning to show.

Seeing that big head arch up and into the air was startling. I had seen this sort of event before in medical school, of course, but now I had to shake myself. I had felt a fetal heel beneath the skin and I had felt it kick through Caroline's belly, and rationally, I knew it was in there, but seeing that surprisingly big wet head, all covered with black hair (which would later fall out and grow in blond) and then the neck and shoulders and runty little body and curled legs —it was simply stunning.

They cut the cord and took him off to weigh him and put him under a heater where the nurse cleaned him off and listened to his heart with a stethoscope. I wanted to listen to the heart, too, but I stayed by Caroline and held her hand.

"Go look at him," Caroline said.

The nurse had pulled a knitted cap over his head so he looked like a Chinese sailor, and she started to wrap him up, but I motioned her to stop. I listened to his heart, and I checked each testicle. His heart sounded strong and fast and it had no murmur. Both testes were in place. He looked like the nude mice I'd once worked with as a Fellow, all wrinkled and raw-looking. He waved his arms slowly and stretched and contracted and all parts seemed to be working. I don't know how much he could really see of me with those big beamers wandering around in different directions, but he seemed to look right at me for a while, looking by turns perplexed, fascinated, bored, but never afraid or disturbed.

It was quiet in the delivery room, considering all the people. The obstetrician had come in and leaned against the tiled wall and there was the midwife, quietly suturing Caroline's bottom, and there was a circulating nurse and an anesthesiologist. And most of all there was Caroline. And now this kid.

They had dimmed all the lights and only the big spotlight on Caroline's bottom was at all bright. This baby seemed to take his cue from the adults around him, and he was quiet. He was like someone who had just awakened and was trying to get his bearings.

I wrapped him up and carried him over to Caroline. She put him to her breast and he knew exactly what to do.

"Poor guy," she said. "He doesn't even have a crib at home."

"He'll have one."

"What's his name?"
"What's he look like?"
"Definitely not an Emily."
"No."
"Max, I think. A definite Max."
And so he was.

19

THE LAW

Caroline and the new kid, Max, were still at the hospital, the next day. I was trying to get out of my office early, so I could get over to Crib n' Cradle and pick up the crib and the dresser and then go see the family before visiting hours ended on the postpartum floor, when my secretary buzzed.

"There's a man out here who says he has to see you," my secretary said. "I told him you were with a patient. He doesn't have an appointment."

She was speaking over the intercom, but the strangeness in her voice came through. I excused myself to the patient and stepped into the waiting room.

I didn't see him at first. He was standing around the corner, in front of the reception desk. I saw two patients I knew, who smiled and waved. He was wearing a cowboy hat and brown cowboy boots, all intricately carved with white inlays in the leather, and he had a droopy mustache. I wouldn't have been surprised if he had drawn a six-gun on me.

Instead, he asked me if I was Dr. Brendan O'Brien, which I thought odd. Who else did he think I was? There was only one name on the door and I was the only one in the white coat. I said I was, and he drew a large manila envelope from his imitation flight jacket and handed it to me. "There now," he said. "You've been served."

I stood there staring at the envelope and he tipped his hat to me and to my secretary, as if he were Marshal Matt Dillon and he had just shot the bad guy, and he stalked out of my waiting room. My patients sat there staring at me with looks of what I imagined to be fear, embarrassment, and reproach. I walked back into the examining room, which was the only place I could be alone, and opened the envelope.

YOU ARE HEREBY SUMMONED to answer the complaint in this action . . .

I knew I should fold this all back into the envelope and go back to my patients and not think about it until after my last patient. I knew if I continued reading my heart rate would just get faster, and the sudden headache in both temples would get worse and my mouth would get drier and taste even more brassy.

Naturally, I kept on reading.

IN THE UNITED STATES DISTRICT COURT FOR THE
DISTRICT OF COLUMBIA
Civil Division
Brendan O'Brien, MD
Defendant

I read and I read, all the nice pithy phrases lawyers love when they are hot on the scent. It took me a while to understand, but gradually I understood. This was no mistake.

My secretary popped her head into the examining room. "We are coming out to play today, are we not? The natives grow restless."

I looked up at her and flipped the envelope to her.

"Who was that bizarre man?"

"A summons server," I said. "There's a file for my malpractice insurance. In the file is a number to call when you get sued. Call it and I think they'll want a Xerox copy of this thing and a copy of our chart on John Lockhardt."

"John Lockhardt's suing you? And I thought he was so nice."

"He's not suing me. The father of the kid he ran over with his car is suing me."

"For what?"

"For signing his driver's license application, which since he is a diabetic, he has to have me sign. To attest to the fact that he was in good control and had not had an insulin coma in the previous year."

"Oh, don't be absurd," said my secretary. "They can't sue you if one of your patients runs someone over."

"You obviously are not a student of the legal mind."

"Seriously. How could you know he was going to run someone down?"

"What they are saying is that I should have known he was going to go driving in insulin coma someday."

"Has he ever been in insulin coma?"

"Not that I know of. But did I write down in his chart that he had told me he had never been made hypoglycemic by his insulin? I don't remember whether I wrote that down or not."

"Run that by me one more time. You sign his driver's license form and then if he runs someone down, you get sued?"

"Now you've got it."

"But how can his driving be your fault?"

"You don't understand the concept of deep pockets. John Lockhardt pumps gas for a living. He's got maybe ten dollars to his name, less after payday, and he hits the bars. He goes out and gets loaded and runs over some poor kid and the family goes to sue John Lockhardt and discovers he's uninsured and there's nothing to go after in his bank account. So they get a lawyer who says to John, 'Look, this isn't your fault. You weren't drunk. You were in insulin coma. This is all your doctor's fault.' Now, John is most happy to learn this. And the family is most happy and most of all the lawyer is happy, because now they can all sue me. And I've got deep pockets. I've got malpractice insurance."

"You must be terribly upset."

"No," I said. "Not anymore. Just at first, when you open the envelope. Then you have to have a talk with yourself. You have to say, I've been sued before. I will be sued again. I've still got people from Tinker, Mudwater in New York calling me every couple of months about that suit from when I was a resident."

"That awful lawyer from New York who calls with his imperious commands for you to appear for depositions and then cancels the night before?"

"The same. That isn't the worst of it. You should try getting a mortgage or a loan when you've got a case pending against you for ten or fifteen million dollars. The bankers love that. Makes you a real good risk."

"I cannot believe you're being sued because your alcoholic patient ran down some poor child. Surely they cannot hope to win."

"They cannot lose. Try this before a jury of twelve retired postal workers, inner-city people. They sit there looking at the bereaved father and they look at me, a doctor with deep pockets.''

I walked back into my office where a patient waited to tell me about her headaches. She had had headaches for twenty years. But now she had headaches and a new doctor, and she wanted to tell me all about them. She thought her headaches might come from stress.

Lady, you don't know what a headache is.

Norman the Chief warned me about the Real World. But I wanted to practice real medicine, to be a real doctor.

Then I thought about that new kid, who looked like a nude mouse, all wrapped up under the heating lights downtown, whom I was going to get to see later that evening, and I felt better.

20

THE WORKING MOTHER

Those next two years we pursued the ordinary life.

"Who would have thought," Caroline said, "being a mommy could be such a kick?"

"I remember all those people I thought were such fools," I said. "They thought all they had to do was get married and have babies, and they'd be happy. Christ, I thought, what a bore. And so many of them did seem disappointed, later."

"If you had told me, ten years ago, when I was backpacking through Europe, living in hostels, or when I was in the Peace Corps, or even when I met you at Whipple, that I'd be playing Mom, buying Pampers and reading articles about toilet training, I would have laughed rudely in your face."

"But you're not laughing now."

"Oh, no," Caroline said, looking over at Max destroying a cardboard box. "I'm having a wonderful time."

We did all those things so many people do as a natural progression in life, but which, for us, seemed strange and exciting and a little overwhelming. We even decided to forsake the city for suburbia. After many Sundays in the car with the real estate ads, we found a house we thought might be within reach.

We applied for a mortgage, but the loan officer was most unhappy about the two lawsuits pending against me. There was a lot of letter writing to the law firms defending me, and to the malpractice insurance people.

"How ironic," Caroline said. "We may get turned down for this mortgage because you're a doctor. And if we get it, it'll be because they've overlooked that and accepted us because I've got a job—as a nurse."

Eventually, after some restless nights, they approved the mortgage, and we got the house. It was a three-bedroom frame house and everything about it seemed small except the mortgage, but it was where we wanted to be. It was in Montgomery County, where people moved when they had kids, for the good schools.

It was a pretty neighborhood, though, with big trees and lots of little kids and a park in back of the elementary school filled with swings and playground equipment, and it was all an easy walk from our house along the quiet neighborhood streets. We'd wheel Max up to the playground and watch him stumble around and try to keep him from careening into the swings, and we'd watch the three- and four-year-olds running around and sliding down slides and we'd imagine how Max would do that someday.

We were watching a group of mothers one day, all dressed in pink and green Fair Isle sweaters and down vests and those L.L. Bean rubber shoes with the leather uppers. They were standing and talking, holding mugs of coffee, and they looked young and affluent and happy.

"None of those women work," Caroline said. "I've met each one of them before, up here. That one with the black hair is an economist. The mousy one with the mousy kid is a lawyer and the other one is a social worker. They all decided to stay home with their kids."

"Would you want to do that? If I could support us?"

"Max is growing up," she said. "And I'm missing it."

"I ought to get a real job," I said.

"You keep at the practice," she said. "It'll grow."

Caroline was very nice about it, but I felt sad, seeing her all dressed in the morning, rushing around, feeding the kid, ulcerating over her chronically late hired surrogate mother, Lurlene, who drove out from Prince Georges County every morning, and was late whenever it rained or whenever there was an accident on the Beltway. Max seemed to think it was normal to have Lurlene arrive in the morning and Caroline come home only at night. But Caroline missed her kid.

We avoided spending money. We never went out. We invested in a VCR so we could rent movies and watch them at home. We rationalized that it would save us money in the long run, what with baby-sitters and the price of admission. But we felt guilty plunking down the money. The rental movies were cheap, though, and it was something to look forward to Saturday nights. We were poor again. House poor.

My practice grew slowly, never enough to make us feel flush, but just enough to get by each month and not fall behind. But we had no cushion at all. A big increase in my malpractice insurance, a major car repair, the loss of a moonlighting contract, anything at all, and the whole house of cards would fall apart. We lived month to month.

There were fights, but strangely enough, not about money. We fought about the division of labor and about time. It was Caroline's job to keep the house at least livable, but she was never much of a housekeeper. Those were the worst fights. I'd get home at eight and she had just fed and bathed Max and I'd open the door and slip on one of Max's cars, look around the living room, littered with toys, every counter space covered with the litter of daily life, nothing in its place.

And I'd start to pick up, thinking this was no way to come home, and Caroline would come down carrying Max, both of them smiling, oblivious of the pigpen I was trying to put into order.

"Say good night to the big boy," Caroline would say.

"Good night," sullen, without joy from me.

"What's wrong?"

"Look at this place."

Crestfallen looks.

"Well, welcome home. It's a joy to see you."

"Your mother is a pigpen proprietor."

Later, after Caroline had carried Max upstairs and put him to bed, cold wrath seething, she went around whatever room I was in, making great dramatic gestures as she picked up things and stuffed them in place.

I refused to react.

Finally, Caroline said: "Why do you do this? We haven't seen each other all day."

"Because I'm pissed off."

"I do a pretty good job. So bug off."

Those were the weekly fights. We had to blow it off and let out the bad blood and then we'd be okay for a while.

Some Saturdays Caroline worked. On these days I'd take Max and we'd wander through the zoo. We'd start up near Connecticut Avenue and wander down the hill, through the panda house, into the gorilla house, watch the orangutans swing around in their

cages, and on the warm days, we'd go over and listen to the gib-
bons shriek.

Then down to the lions and tigers.

Max was just a few months past two, but he was a decent talker,
really very good for his age, and you could almost have a conversation. The lions and the tigers were outside. You looked down at
them, across the moat, protected by the water and the sheer stone
walls, as if they were in the pit of a coliseum, and you were safe
high in the amphitheater. Max and I stood watching a solitary tiger
pacing up and down along the waterline and he seemed to be
keeping an eye on us. Max stood by me, watching the tiger eye us.
Max studied the tiger examining him as if he were watching a
goldfish in a bowl.

"Tiger by himself," Max observed.

"That's the way tigers are," I said. "Lions hang out in groups.
But tigers are alone."

"Where his mother?"

"I don't know."

"At work," said Max. "The tiger has a mother what works."

I told Caroline that story and she listened, as she always did,
with a smile of sheer pleasure, hearing any story about the brilliant
things her boy said. But when she heard the punch line, the smile
vanished and she buried her face in one hand and she sobbed.

21

BLIND JUSTICE

Once every three or four months, the lawyers for the hospital, who were supposed to be defending me in the Roundtree case, would telephone with a date for a deposition. I was instructed to drop everything, reschedule my office patients, and hop a plane to New York to testify. The first three times, the deposition was canceled for reasons that were never made clear.

Finally, one May, they managed to pull it off.

The lawyers' offices were vast and sumptuous. The law firm employed two hundred lawyers, and I marveled, as I walked down the deep-pile-carpeted hallways, that so many lawyers could be employed by one firm. There were as many lawyers employed by this firm as there were doctors employed by the Manhattan Medical Center. And from the looks of the appointments, they were making a lot more money than the hospital was.

The hospital lawyer shook my hand in a conference room before we set off to do battle with the plaintiff's attorney.

"Just tell the truth. And remember this suit's for twenty million dollars."

"I'd almost forgotten."

The Roundtrees' lawyer was a fat sweaty man who, at first, didn't seem to know where he was or which case he was supposed to be thinking about or even who I was. He asked me a lot of questions to establish who I was and what my credentials were and what my position in the hospital was at the time I was taking care of Mrs. Roundtree. When he finally got rolling, his intentions seemed to peek through his questions.

"Now, you were a resident at the time Mrs. Roundtree was your patient?"

"Yes. Actually, she was Seymour Freudenberg's patient, and I was the resident assigned to her case."

"Then she wasn't your patient?"

"Dr. Freudenberg was her physician of record."

"Now, what does that mean? Physician of record? Was she your patient or was she not?"

The hospital lawyer broke in. "You know what he's saying. Dr. Freudenberg had ultimate responsibility for her care. Dr. O'Brien was still in training and he was carrying out the plans formulated by Dr. Freudenberg. Dr. O'Brien was not making the basic decisions."

"I think Dr. O'Brien can answer for himself."

"It's just as he says," I said.

"Then you were not making the decisions on Mrs. Roundtree's case?"

"I made day-to-day decisions. Decisions of therapy and the big decisions were made by the attending, the physician of record."

"Now, on March ninth, you performed a thoracentesis on Mrs. Roundtree, did you not?"

"Yes."

"Now, Dr. O'Brien, what exactly is a thoracentesis?"

"A needle is passed between the ribs to drain fluid from between the lungs and the coverings of the lungs called the pleura."

"And what are the potential complications of this procedure?"

"Pneumothorax and laceration of the lung are the major risks."

"And pneumothorax is what, in English?"

"Pneumothorax is English."

"Well, what does it mean?"

"It refers to air collecting between the lung and the chest wall."

"Air that can compress the lung beneath it, so the patient cannot expand the lung. So she cannot breathe? Pneumothorax can be fatal, can it not?"

"If it is massive and sudden, yes."

"Now, why exactly did you do this procedure on Mrs. Roundtree?"

"Because it was indicated."

"Indicated?"

"Her medical condition required it."

"And how did you know that?"

"I examined her."

"Did Dr. Freudenberg examine her with you?"

"No."

"Why not?"

"He was in his office and there was no time to waste. Mrs. Roundtree was in acute respiratory distress. She was gasping for air."

"Were you surprised by this?"

"Yes and no."

"Why yes and no?"

"She had a pleural effusion making her short of breath. Fluid was weeping out of her lung and collecting between the chest wall and the lung, compressing the lung. This is a fairly common complication of metastatic breast cancer, when it goes to the lung. So if you're hanging by a thread, you're not surprised when it breaks, but you're always surprised at the moment you fall."

"Was Mrs. Roundtree hanging by a thread that morning?"

"She was hanging by a thread every day of her life, once her breast cancer metastasized."

"Is a ward floor the proper place for a patient whose life is hanging by a thread?"

"That depends on the circumstances. Home may be the proper place for her under some circumstances, home or a nice tropical island in the sun. Or maybe a ward or maybe an ICU. I think Mrs. Roundtree was in the appropriate place for her that morning. She didn't belong in an ICU, which has dangers of its own, and there was still reason to treat her, so the hospital was the proper place."

"And you knew, and Dr. Freudenberg knew, Mrs. Roundtree had metastases in the lung and so it was no surprise she had pleural effusions?"

"That's not what I said. I said knowing she had metastases to the lung, I knew she was at risk for developing pleural effusions and I wasn't surprised to discover she had developed this complication. I had seen this complication many times before."

"Now, you have read the notes Dr. Freudenberg made that morning when he made rounds and examined Mrs. Roundtree?"

"Yes."

"Did he note her pleural effusion?"

"Yes."

"Did he mention this effusion to you before he left the hospital?"

"No."

"But why not? You've just described a patient who had a potentially lethal complication and who required a thoracentesis, a potentially lethal procedure, under emergency circumstances, and yet Dr. Freudenberg did not call you when he discovered a diagnosis of such significance, a diagnosis that you discovered yourself only two hours later on rounds? A diagnosis on which you had to take potentially life-threatening action?"

I took in a deep breath. Calm yourself. Be reasonable. "Half the patients on the ward had pleural effusions at one time or another. Usually pleural effusions collect slowly and cause no trouble. Sometimes they suddenly expand or cross over from a well-tolerated state to one of decompensation, and you have to act. But it's like cleaning your gutters: usually they don't overflow, but sometimes they do."

I knew that was a poor analogy as soon as I said it, and he pounced on it.

"Then Dr. Freudenberg hadn't kept his gutters clean? He hadn't done the routine maintenance?"

"No, that was a poor analogy. It's more like a rowboat. Usually there's a little water in the bottom and it causes no trouble, but if a squall comes up the boat can fill up. The fact that she had a pleural effusion was not a red flag. We were keeping an eye on it. She just filled up that morning, which can happen. There's no way to predict it. But it happened, as bad things do to women with breast cancer, and we took care of it."

"You mean, you took care of it. Dr. Freudenberg wasn't there to make the diagnosis of the effusion when it got to be a problem, was he?"

"He didn't have to be."

"Why not?"

"The fact speaks for itself. I was, as a senior resident, perfectly capable of making that diagnosis and treating pleural effusion."

"Either that or you were just lucky."

"Luck has nothing to do with it. I was well trained."

"But if she had suffered a pneumothorax, you would now be claiming it was just bad luck, wouldn't you? You'd still claim you were the right man for the job, even if the outcome had not been good?"

"Let the record show," said the hospital lawyer, "that I object to that statement—it was not a question. The doctor is not here to answer questions about what he might have said if things happened in a different way than they actually happened."

"I am simply trying to establish that Dr. O'Brien is not a thoracic surgeon, that Dr. Freudenberg never called a board-certified thoracic surgeon to see Mrs. Roundtree, and that Dr. O'Brien, who was then still in training, was left to do a potentially lethal procedure on Dr. Freudenberg's patient for a diagnosis that only he, a physician still in training, had made without confirmation by an attending physician. I am trying to establish that Mrs. Roundtree was left in the hands of a trainee who made a diagnosis that placed her fate in his hands for a potential lethal procedure."

"Are you questioning the fact she had a pleural effusion?" I asked.

"I'm questioning your diagnosis, yes. You were still in training. Was it ever verified by an attending physician?"

"The nurse's notes, as well as my own, document that we drained off three hundred cc's of bloody pleural fluid. The medical record also documents that she was breathing thirty-five times a minute before I drained that fluid off and she was breathing twelve times a minute after the thoracentesis. Have you had any doctor look at that record?"

"I'm not here to answer your questions. You're here to answer mine."

"Well, you obviously have some homework to do. If you have any physician who knows what he's doing look at that chart, he'll tell you there is no other conclusion you can draw except that she had a large pleural effusion, correctly diagnosed and correctly treated in a timely manner."

"We'll have expert testimony on that point," said the plantiff's lawyer.

"I should hope so," I said.

"Let's go back to that morning," he said. "Did Mr. Roundtree ask you to call his wife's physician of record, as you call him, that is, Dr. Freudenberg?"

"Yes."

"And did you?"

"I pointed to Mrs. Roundtree, and I asked if Mr. Roundtree, seeing the distress she was in, really wanted me to delay the thoracentesis while we got Dr. Freudenberg on the line. He said no."

"So you went ahead under emergency circumstances and did the thoracentesis?"

"Yes."

"Because you were the only doctor available to care for Mrs. Roundtree in the entire Whipple Hospital."

"Because I was in the best position to care for her at that moment."

"Did you call for surgical backup?"

"Did I what?"

"Did you page a surgeon?"

"No. I did the tap."

"Do you have your . . . Let me rephrase that: Do you now or did you then have your boards in thoracic surgery?"

"No."

The hospital lawyer interjected, "If I may interrupt?"

"I'm pursuing a line of questioning here."

"I can wait, but in the interest of time it might be better if I asked Dr. O'Brien whether a thoracentesis is a procedure you need to be a thoracic surgeon to do, since that is the clear thrust of your question."

"Why don't you let me finish? You can ask all the questions your heart desires then."

He went on to ask a lot of questions about how often Seymour Freudenberg came in to see Mrs. Roundtree and about who made which decisions when. It was pretty clear he was trying to build the case that Seymour had admitted Mrs. Roundtree to the hospital, where she was left to the care of a bunch of unsupervised neophytes. It was all rot, of course, but I imagine he could sell it to a jury of retired postal workers or a jury of Guido, the rental-truck man. You could sell the Brooklyn Bridge to Guido, if you said it belonged to a bunch of millionaire doctors who were trying to unload it to buy themselves new Rolls-Royces.

He never asked why we let Mrs. Roundtree walk on her metastasis-riddled legs so she broke her tibia and got phlebitis and a lung clot and died. That wasn't part of his case. He was making an argument and it had nothing to do with whether or not the process of Mrs. Roundtree's care was a careful or well-thought-out one. It had to do with appearances, with words and with images. He was spinning out a story, and it had its own life and its own reality, which had nothing to do with Mrs. Roundtree or what we had or had not done for her.

After it was all over, the hospital lawyer smiled and shook my hand.

"Thanks for coming up," he said.

"That's all?" I said.

"Yes."

"Do you think he got what he wanted out of me? Or did I derail him?"

"No, you didn't derail him. He's trying to say Seymour Freudenberg should have been hovering by Mrs. Roundtree's bedside. And he's going to imply Seymour Freudenberg didn't care: he just dumped Mrs. Roundtree in the hospital and he flew in and out of her room every day and charged her a bundle for the hospital visit, but he abandoned her to the care of you young interns, fresh out of medical school."

"But that's not true."

"Truth? Whose truth? Truth has nothing to do with it. All he's got to do is to plant that seed. Nobody on this jury has ever done a medical residency. They're not going to see this case through your eyes, much as you might like them to. They know doctors. They've been in that bed with their fifty questions and the doctor runs away from them."

"So you think he's going to win? Twenty million dollars."

"He'll settle. You're an appealing witness. The jury just might like you. He's got to weigh that. He'll settle."

"The jury might like me? I don't care if they like me. I care about the truth."

"There you go again with the truth. Jury trials are about impressions. They are theater. The winning side is the side that makes the best impression. Roundtree's lawyer knows that. He'll settle."

"For how much?"

"We've already offered fifty thousand. He took that back to his client, who turned it down."

"Fifty thousand?" I said, trying to control my voice. "But we didn't do anything wrong."

The hospital lawyer sighed, and begin speaking as if he were speaking to a very slow child, very patiently and slowly: "You haven't been listening, Doctor. This has nothing to do with technical questions. The jurors are not going to be technical people."

"A jury of my peers."

"You may not think they're your peers, but the law does."

"Some system."

"No system is perfect. Cynics say if the laws could speak for themselves, they'd complain about the lawyers. But it's the best we've got. Look at it this way: If they settle for half a million, we've saved the hospital nineteen and a half million."

"You'll go far," I said. "There's always a demand for a man who can make wrong seem right."

"Now just a minute," he said, the color rising to his cheeks.

"This is a real nice industry," I said. "Everybody's happy: Mr. Roundtree gets his share. His lawyer can't lose, and the insurance company breathes a sigh of relief it wasn't ten million. And you, of course, you get paid, win, lose, or capitulate."

"What are you saying? That doctors are always perfect? Nobody should be able to lodge a complaint?"

"What I'm saying is that I don't like to see the Good Samaritan with a rope around his neck, swinging from a tree. You may be able to stomach it, but I can't."

"Are you so sure nothing more could have been done for Mrs. Roundtree?"

"What I'm saying"—I don't know why I was arguing with this man— "is that Seymour Freudenberg did not give Mrs. Roundtree breast cancer."

22

ATLANTA BURNING

"It boggles the mind," Caroline said, when I told her about my day at the deposition. "I'd sure as hell rather have had you doing my thoracentesis than Seymour Freudenberg, much as I loved Seymour. You did, what? Three or four a week? Seymour probably hadn't done one for years."

"No," I said. "Seymour's great mistake was not having a thoracic surgeon posted by the bedside of any patient who had a pleural effusion."

"The whole thing sounds too silly to be believed."

"Twenty-million silly."

"That hospital lawyer had a point, though, about juries. Can you imagine if the ladies of our puff-and-pant class were on one? All Mr. Roundtree's lawyer would have to do is bring the Roundtree kids to court and the verdict would be a foregone conclusion."

"The ladies of the puff-and-pant class," I said. "A jury of my peers. I wonder how they all did," I said. "Cast out upon the various maternity wards of the metropolitan area, subjected to intravenous-line insertions and other heinous acts."

Caroline leaned back with her hands behind her head. "Uh, I don't know how to tell you this. But about those maternity wards, of which you speak so lightly. We are going to be making our own visit."

And so it was I learned of the next major agenda item, Samuel Bates O'Brien, who arrived March of that next year, after a booming two-hour labor.

Oh, the perishability of novelty. While Max's every sigh and gurgle had been the subject of wonder and fascinated observation, poor old Sam was more or less shoved off into his hand-me-down crib and left to fend for himself. We had stood over Max, staring down into his crib, as if he were some creature from outer space, watching him sleep, terrified he might stop breathing (Caroline laughed at me, but I noticed she had a dozen articles on crib death in her briefcase). I had Max's crib next to our bed so I could hear him breathe. Sam was off in his room down the hall. With Max, *Consumer Reports* articles were read before paper diapers were purchased and applied to his bottom. With Sam, we bought whatever was on sale. Sam was fed and changed and powdered, but few pictures got taken and he was hauled around as if he were nothing more remarkable than a new pocketbook.

But, of course, he was remarkable. As Sam grew, he asserted his individuality.

"They are as different as day and night," Caroline said.

Caroline took three months off and went back to work, but after our third visiting surrogate mother simply did not show up for work one day, Caroline finally gave up and resigned her job at NIH. My income from the office practice and from the moonlighting jobs was just enough to get us by, and Caroline said, "They are, as we have heard so often, only young once."

"And so are we," I said.

"I don't know about you," said Caroline. "But I am no longer young."

"You are forever young."

"Were it only so."

"I am older. You are simply a little riper."

"Oh, I am ripe now, am I?"

"You are lovely."

"And your temples are turning gray, which makes you so attractive."

"I'm getting old."

"It's not so bad," Caroline said. "Getting older. The kids get older along with us, and it's like reading a good novel. I just don't want to put it down. I want to see how they turn out."

For some reason it struck me: Mrs. Roundtree had said something like that once, in one of her clearer moments. She had asked me what it would mean to me to know I was going to die tomorrow. I had been thrown off-balance by the question and stammered something about how I felt I hadn't really lived, I had been in training, in preparation all my life, so I would feel cheated.

She had listened, studying me with her full brown eyes, smiling as if she understood. Then I asked her what it would mean to her, and she had said, "It would mean I'd never get to see my children grow up. That's what I'd really miss. Like having to leave halfway through the movie. Like having to leave with Atlanta burning and Scarlett and Rhett riding through it in that buggy, and me being told to leave the theater. And knowing that the movie was still going on inside the theater, but I'd never find how it turns out."

At the time, I told her I understood, but I hadn't really.

23

JUST ABOVE MY HEAD

Once a week, Caroline dragged both kids to the library at Little Falls, where they could run around in the downstairs children's section and Max could choose five books for his bedtime stories.

"Wait till you see this week's selection," Caroline said, pregnantly.

"Let me guess: *Warriors and Their Weapons. Great Battles Through the Ages. Good Guys and Bad Guys. He-man Conquers Skeletor and Rips His Guts Out.*"

What Max had chosen and was now demanding to be read was a book with the innocent enough title *Legends Through the Ages.* It had a wonderful full-color picture on the cover of Saint George dispatching the dragon with a spear. There was Beowulf holding the severed head of Grendel. There was Perseus chopping off Medusa's head, and there were more hackings and choppings and eviscerations than I have ever seen between the covers of any book.

"This is not what I had imagined reading my child as his bed-time story," said Caroline. "Why doesn't he like *Goodnight, Moon?*"

Max delightedly thumbed through the mayhem, stopping at each gory picture, demanding to know who was the good guy and who was the bad guy. He was very concerned only the good guys should win. Finally, I stopped him at the least gory picture he had encountered, showing two men in Greek frocks soaring above an azure sea, each with his own pair of wings.

"That's Daedalus and Icarus," I said. "The father made two sets of wings, one for himself—"

"No! No! Read!" Max would not accept an adaptation.

I read aloud, " 'No story more foreshadows the direction West-ern culture would take than the Greek myth of Daedalus.' " I stopped reading and looked up to Caroline. "I don't think this is written for four-year-olds."

"Go on," said Caroline. "It gets more interesting."

"Read!" Max demanded.

"For the Greeks, and for Western man, the hero rises above his difficulties and escapes peril, not by invoking with magical incantations the intervention of gods, but man escapes his bonds through his own works, his own science and art and craft."

I looked up again to Caroline, who was standing in the doorway, leaning against the jamb. She was smiling, watching us.

"Keep reading!" Max demanded.

"You following this?"

"Daedalus is the good guy."

"He's got it," said Caroline.

I looked up and saw Caroline was grinning now.

"Remind you of anyone?" she asked.

"Our friend," I said. "The professor. He wanted to break free of his bonds and fly around the Upper East Side."

"Look who wrote it," she said.

"What?"

"Look at the initials down at the bottom of the page."

"P.S.T."

"He's the editor, Professor Patrick S. Toomey."

"No!" I turned to the front cover, and sure enough, it was the professor. "Did you know?"

"No, Max picked it out. I didn't notice until we got home. I wasn't sure even then, but it says 'Professor of Classics, City College.' And when I read that part on Daedalus, I was sure."

"Good old Professor Toomey."

"Who's he?" asked Max.

"A patient of your mother's."

"Did he die?" Max knew that mother's patients tended to do that sort of thing, even if he wasn't quite sure what dying meant. He had picked up the idea of going to heaven from his school friends.

"Yes."

"Was he a good guy?"

"Yes," I said.

"And is he in heaven?"

"I imagine."

"You know," Max informed me solemnly. "You keep your arms when you go to heaven. D'you know why?"

"No, I didn't know that. Why?"

"Because you need to pick things up."

"I see."

"He's been talking about this," said Caroline. "I haven't known what to say. I leave the theological instruction to you."

"I like to think of Mr. Toomey as being in heaven," I said. "The Eternal Care Unit."

"What's that?"

"Another name for heaven. Where they take care of you forever."

"He drew the pictures?"

"No, he chose the stories."

"D'you know what he's doing in heaven?" Max said. "Talking to Davy Crockett."

Max had seen the Walt Disney version of Davy Crockett at the Alamo, and he understood Davy had died there and gone to heaven.

"I hope he is," I said.

"I don't think he'd waste much time on Davy Crockett," said Caroline. "He'd be hanging out with Homer and Euripides. Talking with them in their native tongue, having a wonderful time."

"Why not Davy Crockett?" Max demanded, indignant at the thought that anyone would not want to hang out with Davy Crockett.

"His interests ran to the classics, the professor's did," said Caroline. "Latin and Greek. He taught Latin and Greek in college."

"I'm going to college when I get twenty."

"Before then even."

"Oh, no! I'm staying here until I get twenty."

"He doesn't like the idea of breaking up the family," Caroline told me. "We've discussed this in great detail."

"Good man. You'll keep your mother company in her dotage."

"What's dotage?"

"Her old age."

Max laughed heartily at that idea. "Mom's not going old."

"Well, by the time you're twenty . . ." but I caught a look from Caroline that meant: Stay off this topic. Max was studying me carefully. "Oh, stay at home then," I said. "Your mom will appreciate it."

"Mom isn't going to get old like Mrs. Welch."

Mrs. Welch was a very nice seventy-year-old woman who lived next door.

"When you get old, you die," said Max. "Mom won't get old."

Caroline and I shared a hopeless eye-to-eye exchange.

I stood up and announced that it was bedtime.

Max tried to delay the inevitable by demanding to pee, and then by demanding the presence of some stuffed animal he had left downstairs, in a location only he could find. After these delaying tactics were exhausted, he climbed up into the upper bunk of his Cargo bunk bed and flopped over and fell asleep.

"He does not like the idea of leaving home or separation from mother or the dissolution of his rigid, ordered little world," said Caroline. "It's typical for his age. It's in the book."

"Oh, Christ, the book."

"He's very typical. He follows all the patterns as if he'd read the chapters."

"Good. We have a normal child."

"We have a wonderful child. Two wonderful children, whom you never see because you work too hard."

"Right now, I'm building a practice," I said. "I'll get to know them later."

"They'll grow up and go away to college and you'll miss the whole thing. They'll move out and all you'll have is me."

"That wouldn't be so bad," I said. "After all, you're all I started out with."

BEFORE MEMORY

Later that night, Caroline and I went in to look at the babies sleep. It was one of our favorite things.

We went into Max's room first, and watched, then to Sam, who slept on his back like a little man but with one thumb in his mouth and the other hand on his soft belly. Flashing by, as I watched them, was the image of that ward at Whipple where they kept the kids. And the kid who vomited the chocolate doughnut. The kids hooked up to IV poles who chased each other down the hallways never knowing what life without leukemia could be. And a dread deeper than anything I'd ever known took hold.

I looked at Caroline, and she was dabbing away tears with her sleeve.

"What's wrong?" I asked.

"Nothing."

"Oh," I said. "Nothing. Just stand there and sob."

"I was thinking about Mrs. Roundtree."

"Mrs. Roundtree?"

"Yes, and Mr. Roundtree, too."

"Mr. Roundtree! Spare me."

"I was thinking about how he must feel."

"What?"

"If I died tonight, these kids wouldn't even remember me."

"Max would."

"Only dimly. And I'd want you to remarry, so they'd have a mother."

"Naw," I said. "It'd just be me and the boys. No intruders."

"Don't say that. Promise me you'd find them a mother."

"No way."

"Promise! I am not kidding, you dirtball. I don't want my kids growing up without a mother. You'd ruin them. You'd make them as phobic and neurotic as you are. They'd never travel. They'd never learn a foreign language."

"Well, maybe a Swede. Or a Dane. I've always liked Scandinavians."

"No, French. I'd like that. Marie Claire. Marry some Marie Claire."

"Okay. My kids will speak French and I won't know what the hell they're saying."

"You don't know now, and Max speaks English."

"That's being very generous. Max speaks whatever language he speaks."

"Promise me."

"Okay."

"They'd forget what I look like. You'd have to show them old yellow photographs, and Max and Sam would look at you like you were some pitiful old moron and they'd humor you, but they'd have absolutely no recognition in their eyes. And they'd grow up never knowing how much I loved them."

"What's this have to do with Mr. Roundtree?"

"Everything. Doesn't it make you sad? Thinking about that family?"

"I try not to."

"But, it would be something that separates you from your kids, see? You'd have known their mother and they're looking at you like you're some old fart halfway to senility."

"Mr. Roundtree's kids were older. They'd remember their mother."

"Maybe for a while, but the memory would dim very quickly. They'd all forget eventually. Even the ten-year-old, by the time he's twenty, nothing left."

"Max would remember you."

"Maybe," said Caroline. "But so many memories would compete. So much to follow, to crowd out our time together. Which is so lopsided. I'd think back on life and what I'd remember is Max. And now Sam. They crowd out everything else. But for Max, I'd be like some preschool sweetheart. He wouldn't even remember the color of my hair."

"He'd remember," I reassured her. "Or I'd beat the shit out of him."

"Oh," Caroline said, holding my arm, putting her head on my shoulder. "I knew I could count on you."

BOOK III

Mere Mortals

But I always thought
That I'd see you again.

—JAMES TAYLOR

— 1 —

COLD QUARRY ROAD

That year the winter could not seem to get started. It was mid-January and it had not yet snowed or been bitter except for a few days at a time, and on the Friday of the party it had been warm enough to go without an overcoat during the day, although it got colder when the sun went down. I was late getting home. Friday night I was always late.

I was always late answering the Friday phone calls from all the walking worried who were seized by the intense desire to speak with their doctor before the weekend. Patients thus seized almost always suffered a strong aversion to making appointments they had to pay for, and so the only way they could get my attention was by the time-honored Friday afternoon call.

Caroline had called twice, reminding me it was a surprise party and we had to be there before the surprise-ees, and we could definitely not be late and I snapped at her. I said if she'd stop calling and let me see a few patients, I just might make it home in good time. And she hung up on me.

Nothing too unusual for a Friday night. Caroline was taut as a Doberman's leash after a week alone at home with the kids, and now we had an actual party to go to, with living, breathing, mentating adults, and she got a little frantic at the first signs that I might spoil it all, that I might just stroll in around nine-thirty and expect her to be the good wife of the doctor and understand why we couldn't make the party after all. But I knew the dedicated-doctor-got-held-up-at-the-office wouldn't play with Caroline. It wouldn't play even if it were true, and I had a patient in pulmonary edema. After five days with the kids, Caroline was in no mood to listen to reason.

It was seven-thirty when I pulled into our driveway and I knew Caroline would be in a fine state of fury. Caroline had her hands

full trying to get the kids fed and bathed and get herself dressed
for the party with no help from me.

Stepping into the house, I became momentarily disoriented—
the place was immaculate, a condition so rare, the place was almost
unrecognizable. The woman who lived above our neighbor's garage across the street was coming to baby-sit and Caroline had
spent the day getting the house in order: cleaning grimy finger-
prints off walls, washing dishes, clearing from underfoot the drop-
pings of two children, stacking two weeks' worth of newspapers in
the garage for disposal, vacuuming, and doing all this while the
kids did their best to undo it even as she worked.

"Where have you been?" Caroline said, biting off the words,
trying to keep it under control. "You know we have to be there
before eight. Look at the time." She was still in her bathrobe.
"Sam's asleep. Read Max."

She shoved me into Max's room with a book, *Where the Wild
Things Are,* and she went off to change. Max had been bathed and
dressed in his blue cotton zip-up single-piece pajamas with the
bear embroidered over his breast and he smelled clean and fra-
grant from the shampoo. We sat in his reading chair and he took
his customary position in my lap and I read using all the different
voices and Max concentrated on the pictures, correcting me when
I got a sentence wrong. He couldn't read, but he knew the book
by heart and would catch even the smallest error of rendition.

Caroline stepped back into Max's room all dressed up, in her
black wool dress, high heels, the dark gray Ann Taylor lamb's-
wool jacket, and her Jackie Chalkley black beaded necklace. Her
hair was shining and her skin luminous, and she looked wonderful.

Max took one look at her and burst into tears.

"Don't go!" he wailed. "You're going to leave me!"

Max was no dummy. Max knew his mother didn't get all
dressed up and looking like a million dollars for him or for me.
Mother was going out and leaving Max, no doubt with some toad
of a baby-sitter.

He clung to her hemline, looking up with tears glistening, imploring, "Don't go."

"I'm going to a party," Caroline said, stroking his cheek, trying
not to laugh, and trying not to scream, trying not to shout "I am
escaping!"

"I hate parties," said Max.

Caroline sat down with Max on his bed.

"Don't leave me," said Max.

Max was two months past three, and on one thing Caroline's many child development books agreed: Three is an age children do not suffer gladly separation from mother.

"I am not leaving you," said Caroline, peering into the most somber three-year-old face I had ever seen. "I am going to a party and I am coming back."

That was in the books: Reassure the child the separation is only temporary. The bond is not broken. The child must be made to understand that because you are out of sight does not mean you are not thinking of him.

"You're going."

"I am not leaving you. I would never leave you. I always come back."

She kissed him good night and his lower lip started trembling again. And Caroline put a finger on his lips, and she said, "I always come back," and he stopped.

I read him some more and he fell asleep before the last page and I lifted him into bed and looked at him and kissed him, between his eyes. I loved the way he breathed through his mouth and the way his eyelashes fluttered.

Slipping into our bedroom, I changed for the party. There was no time to shower, but I changed my shirt to a fresh white one, and I drew out a tie I almost never wore because I had bought it one Friday the thirteenth, which made it a bad luck tie. But it was a regimental striped tie in the colors of the Wimbledon Club. The party we were going to was for an Englishman, a diplomat, who belonged to the Wimbledon Club and he always got a kick out of the tie, and anyway, it was a nice tie, purple and green. I pulled on a thick gray tweed jacket and presented myself to the mirror for inspection and passed marginally. I was dog-tired and would have stayed home in an instant if Caroline had said she didn't really care about the party.

But Caroline cared. She was all dressed up, wearing eye makeup and lip gloss and she needed some adult company.

I walked down the hall to Sam's room and pushed the door open silently. Caroline was sitting in the chair next to the crib nursing Sam, whose eyes were closed and who looked asleep, except for the puffing of his cheeks as he sucked. He wasn't sucking often. Caroline stood up and lowered him into his crib. We looked at him sleep for a few moments and she kissed him and we slipped out of the room. Caroline slid her nursing pad back into her bra, buttoned up her dress, and rearranged herself in the hall and we heard the knocking at the door.

I ran downstairs, afraid the sitter would not read the sign over the doorbell: "Knock. Do not ring. Children Asleep."

She did not ring and I let her in. Caroline went over the instructions: telephone numbers, my beeper number if there were some problem reaching us at the party in some emergency, the bottled breast milk for Sam, if he should wake up.

I went out to warm up the car. It had got colder with the dark. I started to warm up the Buick, but Caroline came out and said, "No. Let's take yours."

Caroline hated her clunky old Buick and the Buick's heater didn't work. The Buick was a big, heavy car, and on its last gasping miles, but it was the closest thing to an armored truck, and with the kids strapped into their car seats in the back, it felt safe, so Caroline agreed to keep it. But this was our night out together, she wanted to go in style, and in warmth, although the Honda was a light car for winter driving.

I started up the Honda, and let it heat up. After a few minutes, the engine was warm and I switched on the heater. The Honda had a very good heater and the car got very nicely warm. Then Caroline came out of the house, wearing her thick Benetton winter coat over her jacket, carrying a bottle of wine, and she slid into her seat.

"Put on your seat belt," I said.

"Not with this coat," she said. "We're late. Let's get going."

We drove down to Potomac Road, and stopped at the traffic light waiting for the left-turn signal, and Caroline looked conspicuously at her watch and I said, "What do you want me to do, run the light?" She said nothing. The light flashed green and we headed out toward horse country, where the houses were zoned for two-acre lots, and backyard pools were de rigueur. We turned off, onto Cold Quarry Road, at the old stone blacksmith's house, and headed straight up.

* * *

Cold Quarry Road is like many east-west roads in that part of Montgomery County, two lanes and narrow, but it was narrower than most, and had no shoulders at all, tall pine trees rising straight up from the road, almost touching the asphalt, and it was steep as a roller coaster and winding. Every once in a while a big truck would come around a curve too fast and its wheels would cross the double yellow line and you had to veer off into the pine trees on the right where the shoulder should have been.

"This is really sort of a dangerous road, when you think about it," I said as I shifted down into second gear. The Honda was automatic, but even the automatics needed to be down-shifted on that steep part near River Road. We came to the top of the rise and off to the sharp rightward curve in the road and down.

"One of those big garbage trucks almost ran me into the trees this afternoon," Caroline said. "I had the kids in the car going off to Montgomery Mall, and this truck came across the double yellow line and I swerved and the kids didn't stop screaming until we got to the mall."

"Probably ought to take the Beltway," I said.

"Oh, sure. With those big eighteen-wheelers running up your rear end doing eighty miles an hour."

The party was for a couple we liked, who were being transferred back to England. We were all going to be kept hiding in the basement while the couple, who thought they were simply coming to a quiet dinner with two friends, would be brought in through the front door, given cocktails in the living room, and once they were comfortably ensconced, were then to be stampeded by everybody they had ever met in Washington. It really was fun. We all huddled in the basement, whispering to strangers caught up in the same ridiculous circumstances, giggling and trying to carry on introductory conversations, being shushed every few minutes. Then, at the signal, we thundered into the living room taking them totally by surprise.

They responded perfectly, of course, with great protests about being duped, but with pleasure at seeing all their friends. Caroline and I talked to a British diplomat and his wife for a long time. She was a doctor, with two kids almost exactly the same ages as our kids, and Caroline got her phone number for a "play group." He was very funny and apparently had some function at the embassy having to do with trying to persuade our Congress that whatever trade concessions they made toward England, they weren't nearly enough.

A little before midnight, I started looking at my watch, thinking about the baby-sitter. We thanked the hosts, and said good-bye to the guests of honor.

"Do come visit us in London."

"Oh, of course we will," said Caroline, with a look of vast irony to me, knowing she would never be able to get me to fly in an aluminum machine across the ocean.

Then we walked out into the wet cold night.

"Let there be heat," Caroline said, when we got into the car. She started flipping on the switches for the heater.

"The engine has to warm up," and I flipped the switch off again. "Seat belt."

"Just let's get home." She wrapped her coat around her tightly.

The road was just as narrow and winding as it had been the way out and we got the green light at Bradley Boulevard and headed down for the last mile home.

"Who was that couple we were talking to?" I asked. "I never got his name in all the noise."

"Derrick Tinker. Her name's Christine. Her first kid was born five days before Max, and the younger one's two months older than Sam. She's still breast-feeding. We talked about trying to get out of the house with one last suckle for the road."

"Inevitable," I said. "Go out for some adult company, and what do we talk about? Breast-feeding."

There was a car coming down the hill in our direction. It lurched toward the right then toward us, then back toward the right. Suddenly it swung across into our lane, the headlights blinding.

Caroline said, "Uh-oh."

I remember swerving hard to the right, toward a driveway. The car seemed to be broadside in our lane, but somehow coming straight at us.

ALIVE AS YOU OR ME

When I regained consciousness, I thought: Christ, he hit my car.

Then, another thought: I cannot afford to fix this car.

That was probably the single most connected sequence of thought I had that night.

That was before I discovered Caroline.

I remember a wave of dread that I might be given a ticket or even arrested, when the cops arrived. Why I thought that, I have no idea, but I began to rehearse my protestations of innocence. The fact is, I wasn't sure, when I first came to, about anyone's innocence. I had no clear idea what had happened.

Then I looked over toward Caroline.

She was curled up on the floor, her head on the seat where she had been sitting. She seemed to be growling, "Uh-uh-uh-uh."

"Caroline."

She didn't answer at all, she just kept making that strange guttural sound. My door wouldn't open. My seat belt held me and I popped it open. I climbed over to Caroline, noticing the spiderweb pattern on the windshield on Caroline's side. I lifted her head up. There was that dent in her forehead, the wash of blood down her face to her chin. Her eyes were rolled up into her head.

"Oh, God, Caroline."

"Uh-uh-uh-uh."

Not here, please not here. Don't let this happen.

She's going to seize. Grand mal, right here, tonic clonic. She's hurt inside her skull. She's bleeding into her brain. Her legs are curled up below her.

The car's going to explode.

I crawled over her, got her door open and got out her side and leaned back in and put one hand under her knees and one under her arms and lifted her out.

She cried out. No words—just a cry. I couldn't hold her and staggered with her a few feet away from the car. Screaming from somewhere else. Not a scream, a wail, somewhere, nearby but from somewhere invisible, like the sound track in a movie. Sounds from nowhere.

I laid her down on the black glistening asphalt. There was a mist, and in the streetlight everything seemed to shimmer and the black of the asphalt seemed to sparkle. For mid-January, it wasn't that cold. No ice. A wet chill.

Caroline lay on her back, not moving her arms or legs. I knelt over her. She seemed to be trying to open her eyes.

"Oh, oh, oh."

"Caroline, Caroline."

I put my finger on her wrist pulse. I couldn't feel it. She was all vasoconstricted. Her neck pulse was throbbing. Her heart was going.

Her eyes rolled down under her lids, but the lids did not open. "Cold," she said. "I'm so cold." Lovely words. Speech. A living brain.

"Caroline? Caroline?"

Eyes opening. Eyelashes fluttering. Come on. Open. Look at me.

"Uh?"

"Caroline."

"What?"

"Caroline."

"What happened?"

"Car crash. You were out. Oh, God, you were so out."

"What? What happened?"

"I've got to get you away from the car. It might go. It might explode."

I put an arm under her neck and the other under her knees and started to lift.

"Oh, God!" Caroline shouted, reaching for her knee. "Don't! My knee!"

I stood with her in my arms. I've heard you get power you never know you had in those situations, but she felt heavy in my arms. I staggered with her up the driveway, toward the house above us.

We passed the other car, the one that hit us. It was flipped over on its roof and the wheels were not spinning. It was lying at right angles to what was left of my car, in my lane, so the two of them formed a T. The other car was a big American car. It looked dark and coffinlike. I didn't see anyone moving inside. I thought the wail must have come from inside that car.

I continued up the hill toward the house. It seemed a long way off, but there was a front light on, and there was a flagstone sidewalk running up to the door. When I reached the door, it opened, as if they had been watching me approach.

There was a woman in a bathrobe, but she didn't say anything. She opened her mouth and stared at Caroline.

"My wife has been hurt. May I bring her in?"

She shrank back. I stepped in, and the woman whisked away a carpet from the front hall, so Caroline wouldn't bleed on it, I suppose. I lay Caroline on her back on the black-tiled floor.

"My knee." Caroline reached down toward her left knee. "God. My knee."

"You're talking, thank God."

"Oh, my back."

Oh, wonderful. A spinal injury. And I had just carried her twenty yards.

"My leg hurts. God, I can't believe the pain."

I looked at her leg, halfway between the knee and the ankle was a deep depression in the shin. The leg was clearly broken. The back worried me more. But she was talking. The back could be dealt with. The leg just has bones. Bones heal. The skull contains the brain. You can bleed into a brain.

"What is it?" she said.

"Your leg is broken."

"But what is it? Oh, my chest."

She wasn't focusing on my eyes, although I was staring right into her face, trying to give her a focal point as we had never been able to do in puff-and-pant class. "Caroline, keep your eyes open."

She opened her eyes, but she wasn't focusing.

"My leg. Where are the kids? Brendan?"

"I'm right here."

She was like Vince Montebelli, when he went all delirious and thought he was at home and his mother was in the kitchen. Her brain was all scrambled.

A piercing shriek right above my head. An adolescent girl in a leather jacket and black tights looking down at me and Caroline. She was screaming, "God! God! God!" The girl stepped around us and raced up the stairs.

"I'm so cold," Caroline said.

I took off my jacket and laid it over her.

I looked up. The woman in the bathrobe stared down at me. Her face looked twisted and terrified.

"Do you have a blanket?" I said. "My wife's been hurt."

She disappeared.

Caroline's face was awash in blood, but nothing seemed to be pumping actively. There was the dent in her forehead, and the wash of blood from that down her nose to her lips. But she was looking better.

I put my finger on her wrist pulse. It was strong and fast now.

A young man, about twenty, big chested, came through the door. He was wearing a T-shirt with "BCC rescue" printed on the front.

Why is he wearing nothing but a T-shirt in the middle of January?

He carried some sort of metal case.

He began to examine Caroline, feeling her chest. "I'm a paramedic," he said. "You're going to be all right now."

A cowboy, I thought. Still, it was somehow reassuring he was here. On the other end of his truck was the hospital.

I think Caroline might have smiled. She looked at me. "What happened?"

"Car crash," I said.

"She says her chest hurts," I said. "And her knee and her leg's broken."

"Your chest?" said the cowboy. He felt her chest wall, very skillfully, I thought.

"Broken ribs," he said.

I hadn't even thought of broken ribs. Of course. That's why her chest hurt. And I hadn't even thought of it.

"Can I take her blood pressure?" I asked, pointing to his stethoscope.

He looked at me. "Sure." He handed me a blood pressure instrument from his case. "What is it?" he said.

I told him. It was decent. "She was unconscious," I said. "Until just before you got here."

"Out cold?"

"Unresponsive to deep pain," I said, using that phrase we had used so often at Whipple to mean that a patient was in deep coma. At Whipple, we had said that when we meant we didn't think the patient had a snowball's chance.

"You a doctor?" The paramedic looked at me with no special interest. He had picked up on the phrase, and he put that together with seeing me take Caroline's blood pressure, but he wasn't about to defer to me. He continued his probing of Caroline's rib cage.

"Yes," I said. "She's a nurse." I have no idea why I thought that was important to say.

The cowboy began examining her, listening to her lungs with his stethoscope. Maybe I was saying, She's one of us. I don't know. I said a lot of things that night.

Then I thought about the kids. I stood up and looked around and the woman in the bathrobe stared at me, mouth still agape, saying nothing.

"Do you have a phone?"

She looked at me dully. "A phone?"

"A phone." I made a dialing motion and held an imaginary receiver to my ear.

She pointed through a lighted door. I walked through it to a kitchen.

I punched in my number. Busy. I looked at my watch. Twenty past midnight and the sitter's on the phone.

I stepped back into the hallway where Caroline was lying. The paramedic was still going over her. The woman in the bathrobe was still staring at her. There was shrieking upstairs.

I walked back and tried the phone again. Then it hit me: Max had been up to his old tricks. He had been playing with the phone again and the phone was off the hook. Probably had been off the hook all night. I tried to remember Bob and Florence Goldenheim's number. They were neighbors. Friends and neighbors. I tried a number.

Sleep drunk voice, Bob's. "Hello?"

"Bob, this is Brendan."

"Brendan?"

"Brendan O'Brien. We've been in an auto accident. The phone is off the hook at our house. Max probably was playing with the phone. Could you go over there and tell the sitter what's happened? Ask her to stay. We won't be home tonight."

"Brendan? What happened?"

"Bad accident."

"You okay?"

"Caroline's hurt. Bad."

"Where are you?"

"Cold Quarry Road."

"We'll go over."

"Thanks."

"Brendan? Is Caroline going to be okay?"

"I don't know," I said. And saying it, I realized it was true. The paramedic and I were talking as if things were in control. I was on the phone, as if I were cool and collected and arranging a shift change for the baby-sitter, but the fact was, I really did not know the answer to that question. The matter was still in considerable doubt. Caroline had been unresponsive to deep pain.

I hung up and walked back into the hallway.

Another cowboy, short and fat, with the same T-shirt but wearing a rubber fireman's raincoat, jumped through the door. "Seven in the car," he shouted. "What you got here, Dale?"

"Broken ribs. Head injury. Broken leg. Knee. What's in the car?"

"Nothing much. We got 'em on the lawn. Nobody bad."

"Then this's the worst, here. Call 'em in."

"Dust-off?"

"Yeah, yeah. This one here. Let's go as soon as they're ready."

"Your wife has to go to the hospital," the cowboy told me.

"I don't suppose I could persuade you to take her to University."

"No way. She goes to the Medical Center by chopper."

I knew it didn't matter what I said.

The other cowboy brought up an aluminum gurney stretcher and some dark wool army blankets. They slid the mat from the gurney under Caroline and hooked it up to the aluminum side bars and cranked it up and lifted her off the floor that way. It was calming to see them do something I had seen done so often. I knew how that gurney worked, and their calm efficiency working it reassured me. They might be cowboys, but they knew how to work that gurney.

They rolled Caroline out of the front door and lifted her off the cement porch and set her gurney down on the lawn with a little jolt.

"Oh! God!" Caroline shouted, lifting her hand to her forehead. "Don't drop me like that."

"Sorry, lady," said the short, fat paramedic. The muscular one pulled the gurney from the head end and the fat one took up the rear. I tagged along near Caroline's head, trying to talk to her. They rolled the gurney down to the asphalt driveway and rolled her down to the ambulance that they had backed in, at the bottom of the driveway.

Funny the things you notice: As we came down the driveway I saw the plates on the upside-down car that had hit us. They were the distinctive red, white, and blue plates of the diplomatic corps.

THE DUST-OFF

They lifted Caroline's gurney up into the ambulance and they did not jolt her at all, setting her down. The muscular paramedic sat by her head, taking her blood pressure, and I got in and sat on the platform beside her.

"Are you okay?" she asked.

"Not a scratch," I said.

The ambulance lurched into motion and Caroline said, "Where are we going?"

"The helicopter's coming," said the paramedic.

I noticed that the second paramedic, the short, fat one, had been assigned to me. He sat right next to my elbow and took my pulse as we rode.

"You look frightful," said Caroline. "Your face is all blood-streaked."

"How are you?"

"The leg is killing me. My knee. What happened?"

"Car wreck."

The ambulance headed back toward Bradley Boulevard. I remember thinking we were less than a mile from home. The timing had to be perfect for us to be hit by that car.

"What happened?" Caroline asked again.

"It came across the road, rolled right into us."

"I don't remember. Did I see it coming?"

"Even before I did."

"How could it happen?" Caroline said. "We were almost home."

"Everything is written," I said.

"It's all luck," said Caroline.

We could hear them talking into a radio in the front of the ambulance, all the static and all the gibberish the cowboys love. They weren't using the siren, for which I was glad, because it would have frightened Caroline and made things even more difficult.

They pulled off into the driveway of an elementary school.

"Where will they land the helicopter?" I said.

"In the field, behind the school," said the first paramedic. He seemed to be in charge.

The ambulance stopped and the head paramedic climbed past us and he got out through the rear door. The other paramedic followed him and he stood at the open doorway looking toward the front of the ambulance, squinting into the night.

"They're taking us in a helicopter?"

"Yes."

"Where?"

"To the Medical Center."

"In Washington?"

"Yes. They have a trauma center there."

"In a helicopter?"

"Yes."

"You'll come." Caroline looked up at me, and for the first time in our life together, she looked really afraid.

"They'd need a crowbar to pry me away from you."

In a few moments we could hear the unmistakable thump-thumping of a helicopter. It seemed like a long time before anything happened. Caroline and I sat in the ambulance and I held her hand. It was cold and bloody, but when I squeezed, she could squeeze back. We sat and waited.

Caroline listened to the thump-thumping, as the blades slowed and her eyes searched around, but we were inside the ambulance and neither of us could know what was happening outside.

"They called in a helicopter?" Caroline asked.

"Yes."

"For me?"

"Yes. I think the others are going by ambulance."

"Then I really am in trouble." She looked me in the eye, and I had to look away.

Then I caught myself and made myself look at her. "You look much better now. But you were really out before. So they aren't taking any chances."

"You think they'll do a CAT scan?"

"Oh, I don't know. Eventually, maybe."

"My leg hurts so much. I never knew anything could hurt so much."

"It's broken."

She tried to look at it, but she couldn't lift her head well. They had snapped a cervical stabilizer under her chin.

"I never saw much orthopedics," she said, looking at the ceiling of the ambulance. "Except for Mrs. Roundtree that time."

"Yours isn't like that. They'll set your leg and it'll heal. There's no tumor in your bone."

"Remember how it sounded with Mrs. Roundtree that time?" She looked at me. "Like a tree snapping in the wind." She looked off into some distant place. "I'll never forget that sound."

We sat there in the ambulance and listened for the paramedics. But it was quiet now, not even the helicopter sounds.

Finally, we heard footsteps and voices and the head paramedic stepped into the doorway.

"Let's go," he said.

I jumped out and helped them lift Caroline's stretcher down. It landed on the ground with a little jolt and she cried out.

"Oh, God! My leg. Please, my leg."

We started rolling her stretcher toward a very dark field. I could see the outline of the helicopter, its blades slowly revolving, and a wire fence directly ahead of us.

There was a man in a jumpsuit who looked like a pilot of a jet fighter standing at the fence, talking to a fireman in a long black coat. When we reached them the fireman put out his hand and touched my chest.

"Just the patient," he said.

"I'm her doctor," I said.

"Just the patient."

"Come on, buddy. She's my wife. I'll just sit with her."

They were rolling her away. Caroline looked back and reached an arm out for me. "Brendan," she said.

I started around the fireman, but he stepped in front of me and two more firemen I hadn't noticed came in from either side.

"Just the patient, buddy," the fireman said. His face was hard. He meant business. "It's the law."

They had her moving toward the helicopter, and their forms were getting dimmer as they receded into the darkness.

"You're not taking my wife anywhere," I said. "Unless she lets you and unless I let you. That, good buddy, is the law. They call it informed consent."

The fireman glanced at his companions, and looks were exchanged.

"You a lawyer or something?"

I looked over his shoulder. I could no longer distinguish the shape of the stretcher or the paramedics who were rolling Caroline toward the helicopter, only the outline of the blades and body against the mist.

"Yeah, and you're all going to have to explain in court why you transported a patient against her will. That's called assault and battery, if you lay hands on a person against her will. That's a felony."

"Look, mister," said the first fireman. "You got kids?"

"Yes, two."

"Well, the thing is, every once in a while, one of those whirlybirds goes down. And well, if both your wife and you are in it. Well, then your kids got nobody to take care of them."

"Then don't take her in the chopper." I could hear the propellers moving now, getting louder. They were getting ready to lift off. "Take her in the ambulance," I said. "To University Hospital."

"She's too bad hurt," he shouted over the noise. "She's got to go to the trauma center."

"I know how bad she is," I shouted. "I'm a doctor!"

"I thought you said you were a lawyer."

"I'm both."

It didn't matter what I said. I could see it now, the helicopter's black form lifting up into the dark, misty night sky.

— 4 —
BACK TO THE SCENE

They took me back to the car in the ambulance. I kept thinking about Caroline up there in the air in that helicopter. Now the helicopter will go down. That's all we'd need. It is all written. It is all luck. They had taken her right by me. I had been led around like a lamb.

When I got out, a fireman came up and spoke to my paramedic.

"You got the driver of the Honda?"

"Right here."

"The cops want him."

The paramedic walked with me silently toward a white police car. We passed my car and I stopped to look at it. The front part of it was compressed and it was clear it would never drive again. The other car lay upside down, like a large dead animal, belly up, completely blocking the road. There was nobody in it.

We reached the policeman. He wore the smart khaki uniform of the Montgomery County police with his gold badge and his silver buttons. He was sitting bareheaded in his white police car with the door open and the blue light on his roof flashing slowly.

He looked up and the paramedic said, "This is the other driver."

"Get in the other side," the cop said.

I walked around the other side of the car and slid in.

He continued writing on his clipboard. There was a plastic photo ID driver's license clipped under the clip.

"You were driving the Honda?" he said.

"Yes."

"Let me see your driver's license."

For a moment I thought I had left my wallet in my jacket, which was still on Caroline, in a helicopter. But it was in my back pocket. I fished it out and handed it to him and he clipped it next to another license and copied down my name and address.

"What happened?"

"I was driving toward Potomac Road," I said.

"East to west?"

"I don't know. Toward Potomac Road. Is that west?"

"Yes."

"Toward Potomac Road. And this car was coming toward us in his lane, until just before he got to us. He was just about to pass by. Then he seemed to lurch right and then left, right across in my lane. I must have hit him broadside. I think I tried to swerve right, but there's not much shoulder."

The cop wrote for a while. He had a form with a generic road diagram and he had drawn the paths of our cars and where they had landed.

"I can draw you a picture," I said.

"No," he said. "Just tell me."

I stopped talking.

"How fast were you going?" he asked, without looking up.

"The speed limit."

He looked up, and for the first time he met my eyes.

"There's a sign thirty-five yards up the road that says 'Curve, twenty mph.' "

First the fireman, now this cop. I was in the hands of the authorities tonight. I had been an authority once, I thought, in that ER in Charlestown, where I dreaded the auto accident casualties, and Caroline had told me to quit, if I didn't feel competent to deal with auto accidents. I thought about the guy on the other end of the helicopter ride, the guy in the ER who'd get Caroline. I hoped he was a real ER doc. I hoped he'd know exactly what to do.

"I said the sign said 'Curve, twenty,' " the cop repeated.

I looked at him, "And I said I was doing the speed limit."

"Was it raining?"

"No, it was misty. But not raining."

"Where were you coming from?"

"Near Rockville."

"Movie? Party?"

"Party."

"Had anything to drink?"

"No. I was driving."

He wrote that down.

I was being led around that night, and sitting there in that police

car, I decided I'd had enough of the docile-citizen role. First they
wheel Caroline away, and I just stand there gaping, now the cop is
ragging me and my car is flattened in my own lane.

"Look," I said. "His car is sitting on its roof in my lane. My car
is over to the right of the road. How much investigation does it
take to figure out what happened?"

He looked at me for a moment, then went back to his clipboard.
"Kid driving is sixteen. He had eight kids, besides himself, packed
in that car. They'd been at a party at his father's farm in Potomac,
come back by Potomac Road. I wrote him two citations: one for
overloading the car, one for exceeding prima facie speed limits on
a wet road."

"He drinking?"

"He denies it."

"He denies it? You don't know?"

"No point in finding out. Father's a diplomat with the Turkish
embassy."

"Father's a diplomat," I repeated dully.

"Yeah, fat little greaser, got here before I did, waving his diplomatic card around at everybody. Can't touch his son. We might
haul his innocent baby off to the station house, you know. Work
him over or something. He's got his kid now."

He opened his door and got out of the car. Our interview was
over. I got out my side and walked back toward my car. I heard
heavy footsteps behind me and I turned. It was the cop.

"You forgot your license."

"Thanks."

"How's your wife?"

"I don't know."

"And you're a doctor, right? You should."

"How'd you know that?"

"Hospital parking decals on your left rear window."

"Good pickup," I said, with an irony that escaped him.

"I'm an old hand at this. Been doing it six years."

"Investigating accidents?"

"Yeah. Four others before yours tonight. I was standing out on
East West Highway tonight and a drunk came along and took the
door right off my car."

"Tough night for you," I said.

"Naw, happens all the time."

I looked at him and thought: You're a schmuck. Then I thought: No, you're not. You just see this all the time and you can accept it as something that happens to people. Mr. Roundtree must have felt the same way about me when he first brought Mrs. Roundtree into the hospital. I must not have seemed any more sympathetic or attractive than this cop. When I was at Whipple, admissions rolling up to my door were just more work. That's what auto accidents were to this cop: nothing to wring hands about and say, "I'm so sorry," like some phony funeral director. This was the kind of thing this cop dealt with, and he wasn't wasting any emotion on it.

I walked over to my car and noticed the crowd of neighbors on the lawn, and a camera crew from some local TV station with their bright lights. I crawled in through the right-hand door, and reached in for my keys, still in the ignition, and pulled them out. Then I looked at the windshield again. Caroline's head had hit that windshield and the force with which she made contact was plainly written there. There were the kids' safety chairs strapped on the rear seats. I'd have to get those later. I looked in the trunk, but it was empty. The paramedic, who must have shadowed me the whole time, stepped forward, holding a black plastic garbage bag.

"We emptied it out. Everything's in here."

I looked in: Caroline's coat, and her Jackie Chalkley necklace and her shoes.

Then I remembered my tie. My bad-luck, bought-on-Friday-the-thirteenth tie, and I pulled it off and threw it back at the car and it landed there, on the roof.

The paramedic looked at me closely. "You okay?"

"Never liked that tie," I said.

MINOR MORT...

— 5 —

THE EMERGENCY ROOM

They took me to the nearest emergency room. The only thing I remember about the place was the cement helicopter landing port right in front of the ER door, which was lighted with big spotlights. The landing pad was painted in various primary colors and it looked very efficient, as if a dozen helicopters could land in close-order drill, if necessary. They could have landed Caroline there, if the medical situation had been right. But the paramedics had decided Caroline's injuries were too severe to be taken care of locally, and she had to go to the Medical Center.

I phoned Bob Goldenheim from the ER and he drove me across Washington in the black night to the Medical Center, which was in the cut-and-slash part of town. We drove past the boarded-up, burned-out blocks, and I comforted myself with the thought that all the best trauma units are in combat zones. When she was stable, we could have Caroline transferred over to the university hospital in the upscale part of town where I practiced, but now she was better off here. I kept telling myself all this, but I wasn't believing a word of it. This was the part of town where even the police rode around with their windows up and their doors locked and there was no place to hide.

We parked in a parking lot marked, "Trauma Center," and we trotted up to the sliding glass doors.

I stopped right before we walked through them and Bob almost ran into me from behind. I stood there with the doors yawning open in front of me, trying to work up the courage to step through them.

"Maybe I better go in first," Bob said. "And ask about Caroline."

"No," I said. "I'll be okay now."

As soon as I stepped into the emergency room, I felt better. It was all so familiar. Bob, on the other hand, blanched noticeably and hung back, his eyes jumping from stall to stall where nurses struggled with patients on stretchers, bloodied, battered, cut and slashed patients, and he looked at me and said, "Welcome to the Real World." But I saw nurses in blue scrub suits, and along one wall was a bank of X-ray view boxes, and EKG machines, a defibrillator, all the usual equipment. It looked like the Manhattan Hospital emergency room, like the ERs in Boston, as all emergency rooms all the way to California must look.

It looked like home.

A man in a white coat and blue scrub suit came toward me. He extended his hand toward me but suddenly withdrew it to sneeze into a tissue. Then he said, "Dr. O'Brien, I presume."

We shook hands.

"Your wife's CAT scan was fine. No intracranial bleed."

"Thanks," I said. Then I realized he had told me he had already got the CAT scan of Caroline's head and she hadn't bled into her brain. She had been unconscious and there was that ghastly spiderweb on the windshield, but somehow her brain had come through undamaged.

"She's in there," the ER doc said, pointing to a glass-walled stall. "Jack Thoreau's just cleaning up her face a little. Know him?"

"No."

"Plastic surgeon. Really good. He's been working on her for about an hour and a half. She's going to look just fine. I know it's hard to believe, but she really will look just about the same, Jack says."

"I don't care," I said.

He looked at me, uncomprehending.

"I mean," I said. "As long as she's alive." He looked at me as if he could not quite hear me. I tried to explain: "She looked so bad. She was really out for a while. I couldn't get her to say a word. I thought she must have bled into her head."

"They often look real bad at the scene," he said. "But she'll be fine. Her leg's pretty smashed."

His name was Jack Marks. He was a trauma doc. Later, Caroline would call them her pair of Jacks, the plastic surgeon and the trauma doc. Trauma Jack—T.J. for short—would take care of her from the moment she hit the emergency room and afterward on the trauma ward, until she was transferred to the orthopedic ser-

vice. Trauma Jack had examined her when she arrived and he had
sent her down to CAT scan and he had called the plastic surgeon,
who was now sewing up Caroline's face in what looked like a full-
fledged operating room with a glass wall so you could see everything happening inside.

I had never seen an emergency room with an operating room
built right into it.

"It looks like an OR," I said, in wonder.

"Yes, it is," said Trauma Jack, his eyes dancing. "We can do
everything right here in the emergency room. Never have to
leave. We can open a chest right here. Done it plenty."

Trauma Jack was obviously very proud of his emergency room.

"Amazing," I said. "I thought I saw some kind of X-ray machine when I came in."

"Oh, sure. We develop 'em right here. Never have to leave."

He gave me the grand tour, like Captain Nemo showing off his
state of the art submarine. He led me to the X-ray view boxes.

"These are her films," T.J. said, pointing to a set of chest X rays
and leg films. He sneezed three times, violently, into a cloth handkerchief. "Rotten cold," he said. His eyes turned rheumy-looking,
and his nose ran, but he smiled at the films. He was very proud of
their high quality. "Real nice films, aren't they?"

They were Caroline's chest and Caroline's leg. You didn't need
four years of medical school to see what was wrong there. The
tibia was in pieces and the fibula had a spiral fracture. That didn't
bother me. The CAT scan was normal, he had said. As long as her
brain was okay, the rest was just orthopedics.

The chest film was more of a blow. It looked like every rib on
the left side was broken. They looked just like broken twigs. The
ends of the ribs were jagged and poking out at all different angles,
not aligned at all. I couldn't imagine how they could ever heal.

"Oh, they heal up fine," T.J. said. "But they'll hurt like suckers
for a good long while. And the lung. Look at that."

Soft-tissue injury is harder to appreciate on plain film, but you
could see her lung injury clearly and there was an effusion, a collection of blood at the base of the left lung.

"Her gases are fine," said T.J., anticipating my question. Her
blood gases, he meant. The measure of how well she was getting
oxygen into her bloodstream. That's what the lungs are for, and as
long as she had enough lung to aerate her blood, she was okay.

I looked at that effusion on Caroline's chest film and the image of that Spanish lady at Whipple popped up, the lady with the effusion. Caroline tapping out the effusion. Caroline sticking in the needle and the fluid rushing out and Caroline being so proud and feeling so accomplished. And then I thought of Mrs. Roundtree with her effusions, and suddenly I felt nauseated and the lights seemed to dim.

Then I heard Trauma Jack say, "Are you okay?"

"Oh," I said. "Sure."

He looked at me appraisingly. "You were driving?"

"I'm fine. They took me to Memorial. You know, they never took my blood pressure in both arms," I said.

A great sly grin crossed T.J.'s face. He looked to a nurse standing at his elbow and said, with great irony, "The renowned trauma center at Memorial General Hospital. For Chrissake."

In any deceleration injury, when the driver strikes the wheel with his chest, you worry about aortic tears. I had been wearing a seat belt and had probably not hit the steering wheel, but one of the things you always check is blood pressure in both arms. Nobody had done that at Memorial. Nobody had done squat at Memorial. They were designated a trauma center and they had a fancy helicopter pad with painted patterns and they had bright lights and everybody wore spiffy-looking scrubs, and, for all the world, they looked like a trauma center, but the proof is in the details of what you do, and they had done nothing but look the part.

"They do a neurological on you?" asked T.J.

"No."

"They get a CBC?"

"No bloods were drawn."

"What the fuck did they do?"

"A urine," I said. "And some old gomer doc came in and rolled my head around. I was in a pretty big hurry to get out of there. It wasn't his fault."

"You don't let the patient tell you he's well. You tell the patient," said Trauma Jack. He sneezed again and smiled at a nurse who stood at his elbow. "Some trauma fucking center." Then back to me. "Step over here. Take off your shirt."

I took off my shirt, and for the first time saw myself in the mirror. The imprint of the seat belt crossed from shoulder to waist in deep purple bruises.

Within five minutes I had a chest X ray, an electrocardiogram, bloods drawn, and neck films done. T.J. hardly had to say a word: his team simply swung into action like the proverbial well-oiled machine. I owed that paramedic who called for the helicopter that took Caroline to this place. They were good here.

T.J. looked into my eyeballs with his ophthalmoscope.

He finished with me and started sneezing again.

"I always get the flu," he said. "Your wife said you were in ID."

"I'm surprised she could even remember," I said. "She was not making much sense. Her head must have cleared on the way in here," I said. "She kept asking me the same questions when we were in the ambulance."

"She was fine, really. I did a neurological on her too. I know she was fine. The CAT scan just confirmed it."

"Maybe I could gown up and go in and see her."

"No. Let Jack finish up. He's nearly done anyway."

I got dressed and walked out of the stall and stood at the glass wall and watched the plastic surgeon's back as he worked over Caroline. I couldn't see her, just the form of her legs under the green paper surgical drapes.

I looked over my shoulder at Bob. He was sitting on a metal chair drinking coffee, looking around him like a man taken aboard a space ship surrounded by alien life forms. I walked over to him.

"Why don't you go on home," I said. "I'm apt to be here a while."

"This place," Bob said, waving a hand. "Like Hiroshima after the bomb."

"Like the black hole of Calcutta," I said. "Caroline had a patient once who described hospitals that way. That's the way he saw it."

"But you don't see it?"

"Caroline and I spent a lot of time in places like this."

"Somehow I can't see Caroline working in a place like this."

"Oh, she did, once."

"In another life."

"You just didn't know her. She's always been Max and Sam's mother to you. Suburban housewife. But she'll feel right at home here."

"Hard to believe," Bob said, shaking his head.

"At least go get something to eat," I said. "They usually have all-night vending machines."

Bob said he thought he would, at that, and he went off with a nurse who was going to the machines for bagels for the night shift.

Jack Thoreau, plastic surgeon, came out of the operating room peeling off his rubber gloves and stripping off his blue operating room gown. Beneath this, he was wearing an immaculate white shirt, maroon tie, and a cashmere and lamb's-wool jacket of maroon and blue glen plaid. His hair was wheat-colored and perfectly combed, with a straight sharp part on the left, and he wore gold-rimmed glasses and he looked like he had just had breakfast at the Willard Hotel and was stepping out to meet the day. But it was nearly four a.m. and he had driven in the mist and rain and he was at the Medical Center.

He shook my hand and said, "Lovely lady, your wife." He scrutinized my face, looking for imperfections, no doubt. "She'll look just fine. A little makeup over that left eyebrow and she'll be just fine. I'll do a little dermabrasion over the forehead in six weeks. She'll have to avoid the sun this summer. But she'll look fine. Really, you cannot tell after these accidents. She'll look fine."

I almost laughed. I'm worried about her bleeding into her brain. I'm thinking mortality. Plastic Jack Thoreau's talking about some scars on her forehead.

"I'm sure she'll look okay," I said.

"Oh, she'll look better than okay," said Plastic Jack. "She'll look just about as she did. She'll look fine."

Fine would be wonderful, I thought.

"Can I see her?"

They wheeled her out. She looked up at me from the stretcher and smiled, and raised her right arm. I kissed her hand. They had covered most of the left side of her face with some kind of ointment. After all Dr. Thoreau's work, I was careful to avoid unhygienically kissing the injured side. The right side was almost untouched, and I kissed her cheek.

"How are the kids?" she said. Her eyes crawled up and down my face. She had looked so happy to see me at first, but then her expression changed and she looked very frightened.

"The kids?" I echoed.

"Yes. Are they okay?"

"They're home in bed. They're fine. They don't know anything's happened."

"They're home?"

"Yes, they're home. Florence's with them."

"They weren't with us?"

"Just you and me, babe. The kids were home in bed."

"Thank God," she said. Her face relaxed. "They wouldn't tell me where the kids were. All I could think was: Well, then they're dead."

"Christ, Caroline."

"And you too. Of course, nobody here knew anything. I was the only one they got from the accident. They didn't know anything about anyone else. But I didn't believe them. I thought it was like we used to do at Whipple, you know: call the relatives at home and say, your mother's taken a turn for the worse—better come in. And then, later, you break the news. I thought you were dead and they weren't telling me."

"But I went with you to the helicopter."

"I don't remember that at all," said Caroline.

"I carried you up to that house."

"I just remember the helicopter ride, and I kept asking about you. And they kept saying, 'Sorry, lady. Don't know anything about your husband.' And I thought, that's it. I'm alone now. You, the kids, all gone. I knew it couldn't last."

"But I came with you in the ambulance to the helicopter."

"Isn't that strange?"

"It's normal," said Trauma Jack, who had been standing behind us. "You've got posttraumatic amnesia."

"I can't remember a thing."

"Football players get it," T.J. added.

"Very strange."

"It's all normal," T.J. said, and he wandered off with Plastic Jack Thoreau, leaving us alone.

"It was just you and me," I said. "We went to the party."

"Party?"

"What do you remember?"

"I remember the helicopter ride. I remember breast-feeding Sam tonight."

"We went to a party for the Duffields. We were driving home along Cold Quarry. There was a car coming the other direction, then it swerved. You said, 'Uh-oh.' You saw him come at us before I did, really."

"Don't remember a thing," she said. "I guess the car's smashed?"

"Totaled."

"Christ, what'll we do?" Her eyes searched my face. "We can't afford a new car."

"We'll think about it later."

"My leg's broken."

"I'll get Norm Levinson." Norm was a friend, and an orthopedic surgeon.

"Good."

"The leg hurt?"

"Unbelievable."

"I'll call Norm in a little while. No sense waking him up. He can't do anything about it until your lung's better."

"What's wrong with my lung?"

"Contusion."

"What's that?"

"Bruised lung. Broken ribs."

"No wonder. My whole left side feels numb."

"Can you move your arm?"

"Oh, yes. Dr. Marks went over me with a fine-tooth comb. He did a very compulsive neurological, like Ludvik Novotny used to do, remember? Every centimeter. I can feel pain on both sides. It's just my side, over the ribs, is numb with the pain, I guess. But I'm neurologically intact. The CAT scan was really weird. They put you in this little tube, like a tunnel."

"I haven't seen the CAT."

"Go look at it," she said.

"I wouldn't know what I'm looking at anyway. They say it's normal," I said, laughing a little. It was so good to hear her talking. Not just talking, but sounding like herself.

"I'm sure it is. Except for the memory lobes. Really, it's so strange, I remember nursing Sam, and then the helicopter."

"Don't you remember promising Max you would come back? He was crying because you were going out and you said, 'I always come back.' "

"No, I don't remember, but that sounds like Max. You've got to tell him about this very carefully. He's not going to ask a lot of questions. He'll just curl up into a ball and think bizarre thoughts. He'll think he did this to me or something weird. You've got to talk to him."

"Okay."

"Who's with the kids?"

"Florence."

"Good."

"She and Bob have been rocks. Bob drove me here. At four a.m., or whatever hour it was."

"You thank them."

"We owe them for tonight."

"I'm glad you're not dead," she said suddenly, reaching up for my face with her good hand.

"I wasn't hurt at all."

"You sure?"

"I'm fine."

"Me too, except my knee and my leg."

"I'll get Norm."

"Who hit us?"

"Some kid. Nine kids packed into his car, coming home from a party."

"Drunk?"

"Probably. I didn't see him. Cop told me."

"The kids weren't with us, though."

"It was just after midnight. We were at a party. The kids are home."

"Thank God," said Caroline. "That's all that matters."

"Oh, no," I said. "You matter."

"Was I very out?"

"You weren't talking to me, Caroline. You were so far away."

"Don't look so sad. I'm okay now."

I leaned down beside her so my face was closer to hers. She did look better. But a normal CAT scan is not a written guarantee. She could still seize, days, even years, later, from undetected damage to her brain. And that leg would take some work. She wasn't out of the woods with the leg. Or with the lung. Or the ribs.

"Remember how the Roundtrees used to travel in separate airplanes?" Caroline said. "So they wouldn't be killed in the same crash and leave their kids orphans?" She studied my face. "Remember how we used to laugh at that?"

"Sure."

"Maybe they weren't so crazy."

"I don't like that idea so much."

"Why? You used to say how sophisticated and prudent that was."

"I just don't like it."

"Brendan," she said. "I think maybe you better make some plans."

"What plans?"

"I think maybe it's time for Marie Claire."

"You're crazy. You're going to be fine."

"I know, I'm not right in the head. But you promised, remember? Marie Claire? The kids will not grow up motherless. They'll learn French."

"You're crazy. We better do another CAT scan."

"You promised."

I couldn't look at her, I looked at the nurse coming toward us, so I wouldn't have to look at Caroline.

Caroline tugged on my sleeve, "Promise, Brendan."

"You are not in trouble," I lied. "You are just a little busted up. I wouldn't let anything happen to you."

"I know."

"Your problems are just orthopedic, that's all. Just bones. Bones hurt, but nobody dies from bones." I said that and regretted it as soon as I did, remembering Mrs. Roundtree, and knowing she was thinking the same thought.

"But sometimes there's nothing you can do. Promise me, Brendan."

I promised, but I still couldn't look at her. I swallowed hard and I was glad when the nurse came up and said they had Caroline's room ready on the trauma ward.

THE TRAUMA WARD

The emergency room nurse gave me a paper bag containing Caroline's Timex watch and what was left of the clothes they had cut off her in the ER and two plastic bottles with saline and her soft contact lenses. A security guard thrust some form at me and asked me to sign, attesting to the fact I had received her "personal effects."

Bob arrived back from the vending machine room, and we trailed after the nurse as she wheeled Caroline down the hallway to the elevator. There was nobody in the hallway at that hour, and only every third overhead fluorescent light was lighted. It gave the hallway a dark and stealthy air.

"Christ," said Caroline. "Where are you taking me?"

"The trauma ward," said the nurse.

"Looks like the tunnel to the morgue," said Caroline.

She was right, too. It looked like the tunnel under Whipple.

We reached the elevator bank and the nurse pushed the button and the elevator door sprang open. We all crammed in around the stretcher. Up we went, in the hospital elevator. How many times had I been hauled up and down a hospital elevator at some dark hour? The elevator lurched to a stop on the third floor.

Rolling the stretcher over the elevator threshold jolted Caroline's gurney and she cried out.

We rolled the stretcher toward a set of double doors and the nurse pushed a metal plate on the wall and the doors swung open and we pushed the stretcher down a long, shadowy ward hall. I was surprised by the number of nurses moving in and out of rooms. For some reason, I thought of that ward at Whipple where I first met Caroline. She was one of only two nurses working night shift covering the whole ward at Whipple.

Caroline looked up to me, smiling. "I counted five. How many did you see?"

"Nurses?"

"Yes."

"Five."

"This is some place," Caroline marveled. "What I would have given for five nurses for one ward at night, at Whipple."

A Filipino nurse appeared. She wore a green scrub suit and she had acne. She spoke to the ER nurse, not looking at Caroline or me.

"This the car wreck with the lung?" the nurse said, meaning Caroline.

"Bates," said the ER nurse. "Multiple fractures. Private ortho doc will see her. She can't have surgery until the lung's cleared. Seven ribs. CT of her head was okay. No allergies."

They were pushing Caroline's stretcher around as they spoke, guiding it into a room. Once they had her in the room with the stretcher parallel to the bed, the night nurse got on the opposite side of the bed and she told Caroline to shift her weight over to the bed.

"You've got to be kidding," said Caroline.

"She can't move real well," I said. "You'll have to pull the sheet from your side and I'll lift her leg."

"Don't pull," Caroline said. "Get more help. Lift me."

"We don't have orderlies at night," said the night nurse. "We'll be gentle."

"Not if you pull me, you won't," said Caroline.

"We have to transfer you to the bed."

"I'll wait for the orderlies," said Caroline. "I can wait on this stretcher until morning."

"But I have to do some things for you, I cannot do them on the stretcher."

"What time is it?"

"Five-twenty in the morning."

"When does the morning shift come on? Seven?"

"Seven-thirty."

"I can wait two hours."

The night nurse stuck her arms akimbo, and glared at Caroline.

The nurse from the emergency room said, "She's a nurse. She knows the score."

"Look," I said. "Bob can help. And I'll lift your leg."

Caroline looked doubtful.

"We'll go very slowly," the emergency room nurse said.

"Just don't push it," Caroline said.

Caroline was lying on a sheet and the night nurse and Bob grasped this from their side of the bed and pulled very gradually toward them with the ER nurse lifting from the other side and I held her leg, which they had wrapped in the ER in a huge soft cast swathed in big Ace bandages.

"Oh, God!" said Caroline. "My leg."

It took about ten minutes. I'd never seen a patient moved from stretcher to bed so slowly. Then again, I hadn't seen too many orthopedic cases.

The ER nurse said good-bye.

"Sorry I was such a baby," Caroline told her.

"You'll be fine," said the nurse.

"You cannot imagine what that leg feels like," Caroline said, after the nurses were gone.

Bob stepped out of the room to let me have a moment alone with Caroline. We weren't quite alone. Caroline had a roommate, a teenage girl in traction, who had the window bed and a teddy bear with a ribbon, who never stirred during all the commotion transferring Caroline to her bed.

"You better get home," Caroline said. "I want you to be there before Max wakes up."

"Okay."

"Bring my phone books and my toothbrush and my glasses."

"Okay."

"Call my dad," said Caroline.

"Okay."

"And don't look so worried."

"Okay."

"I wish to Christ Norm Levinson were here right now to fix this leg."

"I know."

"Go home."

I stood there. I was afraid to leave her.

"Jesus, O'Brien, it's not like I've got breast CA or AIDS or testicular CA."

I should have laughed, but I couldn't bring it off.

"The time to have worried was when I couldn't talk to you. I'll be fine now."

"I know. You'll be fine."

"You're thinking too much."

"I can't help it," I said, brushing her good cheek. She was right, of course: I was thinking of all the complications for which she was such a setup. She could get pneumonia in that contused lung, phlebitis in the fractured leg, fat emboli when they tried to set the bone. Or she could have a late bleed into her brain, a missed subdural hematoma. She could get a urinary tract infection from being bedridden, and die in gram-negative sepsis. One of those sharp ends of a fractured rib could puncture her lung and she could die of a pneumothorax. She could bleed when they operated to set the leg and need transfusions and die of AIDS. The list went on and on.

She reached up around my neck and pulled me toward her and kissed my forehead. "I am going to avoid complications," she said. "Like the plague."

"Do that."

"I am young and healthy and I will bounce back."

"I know."

"Then why do you look so sad?"

I tried to smile, but I couldn't. I knew it would be worse to force it. I just shook my head. She looked so broken and so battered and I had the feeling a bad time was coming.

"Go home, gloom face."

I walked to the door and turned and said, "I'll call."

Caroline held up her hand, "Tell Max . . ." but she couldn't think of how to finish it.

7

WHERE THE WILD THINGS ARE

It was still dark at six-thirty that morning when Bob and I arrived back at my house. Florence sat up on the couch in the family room when we came in. She had been sleeping under a quilt.

"How is she?" Florence said.

"Alive," I said.

"Her CAT scan was normal," said Bob. "She was wide-awake and talking to us when we left. But her left lower leg is broken and they haven't set it because her lung was injured and she's got seven broken ribs on the left side. The plastic surgeon worked on her for two hours and her face is scratched up but he said it would look fine, once she heals."

"All true," I said. If Bob had been my intern I would have said, "Good report."

I sat down on the long couch and Florence sat on the short couch and Bob stood in front of us.

I asked her where her son was.

"In the living room, asleep."

"Thanks for coming over."

"Oh, good Lord."

"She looked dead for a while tonight," I said. "I've seen that look often enough."

Florence sat down next to me and Bob sat down on the floor.

"But she's okay now," Florence said.

"She's not out of the woods," I said. "The leg has to be set. She could get phlebitis, fat embolism, sepsis, pneumonia in that lung."

"She made it to the hospital."

"Yeah. She made it that far," I said. The long night was beginning to catch up with me. I wasn't an intern anymore and staying up all night took its toll. "I better tell Max," I said. "I don't want him getting out of bed and wandering into our room and finding the bed empty."

"Right," said Florence.

"Before we left for the party," I said, "Caroline told him, 'I always come back.' Now what am I supposed to say?"

Florence smiled and shrugged her shoulders. "Just hold him."

I trudged upstairs and went to Max's room and stood over him and watched him sleep. He slept on his back, like a little man, with his head on his pillow and the cover down to his chest. He looked very peaceful and contented.

I lifted him up and carried him out of his room, down the stairs to the family room, and I sat down with him in my lap on the couch. Florence sat by us.

Max woke up by bits and he looked blankly at Florence and at Bob, trying to figure out why they were there. He looked a little dopey, but his eyes were wide open. He was awake.

"Mom is in the hospital," I said.

Max looked at me and then at Florence and he looked back at me. He said nothing. Caroline had said he would be like this.

"We had an accident last night, in the car." I said. "We had to take your mom to the hospital, so they could fix her up."

Max listened. He still wasn't talking.

"Do you understand? Mom's in the hospital."

Max nodded.

"She's there now, and she told me to tell you she'll talk to you on the phone."

"Now?"

"No, later in the morning."

"You and Sam are coming to our house this morning," Florence said brightly. "Would you like to come visit at our house?"

Max nodded solemnly.

"As soon as Mom's better," I said, "we'll go see her."

Max looked at me.

"She's not coming home?"

"She's in the hospital now," I said. "She's getting better."

Max said nothing. I stood up and sat him down on the couch and he sat there in his blue one-piece furry pajamas with his feet out in front of him and his arms beside him.

"I'll feed the kids," I told Florence. "I'll bring them over after breakfast."

"Okay," said Florence.

Florence and Bob gathered up their kid and tucked him into the back of their Volvo and drove off.

Max sat alone on the couch and stared at his feet.

I sat down next to him and put my hand on his head. What does a three-year-old think at that hour in the morning when he's just been roused from sleep and told his mother's in the hospital?

8

NORM LEVINSON

After the Goldenheims left, I put Max back to bed and I walked into our bedroom feeling like an intern after a bad night at Whipple. I looked at the bed where Caroline and I slept. I didn't want to sleep there alone. On her bedside table was an open paperback, facedown. I picked it up and put it on the bookshelf. Her things were scattered around the room, as usual. Except there wasn't anything usual about her things this morning.

I went back to the stairs, and stopped at the door to Sam's room, pushing it open slowly. Sam was a good sleeper and I backed out the door. I went downstairs and stretched out on the couch. Starting to close my eyes, I felt a wave of dread. What if I dreamed about the accident? To hell with it. I had to close them.

The car was coming at us in our lane again, and there wasn't any stopping it. I hit the brakes but we didn't even slow. I was sitting up, batting my eyes and the room was sunlit at nine-thirty. I had slept two hours. Neither kid was howling.

I walked up to Max's room. Max was awake, sitting in his bed playing with two He-Man figures, Skeletor, the prince of darkness, and Awful Clawful. Skeletor was in his Land Shark, his menacing automobile, and he was taking a beating from Awful Clawful. Max struggled with Skeletor, whom he could not extract from the Land Shark. He didn't look up when I stepped into his room. I don't think he noticed me. He said, "This goddamn thing won't move."

Caroline groaned whenever Max used that incriminating phrase. Aside from Max, Caroline was the only person in our house who ever said it. Max hadn't heard it from me or from TV or at the day-care center. Caroline had to take full responsibility for that one. She could blame me for his indifference to any sort of tooth-brushing regimen. But for that phrase, which Max used with perfect intonation and in exactly the proper context, Caroline had to accept full credit.

"It's cartoon day," I told him.

He looked up, without his usual enthusiasm. "Okay," he said. I looked at that solemn face and felt immediately sad.

"Did the maniacs get Mom?"

"The who?"

"The maniacs in their cars."

"Oh, the maniacs. Yes, A maniac hit us."

Another phrase Max must have absorbed from Caroline. He sat silently in that safety seat in the back of the car and soaked it all up, every muttering from his mother as she dealt with Washington drivers. The maniacs on the road. The drunken son of a diplomat maniac had got us with his Land Shark and the guys from Snake Mountain had dealt the decent denizens of Eternia a blow.

He followed me past Sam's room and I made a sign with my finger to my lips. If I was lucky, Sam would sleep for another hour. Then he'd be up howling for the breast. This morning he'd get the bottle.

We went to the stairs and I said, "Piggyback?"

Max didn't say anything, he just hopped on my back and I carried him down, looking at him in the mirror along the way. He was on my back, but there was no joy in his face. There were no demands for more piggyback, and there was no screeching and beseeching for an extended romp through the house, out-of-doors and back again. There was just a silent three-year-old, clinging to my back.

I turned on the TV and Max sat down in his blue folding chair, slump-shouldered, and he stared blankly at the TV. I poured him orange juice into the plastic cup emblazoned with Superman leaping a tall building in a single bound. Max sipped at it, never taking his eyes from the TV, not so much from interest in what was going on on the screen, I thought, but more as a way of not looking at me.

I sat down in the dining room and made a list on a three-by-five card. Then I went downstairs to the basement and fished around Caroline's desk for her looseleaf phone-number book, found it, and ran back upstairs to check Max. He hadn't moved. Using the kitchen phone, from which I could keep an eye on Max, I started to dial the first number.

Ordinarily, I'd have to keep an eye on Max to be sure he wasn't using the couch as a trampoline or taking up position a nose length away from the TV screen, frying his eyes and affecting untold generations of retina cells. But this morning he sat unmoving, narcotized six feet from the TV, not laughing, not stamping his feet, just staring.

Then I realized I'd have to tell the whole story within hearing of Max, and Caroline always said Max hears everything. You don't think he's listening. He seems to be off in his own world, but he's listening and a week later he'll ask, "What's unconscious mean? What's head-on mean? What's brain damage?" I walked back downstairs and used the phone in the basement.

The number rang. I looked at my watch. Seven forty-five. Saturday morning. Too early to call most people, but Norm Levinson might be dressing to make rounds in the hospitals and I wanted to catch him. A very sleepy woman's voice answered the phone.

"Judy? Brendan O'Brien. Sorry to wake you. Is Norm around?"

"Brendan? No, he's in the car. I think he's headed to University."

She gave me Norm's car phone number and I got him as he was tooling down MacArthur Boulevard.

"Brendan? What can I do for you?"

He sounded fresh and bright, as if it were midday, midweek rather than early Saturday morning.

"Personal favor."

"Shoot."

Where to begin? "My wife," I said.

"Caroline? How is the lovely lass?"

"Not real good."

"Oh?"

"She had. That is, we had. We were in an auto accident last night. She broke . . . her leg was broken. They helicoptered her off to the Medical Center."

"Uh-oh."

"Yeah."

"Poor baby. Where is she? Why the fuck didn't you call?"

"I'm calling. I didn't want to wake you. They said she couldn't have the leg touched anyway. She's got a lung contusion. Broken ribs. She was out cold. CAT scan was negative. Head CT."

"Good Lord. Were you in the car?"

"Driving."

"You okay?"

"Not a scratch."

"She wasn't wearing a seat belt?"

"No."

"Where'd you say she was?"

"Medical Center."

"I'm on my way. No, hold it. I'm due at University. Got to discharge a lady and make lightning rounds. Then I'll head over there. You shoulda called me. I can't believe you wait to tell your friends."

"They said you couldn't touch her anyway."

"Sometimes I can sneak one by 'em and fix the leg before the lung gets to be a problem. She's on the trauma service?"

"Yeah. Marks is the attending. He saw her in the ER. And a plastic guy named Thoreau."

"Marks is okay. Thoreau is a prince. Guy never has a hair out of place, which I consider weird. But a very good surgeon."

"He was with her from two a.m. to four."

"I could bust you, for not calling me. The fucking plastic surgeon gets out of bed and you never call me. What kind of fractures?"

"Lots of ribs."

"Nothing in that for me."

"Tibia, fibula, patella."

"Now I can help you. What kind of tibia break?"

"Not compound. I don't know how you describe a fracture."

"I'll see when I get there. You going over this morning?"

"As soon as I can get the kids taken care of."

"Go drop 'em off at my house. We've got a woman who lives in now. No problem."

"Some neighbors the kids know offered. I'll drop them off on the way to the Center."

"I'll probably beat you over there," he said, and we hung up.

The next call was to my father. By that time I had my story down and got it out more fluently and more coherently. He asked if there was anything he could do and I said no. There really wasn't. I don't know why I called him, but I felt like talking to my father. He gave me the name of a lawyer, a family friend.

Then I called Caroline's sister, who took down the name of the hospital and said she would call Caroline. She told me to call their father, but she didn't have his number and it wasn't in Caroline's address book. "Try the State Department," she said. "They ought to at least know what country he's in." I tried State, but got nowhere and gave up. I called the auto insurance people and got a recording and I called the HMO Caroline belonged to, and they said they'd talk to Norm Levinson.

There was only one more call to make.

Sally answered on the second ring.

"It's Brendan," I said. "In Washington."

"Brendan? Forrest, get up you lazy bum. It's Brendan."

Forrest's burly voice came across the line. "You guys in a different time zone down there or what? We never hear from you and now you call in the middle of the night."

"Caroline's in the hospital."

"I didn't even know she was pregnant," said Sally.

"Auto accident. We had an auto accident."

"What!" Two voices as one, in alarm.

"Is she all right?"

"Not by a country mile."

I told them about it, more calmly than I had been able to tell it so far. I guess I had had more practice. It seemed to grow more distant, less personal in the retelling, as if I were presenting a case at morning rounds, as if all this had nothing to do with me. And I knew they would listen.

"I am on the next shuttle out of La Guardia," said Forrest. "You got any good orthopods down there? We'll bring her up to Special Surgery."

"I'll be down," said Sally. "I've got to make some arrangements for the kids. Don't worry. What do you need?"

"Child care."

"Don't they have day care?"

"Just half days, I think. Caroline hadn't gone back to work. Sam's just nine months. I don't know."

"Just take care of Caroline. Don't worry about the kids. If worse comes to worst, they can both come visit Aunt Sally and her kids in New York for a while. Don't worry about the kids."

I felt much better when I hung up.

And then I felt much worse. For the first time it struck me that I might have to send off my kids.

9

THE TRAUMA WARD

Sam awoke screaming, but he calmed down instantly with the bottle, and I had him and Max dressed and strapped into their car seats in the back of Caroline's car and, in the winter's first snowfall, we drove to Bob and Florence Goldenheim's house.

From the backseat, Max's voice: "Are we going to see Mom?"

"I am," I said. "Not you. You are going to the Goldenheims'. You can play with Michael."

"I don't want to. I want to see Mom."

"You will. As soon as she's better."

"When?"

"Soon. They have to fix her broken leg."

"When?"

"Today, I hope."

"Then she'll come home?"

"Soon. But you'll see her in the hospital before that."

"She's not in heaven, is she?"

"No, she's in the hospital."

"You need your arms in heaven."

"To pick things up," I said. "I know."

I didn't know if I was too early for visiting hours, but I didn't care. I had worn a jacket and tie and I took my stethoscope out of my pocket and draped it around my neck. Walking down the hall as if I knew what I was doing and where I was going, I found Caroline's room after one or two false entries. The ward had looked so different at night. In the daylight, the profusion of equipment and medical paraphernalia in the hallway was much more striking. I saw only two nurses and they were too busy to bother with me.

Caroline was asleep. Her leg was wrapped in the biggest soft cast I'd ever seen, with only her toes sticking out. Her roommate, the teenager in traction, was asleep too. I found a chair and sat down next to Caroline's head. Her white arm was next to me. It looked to be the only uninjured part of her. They had put an IV in the forearm, and it was a neat job. I laid my hand next to her hand, but didn't touch her, not wanting to wake her.

She seemed to be breathing easily. Her face looked more battered than it had the night before. Her forehead looked as if someone had taken a wood file to it and her chin was crisscrossed by a long line of black sutures. Her left cheek had a spray of small lacerations, apparently where tiny glass shards had lodged. That was what Thoreau had spent so long doing: picking out each glass sliver, bit by bit.

Her eyes opened and she smiled. "Hello, darling."

"How are you?"

"Not bad. Where are the kids?"

"With Florence and Bob."

"What did you feed them?"

I told her. She nodded.

"What is Sam wearing?"

I told her.

"And Max?"

I told her, each detail.

"Would you bring me a picture of those two snookers?" she said. "I miss them so much. It's like something physical. I woke up this morning and for a moment I didn't know where I was and I thought: Where are the children? It was awful, not hearing them in the next room."

I pulled out a picture for her.

She looked at it and smiled and kissed each face. She clearly recognized her kids, not like Mrs. Roundtree that time. Caroline's parietal lobes were working. She had taken quite a blow to her skull, and I was still more worried about her brain than about anything. But that would be a worry forever. She could have her first grand mal seizure five years from now. Right now all that mattered was that she could talk and she could recognize her kids.

"Put it over there," she said. "Where I can see them."

She looked at the photo. "I can still recognize those two beauties. No damage to my parietal lobes."

Great minds think alike.

"Were you worried?" she asked. "I wouldn't know my kids?"

"No," I said, lying only a little. "How's the leg?"

"Killing me. They don't want to let Norm set it until the lung is okay."

"I'm not sure they're going to let Norm set it," I said. "The HMO has its own orthopods."

"Oh, Norm was just here," Caroline said. "He didn't say anything about that."

"Well, maybe he's talked to them."

"Norm is such a prince. He said he'd have me skiing by next year."

"How's your lung?"

"My side hurts. It's hard to breathe."

"You've got some broken ribs."

"I can believe that."

"Are you short of breath?"

"No, it just hurts to breathe. It hurts to do anything."

"I called your sister."

"How is she?"

"Okay. Worried about you."

"Did you speak to my father?"

"I tried. The State Department wants to know what section he works for."

"He's in Cairo," sounding, for the first time, fussy and irritable. "Tell them the Middle East desk," she said. "Actually, I'll do it. I can use the phone, when I can get the nurses to move it over to my bed." She looked around and lowered her voice, "The nursing here is not exactly what you would call world class." Then she dropped the ironic tone and said, "What are we going to do with the kids?"

"Christ if I know," I said. The kids, of course, were the big problem. The kids and Caroline. At least I knew who was taking care of Caroline. "I can't stay home. I've got to go to the office every day. And what if I get called out at night and have to go to the hospital?"

"Don't get so worked up," Caroline said, taking my hand. "One step at a time. Can the Goldenheims take care of them today?"

"Yes. And I called Forrest. Sally's coming down. She might be able to plug her finger in the dike for a few days."

"Where will you put her?"

"In our room. I'll sleep on the couch."

"She's got Jason in school. She won't be able to stay long."

"I'll have to find someone for the kids."

"Where are you going to find someone?"

"I have no idea." I didn't want to worry Caroline with this. I got chest pain every time I started thinking about it, but Caroline smiled and stroked my hand.

"Don't panic," she said. "You're hyperventilating."

"I just don't know what to do."

"If Sally can come down, that'll give us some breathing room. Once they fix my leg, I can get out of here and once I'm home . . ."

"Oh, Caroline," I said. "Be realistic. Even if they set that leg today, and you came home tomorrow, you couldn't get out of a chair. Those kids would be running around. We need somebody to come in and watch them, and take care of you, and you're not even home yet. And where are we going to find somebody? And how am I going to pay her?"

"There must be agencies for this," Caroline said. She was trying to smile and look upbeat. "And we can get a loan."

"Yeah, on my good name and bright prospects."

"I'd bet on you," she said.

"Thanks, but it's the bank who has to bet on me."

"You are a board-certified genius internist and infectious disease specialist," Caroline said. "I'm impressed every time I walk in your office and look at all your diplomas. Go show the bank a photo of your diplomas. They'll back us. You're a winner."

"I don't feel like much of a winner right now."

Caroline looked genuinely surprised. "Why not?"

"I don't know."

"Because you were driving?"

"That. I don't know. Everything."

"Mario Andretti couldn't have driven the car any better. Car comes into your lane, no time to react. Don't be like that."

"It's not just that."

"What else?"

"I don't know. I let some drunk sixteen-year-old son of a Turkish diplomat wreck my whole goddamn family. If I'd had a real job, this wouldn't be such a big deal. I'd take some time off the office—the checks would keep coming in."

"Our family is not wrecked."

"Oh, Caroline, we're breaking apart like a boat in high seas. There's no way I'm going to be able to find someone for the kids. I'm going to wind up having to send them to New York, with Sally."

Caroline's face changed. "I don't know," she stammered. "Sam's so little. New York. They'd be so far away from me."

"Would you rather have them with some illegal alien in our house? That's all we're going to get for child care. I'm not sure how we're going to afford even that."

"We'll see who we can get," said Caroline. "But promise me you won't separate the kids. If anything should happen to me, don't separate the kids."

"Nothing is going to happen to you."

"Promise."

"Nothing," I said, "is going to happen to you."

"Promise."

I promised.

"They stay together."

"Nothing's going to happen to you."

"Christ, I wish they'd fix this leg."

We sat there looking at each other.

"My face must look awful."

"No."

"You know what really kills me?"

"Your leg."

"Besides the leg. My breasts. I think I've got mastitis. They had to put ice bags on them this morning. Did Sam take the bottle all right?"

"Like a champ."

"I've got breast milk frozen in the freezer."

"He took the cow offering this morning."

"And, of course, like clockwork, my period started this morning. Except for the pregnancies, I have never, ever missed a period or been a day late or early."

"What a comfort."

Three doctors stepped into the room. One of them was Jack Marks, the emergency room doc from the trauma unit. The others followed like a row of ducks. Marks smiled and offered me his hand. He had a surgical scrub mask dangling from his neck.

"Hey, she looks better," he said. "We'll have another chest film this morning, see about the lung."

"Norm Levinson's seeing her," I told him.

"Yeah, I understand he's still trying to get the HMO to approve him to do the surgery."

"I can't comprehend why the HMO cares. Norm isn't going to cost them any more than anyone else," Caroline said.

"With the HMOs, you can't ever tell," said Marks. "Sometimes I think they just like to jerk you around, to show who's in charge. You say you want X, so they say no, it has to be Y."

"Well, I wish they'd stop it. I want my leg fixed."

"We have to wait on your lung anyway. How you feeling anyway? Getting any more of that breathless feeling?"

"What breathless feeling?" I asked.

Caroline flitted a look in my direction, and arched an eyebrow at Marks. "Nothing. I had a little dyspnea last night. Hyperventilation, most likely, thinking about child care and bank accounts."

"What?" I said.

"I told you," Caroline told Marks.

"Sorry," Marks said sheepishly.

"I like to be kept informed," I told Caroline. "Since when have you had dyspnea?"

"It's all gone now."

"Yeah, like Mrs. Roundtree's breathlessness. It got all better until she got dead."

"We had this patient once," Caroline explained to Marks. "Broke her leg and got phlebitis and died of a big PE. So all Brendan can think of when he looks at my leg is her."

"It's not clot you got to worry about right now," laughed Marks. "We got to get the lady to surgery and get that leg set."

"But that can't happen until her lung looks better?"

"Just so. We'll get another chest film today."

Marks started to prod her abdomen, in the vicinity of her spleen, but he stopped abruptly and then sneezed three times.

"Bless you," Caroline said.

"Thanks," said Marks, stepping to the sink to wash his hands.

One of the other doctors, an Indian with a maroon turban, stepped up to examine Caroline's belly.

He poked and prodded and he scowled the whole time, as if he were dipping his hand in very hot water. He shook his head. "I would, personally, if it were me, I would get the CAT."

Marks explained to me. "Dr. Singh here thinks we ought to do a belly CAT to be sure her spleen's okay."

"Oh, don't get Brendan going," said Caroline. "We had another patient, a girl we stopped for on the road in Connecticut. Auto accident. She had a spleen. Brendan called it, right at the scene. She died."

"But not from the spleen," I said. She died from the brain injury she got from the windshield. I tried to remember if that girl's head CAT scan was normal, as Caroline's had been. I couldn't remember if they had ever told us. How many people put their heads into windshields and have normal CAT scans but die of undetected brain damage? I didn't know. I didn't ask. And Marks would probably have known the answer to that one.

They moved on to Caroline's roommate. Caroline and I listened while they examined her. She apparently had a broken femur and had bled around it and she required several units of blood. She slept through their visit. They finished with her and filed out and Marks waved good-bye. The doctor in the turban still looked dissatisfied. He wanted Caroline to have the abdominal CAT scan, but Marks was in charge.

"Who's he?" asked Caroline.

"Jack Marks, the ER doc, from last night. Don't you remember?"

"All I remember is Dr. Thoreau and you," she said. "Maybe I should have that CAT scan."

"Don't play doctor. Let Marks decide."

"They did a CAT on my head, the nurse told me."

"You don't remember?"

"Zero."

"You remembered having the CAT last night. You told me all about it."

"All I remember now was you showing up and Jack Thoreau. Thoreau was very nice. He came by this morning, all fussy about my chin. He had a goddamn magnifying glass. He says I'll look just the same, except my forehead, and I can wear bangs."

"He came in at two in the morning. He worked on you for two hours."

"Oh, I remember him, all right. He's so nice. He looks so sleek and well groomed. Like a very earnest seal."

I kissed her hand. She sounded like Caroline again. She had been so different on the street, not talking to me, eyes rolled back up into her head.

"Can we call the kids?" Caroline said. "I've got to hear Max's voice."

I reached for the phone and dialed Florence and Bob's number.

Florence answered and she talked to Caroline for a few moments and then she put Max on. I wasn't on the phone, but I could tell Max had come on the line by Caroline's face.

"Yes, yes," Caroline said. "The maniacs? What maniacs? Oh, yes, the maniacs. Yes, the maniacs got me."

She looked up at me as she listened to Max. He was talking a blue streak.

"Yes," Caroline kept saying. "Yes, yes."

She looked at me as she spoke, and there was joy in trauma ward room whatever.

She kept listening and saying yes, yes, darling, but tears were welling up in her eyes and pretty soon her yesses were nothing more than sobs, and I knew it was time to end things. I tried prying her fingers gently off the receiver, but she wouldn't let go. Then finally, she relented and I put the receiver to my ear and she put her face in her hands and her shoulders shook and I could hear Max's happy voice running on about monsters and maniacs and questions about the hospital and finally I got a word in and he realized his mother was gone again and he said he wanted to talk to his mother and I told him she would call again.

I did not tell him his mother was weeping by my side.

I hung up and sat on the bed and put my arm around Caroline's shoulders, being careful not to squeeze her thorax with the broken ribs and injured lung.

She got hold of herself and I gave her a Kleenex and she blew her nose and she said, "The sweetest sound I'll ever hear." The tears kept coming.

Tears were still streaming down her face when Norm Levinson walked in.

Norm looked as trim and vigorous as ever, wearing a light gray jacket with a crisp blue shirt and striped tie, dark hair neatly shorn and dark brown eyes sparkling. "What's this?" he said, looking at

Caroline. "Didn't they give you the morphine? I will not have my patient crying in pain."

"She was just talking to the kids," I said.

"Oh," said Norm, uncomprehending.

"But I could use the goddamn morphine," Caroline said.

"Is she your patient now?" I asked. "Officially?"

"I'll do her. Screw the HMO. I'll do her as soon as Trauma Jack Marks lets me. I just saw Marks on the way in here. He won't let me touch the leg until the lung looks prettier. I don't know what he's so fussy about. You only need one lung anyway. Want to see her films?"

"I'll be back," I told Caroline. She waved.

We walked down the hallway to the conference room and Norm fished out some X rays from a big manila envelope. He threw them up on the view box.

"This is what's called a pilon fracture," he said, pointing to her leg X rays. "Nasty. It's like what happens when you fall out of a tree and land on your feet. Parachutists get them, when the chute doesn't open completely. It's like a telescope collapsing. The bone isn't just broken, it's compressed."

"So what do you do?"

"Probably need a bone graft to fill in the spot, so the legs will be the same length."

"Where's the bone for the graft come from? The hip?"

"Yeah. And I'll throw in a few screws to stabilize things."

"I'm still worried about her brain."

"CAT looked okay."

"For what that's worth."

Norm turned and looked at me, as if he were seeing me for the first time. "You got to know good news when you see it," he said slowly. "Don't make up things to worry about. We got enough real things to worry about already. As soon as I get the word from the trauma boys, I'll let you know. Where can I reach you?"

I showed him my beeper.

"Good."

"Thanks for coming in on a Saturday, Norm."

"I was here yesterday from seven a.m. to ten p.m. Eight cases. This is ice-and-snow season, big boy. This is my season."

"I'm sorry about this HMO business."

"Well, what can you do? Live and learn. When this is all over, get some real insurance. Get the docs you want."

"Now I know."

"How's she taking all this?" Norm asked, and he gave me a long look. "I mean, you know what I mean."

"Like a trooper," I said. "Like a trooper with two kids."

10

A SURGICAL POSTING

Sunday, it snowed hard. I hated that drive to the Medical Center. Since the accident, I hated driving period, but I really hated driving in the snow. The snow was a typical wet, blinding Washington snow, and it made even the most ordinary drive a heart-pounder. Until the night of the crash, it had been an easy, warm, snowless winter, but as Ira Bloomstein used to say, when it rains it pours. It was a hard time now, and the snow was simply part of all that. Like that month at Whipple, when things would just keep going wrong and getting worse and you had to be very careful and you had to take things one step at a time and concentrate on each step, and not worry about the big picture, but just face each new thing as it happened.

Norm Levinson was with Caroline when I arrived and he said, "The system is go. All we need is OR time."

"OR time?" I said. "It's Sunday. Are the operating rooms that busy on a Sunday?"

"Welcome to the Medical Center," said Norm. "At the Medical Center the operating rooms are always that busy. The only problem is, you can't get OR nurses to work seven days a week, so it's emergencies only on weekends. Emergencies only, which is what Caroline was when she rolled in in the wee hours Saturday, but which I'm having a harder time convincing the posting nurse about every hour that goes by since the accident."

Caroline flipped me a look, meaning, don't say anything. Let me. She smiled at Norm. "I know you're doing whatever you can."

"I'm sorry, Caroline," Norm said. "Really."

"It's okay."

"Most places, a fractured leg is ipso facto an urgent problem. But here, if you don't have a bullet in your left ventricle, you're considered an elective procedure."

"I'm not going anywhere," said Caroline. "When you can get me into the OR, I'll be right here and ready."

Norm said he was sorry for the nth time and left, the perfect picture of frustration.

"He really does feel bad about this, I think," I told Caroline.

"I know." She smiled. "That's why I was trying to be so understanding."

"Yeah, but I think he would have felt better if you'd bitched and complained. That's what he's used to: patients ventilating, rampant indignation. All the warmth and forgiveness just drives him up the wall."

"I know." Caroline smiled.

"So that's why you were so nice?"

"I figure he's had all the niceness he can take. I figure his duodenal acid level's reached ulcer proportions—which is where mine has been for at least twenty-four hours—I figure he's on his way to blast the OR posting nurse right now. She's going to post me for surgery or Dr. Levinson is going to have her head."

Half an hour later, a nurse came in and told Caroline she was officially on call for the operating room, which is to say, the countdown had begun and she was on the launching pad for surgery. They made Caroline NPO—nothing by mouth—in preparation for her anesthesia.

"Oh, great," said Caroline. "Today's the first time I felt like eating anything. Now I'm NPO."

"I'm glad you're hungry, though," I told her.

"I know," Caroline said. "It means I'm starting to heal."

"You're such a clinician," I said. "Oh, I almost forgot to tell you: Forrest and Sally are here."

"Thank God."

"Yes."

She asked about when they arrived and I told her how they were parked outside in a rental car in the cold with their kid, locked out of our house, when I got home from the supermarket. I hadn't expected them until Sunday, but they had packed up and caught the first flight to Washington without wasting a moment.

"I just couldn't sit around New York thinking about Caroline in that hospital bed, and her kids at home and nobody to take care of them," Sally had said. So she packed up her kid, and Forrest, and they jumped in a cab to the airport.

"You must feel better," Caroline said, "having Forrest down here."

"Infinitely," I said. "It was amazing: just seeing him step out of that car. It was like the cavalry arriving in those old westerns. What a relief. He wanted to come this morning, but Sally put her foot down. She wanted to call you first, make sure you were up to seeing people."

"Maybe after Norm fixes the leg," Caroline said.

"Really?" I was astonished. "I thought you'd say come right over. Bring the kids."

"I'd love to see the bambinos," Caroline said. "But people wear me out. Except for you."

I could see she was right. Just getting those few sentences out left her breathless. She had been breathing twenty-four times a minute—I had counted—which is about double the normal rate, owing I supposed to her broken ribs and the lung injury, and the physiologic stress of the pain. Those were the optimistic explanations. Small blood clots from inflamed and clotted veins around her fractured tibia might be traveling to her lungs, making her breathless. She might be developing a pneumonia that wasn't visible on chest X ray yet. There were all sorts of possibilities.

"I'll call Sally, later," Caroline said.

"You look exhausted."

"I'm okay. Tell me about the kids. You went shopping?"

Caroline had dictated me a grocery list. She knew the vast Giant Food store (aptly named) at Westbard by heart. She listed exactly what I should buy and where it would be, aisle by aisle.

"The big problem was the cereal aisle," I told her.

She laughed, but she had to hold her broken ribs with a pillow. "Max wanted some horrible cereal," she gasped, coughing. "I told you he'd throw a fit."

"Max starts climbing out of the shopping cart—I've got Sam in the Snugli and Max's in that seat in the cart—and he's bellowing his mother always gets him Ghostbusters or bubble gum–flavored whatever. I just about had to bludgeon him back into his seat. I thought they'd probably arrest me on the spot for child abuse."

"Now you know," Caroline said. "What I go through every week."

*　*　*

A nurse came in with Caroline's morphine, and I thought it might be her pre-op medication. They call down from the operating room to medicate the patient twenty minutes before surgery, but the nurse said the OR had not called. It was just Caroline's regular morphine dose. Caroline dropped off to sleep once the morphine took hold and her pain subsided. When she awoke, I was still by her bed and she asked if the OR had called and I told her no. We telephoned Sally and Caroline spoke with Max again and we hung up and we waited for the OR to call.

They still had not called at dinnertime. Of course, it wasn't really dinner for Caroline: she was still NPO, on call for the operating room. Dinner for Caroline was intravenous glucose.

I paged Norm Levinson, who was still in the hospital, fit to be tied. "They keep telling me she's next," he told me. "We are on call and on hold."

Sally telephoned from our house at six that evening. Forrest got on the extension. We could hear the kids screaming in the background.

"The kids are fine," said Sally.

"What the hell they waiting for?" Forrest cut in. "Don't they know she's a fucking doctor's wife?"

"This isn't my turf," I said. "I don't even have admitting privileges here. We're just ordinary folks around here."

"Let's fly her up to New York, then. We'll take care of her properly at the Manhattan Hospital."

"If this goes on much longer," I said. "I just might think about it."

"I'm taking a plane back in an hour," Forrest said. "Let's all go."

"Thanks for coming down, buddy."

"No problem. I'm leaving Sally the car, so she'll be able to do the shopping and all that good stuff."

We both thanked them again and hung up.

"That's a relief," said Caroline. "Having Sally at home with the kids."

At eight p.m., Caroline said, "I don't think I can take this pain anymore."

I did not want to call Norm Levinson again. You don't get

things to happen any faster by establishing yourself as a whiner. But Caroline was getting desperate. I paged Norm.

"They were going to let me take her in around seven, but then the helicopter brought in some wreck from the GW Parkway and we got bumped. I just can't get her into the operating room."

Around nine p.m., Norm called again. "One more glitch," he said. "The HMO just brought me to my knees."

The problem was, the HMO had rules. Caroline's health insurance was through a prepaid health maintenance organization, and the HMO had its own way of assigning doctors to its patients. Norm had to get approval from some HMO official before he could operate, and the HMO official said no. Not just no, but really no. If Norm did the surgery, the HMO would not only refuse to pay Norm for the operation, they'd refuse to pay for a single minute of Caroline's hospitalization. It's not that they didn't like or trust Norm at the HMO: in fact they sent Norm cases frequently. But Caroline's ID number made her the property of some other orthopod, according to the HMO rules. Norm had called the orthopod, who was watching a basketball game at home and who was only too happy to let Norm do the case, but the HMO official was immovable: Caroline's ID number ended in 084, and all 084 cases belonged to the doctor watching the basketball game who didn't want to drive in at all hours to do surgery on some lady with a broken leg he'd never even met. Norm gave me the number of the HMO official and after a twenty-minute phone call and a not so veiled threat by me to sue the official for all she was worth if anything happened to my wife, the HMO official saw the light and gave permission for Norm to do the surgery.

"Reason prevails," I said, hanging up the phone.

"The iron fist in the velvet glove," said Caroline, who had been listening to my end of the conversation.

I called Norm and told him he had permission. All he needed now was an operating room.

Ten p.m. came and went and still no call from the operating room.

"Call Norm," said Caroline. "Tell him to go home. Even if they called now, he'd be in the OR with me until midnight."

"Hell, no," said Norm, when I called. "I take whatever time I can get. They brought in three people from a wreck on the

Beltway around three p.m. and I've done three cases. I'm heading for the on-call room, get a couple of winks, and when they call, we'll go."

"You've already done three cases today? You must be exhausted."

"I'm not exhausted. I'm pissed. I wanted to take Caroline up before the last case, but they wouldn't let me. Caroline's not an emergency anymore, see? So getting her in past all the emergencies is going to get tougher and tougher. The longer we wait, the less urgent she is."

At midnight, they came: the OR nurses in their blue scrub suits with a gurney. The floor nurses and I shifted Caroline over to the rubber sheet.

"Oh, God!" Caroline screamed. "Watch the leg." Then, to me, "I'm sorry. It just kills me whenever they move it."

They hoisted her up and we rolled out of there. We took the elevator up to the OR floor and the nurse stopped me at the OR suite door.

"This is where you get off," said the nurse.

Norm came through the automatic doors, in his scrub suit. "Go home," he said. "I'll call you afterward."

"I could wait in her room."

"Go home."

"Norm, you must be exhausted. You sure we shouldn't wait and do her tomorrow?"

"Tomorrow will be just the same. We've got her an OR spot. We do her."

"I'll wait out here," I said.

"Brendan," Norm said, putting his hand over my shoulder. "You are not making this any easier."

"I'm sorry."

"That's okay. You want to be a big help?"

"Anything."

"Go home."

— 11 —

WITH NEEDLE AND THREAD

It snowed the whole way home. I drove through the gloom of Rock Creek Park thinking about the anesthesiologist trying to slide the endotracheal tube into Caroline's trachea so they could breathe her while she was asleep. I remembered a patient from medical school—the anesthesiologist had missed the trachea entirely, and had unwittingly slipped the tube down the esophagus instead, so all the oxygen went into the stomach for an hour and none got into the lungs and the patient woke up with mush for brain.

It was all I could do to keep myself from turning around and driving back and charging into that operating room to listen to Caroline's lungs for myself. Why hadn't I insisted? I should have gone into that OR with her. I had let them take her away from me in that helicopter and now they had taken her away from me again.

Calm down. Do not panic. You have to allow people to do things for you. At some point, you must simply have faith. But things go wrong, even if you try like hell to be careful. I wanted to stay with Caroline the whole time, like a gypsy. In New York, whenever we admitted a gypsy to the ward, the whole family would move in. They'd try to camp out in the patient's room and they got in the way. Now I could see it from the gypsy's point of view: why trust any person to take care of your wife just because that person works in a hospital and wears white? But you could get in the way. People did that in the emergency room all the time. Fathers who fainted while you sewed up their sons. I wouldn't be like that, though. Why couldn't I simply stay with Caroline like a special duty nurse, round the clock, until she could come home? Because they'd evict us when I missed the mortgage payment and there'd be no money to buy the groceries. Be practical.

But what difference would making mortgage payments make if

anything happened to Caroline? Nothing will happen to Caroline. Norm will fix her leg and she will be fine and she will come home and she will heal up. She'll walk with a limp, Norm had told me. But she'd be fine. Don't make up things to worry about.

Sally was asleep on the fold-out couch in the living room, when I arrived home. I went straight up to bed and didn't bother to undress.

When was the last time I actually slept? Lashes lowered. Burning under the lids. (Doctor, my eyes cannot see the light. Is this the price to keep them open for so long?) Who was that? A song long ago. When I was young, long ago. Jackson Browne. Lashes fluttering. Headlights growing larger in my lane. Caroline on the asphalt road, eyes rolled up, with that noise leaking out of her mouth. A noise in the distance, urgent as a siren, and the noise would not stop. And there was that car again, sliding sideways, and the noise louder. The noise was the phone, next to my ear.

"It's done." Norm Levinson's voice. "We got everything in place."

"Norm?"

"Wake up, Doc. It's your buddy, Norm. Your wife's okay. Her leg's back in one piece, more or less. Lot of hardware in there."

"She's okay?"

"Sure. Her leg looks like a Tinkertoy factory, but everything's connected again."

"She's awake?"

"Yeah, she's in the recovery room. She'll stay there for now. They'll move her down to Ortho when the shifts change."

"Did you do the bone graft?"

"Didn't need to. Opened it up and measured everything a hundred times and I figured we could get away without it."

"How is she?"

"She's fine. The knee's another story. I did a fancy little thing with the knee. I'm not sure I got that posterior surface completely flat. We'll see the good films in a couple of days."

"The knee?"

"You know: I showed you the patella. That posterior surface where there was that step down. I kind of wired the whole thing and tied it up like a bow and laid the end right under the skin so all the HMO doc'll have to do is make an incision and yank it out.

I don't know, though: maybe I should've been a little more conventional."

"What time is it?"

"Four-thirty."

"You've been in there four and a half hours?"

"Masterpieces are not to be rushed."

"Four-thirty? I hope you have the day off tomorrow."

"No way, José. I got a full load in the office, starting at eight. I'll sleep here and go right over to the office."

"Your wife ever ask you where you spend your nights?"

"She's too busy spending the money I never see."

We hung up and I set my own alarm clock for seven. I had patients beginning at nine.

More sliding cars and flashing police car lights and helicopters and more of Caroline not opening her eyes and I awoke before the alarm. I took a shower, shaved, and dressed.

I tiptoed into Max's room and watched him sleep. I wanted to kiss the kid, but I was afraid I'd wake him. Next door, Sam was rolling around in his crib, so I stood at the door and watched him and didn't set foot in the room.

Downstairs, Sally was in the kitchen, making coffee.

"Who called at four a.m.?"

"Caroline's surgeon. They fixed her leg."

"Thank God."

"I'm going to run over and see her. I've got patients today. I'll try to cancel out the afternoon and get home, give you a break."

"Don't be silly. Florence Goldenheim called last night. She's coming over to show me around suburbia so I can find the supermarket and the day-care center and all those essential places. You go to work. I'll be just fine."

"Thanks, Sally."

"And stop saying thanks. Something like this happens, you can hang a sign around your neck. Just go see Caroline."

The snow was coming down in slanting sheets across the road, and the drive to the Medical Center seemed to take a year.

She was asleep when I arrived. They had transferred her to the orthopedic ward. Her leg was in a smaller, plaster cast now. The cast over the knee had a drain running out of it. She looked like one of her kids, breathing softly beneath that generic hospital gown with the pattern that looked like little generic flowers.

Her teenage neighbor still had one leg in traction and the other in a cast to the hip. At least Caroline's cast ended midthigh.

I wrote Caroline a note and propped it on her bedside table. "You were asleep. Your cast looks wonderful."

I planned my route to the office, with several alternates in case of snow snarls. It was still early and I was going against the major in-town flow for rush hour. But Washington has the most complicated rush hour traffic patterns devised by the mind of man— entire streets that ordinarily carry traffic in both directions, become one-way during rush hour, and even major arteries like Connecticut Avenue close down to one lane going away from town and four lanes coming in. I took side streets to my office. This was more hazardous because the side streets were icy and unplowed and full of potholes, but I did not want to risk finding myself heading the wrong way with four lanes of traffic coming at me. I'd had enough of headlights coming at me.

Usually, my secretary arrived before me and opened the office. But this morning I was the first to arrive and I turned on the lights, set up the coffee machine, turned on the Xerox machine, and got things going. All the routine things. It felt good. Life was coming together: Caroline's leg was coming together. Now if the wound didn't get infected, and if she didn't get phlebitis, and if a thousand things went right and nothing went wrong, we might just make it through all this.

I sat at my window and watched the snow falling on Wisconsin Avenue and the cars moving slowly with their lights on, making large arching turns, leaving tracks. The snow was falling between Caroline and me, making every trip to the Medical Center a calculated risk.

My secretary came in at nine exactly, as she always did, snow or shine, and the ordinary rhythms of the office swung into motion and for some moments that morning I did not think about Caroline. Upon learning about the accident, my secretary, ever efficient, generated a list of things to do, people to call, and she set about organizing my life, between patients. I cannot remember a single patient from that morning. So many insignificant details are still etched into my mind about that time, the immediate aftermath of the accident, but so many things blur together. I'm not sure I really listened to any patient, that morning. But it was very therapeutic to be in the office, to force myself into action, to force worry out of my mind temporarily and to concentrate on the details of running a medical practice.

While I saw patients, my secretary managed to ascertain certain facts: (1) I could get a copy of the police report only by going personally to the police station in downtown Bethesda. (2) My car was in a lot in Rockville, to which she had directions and I had better go there, the sooner the better, and remove any personal belongings I might have left. She had already called the insurance agent back and the insurance company would go out to look at the car and assess the damage sometime before the end of the century. (3) A rental car could be delivered to my office and left in the parking lot, but I would have to pay for the special insurance policy by check when the car was dropped off, unless I desired to drive uninsured in the snow in Washington. If I were found to be at fault and my insurance company decided not to pay for the rental car, I would be responsible for the entire bill, which would be a small fortune. But it was better to rent a car than to risk our one remaining clunker in the snow on Washington streets.

At noon, my secretary buzzed again: "Your wife is on the line."

"How are you?" I said.

"Okay. Dizzy."

My mouth went dry. "What kind of dizzy?"

"Just spacey. I have trouble describing it. I sound like some kind of crock."

"You're no crock."

"Stop worrying. Post-anesthesia dizzy. Norm was down and he said everything went fine."

"He worked on you until four-thirty in the morning."

"He didn't get to start until one."

"But we brought you up at midnight."

"Yeah, and a helicopter came in with some more highway wounded and we got bumped for an hour. I had to wait in the hall. That was kind of scary. Norm was fit to be tied."

"What a place."

"When are you coming by?"

"I'm canceling out the afternoon patients. There were only two anyway and with the snow nobody's kicking. But Mrs. Salerno's due in. She called this morning and wanted an emergency appointment."

"I do want to see you. I feel so alone."

"Have you called Sally?"

"Yes. Max got on the phone. He thinks he's coming to see me today."

"He says that every day."

"Bring him. I miss him so much."

"When you're better."

"What's wrong?"

"Caroline, you look like you've been mugged. You might scare the little bugger."

There was a silence along the line.

"He's got to see me sometime."

"Let the swelling go down a little."

"No, I've got to see him. I've got to hold him. Sam too."

She had that steel in her voice, the same tone she had that time when she insisted Mrs. Roundtree's kids were going to visit. There was no arguing with Caroline on the subject of maternal visiting rights.

I told her I'd bring the kids.

"Tomorrow?"

"Okay."

"But I don't like you driving my babies around in the snow. Be sure they're in their car seats."

"I will."

"Sally will want to come."

"Sure."

"Brendan?"

"Make Sally wear her seat belt."

"I'll strap her in myself."

We said good-bye.

One step forward. Her leg was fixed. But she still wasn't out of the woods. She was in less pain, and her leg was fixed. But she was dizzy. I didn't like dizzy one bit.

12

DIZZY SPELLS

Just as I was leaving my office for the Medical Center, they called from the ER at University Hospital, to say one of my patients was there, needing my attention. So instead of heading directly for Caroline, I had to make a detour, five miles, to University Hospital, in the snow. I made it to the emergency room there in just under half an hour.

I stood there, looking around at all the action swirling in the various stalls of the ER, and thought about how different it would be had Caroline been brought to University instead of to the Medical Center. She would have had the same things done for her at University, but she would now be upstairs in one of those bright, cheery rooms on the private wards, with nurses I knew taking care of her, with residents I knew calling me to let me know how she was doing. And she would be only ten minutes from home. Instead, she was on the other side of the city, forty minutes away in good weather, in the cut-and-slash part of town, on that threadbare ward, in that tumbledown building they called the Medical Center, where she had to wait two days just to squeeze into the operating room on a Sunday night, when the good citizens of Washington stopped killing each other for long enough to free up an operating room. She was in a part of town where most of my doctor friends traveled only under duress.

Before seeing my patient I phoned Sally.

"No problems," said Sally. "How's Caroline?"

"Haven't seen her yet."

"You haven't?"

"I'm at University Hospital."

"Oh, patients," said Sally. "Why can't they let you alone when you've got your wife to worry about?"

"They can sense when I'm not thinking about them," I said. "And they show up at the emergency room."

"Well, I don't know how it looks over there," said Sally. "But outside my window, it looks like a major blizzard."

"It drives like one."

"Take it easy, brother."

Then Max got on the phone demanding to be taken to see his mother. I told him tomorrow and he said I always said tomorrow and after further unproductive negotiations, we hung up.

I phoned Caroline.

"Don't come," she said. "We need one working automobile. All you need to do is to wind up in Rock Creek Park."

"Wild horses," I said, "could not keep me away."

"Be careful out there."

"Has the neurologist seen you yet?"

"Tomorrow."

"You still having dizzy spells?"

"Oh, yes."

"I'll be there."

My patient had come to the emergency room and grabbed everyone's attention by smiling sweetly and then proceeding on to a grand mal seizure. I asked her, almost without thinking, if she'd ever had any head trauma, and she said, yes, four years earlier in an auto accident. Now she had seizures.

Just as I was leaving the emergency room, my beeper went off. It was an outside call and while I waited for the operator to connect me I thought about auto accidents, head trauma, and grand mal seizures, and suddenly I heard the voice of Ira Bloomstein come across the line.

"As I live and breathe, the doctor is making rounds in the hospital!" Ira roared. "Is this life in the Real World?"

"Ira, how are you?"

"I am fat and happy. I am doing eyeballs in Westport, Connecticut. Paul Newman lives here. We're practically neighbors."

"But does he need an ophthalmologist?"

"He hasn't come into my office yet, but we're working on it."

"To what do I owe the pleasure?"

"I just thought you might be interested: I got a call from some very large animal at Tinker, Mudwater etcetera yesterday."

"The hospital lawyers?"

"Yeah, your defense counselors in the Roundtree thing."

"You're right: I'm interested."

"Looks like we won't be spending any time on the witness stand after all. They settled."

"For how much?"

"The large animal would not say," Ira said, then, basso profundo, "but I have my sources."

"What do your sources tell you?"

"Mr. Roundtree got not less than half a million and not more than a million, probably right in the middle between those two figures."

I caught my breath.

"For what we did to his wife," I said.

"Yeah," said Ira. " Course, Mr. Roundtree doesn't get the whole bite: his lawyer gets forty percent. I tell you, O'Brien, we went into the wrong business. The lawyer got, what? About three hundred grand, three hundred and a half, for maybe a week's work, if you add up all the depositions. So Mr. Roundtree did not get it all, but financially speaking, the best thing can happen to you is to wind up in bad shape on the doorstep of a hospital."

"Doesn't always work out that way," I said. "Caroline's in the hospital right now."

"No! What with?"

"Car wreck. Multiple fractures, head injury."

"How is she?"

"She's not out of the woods yet. Fractured tib-fib. Seven ribs. Dizzy spells."

"Dizzy spells? She hit the windshield?"

"Yeah."

"Christ, Brendan. I'm really sorry."

"Yeah, thanks."

"Her leg okay?"

"Well, it's set now. But she's not out of the woods yet with the leg, as Mrs. Roundtree could tell you, if she were around."

"She got phlebitis?"

"None yet. They just set it."

"When did all this happen?"

"This past Friday night."

"Shit. Is there anything I can do? She didn't hurt her eyes or anything? I'll fly right down."

"No. Thanks, though. But maybe you can do something for me."

"Anything."

"Call up that big wheeze at Mudwater and tell him I think he's a slimeball. Seymour Freudenberg never did anything but try to help Mrs. Roundtree and her whole family, and Mudwater caved in. Those defense lawyers are part of the problem. With friends like them, doctors don't stand a chance."

"It's the juries," Ira said. "They don't know squat. They don't want to know squat. Every courtroom's a kangaroo court. You got as much chance as a kosher guy named Cohen in the Third Reich. The climate ain't real good for a fair hearing."

"I still think they're all slimeballs: defense and plaintiffs."

"You're right," said Ira. "They're all slimeballs. You got yourself some ultra-slime for your lawyer in this accident thing?"

"Won't help."

"Your fault?"

"No, he had to come across the road to hit us."

"Then hire a slimeball and hang the guy. For once it should feel good to be sitting at the plaintiff's table. Even if you have to sit next to one of those PI scumbags."

"Not likely: the kid who hit us is the son of a diplomat."

"A diplomat? Christ, O'Brien, the one time you can pump this filthy system for yourself, you go find yourself a diplomat to crash with."

"It's all written, Ira."

"Hey, tell Caroline I still love her."

We hung up.

Caroline's leg was propped up on pillows and she smiled and held out her hand when I came in. Her hair was wet and combed back from her forehead, revealing the full extent of her abrasions and lacerations. She looked like she'd been goalie for the Washington Capitals without a face mask.

A gray-haired man and his gray-haired wife were sitting at the foot of the bed of Caroline's roommate. The roommate was asleep and her parents just sat and watched her. The girl had one leg up in traction and the other in a cast.

"Any more dizzy spells?"

"All the time," said Caroline.

"What are they giving you for meds?"

"Nothing much," she said. "Percocet for pain. Ancef in the IV."

"Let me go look them up," I said. I walked down to the nurses' station and asked the clerk where she kept the *PDR*.

She never lifted her head. "That's for the doctors, mister," she said.

"It's on the shelf behind you," I said. "I'll use it right here."

She went on reading her newspaper.

I looked up Percocet and found what I needed. Then I checked Ancef, just to be sure, and then I walked back to Caroline's room.

The gray-haired man was standing out in the hall with his hands behind his back. He smiled benignly at me as I approached.

"Your wife?" he said.

"Yes."

"My daughter," he said. "Auto wreck."

"Same with my wife," I said.

"Got the midnight call," he said. "The one every parent fears. Doctor so-and-so at the hospital. Your daughter's been in an accident. I thought my wife would have a heart attack before we could get to the hospital. I was more worried about my wife coming over here than I was about Loretta."

"When did it happen?"

"Friday night."

"Big night for accidents," I said. "Us too."

"There were three near Potomac Road that night."

"One of those was us," I said.

"No kidding? Where was yours?"

"Cold Quarry Road."

"Were you driving toward Cold Quarry and the other car came across the line?"

"Yes."

"Same accident. Loretta was in the other car. Backseat. Seven, eight kids in that car, if you can believe it."

"I heard."

"We told her not to hang around with that kid, Sukru. He's had things like this before. My wife had grounded her before, for running around with him."

"I guess Loretta wishes she'd listened."

"They had to give her four quarts of blood, and with all this AIDS around, we're just sick about it."

"What'd she break?"

"Left thigh bone, right hip."

"Poor kid."

"I'm real sorry about your wife."

"Thanks."

"You know the kid's father?" he asked.

"No."

"I got his card," he said. He fished out a wallet from his hip pocket. "Here." He handed me a dog-eared business card.

I looked at it. It said some name, Embassy of Turkey.

"Imagine that," he said. "Them winding up in the same room together."

I walked back in to Caroline.

Loretta's father walked past and smiled at us. He bent over and whispered to his wife.

I took out my ophthalmoscope and looked into Caroline's eyes. Her optic nerves were sharp and clean-looking. If she had bleed inside her skull and the pressure was rising, the nerves might have looked choked and blurry.

"How do they look?" asked Caroline.

"Good."

"What's this dizziness?"

"Don't take any more Percocet," I told her.

"Why not?" said Caroline.

"Because it's right there in the *PDR,* Percocet causes dizziness and episodes of light-headedness in some patients."

"I'm going to need something for the pain. I think I'd rather be light-headed. At the end of the four hours, I'm about ready to climb the walls."

"They can give you morphine."

"Christ, I don't want any more morphine."

"Caroline, you sound like one of your patients."

"With my patients, it doesn't matter if they get hooked."

Caroline's patients all had cancer and were dying. Morphine addiction was not a big issue.

"How are you?" she asked me.

"Wonderful."

"You look exhausted."

"It's just the driving in the snow. Wipes me out."

"How was your patient in the ER?"

"She'll be okay."

"What was wrong with her?"

I hesitated, then said, "Seizure."

"From what? Brain tumor?"

"Not clear yet. I admitted her."

I did not want to talk about this, but she kept pressing me.

"Trauma?" she asked.

"I don't know."

"She ever go through a windshield?"

"Once, years ago."

"And you can get seizures years later?"

"Caroline, you aren't going to have seizures."

"I felt like I was on my way today."

"It's just the Percocet."

"What would happen if I had one when I was driving the boys, on the Beltway, at sixty miles an hour?"

"You are not going to have seizures."

"But if I did get them, they'll put me on Dilantin and I'll get hairy and my gums will swell up."

"Caroline," I said. But I didn't know what else to say, so I just held her hand. She was entirely correct. I couldn't deny a thing.

"You are overeducated," I told her. "That's your problem."

"I'm scared," she said. "That's my problem."

"Of what?"

"Of everything. I wake up scared."

"I know. So do I."

"But why?"

"I don't know. I guess it's normal. I don't know."

"Why did this happen to us?" she said.

"Why did Mrs. Roundtree get breast cancer? Why did Vince Montebelli get testicular CA and then get randomized to the protocol that couldn't save him when some other guy got the protocol that could save him?"

"So, it's all written? Is that what you're trying to say?"

"I don't know. I'm just a humble country doctor."

"What does Max say? He's good at metaphysics."

"He says the maniacs got you."

"Smart boy. I want you to bring him. I miss him so much, it's physical."

"Okay, maybe this weekend."

"Do I look that bad? Would I scare him that badly?"

"You look great to me. But Max hasn't seen that much."

"I haven't had the guts to look in a mirror yet."

"You look fine. Want to see?"

"Not yet."

The gray-haired couple, Loretta's parents, stood up and gathered up their things and walked by us, on their way to the door. Loretta's mother said, "I hope you feel better."

"Your roommate," I said, when they were gone, "was in the other car."

"The car that hit us?"

"In the backseat."

Caroline looked over at Loretta, who was sleeping.

"Poor kid," she said. "They've snowed her with morphine. She sleeps all the time. Her parents come in and just sit and look at her."

"I guess that's what we have to look forward to," I said. "Teenage kids who go out in cars at night and you can never rest easy."

Caroline looked at me and then looked away.

I looked at her. "You okay?"

"Sure."

"What's wrong?"

"Nothing. Just bring Max, okay?"

"What's wrong?"

"Nothing, I just want to see Max again, before he's a teenager. You keep stalling."

"What's the big rush?"

"I just want to see him."

She still was not looking at me.

"Remember what Mrs. Roundtree said that time, about Atlanta burning?"

I didn't think I'd ever told Caroline that story, but I guess I must have. I said: "Yes."

"That's what I feel like now. The show is going on inside, but I'm locked out. I'm not even going to get to see the end, to find out how it all works out."

"Mrs. Roundtree had cancer, Caroline. You've got a broken leg and some lacerations. You're going to live to see your kids have kids."

"I hope so."

"Caroline, it's me, the ulcer king. I know when it's time to worry. You're past it now. Your lung's better. Your leg is set. You're on your way."

"Oh, I'm on my way all right."

"Caroline."

"Just bring Max," she said. "Okay?"

13

SLOUCHING TOWARD LEBANON

Two patients I had to see were scheduled for the office Friday morning, but I had my secretary clear out the rest of the day. I had appointments with the lawyer and the junk man and I wanted the afternoon with Caroline.

I was leaving the office when Caroline called.

"Do you think," she said, "you can get me out of this room?"

"What's the problem?"

"Our friend the Turk came in today," she said. "With a gaggle of young female cuties—his admirers—to visit my roommate, another admirer, who kept telling him it wasn't his fault."

"No kidding? The Turk? The kid who was driving the car that hit us?"

"Oh, yeah. Quite the young prepper. Came in to see my roommate, Loretta. She was in his car, you know."

"I know."

"He's got on his Gucci sweater, basketball shoes with the laces untied the way the kids wear them. One of his girlfriends is looking over at me whispering, 'Oh, how gross.' Do I look gross?"

"Not to me. Maybe to some sixteen-year-old bimbo with teased hair."

"No teased hair. Hot pink lipstick, however."

"I'll call the head nurse."

The head nurse listened quietly and said, "Consider it done."

I hung up and dialed the State Department and got nowhere, as usual, trying to get some word about Caroline's father.

When I arrived at the Medical Center, they had moved Caroline to a private room.

"What did you say?" she asked. "They were in here almost before I could hang up the phone."

"I simply told them what happened."

"You should have seen this twerp," said Caroline. "Laughing

and kissing Loretta. Poor Loretta, she's in traction because of him and she's gooing and eating out of his hand."

"She's got a broken femur. I suppose she can pick her own poison."

"I'd like to slip the young Turk a little poison," Caroline snorted. "But I guess that's what the lawyers are for."

"Let me wash your hair."

"Wonderful," Caroline said.

Caroline loved to have me wash her hair. It was quite a production, with her leg exquisitely sensitive to any motion and with her broken ribs making any shifting of her upper half difficult. But it could be done, and she looked forward to it. It was one of the few pleasant physical sensations in her day.

"Did you see the lawyer today?" she asked as she watched me assemble all the hair-washing implements.

"Did I ever."

"What was he like?"

I slid a clean black plastic bag—a trash bag really—under her head and shoulders and then readied a green molded plastic commode to catch the water and then I poured a pail of warm water over her hair.

"Gray pinstripes and all that, but his gold bracelet gave him away."

"Gold bracelet? Gold chain on his hairy neck, too, I bet."

"He wore a tie. But I'm sure he had a gold chain. The bracelet was one of those thick chain link things like the old ID bracelets."

"Excellent, he sounds like true slime."

"He had that phony sincerity they have, like an undertaker. He's telling me to take a seat, and offering sympathy for my poor injured wife, and the heater next to him started to rattle and he slams it with his fist like he's karate-chopping someone and he turns back to me smiling, all sweetness and light. That kind of lawyer."

"Sounds like the genuine article."

"He brought in some young schlepper to take notes. Secretary's hovering around to pour me coffee. You should have seen the office."

"Sumptuous?"

"Sumptuous is a vast understatement."

"Very good."

I slathered on the shampoo, and massaged it into her hair, then rinsed it with a water pitcher full of fresh water, being careful not to disturb the healing eschars on her forehead.

"Oh, that feels so good. So, what did he say?"

"Well, at first he and the schlepper were very enthusiastic. They had me take off my shirt to show them the burns across my chest from the seat belt."

"You have seat belt burns?"

"Yeah, and the main man sends the schlepper out to get a camera and take a photo of the burns."

"Let me see those burns."

"They're nothing. But they're getting all excited. They're getting me all caught up in their excitement. You know, they had me feeling sorry for myself, as if I were injured. It's all theater for them. They believe. They make you believe."

"You can imagine how it must have gone with Mr. Roundtree," said Caroline. "He goes in with some doubts about his case maybe and by the time they're finished with him, he wants to burn the hospital down."

"Oh, they do get you worked up into righteous indignation. They get you telling the story, dramatizing it. They're looking at each other as if to say, 'How's this going to play to the jury?' "

"Such artists."

"They wanted to come out and photograph you in the hospital bed."

"Lovely people."

"And they want to photograph the car."

"What's that look like?"

"I saw it today in the pound."

"What's it look like?"

"Pretty sorry. You go out to this place in Rockville, and it's just a big fenced-in lot. Wire fence with this big police dog running around among all the smashed-up cars, comes bounding up to the fence and hurtles his body against it. This is one of those dogs hungers for your vital organs. There's this little house next door to the lot with a guy in a torn T-shirt who comes out and ties up the dog to a tree. Dog's name is Duke."

"Duke! I love it. After the man's alma mater?"

"After John Wayne. The guy told me that."

"So then, he lets you go get whatever's salvageable from the car. Meanwhile, the dog is straining at this old leather leash, which looks as if it's just about ready to snap."

"How very pleasant."

"You know," I said. "I was almost hoping that leash would snap."

"What?"

"I don't know why. I had this tire iron in my hand I used to jack open the trunk, and that dog's straining to get at me. And I just wished for a moment he would. I just wanted to take my cut at him."

Caroline looked at me for a long moment and finally said, "But what's the car look like?"

"The car looks like your basic accordion. Not too bad, really, considering it was half the size of the car that hit it."

"A total wreck?"

"Absolutely. And looking at the inside, the glove compartment torn off, and the dashboard smashed, it's easy to understand your X rays."

"Okay, I've heard enough about the car. What about the lawyer?"

I toweled down her hair.

"They were getting worked up, until I told them about the father being a diplomat."

"Then they weren't so enthusiastic?"

"It was like I threw a switch. The main lawyer, the partner, left with some excuse about having to go to a meeting, and the schlepper told me there wasn't much they could do, if the father is a real honest-to-Jesus diplomat."

"So, is he?"

"Oh, yes. I called the State Department and talked to the ambassador. Some guy they call an ambassador who isn't an ambassador to any country. He just deals with diplomats in Washington. He knew all about the accident."

"Already?"

"Oh, yeah. And the kid's the bona fide son of a bona fide high muck-a-muck in the Turkish embassy. There's not a damn thing we can do. Can't sue them."

"But the kid isn't a diplomat."

"I asked the lawyer that. Yeah, you can sue the kid, but he won't have any money. The most you could do is try to attach his earnings if he ever decides he wants to come back to the US of A and work. But there's no money in that for the lawyers and they aren't interested."

"And the Turks don't have insurance?"

"They've got some. But the schlepper lawyer figures it's got to be split eight ways, since everyone in that car will sue for the insurance money. That's why the main lawyer left. It isn't worth his time. The schlepper will handle the case, but it's going to be peanuts."

I started to dry her hair with the blow-dryer.

"Wouldn't you know?" said Caroline. "The one time we can use a lawyer, and we can't sue. But you sign a motor vehicle form for some diabetic and the lawyers are lining up to sue you."

"It's the American way."

Caroline laughed.

"What did the State Department guy say?"

"He said once in a blue moon, the embassy will agree to pay a little compensation, but he didn't think the Turkish embassy would be so inclined."

"Our allies, the Turks."

"I told this ambassador, it's like these guys are aristocrats, cruising around, above the law. And he says he wouldn't put it that way. He says, remember we've got diplomats in Turkey who have to be protected the same way."

"Like my father, whom nobody seems to be able to find."

"And I said I could understand what happens in places like Lebanon where there isn't any recourse to the law. All revenge has to be personal."

"I like it," Caroline said. "Slouching toward Lebanon."

"I figured I'd wear a ski mask and sneak over to the Turk's house and smash his tibia with a baseball bat."

Caroline thought about it. "No," she said. "The whole idea makes me sick. I hope nobody ever breaks another bone in the whole future of mankind."

"How can you say such a thing?" I said. "Norm Levinson would starve."

"Norm would understand."

I combed out her hair.

"The antibiotic ointment they keep smearing over my forehead gets into my hair," she said. "It takes about one day to feel really creepy crawly."

"Tell them to stop the ointment."

"It's Dr. Thoreau's order," Caroline said, making her Dr. Thoreau face, an expression of raised eyebrows and stiff mouth.

"Heaven forbid we cross Dr. Thoreau," I said.

"I think he would decompensate," said Caroline. "The man cannot tolerate a thread out of place. One day he will discover he's gone through the entire day with his fly open and he will throw himself off the Calvert Street Bridge."

"He's just what you want in a plastic surgeon."

"He's wonderful. He comes in every day and tells me how splendidly my face is healing and how I'll look beautiful again—again, mind you—in time and I have nothing to worry about. It's just a matter of time."

She started opening mail I had brought from home.

"Oh, here's a note from Susan Hughes," Caroline said.

"Who's she?"

"The sitter from across the street who was sitting for us Friday night."

Caroline read, "I hope and pray for your quick recovery. Sometimes the darkest clouds have silver linings." Caroline laughed and shook her head. "Susan has a strong streak of Hallmark in her."

Then I noticed her cast. They had wrapped a big Ace bandage around it.

"What is this?"

"Oh, more good news."

"I can't take any more news."

"They bivalved the cast, slit it in half because the leg swelled inside of it. Norm's worried about phlebitis."

"He didn't tell me," I said, and I felt a little dizzy, and I sat down.

"You can look at it," Caroline said.

I did not want to look at it. But I had to look. Unwrapping the Ace bandages and carefully lifting off the top half of the cast, I had the feeling I was unraveling a shroud, a shroud that covered things to come. Her leg was red and swollen and hot. It looked like Mrs. Roundtree's leg had looked when she had phlebitis.

"I think you've got it," I told her.

"Norm started me on heparin today."

"He never told me."

"Don't worry," Caroline said. "This, too, shall pass." Then she smiled and said, "When are you going to bring my babies?"

"Tomorrow," I said. "If you want me to."

"Am I such a gross-out?"

"You're beautiful."

"No, really."

"Remember Mrs. Roundtree and her kids. The kids didn't get much out of that visit."

"Either did Mrs. Roundtree," said Caroline. "But I'm still mentating. And I want to see my babies." She lifted up her photo of Max and Sam.

"Does Max ask about me?"

"What do you think?"

"Does he?"

"All the time."

"Let's call him."

"We called and Sally put Max on the phone, but he wouldn't say a thing. He just listened to Caroline and finally she stopped talking and waited and we could hear him say, "Mom?"

"Yes, darling?"

"Come home."

14

THE VISIT

Saturday morning, I strapped Sam and Max into their car seats and I lashed Sally's kid, Jason, down with a seat belt in between them in the backseat and Sally got in the front and pulled on her seat belt and I snapped on mine and we headed for the Medical Center. It was bright and sunny and warm and the snow had melted from the streets and the drive in daylight didn't seem like the journey across the desolate tundra as when I drove it alone in the dark evenings.

At the Medical Center, I parked in the visitors' garage and I plopped Sam into his-highly-rated-by-*Consumer Reports* Aprica stroller and I strapped him in as if he were being launched into space, which was necessary with Sam, who was always a threat to win the Harry Houdini award for impossible escapes. I held Max's hand in my special vise grip, which was all that prevented him from rushing headlong directly into oncoming traffic. Sally followed with her kid and our squirmy, jumpy, recalcitrant mob negotiated the block between the garage and the hospital without major incident.

"Now, you wait down here," I told Max, when we arrived in the lobby. "I'll go up and tell Mom we're here."

"I'll come with you."

"No, let me go up first. I'll come down and get you."

"You wait with Aunt Sally," said Sally. "Give your mother some time to arrange herself."

I left Sally in charge, and she went off wheeling Sam down the corridor, shouting after her kid and Max as they flew ahead of her, off to explore the hospital.

Caroline was sitting up in bed. Her hair was greasy and dark from the antibiotic ointment, and her face still had that scalded look and her leg cast looked larger and more intimidating this morning.

"Did they rewrap your cast?"

"No, why?"

"I don't know, it just looks different."

"Are the kids downstairs?"

"With Sally."

"Well, bring them up," Caroline said, beaming. "God, I can't wait."

"I'll bring Max in first."

"I haven't seen him for a whole week."

She hadn't looked happy since the accident. It was good to see her look so keen.

I ran back down the stairs and found Sally pacing up and down the long hallway from the lobby to the wards, wheeling Sam, who was sucking on his bottle. Max ran full gallop ahead of her, narrowly avoiding little old ladies, trailed by Sally's kid. Max ran up, when he saw me.

"Okay, big boy," I told him.

Sally waved and restrained her kid, and she called out, "We'll wait down here until you come for us."

Max and I took an elevator up to Caroline's floor.

"Your mother is going to look a little different," I told him. "She's been in an accident."

Max said nothing and when we got off the elevator he held my hand, which for Max was unusual, and we walked down the corridor and through the door to Caroline's ward. We walked to the nurses' station and I told Max to wait there. I wanted to be sure her nurse wasn't doing anything to Caroline and I wanted to be sure there wasn't going to be any trouble about having an underage kid on the ward. There were no nurses in the ward hall. I peered in her room and Caroline looked up and grinned. I motioned to Max and he raced down the hall, flew by me into the room, straight for Caroline's bed, where she held her hands out to him.

Max slammed to a halt as if he'd hit a glass wall and bounced back off it. He stood there a yard from her bed, staring at Caroline, and for one awful moment, I thought he did not recognize her. He clearly had some doubts this woman in the bed was his mother. She did not look as he remembered her. Her hair looked a different color, dark with the grease, and her face was swollen and burned-looking and her leg looked like it didn't belong to her body.

"Hello, Max," Caroline said, holding out her hand to him. "Come say hi to Mommy."

Max swung one leg around the other and looked back to find me and just stood there, staring at her, uncertain, torn.

Caroline's eyes started to fill.

"I'm so glad to see you," she said.

Keep talking. Your voice hasn't changed.

Max stared at the bed, and took a step toward it, eyeing all the wires and mechanical devices on it. He'd never seen a bed like this before. And he'd never seen a woman as beat up as his mother.

"I've missed you so much," Caroline said.

Max ambled around the bed to Caroline's left, looking at her cast and at her bedside table with the photograph of him and his brother. Then, as if he were just hanging around, going nowhere in particular, he slid to her right, past the foot of her bed to look at her cast.

"That's my cast," said Caroline. Her voice was cracking. "So my leg can be all fixed."

"Mom," said Max. "You're scratched."

She smiled, half laughed. "Yes," she said. "I'm scratched."

Max walked over and held her hand, that one unmarked, familiar part of her, and she reached behind his head with the other and pulled him to her, and she cried.

Max sat on her bed and began his usual stream-of-consciousness chatter about all the strange and wonderful things in the room, pointing out the cast, the television set hanging from the ceiling, the console that worked the bed, the IV pole, the flower arrangements on the windowsill, all the things he had taken in, in that instant of stunned silence, which had disoriented him. Not only did his mother look different, she was placed in this strange and unfamiliar setting.

"You were in an accident, Mom."

"Yes. But I'm getting better now. And soon I'll come home."

"When?"

"Soon. But first you're going to get to go to New York with Aunt Sally and with Jason."

"And with Forrest."

"And with Forrest."

"And we're going to go to the Central Park and ride a train."

"A subway."

"A subway train. Aunt Sally told me."

"And then, when you come home, I'll be home again."

"How will you walk?"

"They'll take the cast off by then. Or at least they'll make it smaller."

"It comes off?"

Caroline laughed, and she kept stroking his hair.

He did not move away from her, but he did not move any closer either, as if he were still just a little uncertain this was truly his mother, as if the goblins might have left him an impostor, as if this were all some Maurice Sendak fairy tale, and Caroline might melt like ice or transform.

Caroline saw this, and kept talking, kept stroking, trying desperately to reestablish her connection.

"It certainly does," she said. "I'm not going to have this cast forever. Is that what you thought?"

"I don't know."

"I'll ask the nurse to get you into a chair and wheel you out to the hall," I told Caroline. "They'll freak out if they see the whole kindergarten here in the room. I talked to the charge nurse on the phone this morning before we came. She said it's okay to have the kids in the main hallway outside the ward."

"Okay," Caroline said, never taking her eyes from Max, touching him as if she could hardly believe he was really there, unable to stop touching him for fear he would turn out to be only a dream.

I left them and went out to find a nurse and asked her to help Caroline into the wheelchair and then I went to find Sally and Sam and Jason.

When we arrived back upstairs, Caroline was in a wheelchair in the long corridor, still talking with Max. Sally lagged behind and I wheeled Sam up beside Caroline, so he could see her.

She leaned over and touched his cheek and he held up his bottle and offered her a swig.

But he clearly didn't know who she was.

He smiled and waved at her, just as he did with everyone, but there was nothing of that special excitement he had for her when she was his milk supply.

Sally came huffing down the hall, dragging her kid, and Caroline lifted her arms and they hugged.

Max never left her side. After about twenty minutes, it was evident that Caroline was getting tired and her ribs were hurting. She shifted in her wheelchair, trying to find a comfortable position, but the pain was in her face and her breathing got faster and more labored.

"I'll wheel you back," I said.

"Oh, don't go so soon."

"The kids have to eat. We promised them McDonald's."

Caroline smiled at them. "God, how I would love a McDonald's anything right now. Not the food. Just to be there and watch them slop ketchup all over themselves. Those things seem so important now."

"You'll be doing it all again," said Sally.

They hugged and kissed again and said good-bye.

"You be a good boy for Aunt Sally," Caroline told Max. Then, to Sally, "New York seems so far away."

"Oh, it's just a hop and a skip," said Sally. "And a phone call."

Sally held the door open and I wheeled Caroline back down to her room and Sally stayed in the hall with her kid and with Sam.

Max walked alongside Caroline, holding her hand as I wheeled her chair back to her room.

"Leave me here," she said when we reached the door. "They'll get me back in bed. Max doesn't have to stay for that."

"I'll stay with Mom," Max said brightly, looking up at me, as if he really thought he could put it by me.

"Not today," I said.

"You go with Dad," Caroline said, smoothing his hair.

Max kissed her hand, instinctively avoiding her abraded face, planting his kiss on her unscathed hand, which brushed his cheek.

We left her there, looking after us.

15

NO DIRECTION HOME

That same night, I packed the kids' things.

One suitcase for our kids would be all Sally could handle. She had one bag of her own and three kids to lug around and one suitcase would have to do. I dragged up the big suitcase from the basement, thinking it was going to be a major feat squeezing clothes for both kids in one bag, but I hadn't thought about how small the clothes were: the undershirts looked like dolls' clothes and I folded them and fit them into a corner of the suitcase, taking up no more room than a pack of handkerchiefs. Three pairs of well-worn OshKosh B'Gosh overalls, three sweaters, four pullover cotton turtleneck shirts, six pairs of socks, a pair of Kangaroos sneakers with Velcro instead of laces (which Caroline regretted buying because Sam could rip the shoes off so easily), and one red Tyrannosaurus Rex sweatshirt for Max. (Tyrannosaurus Rex, Max had informed me, was the dinosaur what eats bad dinosaurs and it doesn't need weapons.) All of it fit into a space not much bigger than a shoe box.

Folding each item and laying this stuff in the suitcase, it suddenly struck me that I was sending my kids away. Our family was breaking up. All this stuff Caroline had selected and washed and folded and repaired, all these worn artifacts of family life were being laid out like a body for burial.

And I had been at the wheel.

I had, in a sense, steered the course to this point. Eighteen-year-old kids who get their sixteen-year-old girlfriends pregnant are able to support families, working construction, pumping gas, mopping floors, whatever, but this nearly-forty-year-old physician in private practice was unable to do that basic thing: keep the family intact. After all the training, after all the long nights, after all the preparation, I had stepped out into the Real World, and I couldn't even keep my family together. What competence. What a man.

Sally appeared in the doorway. "Don't pack diapers," she said. "I can buy them. We have Huggies in New York."

I looked up and realized Sally had been watching me, arms folded, she had been standing there watching me, leaning against the door.

"They're just coming to New York for a visit with Aunt Sally," she said. "It's not forever."

"I always come back," I said.

"Pardon?"

"Something Caroline said once."

"Caroline said you'd be like this."

"Like what?"

"She said, 'The kids will be fine. It's Brendan who'll get all morose.'"

"I don't think Sam even knew who she was."

"Good Lord, Brendan. He's only, what? Nine months? He'll have plenty of time to get reacquainted."

"Max didn't recognize her, at first," I said. "Or, at least there was some doubt in his mind."

"Well, they looked very friendly when I saw them."

We put the kids to bed. I read Max *The Cat in the Hat*, and he listened silently.

"You don't like *The Cat in the Hat*," said Max.

"It's okay."

"But you don't like it."

"It's fine."

"You like *Where the Wild Things Are*."

"Yes, but I packed it."

"Did you pack my Tyrannosaurus shirt?"

"Absolutely."

"Can I take my Skeletor?"

"You'll lose it in New York."

"I want to take it."

"Go ahead."

"Are you coming to New York?"

"No, Aunt Sally's going with you. I'll come up to take you home."

"When?"

"When Mom is ready to come home."

"When?"

"A week. While you're in New York, I'm going to find a woman to live with us to help your mother and to help with you when your mother gets home."

"I'm not going to stay in New York to live."

"No."

"I like my room."

"It'll be right here waiting for you."

When they were all in bed, I cleaned the kitchen and Sally drank wine and studied a printed schedule spread out before her.

"I'll drive you guys out to the airport," I said. "You can leave off your car and I'll drive you from the car rental place to the terminal."

"Actually, I was thinking about taking the train."

"Why?"

"Oh, Jason's never been on a train. It might be fun."

"Caroline's been talking to you again."

"You're going to be biting your nails until we get there. I know you're worried about us flying."

"I don't like flying in the winter. Then again, I don't like planes, period. But it's not practical, the train for four hours, with three kids. Maybe I should come."

"Don't be ridiculous. Forrest'll meet us."

"Well, do what you want. Maybe it'd be better to worry only forty-five minutes, and have it over with. You call as soon as you get in."

"From the airport," she said. "And again from our apartment. I'll keep you posted."

We made it to the airport without collisions.

I drove to the short-term parking and we unloaded the kids. We threaded our way through the parking lot and across the walkways to the terminal in the dark. I thought about Caroline lying across town in the dark of her room, while we proceeded to send her kids away.

I got the tickets while Sally checked the bags and tried to keep the kids from wandering off onto flights for Texas, and by the time all the tickets were bought, the plane was boarding: seventy businessmen and -women in gray pinstripe suits, Sally in a parka, and three kids in Kangaroos sneakers and dungarees.

The plane was pulled up to the window so you could look right into the cockpit, and the passengers loaded by walking down a galleyway directly into the forward door. They walked down the galleyway to the plane, Sally pushing the stroller, Jason attempting to swing from one of her arms, and Max clinging to one of the metal railings of the stroller.

Just before they turned the corner out of sight, Max turned around and found me with his eyes and he waved.

I waved back and they were gone.

16

FIRE IN THE SKY

Sally and Forrest called as soon as they made it back to their apartment with the kids.

"The plane did not crash," Forrest said. "And even more amazing, we survived the taxi ride in from the airport."

I spoke with Max and with Sally and we hung up.

The house seemed strange without the kids. I started in the basement and worked my way upstairs, cleaning. I was in the living room when the doorbell rang.

It was my father. He was carrying a bag of groceries.

"I just thought I'd bring some things by," he said. "How is she? Where are the kids?"

"Sally and Forrest have them, in New York."

"Oh, yeah. I guess that makes sense."

"She's doing better. She tells me you call her every day."

"Yeah, well, I really should get over there and see her. But I get sort of claustrophobic in hospitals, you know. Ever since your mother. I just avoid the places."

"She gets pretty tired with visitors, anyway. Calling is just as good."

"I just can't stand hospitals. I tried to visit a friend they had over at Hopkins a couple of years back, and I walked onto that ward and that same smell hit me right in the nose and the shiny hallways, and I never made it to his room. I just turned right around and left and phoned him later. Your mother was in three different hospitals and they all smelled the same."

"It's the disinfectant."

"Well, look. Here's a little something to cover expenses." He stuffed a check inside my shirt pocket.

"Thanks."

"Caroline said her dizzy spells are getting better," he said. "She said they stopped her Percocet, and she feels better."

"We're still waiting for the neurologist to show up."

"Why don't you get one of your buddies to see her?"

"We're waiting for the HMO neurologist."

"Hell, get anyone you want. I'll pay for it."

"I don't think she's got a problem, Dad. I think it was just the Percocet all along."

"What'd the insurance company give you for the car?"

"Nothing yet. They called Friday and said I'd get the blue book value. The Honda was a year old. I can't buy a new one for the blue book value."

"Don't worry about the car. Cars I got. I'll get you a car. I'll get you an American car. She said the kids were going to visit. How'd that go?"

"They warmed up, after a while."

"We were worried about you, when your mother got sick. Of course, you were in college when she first took ill. But she was all worried you'd be upset when you saw her. But you shrugged it off."

"Well, it's never easy."

"Call me if that neurologist doesn't show up. We'll get her a real one," he said, and he was out the door.

Monday morning, Caroline was not in her room when I arrived. The nurse told me she was down in physical therapy. I left and phoned her from the office.

"I walked on crutches this morning," she told me. "I am very proud of myself."

"That is progress."

"Only four steps. But I'm advancing on other fronts," she said. "I've got four people coming in for interviews."

"Interviews?"

She had put an ad in *The Washington Post:* Wanted nanny for two kids whose mother has a broken leg. Live in, full-time. Must be able to drive. Salary negotiable.

"Just be sure you negotiate to the bone," I said. "Room and board and wine on weekends. Our finances aren't real robust right now."

"You really think there's no chance our lawyers will get anything out of the Turk's insurance company?"

"Eight people all clamoring for a piece of a small pie. Our lawyers aren't even interested. There's no money in it for them."

"Not even enough to pay for a girl to come in and take care of the kids?"

"I wouldn't count that money. Even if it came, it would be too late. My father gave me a check, though. That'll help."

Caroline grew quiet. I knew what was coming.

"You haven't heard anything from my father?"

"I called the State Department again today. They say they are trying to get word to him."

"Okay."

"I could wire your mother."

"Don't bother. She'd just write a lovely letter about how much she loves me and how she wishes she could be here, but she cannot leave the prime minister. She's giving a black tie dinner, you see, and everyone's depending on her."

"Okay."

"We don't have any choice. You can't stay home and I sure won't be able to take care of those kids when I get home. Norm says I'll be in a cast and just bed-to-chair for six weeks. We've got to hire someone."

She was right, of course, but my office practice barely covered the office rent, my secretary's salary, and the mortgage. We were living on savings and my father's checks.

"Sally can't keep the kids forever," Caroline said. "We have to find a live-in nanny."

"I know, but how're you going to find anyone through the paper?"

"You got any better ideas?"

I did not.

"I miss the kids," I said.

"I called," Caroline said. "Max got on the phone. He loves New York. Sally took him over to the East River walkway near the hospital. He saw 'a big boat what goes out on the ocean and sees whales.' "

"I always liked those boats."

"When I'm all better, we'll all go back up there. Brooklyn Heights. We'll push Sam along in the stroller and let Max run along the Promenade."

"When we can afford it," I said.

"We'll make it," said Caroline. "We can sell the house."

"Great. Maybe the ambassador from Turkey will buy it, give us a real good price."

"This is like one of those board games you play with dice," Caroline said. "We could patent it: You help Mr. Roundtree, Mr. Roundtree sues you. Go bankrupt, do not collect two hundred dollars. Mr. Ambassador's son gets you, you do not get to sue. Go bankrupt, do not collect two hundred dollars. What do we call it? Double Jeopardy? No, I got it: We Got You, Coming and Going."

"It's the system."

"I don't like it," said Caroline.

"You got any better ideas?"

"War on Turkey."

"I could go for that."

Tuesday morning, Caroline asked me again if I had heard anything from the State Department about her father. I told her I hadn't. She dropped the subject in a hurry and I didn't bring it up again. But I wondered about it. I had left the message that his daughter had been in a serious accident. I couldn't believe they couldn't reach him. I almost asked Caroline if the State Department title was just a cover for some more clandestine activity, but I didn't want to rub salt in a wound. Caroline had enough of those.

We had four patients that morning, which cheered me up, with respect to the issue of how I was going to pay rent, but the patients all had viruses and wanted antibiotics and I had to explain antibiotics don't help viruses to some very dissatisfied customers.

Early that afternoon, Caroline phoned. Her voice sounded wrong, strained and breathy.

"You have the radio on in your office?"

I told her no.

"They finally sent the neurologist by," Caroline said. I was still trying to figure out how that connected to the radio. "He reminded me of Ludvik Novotny. Mr. Warmth and Milk-of-Human-Kindness. And he's doing all those stupid neuro tests Ludvik was so fond of—serial sevens and all—and my TV's on in back of him, and they're showing the shuttle launch, and I can't concentrate on his questions and his head's in the way of the screen. He has his back to it. And the goddamn shuttle blows up."

"What?"

"The shuttle with that schoolteacher. It went up and got up about a mile and just blew up. It was dreadful."

"Are you sure it wasn't some show?"

"No, it really happened. And, of course, I'm trying to look at the TV screen and this neurologist is looking at me like I'm some kind of psych case and I told him, 'The shuttle just blew up.' And he says, 'Uh-huh,' and goes on with his exam. I just about threw him out of the room."

"Christ."

"Somehow, it was like a bad omen. I felt like I was on it."

"You're getting as bad as me."

"I know. But the damn thing was, when I saw that explosion and the thing trailing off in flames toward the sea, I thought about Professor Toomey. It was like a flash. I saw his face."

"Professor Toomey?"

"Yes. I don't know why. But the whole thing is very depressing. And I felt suddenly so frightened."

"You don't sound so good."

"I know. It's like they used to talk about, the sense of impending doom. I suppose it's just the shuttle. They keep playing and replaying that film over and over again on the TV. I've just felt so breathless, ever since it happened."

"What do you mean, you felt breathless?"

"You know, dyspneic. It's like I can't get a deep breath. A real anxiety state."

"Caroline, how long has this been going on?"

"Just this morning."

"You could be having pulmonary emboli. You've got over deep-vein phlebitis. Now you're breathless. Maybe your phlebitis is back. Maybe you've got clots. And emboli."

"Now I'm sorry I mentioned it."

"I'm coming over."

"Don't cancel patients," she said. She sounded breathless to me.

"I'm on my way."

I dialed Norm Levinson, but his secretary said he was in surgery. I paged Norm's orthopedic resident, who was, predictably, also in surgery. I finally got his covering resident.

"Look, this is Dr. O'Brien. My wife's a patient of Norm Levinson's and she's had a tib-fib and deep-vein phlebitis. Norm put her on heparin for a while, but he didn't like doing it because of the fracture and he took her off it. And now she's dyspneic. Just suddenly. Out of the blue. Could you start some heparin on her and get a lung scan? I'm on my way."

He said he would and I ran by my secretary and called back over my shoulder to cancel my afternoon patients.

She called out, "Your wife's on the phone."

I ran back.

"How are you?"

She was breathing faster. She had to pause between words.

"I was okay until this resident ran in here and started poking me for an IV. He says I'm going down for a lung scan."

"Behave yourself. Be a patient."

"Brendan, nothing is happening to me."

"Humor me, babe."

"He wants to start heparin."

"Good man."

"Is this your idea?"

"Great minds think alike."

"Brendan, you are being irrational. You've got Mrs. Roundtree on the mind."

"I haven't even mentioned her."

"You haven't?"

"No."

"That's funny. I thought we were talking about her just now."

"You're the one," I said, "who's got Mrs. Roundtree on the mind."

"Drive carefully," she said. "One of us has to make it through all this."

— 17 —

BLACK IS THE COLOR

Caroline had her first pulmonary embolus before I reached the Medical Center.

I arrived in her room and her bed was empty and my heart sank. It was like finding the bed empty at Whipple on morning rounds. Then the nurse would come in and tell you the bed was empty because the patient was in the morgue. My mind went buzz and I was standing there trying to think when a nurse walked in and said, "Oh, Dr. O'Brien. They took your wife down to Nuclear Medicine for a lung scan."

It was four flights down to Nuclear Medicine and I took them fast, and when I arrived I found myself face-to-face with Norm Levinson, who was standing in his scrub suit looking at Caroline's scan with an orthopedic resident and a nuclear medicine man.

He looked up at me and smiled weakly when I came in. He was staring at the scan up in front of the view boxes, shaking his head. "She's done it," he said. "She's gone and done it."

The telltale wedge-shaped area on her left lung showed where clot had cut off an area from blood flow. It was only a small infarct but looking at it was like a blow. That couldn't be Caroline's lung. Not Caroline. Please, not Caroline. It wasn't just the one infarct: it was knowing that where there was one clot, there were others waiting to break loose from their moorings in the leg.

"She's getting heparin now," Norm said. "Obviously we need an internist. Not you, big boy. Your wife needs a doctor. Tell me who."

I tried to think, but I couldn't bring a name to mind. All I could do was stare at that awful lung scan and wish it weren't Caroline's. I kept checking the name on the film to be sure it was hers. Vince Montebelli had told me about doing that, so long ago, how he couldn't believe it was really his chest X ray, the one that looked so bad. But now it was Caroline's lung scan. And it really was her scan, and there was no denying it. I hadn't seen a lung scan that positive since Mrs. Roundtree's.

My head spun a little but then it cleared and I said, "Maybe we ought to use some streptokinase."

Norm and the orthopedic resident exchanged looks. The nuclear medicine man was staring at me too.

Norm put his arm around my shoulders and walked me away from the other two.

"Uh, Brendan. That's an awfully big gun, streptokinase. You sure you want to be your wife's critical-care doctor?"

He was right, of course. Heparin was the standard treatment for pulmonary emboli. But heparin only prevented the formation of new clot, and she had clots in her leg we weren't doing anything about. She could die. Caroline. It had happened to her. I had seen this all before. But not Caroline. Why Caroline?

The clot in her lung isn't going to hurt her now. Think. Breathe slowly. Think. The clot in her lung will not hurt her now. But the streptokinase could hurt her. It could make her bleed into her brain. The streptokinase was a pretty dumb idea. An idea born of panic. The kind of thing you say when you're not the right doctor for your wife.

"Okay," I said. "But I do think we ought to put in an umbrella."

An umbrella is a plastic device that can be threaded into a big vein to prevent runaway clots from shutting down the lung. But threading an umbrella into the inferior vena cava in a patient getting heparin can be tricky. You can get a lot of bleeding, and other bad things can happen.

"Talk it over with Dan Evans," Norm said. "I'm going to call him right now."

Evans was the critical-care doc.

"Okay," I said. Be calm. Think. Do not panic. Panic will not help Caroline.

But she could die. What if she dies?

"I wouldn't want to be writing that order for my wife," Norm said. "Talk to the doctor."

I spoke with the critical-care doc over the phone, after Norm presented Caroline's case.

"I haven't seen her yet," the critical-care doc said. "But an umbrella's pretty heroic. Why don't you wait till I can see her? They'll bring her up to the ICU in a few minutes."

I said okay.

Then I went in to see Caroline. She held out her hand and smiled. She was still breathless. "Nice pickup, Doc," she said. "You made the diagnosis. Over the phone, no less."

I tried to say something, but I couldn't get the words out.

"What's going to happen?" she said.

"They . . ." I wanted to tell her she was being taken to the intensive care unit, but I was afraid that would frighten her. Then she'd know she was really in trouble.

"I'm causing trouble," I said. "I've been screaming for an umbrella and streptokinase and they've been telling me you're going to do just fine on heparin. So they finally compromised and agreed to take you to the ICU. They're doing it just to keep me quiet."

"The ICU?" she said. "Christ, Brendan."

"It's just to humor me."

"I don't want to go to an ICU. I don't want to go on a respirator."

"You're not going on any respirator. You're just going to get some heparin and I'm going to hover around and wring my hands and drive everyone crazy."

"The ICU," Caroline said. "Right next door to the ECU. Remember? That's what Ira used to say."

"Yeah. Good ol' Ira."

"Brendan, I think I'm going to the Eternal Care Unit today."

"You're not going anywhere. If the ICU scares you, we'll keep you on the ward. This whole ICU thing is my fault."

"No," she said. "I'll go."

I walked beside her gurney as they wheeled her out to the elevator and we rode up together and they rolled her down a long corridor to the ICU.

The ICU looked like every ICU I'd ever seen: lots of glass walls and monitor consoles and lots of nurses. The critical-care doc came up and shook my hand and said hello to Caroline and grabbed her chart so he could go off and pore over it. I went into her room with Caroline and helped the big black orderly transfer her from stretcher to bed.

The orderly was very competent and very gentle with Caroline.

"That's Mr. Washington," Caroline said after the aide left the room. "He's the one who's so good with my leg."

The ICU nurse let me stay in the room while she did Caroline's vital signs.

"How do you feel?" I asked Caroline after the nurse left.

"Tired."

"Breathing any better?"

"Not really. Maybe a little. I can't believe I threw a P.E. Remember when Mrs. Roundtree threw her P.E.? She turned so blue. Do I look like her?"

Your lung scan looked like hers would have looked.

"Everything's under control," I said.

"I know," she said. "Don't look like that. Everything's under complete control. Have you called the kids today?"

"Not yet."

"Me neither," she said. "I've been busy."

I sat by her bed and she slept. Her respiratory rate went up to twenty-four a minute when she was sleeping. Christ. Twenty-four a minute, twice normal. She's probably throwing clots right through her heparin, just lying in bed. And we haven't got an umbrella in to protect her. She's just going to stop breathing. She's going to arrest right in front of me. Do not think that way. Don't give in to it. Right after the crash, every car on the road was coming across into my lane. Now if something can happen, it will. But it can't. Not that. But what if it does? What if she stops breathing? What if that big one breaks free and hits her lung? It won't. But what if it does?

I walked out and found the critical-care doc and told him about the respiratory rate.

"We'll put an A-line in her," he said.

An A-line is a catheter in the artery. You can draw blood gases from it so you can monitor how well blood is getting past the lung clots and how well the blood is being oxygenated. It's nice to be able to monitor, but it's no fun being the patient getting the line stuck in your artery. Don't be too pushy about getting aggressive with Caroline, being sure everything gets done. You could hurt a person, trying to help her.

I went back in to be with Caroline while the critical-care doc put the line in her wrist.

She was very good about it, although it hurt her. After it was sewn in, she said, "Remember, at Whipple, when you taught me how to do arterial blood gases?"

"Yes."

"You were very nice that day."

"Wasn't I always."

"I thought you probably only did it because you had a crush on me."

"You were right."

"So you had ulterior motives."

"Where you were concerned," I said, "I always had ulterior motives."

Early that afternoon, her color turned dusky.

"How's the breathing?" I asked her.

"Getting harder," she said.

"Hang in there, babe."

I walked out to find the critical-care doc. He was looking at a flow chart of Caroline's blood gases with Caroline's nurse. They did not look happy.

"You better look at these," he said.

Caroline's blood oxygen level had fallen to half of its previous level.

"She's getting more dyspneic," I told him.

"There's not much to do. I've asked Joel Conrad to see her about an umbrella, but she needs heparin right now more than she needs an umbrella, and even if he thought we ought to do it with the heparin on board—which would be dicey—that can't be organized until late tonight."

I went back and sat down next to her. Oh, God, don't let this happen. Make her better. Don't let her slip away. Why is this happening? What did she ever do to deserve this? Nobody deserves anything. Not Mrs. Roundtree. Not Vince Montebelli. Not the professor. These things just happen. But why? It can't happen. It is happening. Just because it might happen doesn't mean it will. Nuclear war can happen. But Caroline. So gray. What if she dies? Not that. Don't let it happen. Just save her and I'll be good. Just don't let this happen.

"God," she said. "What is happening to me?"

"Your gases are getting a little worse. Your pO2's dropped and your pCO2's gone up."

"Am I septic?"

"No. But you're having more emboli."

"But I'm on heparin."

"That only stops new clot from forming. You've got to clear out those old clots."

"That's what I feel like," she said. "Old clot."

They came in with an oxygen Ventimask, and Caroline jumped when she saw it.

"Do I really need that?" she said, pausing for breath between each word.

"It might help."

She looked over to me, eyes flared wide. "*Might?* It might help?"

"Sure it will."

"But you don't know anything will help, do you?"

"Just breathe, babe."

"Don't leave, Brendan. I don't want to die alone."

"Just breathe, babe. Nobody's ever died breathing."

I sat by her for an hour and she slept and I watched her breathe. She seemed to be doing no worse, and her respiratory rate stayed in the high twenties, about where she had been since the morning.

Her eyes opened and she looked at me. "You know what I hate?"

"No."

"Not seeing the kids grow up. Missing all that."

"Be quiet, babe. Just breathe."

"There was so much I wanted to see."

"I know."

"Max riding a bike. A two-wheeler." The words were not coming easily. She had to breathe hard. "I was looking forward to that."

"You'll see it."

"I bet he'll be good. No training wheels. He'll just get on and ride."

"You'll be there to see that, babe."

"No," she said. "And that's what I really hate."

* * *

The nurse came in and drew more arterial blood gases and when these came back about the same as her earlier gases, I walked out of her room and went down the hall, looking for a phone booth.

I telephoned Forrest. I told him what had happened.

"Christ, I wish she were up here at the Manhattan Hospital," Forrest said. "We'd have every maven in New York in here to see her in ten seconds flat."

"And what could they do differently?" I asked. I was asking myself as much as Forrest.

"You're right," Forrest said. "She's just got to stop throwing clots. And they've got to get that umbrella in."

I had just hung up when I heard them call the code over the PA system.

Code Blue, ICU.

Oh, Christ, let it be someone else.

I raced down the length of the hall, mind blank. Just let me get back to Caroline.

Don't let her be alone with all of them.

The clerk stopped me at the ICU entrance. Nobody but doctors when there was a code going on. Who was the code on? The clerk didn't know. I told her I was a doctor, but she said I didn't work in the ICU. She knew who I was. She knew who the code was on. That's why she wouldn't let me in. I'd have to wait in the waiting room.

I was the only one in the room. I could see them rushing by with more and more equipment, with respirators and with X-ray machines.

And, from my door at the waiting room I could see they were taking it all into Caroline's room.

No, no, no. Not now. Not so soon. Not like this. Not Caroline. Not with the kids in New York and not now. Not today. Any day but today. Anytime but now. It's not Caroline. Not Caroline.

About twenty minutes later, the critical-care unit doctor came out to see me. I could see it in his face ten yards away. He didn't have to say a thing.

He said, "I'm sorry."

"Can I see her?"

"I'm really sorry. I can't tell you how sorry I am."

"Can I see her?"

"Sure. Just let the nurses have a moment. I can't tell you how sorry."

They let me go in to see her. They had closed her eyes and cleaned up a little. And they had pulled the covers up to her chest and she looked very pale and unreal.

The nurses saw me and they left me alone with her. I didn't have to ask. They just closed the doors behind them.

Are you the girl who called me on the phone? About my intern who was trying to kill your patient? Have we dined above the city at Hotel Whipple? Did we ever walk along the Promenade in the misty rain, and did you carry me home? Could you have been the lady who rode beside me in the U-Haul, all the way to Boston, and carried the sofa up the stairs with that poor resident whose only reward was warm lemonade? Did you cry over that journal article announcing the cure for testicular CA? Are you the mother of my children?

I stood there with her for a moment and looked at her, but it was not really her anymore, not Caroline.

"And now," I told her. "It's happened to us."

After a while, there didn't seem to be anything more to say, and I walked out of the ICU and down the stairs, across the road to the visitors' parking garage.

Walking helped clear my head a little, and I knew what I had to do. I would drive to the airport and go to New York. I would collect my kids.

Put Sam in the stroller and take Max along, and walk over to Whipple Hospital for Cancer and Related Conditions. We would circle the block one time and I would tell the kids about their mother and about how we met on a Whipple ward one dark night, and how it was, and all about it. And I'd tell them, once the whole story was told, how she was resting comfortably now, in the Eternal Care Unit.